THE CHRONICLES OF
PAUNCEFOOT
AND
LONGSHANKS

Visit David Stedman at his website:

www.gradgrind.co.uk

THE CHRONICLES OF
PAUNCEFOOT
AND
LONGSHANKS
THE MAKING OF A KING

DAVID STEDMAN

Matador
9 Priory Business Park
Kibworth Beauchamp
Leicestershire LE8 0RX, UK
Tel: (+44) 116 279 2299
Fax: (+44) 116 279 2277
Email: books@troubador.co.uk
Web: www.troubador.co.uk/matador

ISBN 978 1783063 178

British Library Cataloguing in Publication Data.
A catalogue record for this book is available from the British Library.

Printed and bound in the UK by TJ International, Padstow, Cornwall
Typeset in 11pt Aldine401 BT Roman by Troubador Publishing Ltd, Leicester, UK

Matador is an imprint of Troubador Publishing Ltd

For my mother and father

The first time I met Lord Edward he flung me into the sea. I could not condemn him because I asked him to do so. It was an encounter that transformed my life and the fate of my mother country England and of barbarous Wales and quarrelsome Scotland.

I was born into low station but I moulded myself to be almost as influential as the future king, Lord Edward, himself. I was nothing, but I was steely determined, from a young age, to escape the torment of the life I had been born into.

My wizened soul ached for love, for comfort, for solace, for friendship, for peace, and for recognition of my worth as a fellow human being. Thus I was willing to strive without cease against any obstacle, within me and outside me, which obstructed my ascent from bleak lonely poverty to wealth and influence.

During that ascent I was compelled to risk my life and liberty, time and again, fighting in the bloody encounters that also marked the ascent of my liege lord Edward Longshanks to the throne of England, the subjugation of Wales, and the bitter overlordship of Scotland.

No-one could be allowed to know the full extent of my scheming while I lived. If anyone, especially Lord Edward, had discovered the true extent of my deception I would have been condemned to death, perhaps by his own hand.

But what would be the purpose of achieving, by stealth and guile, all that I did achieve and never anyone knowing of it?

Thus I have committed my life story to this parchment through my amanuensis, a young monk named Brother Godfrey of Tournai. Already he shakes his head in disapproval of my confessions. Well, my young friend, you try shedding the protection of that shabby brown habit and scrabbling for every advantage against a world constructed to keep the low-born firmly in their place. Brother Godfrey is disapproving and believes in morals and ideals, but he is being well paid. Yes, write all that down as well, you tonsured halfwit. I have walked with kings, boy, and what is more, I bent them to my will, so do not presume to censor or censure me.

So, dear reader of the future, it is for you to know and judge what I did. Well, to know anyway. Judge me as you like, I am now foul dust, and your opinion cannot harm me. Just know...

So begins the most extraordinary document ever discovered about the life and times of the English king, Edward I, known as Longshanks because of his unusual tallness. This chronicle was purportedly written by a man who served Edward in the office of jester and musician. He makes claims that, if ever completely verified, must revolutionise our understanding of British history during the second half of the 13th century.

The document, in the form of parchment sheets, was discovered in 2007, 700 years after the death of Edward I, when work was being carried out in a certain university college. The document had been sealed in an airtight lead box and placed in a space behind a wall that had then been bricked over.

The parchment document has given a carbon tested date of mid-14th century and so is certainly consistent with being written when the author claims to have dictated it. Current methods of carbon dating, however, do not allow for dating of the actual ink used to write the document, so the possibility of a later forgery, albeit using an authentic 14th century parchment, cannot be completely ruled out.

What is certain, however, is that the author displays a knowledge of the events of the life of Edward I that is completely consistent with modern historical research, knowledge that is hard to conceive being known to a 16th century forger. The facts revealed by the author that have not been confirmed by modern research must be taken on trust but, apart from a few mistakes that could easily be attributed to the failing memory of an old man, his account of known events is entirely accurate.

At the end of the narrative are brief footnotes to explain some medieval references, arcane to modern minds, which need clarification. The text has been rendered into modern English, hence the presence of words and phrases that were not known to the author but are an attempt to capture the flavour and style of the original account.

My name was Hamo Pauncefoot. I was born in Portsmouth in September of the year 1238. My mother, God protect her shriven soul, died soon after giving birth to me, thus depriving me of the maternal comfort that is the birthright and consolation of most children.

My father was Peter Pauncefoot. He owned a prosperous inn, named the St. Nicholas Inn, Saint Nicholas of Myra being the patron saint of Portsmouth. This saint was supposed to have brought back to life three young boys who had been murdered and then pickled in a barrel of brine, a story that, in the light of a later event concerning my father and myself, has a melancholy resonance.

The St. Nicholas inn flourished and, by the time I was born, the inn was a veritable warren of ramshackle extensions and additions. My father also built a large and sturdy wooden brewhouse, at the back of the courtyard, to make his own ale.

In 1233, when he was well over forty years of age, my father married a young girl who had been working as a kitchen maid at the inn. This kitchen maid was my mother, Matilda.

As far as I know, because my father would never talk about her, my mother married him when she was very young, no more than eighteen years of age, and she died five years later after giving birth to me.

For many years I would make pictures in my head and see my mother as I hoped she would be, if she had lived. I pictured her warm and loving comfort as she held me on her lap and sang songs to me as we sat by the fire. Why is it possible to feel bereaved of someone you have never known? Even to this day, when the darkness of night comes to shroud me, I see my mother's arms reaching out for me, and then I wake to endure the icy aching void in my soul.

I am not sure why my mother married Peter Pauncefoot. Perhaps it was owing to the strongbox full of silver pennies that he kept securely chained and locked in his room. There was little else to recommend my father as a man or a husband. He was a cruel, drunken, cold-hearted tyrant. If he nurtured any love, or even liking, for me then he kept it a secret locked within his shrivelled soul.

From the very earliest age my role in life, as considered by my father, was to be an added attraction and an auxiliary worker in his tavern, and to be the victim of his beatings whenever I displeased him. I hated and resented him for the burdens he thrust upon me but his arbitrary disciplines compelled me to fashion myself into a form that made me indispensable to the most powerful man in the land, Edward Longshanks, by the Grace of God King of England, Lord of Ireland, overlord of Scotland and Wales, Duke of Aquitaine, and close friend of humble Hamo Pauncefoot.

I was fifteen years of age when I first encountered Lord Edward. I was short of stature, no more than five feet tall. Lord Edward, when we had both grown to full height, was fourteen inches taller than me.

My head was topped with a mop of thick black tousled hair that I could never control, although its tenacity has saved me from becoming bald. My eyes, so I have been told, were my most becoming feature. They were cerulean blue before they clouded with old age. Below my eyes came an uptilted nose and a full mouth that provided me with a wide and ingratiating smile.

My visage was one of blithely happy and innocent contentment. That was how most people assumed me to be, especially my father and his drinking cronies, who took malicious delight in taunting me for their own amusement. When I attempted to answer back or stand up for myself, the taunting and beatings became brutal. So, in order to survive, I learned to behave with the sunny accepting bovine stupidity they expected. And that feigned behaviour unexpectedly became the source of my later success.

I realised from an early age that I was more intelligent and shrewd than most of my fellow men, and I was shrewd enough to keep that knowledge secret, even from my father. I presented to the world an appearance and demeanour of gormlessly happy naïvety but I watched, absorbed and analysed everything I saw and heard.

My father, by inveigling his maritime contacts and by greasing palms, sent me every day, from the age of twelve, to work for two or three hours in the sawpits at the dockyard. He desired me to build my upper body strength so that I could entertain patrons at the inn as a tumbler and acrobat, skills at which I displayed high aptitude from the earliest age.

The dockyard sawyers used long and broad double-handled iron saws to cut logs and planks for the ship builders. The logs were placed over a pit that had been dug into the floor, then one sawyer stood on top and the other sawyer stood in the pit and they worked the saw back and forth. The sawyer in the pit was the junior and fast became covered in choking sawdust. A cloth wrapped around the face helped to keep out the worst of the sawdust but I oft-times finished my stint coughing and retching, with my ears ringing from the ripping roar of the saw and the hammering, clanking and shouted obscenities of the shipwrights.

You can well imagine the delight with which the experienced sawyers consigned me down into that hateful pit. At first I could hardly lift my end of the saw. After a few weeks, however, my arm and upper body muscles developed so much that I became as strong as Samson.

When I had finished my stint in the sawpit I ran down to the harbour and dived into the sea, however cold the weather, to wash off the filth before slinking back, as slowly as possible, to my duties at the inn.

Thus, with this newly-developed strength and after many hours of practice, I became skilfully adept as a tumbler and acrobat. The drunks at the inn found it hilarious to watch the grinning little monkey performing back flips and somersaults, or walking around on his hands, or swinging perilously from the rafters before leaping head-over-heels to land on the straw-covered floor.

At the same time as I was learning the techniques of tumbling I was also learning many other more vital skills. I found that my memory was prodigious and my intelligence acute.

My father, although unaware of my true mental acuity, paid one of his more educated regular drinkers to teach me how to play chess and tables so that I could entertain any patrons at the inn who required an opponent.

My father also employed a defrocked monk named Richard Lestrange to teach me how to sing and to play the harp. Lestrange had assumed that I was dull witted and was amazed at the facility with which I learned to play the instrument so skilfully. My singing voice was not strong but was light and pleasant to the ear.

I had secretly collected a small cache of money earned from tips. I paid Lestrange to teach me much more valuable arts. Unknown to my father, Lestrange taught me to read and write, in both English and Latin. Such knowledge was almost exclusively reserved for the clergy and nobility although the nobility regarded writing with contempt as a menial task that was beneath their dignity.

Once I had mastered Latin and English I surreptitiously found other men to teach me to speak and understand the most important language of all, French. In Portsmouth there were many sailors from Gascony willing to converse with me in French and to take delight in correcting my mistakes. It amused them to hear the little English boy trying to speak in their tongue.

French was the language of the court, of the aristocracy, just as Latin was the language of educated men, of the clergy. I knew that if I was to one day seek advancement in the world then to understand French would be an inestimable advantage.

My father was frequently drunk and insensible so I was free to pursue this tuition without him being aware of it. I did not know how I was one day going to use these linguistic skills but I was aware that, just by knowing them, I was attaining an advantage over other men.

So, by the age of fifteen I was equipped to much more effectively entertain customers at the St. Nicholas Inn. My father assumed that he controlled a strong, docile, versatile and amiable son who was thoroughly trained and willing to help him for many years to come as he drifted into old age. What he did not realise was that I detested his vindictive confinement and that I was waiting for any opportunity to escape out into the world and seize any advantage to make a happier and more prosperous life for myself.

Equipped as I was, openly to entertain and delight with my skills as a tumbler, musician, singer and chess player and, secretly, as a master of three languages and with a razor-sharp brain, I was ready to seize any chance for advancement that came my way.

That chance came, sooner than I ever expected, and in the most advantageous way possible, when I first encountered Lord Edward, first born son of King Henry.

AUGUST 1253

On that fateful day when Lord Edward flung me into the sea I had finished my stint in the sawpit and walked out of the shaded dockyard and into the brazen glare of hot August sunlight. The kingfisher sky was marred by only a few white wisps of cloud and the sea swelled gently and smoothly like the skin on some great silver beast.

I had been working stripped to the waist and the white sawdust had mingled with the sweat of my body to form a hideous crust all over me. A group of young children playing nearby noticed my strangely demonic appearance and began to make fun of me by scampering around making faces and monkey noises. I was well used to this sort of mockery, from children and adults alike.

I began to make my way to the harbour to swim myself clean and, as I rounded the defensive stockade of the dockyard, I was dazzled by a breathtaking sight. Out at sea was an armada of literally hundreds of vessels, with snowy sails full set and gay pennants streaming, so many as to blot out the horizon and the hazy view of the Wight Isle.

Then I noticed an excited commotion down at the jetties away to my left. A stately cog was slowly making her way out to sea and a group of elegantly dressed nobles, surrounded by armed guards and scores of townspeople, were watching the ship making more sail as she moved away. I ran towards the crowd, eager to find out what was happening. [1]

King Henry's army had been camped outside of Portsmouth for several days and this huge fleet of requisitioned vessels had gradually been filling Portsmouth harbour to eventually carry them I knew not where. No-one seemed to know where the army was going, or for what purpose, but rumours abounded. The whole town had been abuzz with excitement and lucrative extra trade.

I surmised that the cog now leaving port was the king's ship because it flew colourful royal pennants and was more richly decorated with gilded gingerbread work than any normal vessel. The king, together with the royal family and their noble retinue, had stayed overnight in Southwick Priory. The king was now setting sail to join his fleet and journey to adventures that I ached to know about.

I pushed through the chattering crowd and approached the tight-linked cordon of soldiers. They wore open helmets and chain mail, and were armed with swords, buckled to their sides, and were carrying long spears for prodding back any threatening commoners.

I attracted some ribald comments from the crowd because of my strange encrusted appearance. I rubbed off most of the sawdust from my face, hair and body, pulled my shirt from out of my belt and put it on. Then, adopting my most fawning manner, I asked one of the guards: 'Excuse me, sir, but what is happening here?'

The soldier looked down at me with an amused grin. 'What have you been up to, you filthy little swine?'

'I've been working in the dockyard, sir. What is happening here?'

The soldier, with a grand flourish, pointed to the departing cog. 'Your liege lord King Henry is following his army off to war and that fine ship is carrying him.'

Adopting a suitably awe-struck expression I asked: 'Who is he going to fight?'

'Some foreign prince who is trying to seize our king's lands in Gascony. You should go with him. You would frighten the Devil himself looking like that!' The nearby soldiers chuckled at this comment.

Unabashed, I continued: 'Who are those fine ladies and gentlemen over there by the jetty watching the king sail away?'

'They are the king's family come to bid him farewell.' The soldier pointed again, self-importantly displaying his knowledge to the other onlookers within earshot. 'That fine lady dressed in green is Queen Eleanor herself, who will rule over us while her husband is away. Behind her stands the queen's honour guard, those twelve knights dressed in their finest surcoats and chain mail. The two boys are King Henry's sons. Lord Edmund is standing with his mother and Lord Edward is standing out in front there waving to his father. By the grace of God, Lord Edward will one day be our king, if he is spared the ills of the flesh that all men must endure and the passages of arms that all princes must endure.'

The guards were clearly caught up in the excitement of being so near to the royal family and with the spectacle of the departing fleet.

I looked over at Lord Edward. I did not know how old he was but he looked to be about the same age as me. He was very tall for his age, for any age in fact, but his slim and gangly body had not yet filled out to fit his height. I was looking at his back and his long curly fair hair tumbled down over a striking red and gold surcoat as he waved frantically at his father's departing ship.

Then someone in the crowd shouted: 'Why, Lord Edward is crying! Our future king cries like a baby because his daddy is leaving him!'

The gawpers nearby repeated this remark and laughter began to spread. The more daring onlookers began to make mocking boohoo noises, which served to increase the hilarity.

Someone else said loudly: 'What sort of king will he make if he cries just because his papa is leaving? He should try wading in piss from dawn to dusk at the tanning yard like I do. That would give him something to cry about, the pampered brat!' The crowd roared their approval of this opinion.

Lord Edward had noticed the uneasy sarcastic restlessness in the crowd and looked around frantically. He seemed unable to stem his tears or control his anguish.

In that moment, with a heart-pounding sense of exultation and rightful destiny, perhaps sent to me by God, I realised this was an opportunity I had to seize. My opportunity was to protect this naïve and royally pampered boy from himself, thus attracting his attention and favour. I had to act immediately before the chance was gone forever.

Lord Edward, to escape the mocking crowd, had ran down to the end of the wooden jetty. I ducked down and, using all the strength garnered in the sawpit, I barged between the soldier's legs, sending two of them tumbling over. I wriggled away from hands that reached out to grab me and I was free. I ran past Queen Eleanor and towards Lord Edward standing at the end of the jetty. The queen cried out a warning to her son as I sprinted past.

Lord Edward looked around to see a strange half-encrusted apparition running towards him. He braced himself to withstand the impact of my charge but I suddenly slowed and began capering around him like a demented simpleton. 'Boo-hoo,' I mocked loudly, rubbing my eyes with my knuckles. 'Boo-hoo, boo-hoo.'

Lord Edward gazed at me in astonishment. He was red in the face and red in his eyes but he was not afraid. I ceased capering and Edward immediately grabbed my shirt front with both hands and lifted me off my feet. 'How dare you mock me!' he shouted into my face, his royal spittle daubing my cheek.

I stared back at Lord Edward's handsome features and into his bold grey eyes. Half-choking from his grip I spluttered: 'I come to give you back your manhood in front of these people. It is they who mock your tears, not I. I wish to serve you.'

Several of the knights accompanying the royal family were now surrounding us. They were brandishing drawn swords and daggers but were hesitant to act in case they accidentally harmed the prince. My only route to life and safety was into the sea.

Lord Edward, with surprising strength, was still holding me up by my shirt front. He looked at me in puzzlement as I continued: 'I can be your eyes when your own are closed, I can be your guardian unknown to any who wish you harm, I can be your sword detached from your body to strike down your enemies wherever you command. My name is Hamo Pauncefoot. This is my first service, to restore your manhood in front of your doubting subjects. Now, show them your strength and your courage and throw me into the sea.'

Lord Edward hesitated for a moment but then, with an angry cry, he thrust me away and pitched me into the grey green sea roiling around the jetty. As I bobbed up I heard the crowd roaring their delighted approval of Lord Edward's action.

Two knights were clambering down the wooden jetty to grab me. One of them grasped my woollen shirt and began to lift me out of the water. His grasping hand was within reach of my mouth and I sank my large teeth into his flesh. He yelped and let go but his companion had grabbed my shirt on the other side. His angry face, mouth uttering obscenities, drew down close to mine. Bracing my legs on the thick oak trunks forming the jetty, I arched backwards and then sprang forward to butt my forehead against his nose with all the force I could muster. He let out a scream of agony and released my shirt.

I fell back into the sea and dived under the surface before more soldiers clambering down the jetty could grab me. I was a strong swimmer, thanks to all that work in the sawpit, and I splashed away in one direction before diving down again and reversing course underwater to put my pursuers off the scent.

I swam underwater for as long as I could endure, breaking surface occasionally to suck in lungfuls of air, and then, when my body began trembling with exhaustion, I cautiously surfaced to find my bearings. To my relief I saw that I was now hundreds of yards away from the jetty, well out of sight, and that I had swum near to the place where the fishing boats were pulled up onto the sands.

No-one was watching so I swam to the shore and sneaked up the sands, smoothing my footprints behind me, to hide under the upturned hull of a derelict fishing boat. The hot sun soon burned off the tell-tale trail of water and I dug myself into the sand until I was completely concealed from sight.

I recovered my breath and strength and thought about my encounter with Lord Edward. I remembered his lively grey eyes and how his left eyelid drooped slightly but not so much as to spoil his handsome features. I remembered his voice, sibilant, almost menacing, and with a slight lisp. I had touched his fine clothes and felt the smooth skin of his hands. He was an impressive figure, even though still an adolescent. Physically, he was everything that I yearned to be and could never be.

I did not know what manner of boy he was but I had looked into his eyes and perceived intelligence and determination. I had not sensed cruelty or arrogance, and I was not often mistaken in these estimations of character, even at that young age.

I was gloomily aware, however, that in all probability I would never meet Lord Edward again. My plan had failed, the opportunity wasted. All I had accomplished was to give myself a sharp pain in my forehead where I had been forced to headbutt the pursuing knight at the jetty. After having used such regrettable violence against a member of Lord Edward's entourage, it was unlikely that I would ever be admitted to his presence again.

Exhausted, I slept. When I awoke it was early evening. I knew I must return to the St. Nicholas Inn and I also knew that many in that morning's jeering crowd would have willingly betrayed my identity to the pursuing soldiers. I fully expected that those soldiers would be waiting at the inn to arrest me but, when I arrived, there were none. Why had they not come to take me?

The inn was very busy and Peter Pauncefoot, already drunk and aware of my encounter with Lord Edward, whipped me for my stupidity and for my unexplained absence. I bore the whipping, and his cruel sarcasm, with fortitude.

I did not care about the beating because I had met Lord Edward literally face to face. I had felt his breath mingle with my breath, felt his skin touch my skin and experienced his divinely ordained presence.

I had inwardly accepted that I would never meet Lord Edward again, although I longed to be part of his world. How far I could advance myself, in both wealth and status, under the protection and patronage of such a man!

But, at the very least, I had been blessed by his royal touch and experienced his God-given grace. It was a memory I would cherish until the end of my days.[2]

M AY 1254

For several weeks I waited, tensely expecting to be arrested for my *lese-majesty* towards Lord Edward, but nothing happened. My father chided me every day for my stupidity, no doubt fearing the loss of his trained and unpaid helper. I simply played the amiable dolt and ignored him.

Several months passed. I could not think of any strategy that would allow me to meet Lord Edward again. My dreams of once again looking into his bold grey eyes and using him as a channel to achieve wealth and status began to fade.

Then, one afternoon in May, the harbour master came into the brewhouse, where I was working, to purchase wines and ales. He casually mentioned that Queen Eleanor's ship, the cog *St. Edward*, had arrived at Portsmouth harbour from Yarmouth and that the queen's seneschal had issued orders to victual the ship, with all possible speed, for a voyage to Gascony.

The harbour master, a portly man with a shock of fine white hair and a grey beard, had always treated me with kindness so, after climbing down from the brew tub platform where I had been stirring the wort, I pretended childish excitement in an attempt to glean more information. 'Is the queen already on board?' I asked excitedly.

'Why, bless you Master Pauncefoot,' the harbour master chuckled, 'the queen is staying at the monastery with her sons and they will join the ship tomorrow when all the supplies are on board.'

Her sons!

'Are her sons sailing to Gascony as well?'

15

'Indeed they are, Hamo. Lord Edward is to visit his lands in Gascony and then goes to Castile to be married to a princess!'

'A princess!' I chortled, clapping my hands together with glee. 'When will the ship leave?'

'Tomorrow, with the afternoon tide. Now, if you will be good enough to find your father and ask him to attend me so that I can negotiate my purchases, I will be grateful. I have much to do.'

'Of course, sir.'

I found my father in the inn, directed him out to the brewhouse and then made an excuse to climb down into the dank inn cellar where I could be alone in the darkness and think.

I sat on an empty barrel and applied my mind to the possibilities offered by this unexpected opportunity. I decided that I had to find a way to join the queen's ship as a member of the crew. A voyage to Bordeaux, the port where ships from England to Gascony usually docked, could take, depending on the winds, several days.

On a ship, even a large royal cog like the *St. Edward,* the crew of the ship needs must live in close proximity to the royal passengers, even though the royals would be served, guarded and protected by royal retainers. But how to wheedle my way on board?

I considered that my first step should be to go to the harbour and find out what was going on and whether there was any possibility of being recruited to join the crew of the *St. Edward.* I slipped away from the inn, no longer caring what punishment I might incur from my father, and walked down to the harbour.

The tall mast of the *St. Edward* came into view and I was surprised by the size of the crowd thronging the quay to gawp at the activity bustling around the vessel.

There were several much smaller vessels in port and I soon realised, from listening to the onlookers around me, that these onlookers were sailors from Winchelsea who had recently arrived on the smaller vessels. They were gazing at the royal cog *St. Edward* with angry and envious glances. There was intense rivalry between the seamen of Winchelsea and Yarmouth and it transpired that

Yarmouth had unexpectedly provided this most magnificent vessel for the use of the queen and that the seamen of Winchelsea would be embarrassed and humiliated for supplying such commonplace and weather-beaten auxiliary vessels.

I moved off to locate the crew of the *St. Edward*. A cordon of soldiers was protecting the queen's ship as stevedores moved up and down the gangplank carrying barrels, sacks and casks of provisions.

On the other side of the cordon I saw another group of sailors and, adopting my awestruck dolt attitude, I walked around to them and asked if they were the crew of the *St. Edward*. They confirmed that they were. They became amused and gratified by the young idiot who seemed so impressed with their manly occupation and answered my questions with alacrity.

My interest finally settled on a ruddy-faced lad who was two or three years older than me. He was sitting on a bollard, well apart from his shipmates, eating a simple lunch of bread and cheese from a wooden platter. He told me that he had been taken on as a galley boy that very day. He was clearly not known to the sailors from Yarmouth, which suited my purpose ideally.

I looked at him as if eagerly wide-eyed impressed. 'Could I become a galley boy on this fine ship and sail to foreign lands? Could I, sir?'

The lad laughed, pleased with being addressed as 'sir' at his young age. 'No, mate,' he replied, 'not without a royal warrant.'

I frowned, as if not understanding what he meant. The lad opened a small satchel attached to a leather belt around his waist and took out a folded sheet of parchment. He waved it at me and said: 'This royal warrant gives me, Dick Bailey, permission to board the queen's ship as a member of the crew. You have to get one of these, with the royal seal on it like this one, before you can sail on the *St. Edward*. My father paid handsomely to buy me this warrant. I am going abroad to make my fortune and will repay him when I return as a rich merchant.'

'Can I look at it please, sir?'

'No,' Dick Bailey answered. 'You might run away with it.'

I guffawed and grinned stupidly, as if that very idea was nonsensical, but Bailey carefully put the royal warrant back into his satchel.

'Have to get back to work,' he said, sliding off the bollard and tossing the crumbs from his platter on to the quay where the seagulls eagerly swooped down to eat them.

I had to act quickly before Dick Bailey disappeared back into his ship. Without any clear plan in my mind I said hastily: 'My father owns the St. Nicholas inn, near the old dockyard. If you come to the inn tonight and show me the warrant, I will give you free food and drink.'

Dick Bailey regarded me cautiously. 'Why would you do that?'

'Please sir, I have never seen anything that has been touched by the king.'

'You're touched alright,' Dick Bailey said. 'Free food and ale? You promise?'

'I promise! As much as you can eat and drink. Cross my heart and hope to die.'

'Very well, I'll come, but if you are lying to me I'll kick your arse.'

A strategy was now forming in my mind. I returned to the crowd of sailors from Winchelsea and moved among them to announce that there would be free drinks for all at the St. Nicholas inn that evening. When they asked why they were being awarded such largesse I replied that it was approved by my father, who had bravely served in the king's navy when he was a young man, to welcome them as fellow comrades.

Satisfied that my offer would be taken up, I walked back to the inn to make sure that my father would be insensible and safely out of the way when the sailors of Winchelsea arrived for their free drinks.

When I arrived back at the inn my father cuffed me around the head until my ears rang like Sunday morning bells. I hung my head in pretended shame, apologised, told him he looked tired, and offered to bring him a flagon of ale.

I dosed the ale with a new spirit imported from Spain that the French called eau-de-vie. This drink was distilled from grapes and was much stronger than ale or wine. My father was soon staggering around in a most satisfying manner. I plied him with more laced ale and he soon obligingly disappeared up to his room.

It was only just in time because a few moments later Dick Bailey entered the inn. I was dismayed to see that he was wearing a sheathed dagger on his leather belt.

I sat him down on a bench at one of the rough wooden tables at the side of the inn and brought him a bowl of venison potage and a flagon of ale. He wolfed them down greedily.

Still suspicious, however, he refused to show me his royal warrant. I poured him a beaker of the eau-de-vie and he was intrigued by this unusual new drink. His manner thawed and he took the parchment warrant out of his satchel and handed it to me. 'You can look at it for a moment only.'

I pawed the ivory-hued parchment as if, overawed, I was handling some saintly relic, and satisfied myself that it was genuine. Mindful of the dagger, I handed it back to him with nods of thanks.

I said softly: 'I'd like to buy that warrant. How much will you take?'

Bailey looked at me curiously. 'It's not for sale.'

'One hundred silver pennies,' I offered.

'Are you mad? Where would a pot boy like you get that sort of money? I told you, it's not for sale.'

At that moment the first group of Winchelsea sailors entered the inn.

I fetched Dick Bailey a flask of eau-de-vie and placed it on his table. I whispered: 'Stay and order as much food and drink as you want, sir, but do not tell these gentlemen coming in that you sail with the Yarmouth crew. Think about my offer and name your price.'

I had instructed the serving wenches, as if the order had been issued by my father, to give the sailors whatever drinks they wanted and charge them nothing. The wenches, well aware of my father's tight-fisted nature, regarded me curiously but, reluctant to wake my father from his drunken slumber for confirmation of this odd instruction, they did not argue. They were, in any case, more interested in attracting glances and titillating comments from the lusty Winchelsea lads.

The word spread down to the harbour that my offer was genuine and the inn was soon full of carousing seamen. One of them produced a tabor, another a fife, and, to the disgruntlement of the other paying customers, they began to sing sea shanties at the top of their voices.

After I had judged that sufficient drink had been consumed I caught the attention of the sailors by performing a few acrobatic tricks. They laughed and cheered heartily and threw coins at my feet, which I collected with alacrity.

'Thank you, thank you, kind sirs,' I shouted above the din. 'On behalf of my father, who will shortly be here to greet you himself, I am pleased to welcome you here tonight. My father has happy memories of serving in the king's ships with your fathers from Winchelsea and he is honoured to entertain you tonight to compensate for what the men of Yarmouth have been saying about you. Please enjoy yourselves.'

As I had calculated, the mention of insulting comments by the men of Yarmouth caused a sullen hush to descend on the Winchelsea sailors. One of them asked: 'What have those Yarmouth lubbers been saying about us?'

I adopted an expression of wide-eyed innocence and replied: 'Why, sir, they say that you men of Winchelsea are worse sailors than Spaniards, more cowardly than Frenchmen, more stupid than Welshmen and that Queen Eleanor is mightily displeased with you all for providing her escort with such worm-eaten rotting tubs compared with the fine cog *St. Edward* provided by Yarmouth.'

Another sailor chipped in: 'The little monkey is right. Those

Yarmouth bastards have been saying such things all day. They've been taunting us alright.'

I added more pitch to the flames. 'And they say you are afraid to fight them because you know you would come off worst.'

'You heard them say such a thing?' the sailors asked me.

'Why, yes sirs,' I replied, with an air of imbelic innocence. 'They said you were cowardly scum and that they would beat you all into pulp when it came to a fight. I told them that my beloved father had served with the fine men of Winchelsea and that such talk was…'

But, to my horror, the men of Winchelsea, whipped up to a drunken fury, began streaming out of the inn. This was not what I had intended to happen!

'Wait, gentlemen, wait!' I shouted, but my exhortation was in vain.

I looked for Dick Bailey and, to my relief, he was still sitting at his table. He was clearly very drunk and had been watching proceedings with apprehension.

I needed to act swiftly before the last of the Winchelsea sailors quit the inn. 'Please, sirs,' I shouted. 'Please help me!'

Three of them turned back. 'What is it, lad?' a burly red-haired sailor asked.

I pointed to Dick Bailey. 'That man over there is one of the Yarmouth crew. He threatened me with a dagger and made me give him my leather belt. Can you get it back for me?'

The three men, all brawny and fired to evil by drink, immediately made for Dick Bailey's table. Made dull and stupid by eau-de-vie Bailey was slow to react as the three Winchelsea men charged towards him.

At the last moment Bailey kicked out with his right foot and caught his closest attacker in the stomach. The other two launched themselves at Bailey but, with alacrity fueled by mortal fear, Bailey ducked under them while simultaneously drawing his dagger. The bench and table went flying as the Winchelsea men crashed into them but they were not supple enough to grab Bailey. He rose up from a crouch and began to run.

I was now trapped between Bailey and the door. He dived towards me, his eyes filled with a murderous rage. His dagger slashed up diagonally across my face so closely that I could feel the draught from the movement. But his strike had missed. Thanks to my trained physical dexterity I had managed to leap backwards at the last moment.

Bailey knew that the Winchelsea men were right behind him so he could not stay to finish me off. He roared an obscenity as he disappeared out of the door, his leather satchel containing that precious royal warrant still securely attached to his leather belt.

I was slow to react, still shocked by my narrow escape. The three Winchelsea men, themselves roaring obscenities and angered by their clumsy humiliation, charged out into the night in pursuit. I followed them out in the forlorn hope of catching up with Bailey myself.

The night air was cool and the sky dark, with thick grey clouds scudding across the moon and casting shadows over the sleep-settling town. The darkness seemed to wrap itself around me as I ran towards the harbour. An eerily quiet stillness had now descended around the deserted environs of the inn on this night of lost souls, but in the distance I could hear wailing and keening and screams of agony.

I ran past the chandler's stores, rounded a corner, and then the *St. Edward* was in sight. I stopped abruptly, disbelieving and appalled by the violence I had inadvertantly unleashed.

A vicious mêlée had broken out and had spread on to the ship, along the gangplank, and down on to the quay. The men of Yarmouth, who had been idling or sleeping on the ship, had been taken by surprise by the sudden arrival of the drunken Winchelsea mob.

The few soldiers guarding the queen's ship, reluctant to use keen steel against drunken fellow countrymen, had simply retreated away from the riot.

I could see two bodies lying inert on the quay and could tell, from the agonised cries, the bruising intensity of the punches being thrown, and the moonlight glinting off sharpened steel that there would soon be many more.

I hesitated, fearing to approach this hellish confusion, but I feared more the loss of Dick Bailey and that royal warrant. I moved cautiously nearer, trying to spot Bailey. With several dozen men shouting, wrestling, kicking, slashing and assaulting each other with any weapon they could lay hands on, it seemed an impossible task.

I had to get nearer. I picked up a thick stave of wood for self-protection and moved nearer to the fringes of the mêlée, praying that my obvious youth might save me from being mistaken for a seaman.

'Dick!' I shouted. 'Dick Bailey! Where are you!? I can save you.'

I reeled sideways as a body fell against me. The victim's face was a red mask of running blood. His enraged attacker, wild-eyed blind to my youth, raised an iron bar to strike me. I swung my stave into his rib cage with all the force I could muster. The man grunted hoarsely and sank to his knees. I struck him again, on the side of his head, and he toppled forward unconscious.

I was immediately barged to the ground by two grappling seamen who fell into me, oblivious of my presence. I was now frightened out of my wits and, accepting that my clever plan had failed, all I wanted was to escape this stomach-churning carnage.

I crawled on hands and knees away from danger and then stood up and began to run away, but a movement up on the towering prow of the cog *St. Edward* caught my eye. I looked up. Someone, to escape the fighting, was climbing unsteadily up to the forecastle of the ship. It was Dick Bailey!

I threw away my stave and leapt towards the ship. Bailey had almost reached the safety of the forecastle but he was being forced to climb outwards by stepping on the bracing struts of the overhanging castellated platform. He was very drunk and unsteady but I was sober and a trained acrobat.

Using all the muscle power I had built up in the sawpits, I

clambered up the hull like a squirrel. There were plenty of handholds on the ornate prow and such was my strength that I hardly needed footholds. I hauled myself up with a speed, born of desperation, that surprised even myself.

Just as Bailey was clambering over the castellations to safety, I managed to grab his foot. He looked down at me red-eyed and began shouting angry obscenities. He kicked out with his foot to try to unbalance me but I was too strong and I held on. I knew he could not let go of his precarious handhold in order to draw his dagger so I let go his foot and clambered up further until we were almost face-to-face.

'Don't be a fool, Dick,' I urged him. 'Give me the warrant. I will pay you well in silver pennies. Your father can buy you another warrant but I must have this one. I must sail with this ship tomorrow.'

Dick Bailey looked down at me blearily. 'Silver pennies, you say?' His speech was so slurred as to be almost incomprehensible.

'Yes, Dick! Silver pennies, as many as you want.' I had no idea how I could fulfill such a promise.

The seagulls wheeled and screeched in imitation of the commotion below as Dick Bailey considered his options. My face was pressed hard against the forecastle of the ship and I could smell the newly-applied paint on the wood. Finally Bailey said: 'You would have had me killed in that inn tonight.'

'No, Dick. I acted rashly, on the spur of the moment. I just wanted to frighten you into giving me your warrant.'

'Then you'll kill me anyway. I'll not give you my warrant, you little bastard. I don't want your silver but I'll give you ten inches of steel instead.'

Bailey released his grip on the forecastle with one hand and fumbled to draw his dagger.

'No, Dick!' I cried, but it was too late. Bailey lost his handholds and began to fall backwards. He grabbed my shirt to save himself and, before I could do anything to prevent it, his momentum dragged me away and we were both falling backwards and down towards the jetty.

We landed with a lung-bursting thud on the packed earth. I had fallen on top of Bailey. I was badly winded but otherwise unhurt.

'Dick,' I said hoarsely. 'Are you all right?'

Then I saw the livid pool of red blood spreading around the back of Bailey's head. I realised his head must have struck the edge of one of the wooden support posts forming the edge of the jetty.

Bailey was not breathing. His body was limp. His eyes were wide open and seemed to gaze at me in mute accusation.

I was filled with choking anguish and guilt. 'I didn't mean for this to happen, Dick,' I whispered to his unhearing ears. 'I'm sorry. I didn't mean for any of this to happen.'

Despite my shocked numbness, I became aware that the fighting had increased in intensity. I looked up and saw that, away over on the other side of the quay, soldiers were arriving to quell the fighting.

Also, someone was walking towards me.

I turned back and unbuckled Dick Bailey's leather belt, complete with satchel, my actions hidden from view by my body. I quickly unlaced my shirt and stuffed the belt inside it and under my arm.

Just as I had concealed my prize a voice behind me said quietly: 'You found him then, the thieving Yarmouth bastard. Is he dead?'

I looked up. It was the burly red-haired Winchelsea sailor who had tried to help me at the inn.

'Yes, he's dead,' I replied. 'But I didn't kill him. He fell and hit his head.'

'No matter,' the sailor said, unconcerned. 'You'll still be blamed. The soldiers are here. Better toss him over the side before they arrest you. Or me. Tell you what, you run along back to the inn, boy. I'll take care of this one.'

I stood up and stumbled away, my legs hardly able to carry me. I looked back to see the sagging body of Dick Bailey being rolled into the merciless sea by my Winchelsea benefactor.

I reached the sanctuary of the inn thinking that, thank God, the horror of that night was over. But worse, much worse, was yet to come. [3]

When I returned to the St. Nicholas Inn, all seemed to be as normal. I looked inside the door. There were many travellers staying overnight and there were still many drinkers and diners at the tables. I could not see my father.

I went outside to the back of the inn, pulled up the heavy wooden trapdoor and climbed down the ladder to the dark and dank cellar where I slept. My father would not give me my own room when others were willing to pay for such a room, so I was consigned down to the stink of barrels of ale, fish and salted meats, where I also served as unpaid watchman to keep out intruders. I slept, when I was not disturbed by the noise from the inn, on a pile of straw and blankets in the corner of the cellar.

I lay on my straw bed, in the clinging darkness, thinking about the night's events. I was still trembling with fear. I thought of how Bailey's lifeless and accusing eyes had looked at me after we had tumbled to earth. I relived the bruising sights and sounds of the vicious riot, the first time in my life that I had been witness to such savage violence, savage violence that I had inadvertently caused. All I had intended was to lure sufficient Winchelsea seamen to the inn so that I could manipulate them into intimidating Dick Bailey into handing over his royal warrant.

I thought of my father who, when he awoke from his drunken slumber, would be gleefully informed by any one of those wretched serving women exactly how much money in free food and drinks I had cost him.

I thought of Lord Edward and my scheme to get aboard the *St. Edward* and inveigle my way into his service. What was I thinking of? What was the likelihood that a diminutive common pot boy such as I, however secretly gifted, could possibly be useful to the heir to the throne of England?

In my arrogance and frantic desire to escape a world that had abused me so cruelly I had caused the death of Dick Bailey and several other innocent seamen.

I took out Bailey's leather belt from under my shirt, opened the satchel and felt the smooth parchment of the royal warrant. What if I attempted to board the *St. Edward* and was arrested and unmasked as an impostor? I would be thrown in prison. Worse still, what if the body of Dick Bailey was discovered, or if someone had witnessed our brawl on the bow of the *St. Edward?* I ran the risk of being convicted of murder and executed.

In a timid funk I decided to stay where I was and not to run away from the safety of the St. Nicholas Inn in pursuit of my insane dream. I decided that God had punished me for my hubris.

Then, very gradually, the fear began to drain away from me. Perhaps it was my God-given destiny to serve Lord Edward.

I remembered the stringent efforts I had made to learn all the skills in my possession, all the subterfuges I had undertaken in order to hide my true nature from the scrutiny of others. I had been preparing for this opportunity all my life. Should I now abandon my ambition and spend my life serving food and drink to ill-bred commoners? No, I felt that my blood was different, and I was about to be proved correct, in a most shocking manner.

Exhausted, but fired with fresh confidence and resolve, I drifted off to sleep.

Some time later I was awoken by the crash of the cellar trapdoor being flung back. I saw a figure, illuminated by moonlight and carrying a rushlight, descending down the ladder. I rose to my feet quickly, shaking away my drowsiness, ready for confrontation.

'Hamo!' my father roared. He was still very drunk. 'You moonstruck little idiot. You owe me money.' He raised his rushlight over his head to light his path through the barrels. His ugly vole face was contorted with anger. Eerie shadows danced on the low ceiling as he advanced towards me.

'I'm over here, father, waiting for my punishment. Why don't you come over and beat me?'

My father looked bewildered by my unexpectedly confident and challenging attitude and halted. He had never heard me talking in this manner before and he was confused. Even in the rushlit gloom I could see that his eyes were bloodshot with drink as he peered at me. I was standing, hidden by shadows, in my dark corner.

'Hamo?' he breathed, 'I've never heard you talk to me like this before. What is wrong with you?'

'Why, nothing father. What is a son for but to be trained as a pet monkey to entertain the patrons, to stand exhausted in a pit choking with sawdust, to grow up without a mother's breast to comfort him, to withstand the querulous rages of a drunken cruel bastard who, as my father, should know better. I spit on you and your filthy inn. I spit on the word father.'

He stood swaying in front of me. It was as if he was seeing me, actually seeing me as a person, for the first time in his life. He was baffled but becoming angrier. 'You little turd,' he said menacingly. 'You are not my son. I would be ashamed to have sired a creature such as you. Your whore of a mother gave herself to another. He is your real father. Yes, I have been using you but I also gave you food and shelter and upbringing. Is this fit gratitude for my kindness?'

I was stunned and shocked by my father's life-changing revelation. I felt a tightness in my chest and it was difficult to breathe. Lamely, awkwardly, I responded: 'Do not talk of my mother in such a way. I don't believe you. You use lies to excuse your treatment of me.'

'I tell you the truth, Hamo. Your real father is a nobleman who stayed incognito at the inn one night. He had arrived that day from Gascony. My wife, your mother, became enamoured of his fine clothes, his fine looks, his smooth words and his wealth, and she gave herself to him. Nine months later, in the normal term, you were born.'

I was bereft of speech and I felt an alien emotion, tearful and desirous of comfort, as if I were the child that, in truth, I still was. I could not decide whether to believe Pauncefoot or not. 'You say truly that I am of noble birth?'

'Yes, Hamo, albeit the wrong side of the blanket.'

No, this could not be true. My father considered me a halfwit and this was his attempt to ameliorate me. And yet I desperately wanted it to be true. I asked: 'Who was this nobleman?'

My father's speech was slurred as he replied: 'I told you he was staying here incognito. I do not know who he was and neither did your mother.'

'Does he know of my existence?'

My father laughed scornfully. 'Of course not! Your mother dreamed that he would take her away from me but he never returned. A man like that has bastards in every town and village and would not care about you even if he knew you existed!'

'I don't believe you,' I blustered. 'You must know something about him. Anything at all?' The stunning knowledge that my real father was a nobleman and, if he knew I was his son, could help me achieve my dreams and ambitions was already driving me frantic with curiosity and hope. I asked: 'What did he look like?'

Again, my father laughed scornfully. 'I don't know, boy. I didn't take notice and after all these years I cannot recall. Unlike your mother, I did not care what he looked like as long as he paid his due.'

'You must remember something about him. Tell me!'

My father made a dismissive sound and waved his hand as if trying to brush away the whole subject.

Thinking to play on his greedily avaricious nature, I suggested: 'Perhaps we can extort some money from this nobleman, if we can find out who he is.'

My father swayed blearily as he considered this notion.

'Come on. Think carefully, any small detail might identify him.'

'Perhaps you're right about the money, boy. Let me think... he was dressed plainly, like a common man, but he was attended by two stewards. He was about thirty years old. I peeked into his room and remember seeing his fancy surcoat laid out on the bed. There was a creature displayed on it. This surcoat looked to be made of silk, with gold and… '

'A creature? What sort of creature? What did it look like?'

'Like a dog or wolf or something, standing on its hind legs, with its paws held out.' Pauncefoot put down his rushlight on top of a barrel and mimicked, ludicrously, the rampant stance of the creature. 'And it had a long twisting pointed tail. No, no, it was not a dog, it was more like that fierce creature the priest shows us in his bestiary. Like the creature King Henry was wearing on his surcoat when I saw him take ship.'

'A lion,' I cried. 'The lion of England.'

'Yes, that's it… a lion.'

'What colour was it?'

'God's truth, I can't remember, boy. All this was many years ago.'

'Anything else you can remember. Think, father, think.'

'Wait, wait, there was something about his wife,' my father replied, still stupidly slurring his words. 'I overheard this man's stewards talking to your mother. That is what stirred her interest in this great lord and I was jealous, so I listened to what they were saying. Their master had retired for the night and they were drunk and talking too much. They let slip that their master's wife had once been married or related to another lord. An earl.'

An earl! I could scarcely contain my excitement as I asked: 'Which earl?'

'I can't remember, boy.'

'You must remember! Which earl?'

'I don't know. But I do remember that this wife's former name was the same as some official or other.'

'An official? What sort of official?'

'God's blood, I can't think. Something like steward or chamberlain or sheriff.' My father suddenly had to reach out to support himself on a barrel. 'My head is swimming with all this thinking.'

I stepped forward and grabbed him by his shirt, more to prevent him collapsing than intimidate him. 'Think! What was this woman's name?'

My father gazed at me for a long moment, trying to think of a name, as well as to comprehend my newly-revealed rational assertiveness. His sour breath filled my nose with a noxious stench. 'You stink worse than the Camber marshes,' I said in disgust.

'That's it,' my father whispered. 'Marsh, her name was Marsh… no, Marshal. The wife's name was Marshal.'

'Are you certain?'

'Yes, I'm certain. The lord's stewards said her name was Marshal.'

I deliberately committed this name to memory but I knew I would never forget it. My father's face had turned deep red so I released my grip and he staggered back a step or two

'Can you remember anything else?' I said.

To my surprise, Pauncefoot grinned at me leerily. 'I can tell you one thing, boy. This lord had a strange birthmark on his big cock.' My father noted the confusion in my face. 'Yes, that's right, boy. I caught them at it, just after they had finished making you. Your real father was well equipped, I can tell you. When I caught them he was not in the least concerned. Before his stewards bundled me out of the room I noticed a lozenge shaped strawberry mark on his cock, clear as day.'

As if drenched by icy water my wits cleared and common sense returned judgement to my fevered imagination. 'You are making fun of me, old man. You are mocking me. You tell me lies to satisfy my dreams that I am more than the son of a malignant and drunken potman.'

'You still don't believe me, Hamo?' my father breathed, with a strangely malevolent expression on his face. 'I cannot be your father and I can prove it.'

'How?' I challenged.

My father unlaced his hose and drawers and pulled them down.

That night I had seen men being killed but that was nothing compared to the horror I felt now.

'There, Hamo,' my father whispered thickly. 'Does that prove it to you? Why do you think I was discharged from the king's service with compensation handsome enough to buy this inn. For the loss of my manhood, that's why.'

I could not drag my eyes away from the stump, barely half an inch long, and the badly scarred and disfigured testicles.

'Yes, take a good look, Hamo. I was close to death for weeks. One swipe of a Frenchman's sword followed by a kicking around the deck and my life as a man was over. I have lived in constant pain and humiliation ever since. You call me a drunk. That is the only way I can survive through this wretched existence. Yes, I am a shrunken, drunken shell of a man. And I am not your father.' He pulled up his drawers and hose and relaced them. He picked up his rushlight and barked angrily: 'Now you will give me all the coins you have squirelled away behind that loose plaster under your bed. You will pay for all the free food and drinks you gave away to those sailors earlier tonight.'

I was not surprised that Peter Pauncefoot had discovered my cache of coins. I did not move, the implications of what had just been revealed to me about my true parentage were swarming through my head like Camber Marsh mosquitoes. I was unable to turn my thoughts to what Peter Pauncefoot was saying.

'Give me your money, boy,' Pauncefoot repeated, with unmistakeable menace.

Dragging my mind back to the present, I replied: 'If my actions tonight have cost you money then it is still a fraction of what you have not paid me over the years. You shall not have my money. I have earned it, and I need it. I am leaving in the morning and I shall not return.'

I saw renewed anger blazing in Pauncefoot's eyes as he asked incredulously: 'Leaving, boy? You can't leave me. Where are you going?'

'Somewhere far away where you and your drunken friends can no longer taunt and abuse me.'

'Give me my money!' Pauncefoot roared. His face had now turned from red to purple. 'Give me my money or I shall take it!'

I did not move or speak. Pauncefoot lunged forward and grabbed me around the neck with both hands. Before he could choke me I took hold of each of his wrists and almost effortlessly prised them away from my neck. Pauncefoot stepped back, shocked and bewildered by my unexpected strength.

'Yes, father, you did well to consign me to the sawpits. My muscles have been well trained.'

Pauncefoot was now consumed with a fury that I had never witnessed before. He picked up a heavy bung-stopper mallet laying on top of a barrel and swung it at my head. I ducked, then I caught his wrist and twisted his arm to make him drop the mallet.

I was preparing to strike back with my fist when Pauncefoot made a strange gurgling sound. His face had now turned the deepest purple and, as I watched, the left side of his face seemed to sag and then collapse into a demonic rictus. He sank to his knees and began tearing at his shirt as if possessed by the Devil. His mouth was running with drool.

Then, as if accepting that death had come for him, he held out his arms to me. I kneeled down and took him into my arms. In just a few moments his breathing ceased and his face looked more at peace than I had ever seen it.

Unexpectedly, I wept. I held his frail body in my arms for a long while. Then I laid him down gently on the straw-covered floor. I remained kneeling for a long time, staring at Pauncefoot's gaunt face. I felt a strange mixture of bereavement combined with exultation at my release from his brutal thrall.

I realised that the apoplexy that had carried off Peter Pauncefoot had now presented me with another opportunity and another dilemma. As his only son (in law, if not in fact) I would inherit the prosperous St. Nicholas Inn. But I was a mere fifteen years old. I was aware that many wealthy merchants in Portsmouth viewed the lucrative St. Nicholas Inn with covetous eyes and it would be easy for them to deprive a child of such a prize possession, whatever the laws of inheritance.

It would be easy for such covetous enemies to accuse me of murdering my father. And, even if I could hold on to the inn, did I truly want to spend the rest of my life serving others in such a menial capacity?

No, I was of noble birth. If I could prove that fact then my ascent to wealth and status would be so much easier. I craved adventure, excitement, the chance to be involved in great events together with great men. Lord Edward offered that chance. I resolved that I would continue with my plan to join the crew of the *St. Edward* on the morrow.

If Peter Pauncefoot's body was discovered before I could board the *St. Edward* then the sheriff would be called and an investigation held that would compel me to stay in Portsmouth. I did not want the body found until I was well out to sea or, if my subterfuge in stealing Dick Bailey's identity failed, before I could make my escape away from Portsmouth.

No, I did not want the St. Nicholas Inn but, up in my late father's room, was his strongbox. That was one inheritance that I fully intended to claim.

I prised the lid off a barrel that had once contained fish pickled in brine. The fish had been removed but the brine was still in the barrel. I lifted up Peter Pauncefoot's body and slid it into the barrel. Some of the brine slopped over the top. I replaced the lid tightly. The brine would help mask the smell of decomposition until, whatever my fate, I was many miles away from Portsmouth.

My daintily sensitive amanuensis, Brother Godfrey, now shudders with disgust, crosses himself, and cannot resist chiding me for the suffering I caused on that fateful night. He asks me to repent and asks God to forgive me.

Well, my tonsured friend, should God forgive me, or should I forgive God? The church is quick to claim the benificence of God when it suits, and equally quick to condemn we mortals for our sins.

Were my actions my own? Certainly they were initiated by me but would, or should, have God allowed such a fatal outcome? Or did he approve of my desire to serve Lord Edward, a prince anointed by God? Nothing to say, priest? Then pick up your quill and let us get on.

I buckled on Dick Bailey's leather belt, retrieved my small cache of coins and put them in the satchel, and then climbed up the ladder into the chill night air. I went into the inn through the back door that Peter Pauncefoot had left open. I took a stout leather bag from the kitchen as well as a couple of swigs of eau-de-vie to calm my nerves. I also stashed a bottle in the bag for my journey.

I climbed the ricketty stairs to my father's room, being careful not to let any of the patrons hear or see me. It was very early morning and all the patrons were sleeping soundly, senses dulled by ale and wine.

I entered Peter Pauncefoot's room, which was at the end of a corridor, and drew the curtain closed behind me. Despite Pauncefoot's best efforts to keep it a secret I had long ago discovered the place where he hid the key to his strongbox. One of the finial knobs on his fancy tester bed could be worked loose and the key was secreted in that space.

I opened the strongbox, which was chained to a metal ring set into the floor. I transferred most of the silver pennies into a brassbound wooden box. The rest of the pennies I left. The staff of the inn could fight over them. I had to escape the inn as soon as possible.

I peeped out from behind the curtain to make sure no-one was watching. I silently slunk down the stairs and out of the inn. I did not bother to look back at that hateful place of humiliation.

I fled, hunched like a phantom, through the dancing moon

shadows. I made my way to the graveyard of the church and to the plot where my mother was buried. It was the dead of night and no-one witnessed my passing. I dug down, scrabbling earth like a badger, until I came to the rotted lid of my mother's coffin.

I placed the box of coins beside the coffin. The box would protect the coins until I one day returned to retrieve my inheritance. Dread and superstition would ensure that no-one would dare to disturb the grave and discover the coins, even if they noticed that the earth around the grave had already been disturbed. The shivering and half-starved stray dogs would be blamed.

I shovelled the earth back into place and disguised my handiwork as carefully as I could, then I offered a prayer for my mother's soul.

I hobbled out of the gnarled and earth-stinking graveyard and went down to the sands where the fishing boats were pulled up on the shore. I dug a snug pit under the derelict fishing boat and slept, exhausted, haunted by visions of my mother's arms reaching out to me, of who my real father might be, and tormented by Peter Pauncefoot's face, contorted in death, imploring me to stay.

I awoke with a throbbing headache and a sand-dried throat. I was desperately thirsty and took a swig of the eau-de-vie, as much to bolster my courage as to ease my parched throat. I had to worm my way aboard the royal cog *St. Edward* as soon as possible and without being seen by any busybody who might recognise and betray me.

I brushed the sand off my rough woollen surcoat, splashed sea water on my face, flattened my unruly hair with the palms of my hand, and made myself look as presentable as I could.

I picked up my leather bag and began walking towards the harbour, keeping close to the warming shoreline to avoid the risk of meeting any of the townspeople. The most dread and perilous moment would be when I attempted to board the *St. Edward* using Dick Bailey's warrant.

I had decided to wear Bailey's finely tooled leather belt outside my surcoat. I had to trust to good fortune that whoever was checking the credentials of the crew might remember the belt but not the appearance of the person wearing it. If they did remember Bailey I had a cock-and-bull story prepared about how I had won the belt and royal warrant from him as a gambling debt during a game of dice.

I cautiously neared the *St. Edward*, constantly looking around in order to avoid anyone who might recognise me. I was surprised to find that all was clean and calm around the vessel and that there was no trace of the previous night's mayhem. Everything had been done to ensure that the royal family would not be distressed by the sight of blood and bodies when they arrived from the monastery to board the ship. There was a much more numerous cordon of fully armed soldiers protecting the ship and keeping the peace than there had been the day before.

I approached the cordon and the sergeant-at-arms in command stopped me and asked where I was going. I was tense but I calculated that I would have no trouble at this stage of my deception. I presented my warrant and he waved me through.

On board the *St. Edward*, standing at the top of the gangplank, was a court official and the master of the vessel checking the manifest and the crew list as the last of the victuals were being loaded. The two men looked at me suspiciously as I approached along the quay and then began to climb up the gangplank.

The court official, who was attired in his robe of office, held out the palm of his hand to prevent me stepping on to the deck. 'Name?' he asked.

My heart thumped in my chest as I answered: 'Dick Bailey, sir.' I proffered the royal warrant.

The master, a tall, weather-beaten and grizzled man with a hooked nose, peered at me narrowly and said: 'I don't recognise you, boy. You didn't sail from Yarmouth with me, did you?'

Before I could reply, attempting to keep the tremulous nerves from my speech, the court official said to the master: 'This lad joins the ship here at Portsmouth. His father is known to me as an honest and upright burgher and has vouched for his son as an honest and hardworking boy who is keen to learn.'

Now I knew who Dick Bailey's father had bribed to buy his son's place in the crew. This corrupt court official, thankfully, did not know what Dick Bailey looked like. The master asked me: 'Are you keen to learn, lad?'

'Indeed I am, sir,' I croaked, almost unable to speak through fear and thirst, and giving him my most ingratiating smile.

'Very good,' the master said grandly. 'You are engaged as a galley boy so report to the galley master, do as your betters tell you, and obey orders implicitly. If you displease me you'll feel the kiss of a rope's end on your back.'

'Yes, sir. Thank you, sir,' I mumbled.

The court official moved aside to allow me to step on to the deck. I began to walk away intent on finding any place where I could escape the gaze of the master, but I had not gone more than ten feet when he called out: 'Just a minute, Bailey!'

My stomach tingled with an icy fear. Surely I had not schemed and strived this far only to be unmasked as an impostor when safety was as near as the outgoing tide? I turned and said: 'Yes, sir?'

'Where is your bundle?' the master asked.

For a moment I was stupidly baffled by the question. Then I realised he meant the bundle of clothing, bedding and personal belongings that every sailor carried. Thinking quickly, I replied: 'I gave it to another member of the crew to bring on board overnight, sir, while I went to say goodbye to my mother and father.'

The master regarded me critically. 'Don't be so stupid, boy,' he snapped.

'Beg pardon, sir,' was all I could think to say, now certain that I was about to be unmasked.

'From now on, don't be stupid and leave your bundle overnight unguarded like that. Knowing the rogues and cut-throats who man this ship you'll be lucky to find anything left. Now go and get on with it.'

I humbly knuckled my forehead, as I had seen other seadogs do, and walked away quickly with a surge of intense relief.

I climbed down below deck and found the galley. The *St. Edward,* having been built as a royal vessel, had been equipped amidships with a small fire-proof metal-lined cabin so that a stove could be safely kept alight at all times in order to prepare hot meals for royal and noble passengers.

The galley master was already working in this cramped space. He was a small and stout man, amiable and thorough, who wore an eye patch, having lost his right eye in action against the French, and was a royal servant brought aboard to oversee their food preparation rather than being a member of the crew. He immediately set me to work preparing food for the crew and, much more importantly, refreshments for the royal party when they later boarded the vessel.

Having grown up in an inn that was constantly catering food and drink I had no trouble whatsoever performing my duties and the galley master was very pleased with me, particularly as I plied him with my sunniest and most cheery disposition and kept him entertained with silly jokes and harmless pranks.

I felt exultant and very excited. Not only had I achieved my objective of placing myself in close proximity to Lord Edward, I was also a young man about to depart on my first sea voyage to exotic foreign climes. I had never felt happier, even when the galley master refused me permission to watch the royal party embarking. I was frantically curious to see Lord Edward again but I consoled myself with the thought that my opportunity would soon arrive.

My relief was intense when, confined in the galley as I was, I heard the ship come alive with creaking rigging and the thumping footfall noises of departure and felt the deck moving up and down under my feet. The ship had weighed anchor for Gascony and that, for the moment, was all the contentment I needed.

As soon as I found some thinking time, which was only during the time allotted for sleeping in my warm berth underneath the galley table, I applied my mind to the problem of how to contact Lord Edward and ingratiate myself into his favour. I needed an opportunity to show him, respectfully but unmistakably, how valuable my services could be, but I could not fathom how to engineer such an opportunity. Food and drink for the royal family was fetched from the galley by trusted servants.

I did not see any of the royal family during the first two days of the voyage but, because the winds were not in our favour, I had several days in which to implement any scheme that presented itself. I seized every chance to gossip, in my guise as an awestruck simpleton, with the other members of the crew and glean as much information as I could.

Three days into the voyage the *St. Edward* encountered storms and rough rain-sodden weather. Having grown up in Portsmouth and having often sailed out with the local fishermen I was immune to sea sickness but, judging by the state of the deck, most of our noble passengers were not. As the wind groaned through the rigging and the decks creaked under the strain, the rails either side of the main deck were lined with bedraggled fur-bedecked nobility heaving their guts into the waves smashing against the hull.

One afternoon, a royal servant entered the galley with a bundle of stinking vomit-stained clothing. Laundry for delicate clothing was another duty that had to be carried out in the galley because it was the only place in the ship where water could be safely heated.

The servant dumped most of the clothing on to the deck with the exception of a fine padded linen surcoat which was embroidered with silk. He held it up by each sleeve so that we could admire the armorial emblem finely stitched into the surcoat. 'Be careful with this surcoat,' the servant warned, with a malevolent teasing grin. 'It belongs to Lord Edward's tutor, Bartholomew Pecche, who suffers badly from the mal-de-mer. Master Pecche also teaches Lord Edward the use of the sword and the lance so it would not be healthy to upset such a man by ruining this surcoat, which must have cost him dearly in silver pennies.' The servant grinned again at the enticing prospect of we crude and humble seamen being punished by Lord Edward's virile tutor.

I had already learned that Bartholomew Pecche was accompanying his two sons to Castile where they were to be knighted by King Alphonso at the same ceremony in which Lord Edward would be knighted. This was a very high honour and a reward for Pecche's devoted service to Edward over many years.

I instantly conceived of an opportunity to ingratiate myself with Lord Edward. It was a very risky idea but I calculated that it would be worth the risk and that I had to act boldly and seize the chance.

The galley master was delighted when I volunteered to launder Pecche's surcoat. I explained that, having grown up in a tavern, I was often pressed into cleaning up vomit from all sorts of surfaces and I was adept at so doing. The galley master was no doubt considering that if the surcoat were to be ruined then all the blame could be attached to me.

It took me three days, and several heart-lurching moments when I was nearly caught out, to fully implement my scheme. Now all I needed was an opportunity to talk to Lord Edward. Another passage of rough seas unexpectedly provided a perfect opportunity.

A royal servant, seized in a fit of panic, entered the cramped galley, where I was working alone, and announced that Lord Edward desperately needed a drink made from an infusion of herbs. This concoction was said to quell sea sickness.

The servant was flustered because he had just emptied and cleaned Lord Edward's sick bucket and was anxious to return it swiftly to be refilled by his royal master's retching. I suggested that he return the bucket to Lord Edward without delay and that I would bring the herb drink as soon as it was prepared.

Gambling that I had a much more effective cure, I placed a flask of eau-de-vie and two silver goblets on a tray, then wrapped it all in a linen cloth to prevent them being carried away by the fierce winds up on deck. I climbed the companionway ladder out on to the open deck and gingerly made my way through the sail-flapping howl and across the wildly bucking deck to the doors of the royal cabin, which was installed in the large castellated aft castle at the stern of the cog.

Bracing myself as a wave of green spume-flecked sea roared across the deck, I knocked lightly on the cabin door. The servant pushed open the door against the sighing wind and beckoned me inside.

Despite being the largest space on the ship, the royal cabin was still very cramped. It had been partitioned with a heavy embroidered curtain in order to provide a private compartment for Queen Eleanor, who was suffering very badly from sea sickness. Lord Edward and his younger brother, Lord Edmund, shared the other half of the cabin.

I had never before seen any space so luxuriously appointed. The bulkheads had been covered with wood panelling and hung with tapestries. The furniture was finely made, painted in a profusion of colours, and equipped with embroidered padded cushions for comfort. There were gold and silver plates, and silver goblets rolling back and forth on a small table that had a low pierced rail built around it to prevent such items falling on to the deck. The porthole covers were closed and secured against the storm but even the dark foetid candle-lit atmosphere and the pervading stench of vomit could not mar this first dazzling impression of true wealth.

A lady-in-waiting pulled aside the curtain screening Queen Eleanor's compartment, handed the male servant another bucket of vomit and then preremptorily grabbed the empty one. She silenced protests that it was Lord Edward's bucket with a querulous assurance that the queen was very ill and needed it more. The servant anxiously pushed out of the cabin to empty and clean the sick bucket.

Young Lord Edmund was sitting at the small table reading a book. Having ingeniously braced himself against a bulkhead, he was seemingly unaffected by the motion of the ship and, as ten-year-olds are wont to be, was highly amused by the discomfort being endured by the rest of his family. He was much shorter in stature than his elder brother but was stockier and shared Edward's long fair hair and grey eyes. He was dressed in a simple blue belted tunic but with a gold chain pendant around his neck to denote his rank. He looked up at me benignly and asked: 'What do you want?'

I bowed and replied: 'I have brought a tonic for Lord Edward that will help to alleviate his sea sickness… my lord.'

'He's in there,' Lord Edmund said, nodding towards a curtained-off sleeping alcove on the starboard side and losing all interest in me as he returned to his reading.

My stomach fluttered with excitement and apprehension. I took a moment to try to quell my nervousness. Then I braced myself against the roll of the ship, carefully balanced the tray securely in the crook of my left arm, and pulled back the alcove curtain with my right hand.

Lord Edward lay, with his knees drawn up, on a narrow bunk that was much too short for his lanky adolescent frame. His fair curly hair was spread out on a pillow as he writhed in discomfort. His skin bore the pale green pallor of death. The front of his plain white shirt was stained with puke. He looked up at me, his grey eyes red-rimmed and bleary with tiredness and illness.

I bowed and, summoning all my courage in an attempt to appear confident and relaxed, said softly: 'Good day again, my lord. I have brought you a cure for your sea sickness and warning of a traitor in your midst.'

My statement engaged Edward's attention, despite his suffering, and he half sat up in order to observe me more clearly through his red-rimmed and tear-shot eyes. 'Who are you?' he asked, his adolescent voice a high-pitched and feeble croak. 'I know you.'

'Indeed you do, my lord,' I smiled. 'The last time we met you threw me into the sea.'

Lord Edward's head fell back on to the pillow, his face bearing an expression as if he had resigned himself to his fate. 'What are you doing here? Are you a shade sent by demons to haunt and punish me? Or have you come to kill me in revenge? Death would be a blessed release from this torment.'

'No, my lord, I have once again come to offer my service to you. I repeat that I can cure your sea sickness and also cure you of a foul traitor.'

With eyes closed, Lord Edward asked: 'Are you not afraid that I might have you hanged or thrown into the sea again? You could not swim your escape from here.'

'My life is yours to do with as you wish, my lord. You can kill me or you can allow me to become your loyal eyes and ears whenever you are far away from me. I leave you to decide which would be the most useful course of action. I have taken note, sire, that you did not have me arrested after our encounter in Portsmouth harbour.'

Edward's eyes opened again, but this time they were narrowed with warning. 'By God, you speak brazenly. I admit your foolish antics helped to win the crowd back to my side but I thought you a moonstruck imbecile, that's why I did not have you pursued. What possible service can a moonstruck imbecile render to me?'

'You have perceived the very essence of the service I can offer you, my lord. Everyone considers me an uneducated idiot but, as you can tell from the manner of my speaking, I am anything but an idiot. Great lords are wont to use their jesters as spies and informers. I am a trained fool. I can tumble, perform acrobatics, tell jests, sing and tell stories while accompanying myself on the harp. I can…'

'There are many jesters and fools who can perform such services,' Edward interrupted, losing interest.

'Yes, my lord, but can they read and understand French and Latin as well as English? I have cultivated the impression that I can speak and understand only English. People think I am so dull that I cannot read English, or even speak it with fluency. People often say things in front of me thinking that I do not understand when I understand perfectly. That is how I have discovered the name of the traitor in your service.'

Lord Edward struggled to sit up further and then said, with a hint of sarcasm and a trace of that frightening sibilant lisp I was to come to know so well: 'You are indeed versatile. What else do you do? Perform miracles? Move mountains? Turn water into wine?'

'No, my lord,' I replied, attempting to keep my tone light and unafraid, 'but I can play dice, tables and chess for your amusement, and I...'

'You play chess?' Edward said. This time he was brightly interested.

'Yes, to a good standard, my lord.'

Edward stared at me thoughtfully and then asked: 'Quis est vestri nomen?'

I replied: 'Meus nomen est Hamo Pauncefoot. Meus votum est ut servo vos fidelis?'

'Very well, you understand and speak Latin. Avez-vous également comprendre le français au même degré?'

'Au moins aussi bien que Latin, mon seigneur.'

On a sudden the ship ploughed into a patch of very rough water and I had to instantly brace myself to save spilling the tray. At that moment the royal servant drew back the curtain, shoved me aside and placed the sick bucket on the deck next to Lord Edward's bunk.

Behind the servant, Lord Edmund was leaning forward and peering through the curtain. He asked: 'Is everything all right, brother?' Indicating me, Edmund said: 'Who is this person? Is he vexing you.'

Lord Edward replied by throwing up bile into the freshly cleaned bucket. When he had finished he looked up at me as if considering my fate. Then he replied to his brother: 'No, Edmund. He is a fool come to amuse and distract me, and he says he has a cure for sea sickness. Concern yourself with our mother. She suffers more than I.'

The servant drew the curtain closed as he departed and left me alone again with Lord Edward. He said wearily: 'You babble something about a traitor. What are you talking about?'

'Permit me to suggest, my lord, that I ease your sea sickness first and then you can consider what I have to say with ready wits.'

Edward said distractedly: 'My destiny is to one day rule over the land of England but this unruly sea that surrounds England, like Canute before me, defies all my commands to be still and may be the death of me before I can ever rule the land. God's blood, if you can cure this damnable sickness I will be forever in your debt.'

What encouraging words they were! I had opened a narrow crack in the door of Lord Edward's affections and I now had to kick that door open. I had unwittingly found Edward's Achilles heel. All his life he suffered lamentably from sea sickness and, many years later when he was king, he founded a monastery at Darnhall to give thanks for deliverance from a particularly rough and arduous sea voyage.

Bracing against the heave of the ship I balanced the tray with one hand and poured eau-de-vie into a silver goblet with the other. 'Please take a long drink of this, my lord,' I said, offering Edward the goblet.

Edward looked at the goblet suspiciously. 'You have put poison in there.'

'I anticipated your sensible caution, my lord,' I replied, and drank down the eau-de-vie in one gulp. 'This is a drink called eau-de-vie, my lord. It causes a pleasant numbing sensation and will settle your stomach to give immediate relief. You see, my lord, I still live and breathe. Please drink some.'

I poured more of the spirit into the other goblet and handed it to Lord Edward. After a momentary hesitation he followed my example and drank the entire contents in one gulp. As a proof of burgeoning trust I could ask no more.

I continued: 'Now, my lord, permit me to ask you to rise from your bunk and come out on to the deck of the ship with me.'

'This spirit is good and warming,' Edward answered, 'but why do I have to get up?'

'I have learned, my lord, that if you can watch the horizon while the ship is heaving then the symptoms of sea sickness diminish substantially. Also, the motion of the ship that causes the sickness is less pronounced amidships and the fresh sea air will be better for you than laying in this foetid atmosphere.'

Lord Edward momentarily looked irritated by my presumption but then began to rise from his bunk. 'What is your name again?' he asked, as he sat on the edge of his bunk with his head in his hands.

'My true name is Hamo Pauncefoot,' I replied, 'but I am sailing under the name of Dick Bailey.'

'What reason for such subterfuge?'

'So that I can already be of service to you without the knowledge of others,' I lied.

Edward nodded, accepting my lie, and began to don a fur-trimmed robe to protect him from the cold. He said: 'I'll have you whipped for making me get up, Pauncefoot, if this cure does not work.'

I could tell from Lord Edward's tone of voice that his threat was more light-hearted than serious. 'I promise you it will at least alleviate your suffering considerably, my lord, if not cure you completely.'

Edward stood up and, momentarily forgetting the low deck beam above his tall body, banged his head and groaned piteously. He stared at me, red-eyed with implicit warning but, risking his wrath even further, there was something I had to explain before we emerged from his cramped cubicle.

I set down the tray on Edward's vacated bunk. 'My lord, if I am to serve you in the way that I have described it is vital that the world continues to consider me an uneducated simpleton. Therefore, when we leave here I will continue to act in a doltish manner and I will only talk to you sensibly when we are alone and cannot be overheard, so please forgive me for any transgressions I may make in my guise as your imbecilic fool. We are both young men, my lord, about to fully embark on the great adventure of life. I now offer you my life. It is yours to serve you in any way that I can.'

Edward considered my statement and then nodded in assent. 'This way, my lord.'

I drew back the curtain and stepped out of the alcove. The servant was waiting outside, together with one of the royal doctors, both wringing their hands with anxiety, which increased when they saw Lord Edward stepping out behind me.

Edward waved away their concerned protests and said: 'This fool thinks he can cure my sea sickness so I am going to permit him to try. Do not be concerned.'

Young Lord Edmund looked at us curiously but said nothing. In my newly-granted role as court jester, with all the extraordinary licence that role is granted by princes, I mimicked sticking my fingers down my throat and then dry heaving. It made Lord Edmund laugh, as I hoped it would. Edward was very fond of his younger brother and I judged that Edward would not mind being gently mocked in front of him.

I pushed against the wind to open the cabin door and held it back for Edward to step out on to the deck. There was a flurry of concerned and respectful activity when the ship's crew and those nobles heaving over the side noticed that Lord Edward had emerged from his cabin.

Edward ignored the commotion and asked me: 'What now?'

'We simply stand by the rail amidships, my lord, and watch the horizon.'

The other crew members and passengers, including the Archbishop of Canterbury, hurriedly moved away as Lord Edward stepped towards the larboard rail. Even the fates came to my assistance as the weather gradually calmed and the pitching of the ship subsided. Was this God's sign of approval for my actions?

I said: 'Breathe as deeply and as slowly as you can, my lord. The fresh sea air will clear your head. Watch the horizon and try to relax.'

The master of the ship bustled up to us, bowed deeply, and asked Lord Edward: 'Is this lad bothering you, my lord?'

'No,' Edward replied with irritation. 'He is entertaining me and I am pleased with him.'

I said to the master: 'Lord Edward will soon require a bowl of hot potage to settle his stomach. Have it made ready for him.'

The master appeared as mortally offended by my presumption as if I had struck him a blow. He then looked at Lord Edward for confirmation.

'Do as he says,' Edward ordered. 'Now, leave us alone, all of you!' Edward shooed away the gawping sailors and anxious courtiers to the other side of the deck so that we were alone again. Then he announced: 'By God, Pauncefoot, I feel much better already. Thank you, my friend.'

You can imagine how those words thrilled me! Within a brief time of meeting him again I had manoeuvred the heir to the throne of England into calling me his friend! But now it was necessary to prove to Lord Edward the real value of my services, but if my new friend became aware of my machinations then it would certainly result in my imprisonment, or possibly my death.

'Now,' Edward said, 'what is all this talk of traitors? Do you mean here on this ship?'

'Yes, my lord. There is a gentleman on board travelling with his two sons. I don't know their names. I overheard them talking about how they intend to offer their services to another lord after you have arrived in your lands in Gascony.'

Lord Edward regarded me with a glare that froze my blood. Slowly, menacingly, he said: 'I know of whom you speak. There is only one man in my service who travels with his two sons. What did you overhear?'

'One of them, I think the father, is carrying a letter to somebody named Gaston, whoever that may be. If I understood aright, this letter pledges support, on behalf of this gentleman and his two sons, for the rebellion instigated by this Gaston person to overthrow your rule and expel the English from Gascony. This support is given in return for substantial estates when this Gaston person has prevailed. I know nothing of these affairs, my lord, but I pray that it makes sense to you.'

Lord Edward gripped the rail of the ship and gazed out at the green swelling sea and the grey clouds piling the sky. The high colour had returned to his cheeks with a vengeance. In fact he was now almost purple with rage. Lord Edward was born with the Angevin temper in full measure. I could not tell whether he was angry with me or with the supposed traitor. I feared that I might have badly overstepped the mark with my scheme.

Edward breathed: 'By God, Pauncefoot, you know not what you are saying to me! You are accusing my most trusted tutor and friend, Bartholomew Pecche, a man I have known and respected all my life, with betraying me to my enemy, the Gascon rebel Gaston de Bearn!'

I made a show of grovelling to placate the enraged prince. 'My lord, I am from a humble place and I don't know who these people are or what they do. I accuse no-one. I can only repeat what I heard being said, and if this man Pecche is your friend then I am sorry but, before God, I can speak only the truth as I heard it.'

My words had a mollifying effect and Lord Edward asked: 'Why should Bartholomew Pecche and his sons speak of this matter within your hearing?'

'My lord, conditions are very cramped for the passengers below decks. They did not know I was standing close and they whispered in Latin, not thinking that any humble seaman would understand their conversation. That is what I mean about the unique service I can render to you. I can be your eyes and ears detached from your body.'

Lord Edward looked out to sea and thought for a long time. I waited anxiously to know my fate. He was breathing deeply. Suddenly he said: 'My sea sickness has gone. I thank you for that. Will your treatment have the same effect on my mother, Queen Eleanor?'

'Undoubtedly, my lord.' I replied. 'I have left the eau-de-vie in your cabin.'

Edward was lost in thought again for several moments. Then he asked: 'You say they are carrying a letter?'

'Yes, my lord.'

'Which one of them is carrying it.'

'I don't know. I think the father but I could not be certain. This letter is concealed within some clothing.'

'Very well, this is what you will do. Say nothing of this to anyone and return to your normal duties for the time being. My seneschal will visit you and enrol you in my service as a musician and fool. When we disembark at Bordeaux you will leave this ship and join my entourage. You will not meet me again until after this matter has been resolved, one way or another.' He then fixed me with the gaze that, in future years, would quite literally scare the shit out of some unfortunates, even though he was then still a callow youth, as I was. 'If you are lying to me, Pauncefoot, or even if you are mistaken, you will hang. If you try to run away after leaving this ship, I will hunt you down and you will hang. Do you understand?'

I am not a man easily intimidated, then or now, but all I could say, tremulously, was: 'I understand, my lord.'

'Then go, and pray to God that this letter is found.'

Lord Edward did not need to say anymore. As I bowed and took my leave of him I could almost feel the rope around my neck. Was my scheme too clever, too risky?

I returned to my work in the galley in a sleep-murdering fret of worry. The galley master chided me for my subdued spirits but the gossip spread through the crew and passengers that I had cured Lord Edward of his sea sickness and that achievement earned me enhanced respect.

Edward's seneschal duly visited me to officially, but secretly, enrol me in Lord Edward's service but offered no information as to my eventual fate. In all probability he himself knew nothing about my accusations against the Pecche family. The remainder of the voyage was uneventful except for the ferment of dread churning within me.

I saw no more of Lord Edward, apart from a few glimpses, until the *St. Edward* docked in Bordeaux. It was the middle of June and, after

51

the chilly and turbulent voyage, the weather had turned pleasantly fine and hot.

I disembarked, not bothering to inform the ship's master that I was abandoning my duties, and followed the royal entourage. There was the usual scramble by fawners and courtiers to place themselves as close as possible to Queen Eleanor and the young princes, in the hope of gaining favour, but I held back and tried to remain unnoticed and unremarked.

Lords Edward and Edmund, cheered mightily by the citizens, rode on horseback while Queen Eleanor and the Archbishop of Canterbury, who was elderly, rode in the royal wagon [4] and waved greeting to the throng through the side windows. The rest of us had to use our legs. Under close escort we entered the walled city and travelled through the winding and bustling streets of the seaport.

Despite my apprehension about my eventual fate, it was with youthful light-heartedness that I relished my first journey through an exotic foreign city with all its sights, sounds and smells that were so different from my home town of Portsmouth.

Bordeaux was a wealthy town, abundant with wine and produce sold from gaily decorated street stalls. We passed through the wealthy Jewish quarter and then the royal family stopped to offer prayers and give thanks for a safe voyage at the Cathedral of Saint Andre. After the service we settled into the nearby royal residence of Chateau St. Pierre, an elegant and comfortable fortified manor house within the grounds of the cathedral.

For a day or two I waited for instructions or to be given tasks to perform, but none were forthcoming. Having boarded the cog *St. Edward* in Portsmouth with almost nothing except the clothing I wore and the small cache of silver pennies secured in my belt satchel, I slipped out into the town to shop for some extra clothes and utensils to make my situation more comfortable.

For another two days, nothing happened. Then, early one morning as I lay sleeping on my straw bed in the communal hall with all the other snoring and farting servants, I was shaken roughly by the shoulder. I gathered my sleep-sodden wits and awoke to find one of Lord Edward's most trusted knights, a man named Stephen Bauzan, staring down at me.

'Come with me,' Bauzan ordered.

'Where to?' I asked blearily.

'Shut up and get up,' Bauzan snarled, with a cold stare and a tone that brooked no argument.

Bauzan, a tall, broad-shouldered and darkly handsome man who was attired for combat in chain mail, led me out of the hall and out into the cathedral precinct. There was a group of six mounted and fully-armed soldiers waiting for us. One of them held Bauzan's caparisoned horse and another soldier held a smaller mangy looking beast, which I had no doubt was intended for me. Bauzan ordered me to mount up and we trotted away from the cathedral and quit the walled city through the north gate. Bauzan rode beside me with the escorting soldiers grouped around us.

'Where are we going?' I asked.

Bauzan looked at me with the same cold hard stare. 'We are going to the castle at Blanquefort. It's two hours ride away. If you try to escape, we will cut you down without mercy. And do not speak to me again.'

This was not a good start to the day. Judging by Bauzan's attitude towards me, I had little doubt that my scheme had been discovered and that I was riding to my doom. I cursed myself for my hubris in thinking that a humble-born peasant such as me could outwit and ingratiate myself with a prince.

The morning sun became increasingly hot. I became desperately thirsty but I dare not speak to Bauzan to request water. I rode, in silent abject misery and resigned to my death, through the dusty rolling hills to Blanquefort.

Blanquefort Castle was a small, solid, square castle with round towers at each corner and well situated on a hill to dominate the surrounding land and nearby village. We dismounted in the courtyard and entered the great hall. Bauzan ordered me to wait there with the soldiers and then he walked purposefully through a doorway that led I knew not where.

The servants were clearing away the remains of the morning meal and, despite the fear gnawing at my stomach, I was hungry and tongue tinder thirsty. I offered one of the servants a silver penny if he would fetch me a pot of ale and a hunk of bread. He accepted with alacrity. The soldiers watched impassively but did not interfere as I managed to break my fast.

The sustenance restored my resolve and some of my courage and I determined to be ready to use my glib tongue to talk my way out of any situation that was about to confront me.

A long time elapsed before Bauzan returned and beckoned me to follow him. We quit the great hall through the same doorway from which Bauzan had just emerged and climbed a narrow flight of stone steps to the third floor of one of the round towers. Bauzan threw back a rough curtain concealing the entrance to a small chamber and indicated for me to enter. I went in to find Lord Edward standing looking out of a narrow embrasure. Icy arrows of fear pierced my breast and my heart jumped within my chest.

Edward, who was dressed in the simple habit of a monk, turned to look at me. I bowed deferentially. Up until now Edward had seemed as much a man as a boy but now he looked more like the boy he still was, just fifteen years of age. He was clearly in the grip of some strong emotion. The tension in his manner was palpable, his eyes were shining and near to tears.

Bauzan withdrew and let the curtain drop back. I was alone with Edward. He indicated to a small table placed in the middle of the chamber. On the table was a quill pen, a pot of ink, and a parchment.

'Sit down,' Edward ordered.

Apprehensively, I drew back a crudely made stool and sat down at the table. My animal cunning senses were on full alert. I surmised what Edward was going to command me to do and I knew that my life depended on not doing it. He said: 'I want you to write down what you heard the traitor Pecche and his sons say to each other.'

Edward's use of the word 'traitor' did not fool me. I bowed my head and replied: 'My lord, I am mortified to disobey you but I cannot.'

Edward leaned his hands on the table, drew his face close to mine, and breathed menacingly: 'What do you mean, you cannot? Cannot or will not?'

'I cannot make letters, my lord. I have never been taught.'

Edward's face remained close to mine. 'You told me you can read and write English, French and Latin.'

'My lord, I tremble to contradict you but I said I can read and understand English, French and Latin but I have not had the schooling to be able to write them down.'

'Pauncefoot,' Edward whispered, 'if you do not write down what you heard I will have you taken out and executed.'

'My lord, I don't understand why you are asking this of me? Send me a clerk and I will gladly have him write down what I heard, but if you ask me to use my own hand then I am doomed. I am at your mercy. I cannot write. I beg your mercy for my miserable failing. Please do not execute me.'

Lord Edward regarded me for a long moment and then stood up straight and stepped back to the embrasure. 'Come here, Hamo.'

The use of my first name was encouraging. I stood up and joined Edward at the embrasure. 'Look down there into the courtyard,' he said.

I looked out to see three men, their arms tied behind their backs, standing beneath a gibbet. The three were each standing on a log of wood, placed sawn end upwards, and the hangman's nooses were already placed around their necks.

Edward whispered: 'Down there are Bartholomew Pecche and his two sons. Bartholomew was my tutor and my tutor-in-arms. I would have trusted him with my life. I did trust him with my life. As a child I played with his two sons there. They were to be knighted with me in Burgos before my marriage in a few weeks time. Thanks to your information about that letter I now know they have betrayed me to the rebel leader Gaston de Bearn. I am about to give the order to have them hanged. Before I did so I wanted to satisfy myself that you did not write that letter yourself. Now I know that you could not have done so.' I began to speak but Edward held up his hand for silence. 'You have rendered me a great service. You have insinuated your way into my presence in a most strange manner but you have amply demonstrated your unique ability to serve me in a most useful, albeit personally painful, manner. I have decided to employ you as you have suggested. I am going to appoint you as my chief jester and I want you to use your abilities in my service alone. I want no-one else to know of this arrangement, not my mother, not my brother, not my future wife, not even my father King Henry himself. This sorry business has persuaded me that a prince such as I cannot trust even those servants closest to his heart, cannot trust the friends he played with as a child. It is a bitter lesson, Hamo, and learned in the hardest possible way. You can remark that I am sore distressed by this betrayal, a betrayal that persuades me how I need to protect myself in every way possible, even from those companions I have known all my life. But let me ask you a question, Hamo. I have known Bartholomew Pecche and his sons for many years. I have scarce known you but for two brief encounters. Why should I trust you? What if you become privy to my secrets and plans and then decide to betray me as Master Pecche and his sons have done?'

This was a question that I had anticipated many months ago and I was ready with my answer. 'My lord, I am from a very humble background but I have unusual abilities. Yes, I am ambitious for wealth and advancement. One day you will be the king. You will be the most powerful man in the land. Who better to offer my services to than you? We are of the same age. My safety, my protection, will only exist in preserving your safety, your authority, and your life. If I am utterly faithful to your service, I hope to live a long and prosperous life. If I betray you then I deserve, nay expect, to end up like poor Master Pecche down there.' Edward nodded in acceptance of my speech, but I continued: 'There is one other thing, my lord.'

'What is that?' he asked.

'God sent me to you, my lord.'

'God? In what way did God send you to me?'

I was already aware that Lord Edward was a most pious and God-fearing boy, as was his father, and I was hoping that invoking the will of the Almighty would reinforce my credentials.

'My lord, when I first saw you on the quay at Portsmouth, as you were waving farewell to your father, I was seized by a strange passion and I heard a great voice, as if rolling over the waters, telling me that my life was to be in your service. I require and request no other fate. I swear by Almighty God, whose voice came to me over the waters, that I will serve you faithfully to the end of my days.'

I looked at Lord Edward's face and saw that he was in the grip of religious ecstasy, a look I was to see many times during his endless pilgrimages to Walsingham and other shrines, and was satisfied that I had pitched my speech exactly right.

'I believe you, Hamo,' Edward said.

I looked out at the three men standing on logs of wood, nooses curled around their necks like deadly snakes, and felt heartsick at the fatal consequences my machinations had once again caused. I wanted no more blood on my hands. Yes, I was ambitious for wealth and advancement but let it not be at the expense of the life of three blameless men.

Bartholomew Pecche had treated me with respect and had rewarded me with a silver penny for laundering his expensive surcoat. He would never know that I had forged the letter purporting to betray Edward to Gaston de Bearn. When Pecche had sent his surcoat to be cleaned of vomit, I had carefully unstitched the lining, inserted the forged letter, sewn up the lining, and then gently laundered the surcoat to help prove that I had not known the letter was concealed within if my fakery had been questioned. Whether it ever crossed Edward's mind to question why Pecche would take the risk of sending his surcoat to be laundered knowing that it concealed such a damning letter I never discovered, but my deception had succeeded.

I could not, of course, admit my perfidy to Lord Edward, that would be to sign my own death warrant, but something inside me compelled me to risk my new-found favour to stop this needless execution.

I fell on to one knee and kissed Lord Edward's hand. 'My lord, I tremble to question your authority but is it truly necessary to execute Pecche and his sons.'

Lord Edward looked highly displeased at being questioned by a mere servant but I could also see that he *wanted* to be talked out of hanging his old friends. He replied: 'They have betrayed me. That is a crime that a prince cannot, dare not, overlook. If others become aware of such leniency then they may be tempted to betray me also, without fear of retribution.'

'I accept that Pecche and his sons must be punished, my lord, but could not the punishment be a fine, imprisonment, or banishment?'

'Enough!' Edward roared, visibly shaking with emotion. 'I have been advised that execution is necessary. Why do you concern yourself with the fate of these traitors?'

'Because it is I who overheard their treasonous talk and reported it to you, my lord. I am but a humble boy. I know nothing of these great affairs of state and I could not foresee the results of my actions in reporting this betrayal.'

'You did your duty to your liege lord, as you are required to do by law and precedent.'

'Indeed, my lord, and I do not regret my loyal action. But, if these men are executed, I will feel culpable in their death. God sent me to you, my lord, and I am a God-fearing boy. If my first service to you results in the death of three men it will weigh on my conscience forever and I shall some day have to answer for their deaths to our Redeemer, as you will also. These men were your friends, my lord.

You know full well how the Devil puts temptation in the way of frail mankind. This rebel Gaston de Bearn has been recruited by the Devil. I beseech you to remember the words of the Holy Book. "The Lord is gracious, and full of compassion, slow to anger, and of great mercy". I beg you, my lord, act as Christ would have done, to show compassion and mercy, which are the great glories of kingship, and you shall one day be a great king. Do not let the Devil deceive you into executing three men who, up until now, have served you well. Whoever advised you to execute these men is wrong. You are the prince, you will one day be anointed by God. *You* decide the fate of these men, according to your heart and your conscience, not some adviser who may have an agenda of his own. The Commandments saith: "Thou shalt not kill". I beg you again, my lord, do not lead yourself into sin.'

Brother Godfrey grunts at me sceptically. What reason for the farm noises, monk? Why did I plead so eloquently, earnestly, and dangerously, for the lives of Bartholomew Pecche and his sons? Believe it or not, brother, but I really did feel heartsick at the thought of being the cause of their deaths. In my drive for advancement I had not truly thought through the possible consequences of my deception. I also calculated that if, at some future point, my perfidy became known to Lord Edward, it might save me from execution that I had dissuaded Edward from executing three totally loyal and innocent subjects. May we now continue without you snorting at me, boy?

Edward had been looking at me, deep in thought, as I kneeled before him. Finally he said: 'Raise yourself up, Hamo. I accept that God has sent you to me, and I also accept your counsel.'

I bowed and kissed Edward's hand. 'Truly, my lord, you are a prince I will be proud to serve for all my days.'

Edward went to the doorway and pulled back the curtain. He beckoned to someone outside and, a moment later, Stephen Bauzan followed Edward into the bare little chamber.

Edward said to Bauzan: 'I am satisfied that Bartholomew Pecche and his two sons are guilty of treason but, in view of their past services to me, I have decided on clemency. The punishment will not be execution.'

Bauzan's face clouded with angry concern. 'But, my lord, these men have…'

'I know very well what they have done, Stephen, but they are not to be executed. Their punishment will be the loss of all their lands, wealth and titles within our realm, and banishment, for the rest of their lives, from our realm.'

'My lord, is that wise? If other men seek to betray you then such weakness might serve you ill.'

'Enough!' Edward roared, and slapped his palm on the top of the table with such force that I nearly jumped out of my skin. So did Bauzan, a much more seasoned warrior than I. Edward went on: 'Do not presume to accuse me of weakness, Stephen. Their punishment is severe and still stands as a lesson to all if this affair ever becomes public knowledge. See that my command is carried out. Pecche and his sons are to be escorted, in total secrecy, to the borders of my realm and forbidden, on pain of death, from ever entering again.'

Stephen Bauzan bowed and said: 'At once, my lord. My apologies if I have offended you.'

Bauzan shot me a look of pure venomous hatred that told me clearly who had recommended execution to Lord Edward. Bauzan quit the chamber and let the curtain drop back behind him.

Edward sat down wearily at the table. Now that Bauzan had departed Edward looked once more like a callow youth and less like the dominant prince he had just been obliged to be.

He said: 'Nobody except you and Bauzan knows I am here today. I did not want to execute Pecche and his sons in Bordeaux. They are well liked and their execution would not have been popular. I do not want anyone, except my father, to know how they betrayed me. They will now simply vanish. I could not bear to condemn them to spend the rest of their life in the dungeons. Now they can at least have some sort of life in another country. With their military skills they will have no trouble finding employment. I pray that they will not return to pit such skillls against me one day.'

I could see that Edward was close to breaking down in tears, overwhelmed with grief at the thought of being betrayed by his old and trusted friends, and by the punishment he had had to inflict on them. I remained silent, unable to decide what to say. Besides, I judged I had said enough already. Edward's next question took me by surprise.

He asked: 'Your cure for seasickness, Hamo. Is that cure known to all sailors?'

'Being able to see the horizon, yes, my lord. The eau-de-vie was an addition of my own that I found helpful in easing the symptoms.'

Edward shook his head ruefully. 'And nobody else had the courage to tell me of such a simple yet effective remedy?'

'With respect, my lord, humble sailors are afraid to give advice to princes in case it does not work.'

'Well, you had the courage and my mother's suffering was much eased and she wishes to express her thanks to you. We are dining in the great hall at Bordeaux tonight. You will come and entertain us. But, of course, you must remain in character as an imbecilic fool.'

'Yes, my lord,' I replied.

Now that I could console my conscience with the fact that I had saved the Pecche's from execution, I felt inwardly jubilant at the overwhelming success of my plan.

'You say you play chess, Hamo?'

'Yes, my lord.'

'I am in need of distraction after this business here today. After we have dined I will summon you to my chamber and we will play chess and talk some more in private.'

'Very good, my lord.'

'Are you hungry?' Edward asked, with a sudden smile.

'Yes, my lord. I missed breakfast.'

'Then stay here and take the midday meal. I must now return

to Bordeaux. Bauzan will escort you back to Bordeaux later. Remember, no-one else must know that I was here today and for what purpose.'

'I understand, my lord.'

I bowed deeply as Edward quit the chamber.

I went to the embrasure and looked down to the courtyard. The three Pecches had been released from their nooses and were being led away to permanent exile from their homeland. They were sacrificial lambs, honest men caught up as victims of my first successful scheme to escape my humble origins and attain wealth and influence. I truly was mightily relieved that their lives had been spared and I carry the guilt for my unthinking perfidy to this day. [5]

I had been so wrapped up in the implementation of my scheme that the idea that the Pecches might face execution had not crossed my mind. I had not foreseen that Lord Edward, a sallow boy who I had first encountered publicly weeping for his father, was capable of such ruthlessness. He had been born with the fierce Angevin temper of his ancestors but, when that temper was cool, had been amenable to a rational argument for clemency and mercy, even from an underling such as me, without displaying the arrogant dismissive disdain that many great lords would have shown. Edward did not enjoy cruelty. He was basically a kind and loving man whose natural instincts were often at war with his bounden duties as a prince and king. It was a crucial lesson in my estimation of Edward's character.

My senses were still stunned by the events of the day and the speed with which my fortunes had changed. If I had given Lord Edward proof that I could write then I would have been doomed. He had suspected me of writing the traitorous letter myself. Even before I planted that letter, however, I had decided to keep the knowledge of my ability to write, such a magical and useful skill, a secret from everyone, especially Lord Edward.

I took the midday meal at Blanquefort and then rode back to Bordeaux escorted by Bauzan and his band of soldiers. Once, as were riding along, I caught Bauzan staring at me and he asked me, bluntly, what I had said to Edward to persuade him to remit the sentence on Pecche and his sons from hanging to banishment. I simply played the idiot, denied any such persuasion, and pretended not to understand what Bauzan was talking about.

I would dearly have loved to taunt the arrogant Bauzan with my newly-bestowed influence but I realised I could not. I had to remain in character as the happy dolt and it was not healthy to taunt a man like Bauzan, even if I was protected by Edward's favour.

I entertained the royal family in the great hall of Chateau St. Pierre that night with all the energy and zest I could muster. Somersaults, back flips, walking on my hands and walking crab-wise backwards. I included every trick and comic gesture I had ever learned. Even my fellow jesters were laughing at my antics. Would they still be smiling when they learned the news that Lord Edward had appointed me as his chief jester?

After completing my performance I was presented to King Henry himself, who had arrived that day to be reunited with his family. He was a stocky man of medium height and with a slightly drooping left eyelid, a facial feature that Lord Edward had inherited. He seemed not to care much for my revels and I judged him none too bright.

Queen Eleanor, however, whom I had already seen from a distance, was entrancing. She was a breathtakingly beautiful woman of high intelligence and wit. I pondered on how she could endure being married to such a dull husband but the status of being king of England made up, I suppose, for all of Henry's shortcomings.

Queen Eleanor presented me with a gold ring, set with a ruby, for curing her seasickness. I made my thanks and Queen Eleanor patted me on the head as if I were a pet dog.

I treasure the ring to this day, not because it was given to me by a beautiful, albeit manipulative queen, but as a symbol of the success of my arrival amongst the exalted company in which I was now determined to remain.

Later in the evening Lord Edward summoned me to his chamber and we played chess. He was still cautiously considering how far he could trust me.

When I finally lay down to sleep on the floor of the communal hall I reflected that the day had started with me thinking I would be executed and had ended with a present from Queen Eleanor herself and a private conversation with my new friend, the heir to the throne of England. I thanked God for such a change in fortune and expectation.

Over the next three months I saw Lord Edward infrequently. He was often away with his father and the army suppressing the Gascon rebels. This campaign was Edward's baptism as a soldier and, from all reports, he proved very adept. During military actions he showed remarkable courage and cool judgement for one so young.

These reports were not the usual flattery accorded to the heir to the throne because I heard Edward's knights talking amongst themselves about Edward's *sang froid*. These knights tolerated my presence because they knew that I was a favourite with Lord Edward and were careful not to mistreat me, in the same sense that they would not mistreat Edward's favourite horse or hound or falcon.

I was able to pass many snippets of information to Lord Edward about what people surrounding him were actually thinking and planning, people such as his household knights and sergeants, high-ranking officials such as the Chancellor and the Keeper of the Wardrobe, and sometimes even his own formidable mother.[6]

I marvelled at the change in my fortunes. A few weeks before I had been the downtrodden slave of a Portsmouth innkeeper with only dreams to hold for comfort. Now I was the favourite fool and a close confidante of the heir to the throne. I could never sit above or below the salt but I found that I was being given more comfortable private nooks for sleeping and better food and wine when I ate with the other jesters and musicians.

Only two clouds shadowed my satisfaction. Would the deaths of Dick Bailey and, especially, Peter Pauncefoot rebound on me in any way? By placing the body of my so-called father in the barrel of brine I had made his death seem suspicious.

The shades of Dick Bailey and Peter Pauncefoot took revenge by haunting my dreams and I oft times awoke and cried out, drenched in night sweat, as their death agonies were relived over and over again in my mind.

The more louring cloud was: who was my real father? I fell into the habit of observing every nobleman, and even the knights, and considering whether one of them could be my real father. How could I ever find out who my real father was?

I knew three things: that my real father's coat-of-arms bore a lion rampant with a pointed tail; that his wife or some other relative's surname had been Marshal; and that he had a distinct lozenge-shaped birthmark on his manhood.

The coat-of-arms clue was observable. Most armorial bearings did not include a lion rampant, but some did include a lion in some form, albeit without a long twisting and pointed tail. Perhaps Peter Pauncefoot's memory had been skewed or perhaps he had deliberately lied. If that was the case then any search I made would be futile and fruitless?

When it came to the birthmark, I could hardly approach a nobleman and ask to see his manhood or ask whether he had such a mark on his manhood! Favourite of Lord Edward or not I would doubtless receive a cuff around the ear, or even worse, for such temerity.

I conceived the notion of cultivating the acquaintance of the squires, who might be privy to their master's private parts, and even the physicians. But, as with asking if their wife's maiden name had been Marshal, I was trapped by my own mask as a guileless simpleton. If I made sensible inquiry then suspicions would be raised against me, and it was imperative to my future success that only Lord Edward knew of my true nature.

I determined that I would have to be patient and hope that the truth about my real father would one day present itself to me.

But, for the moment, the sun was shining brightly for me, and it was about to glow with enhanced radiance, kindled by good fortune that I could scarcely believe.

SEPTEMBER 1254

One evening in September 1254, about two weeks before we were due to depart for Edward's marriage in Castile, he summoned me to his private chamber for a game of chess. I was gratified to receive the summons, not only as a proof of Edward's continuing favour but to enjoy the sheer pleasure of the surroundings.

Edward's chamber was furnished with comfortable and brightly painted furniture and bedecked with rich red wall hangings. The barrel ceiling was adorned with gay depictions of hunting scenes, and the chamber was lit with dozens of candles and warmed by a tall bronze brazier. It also contained his canopied bed.

It was a joy to escape the crude and uncomfortable quarters allotted to we menials, although the luxuriousness of this chamber, I later found, was far exceeded by the royal chambers at Windsor Castle and Westminster Palace and such other royal residences in England.

Edward, now fifteen years of age, had matured rapidly in the few weeks we had been in Gascony. That evening I found him pacing up and down his chamber in an agitated mood. He was wearing the simple clothing he habitually favoured, this night a plain blue belted tunic edged with silver trim. He indicated for me to take my place at the chessboard table. The first question he asked me shattered my self-satisfied and complacent mood. He asked: 'Have you ever killed a man, Hamo?'

I was fired alert with the gut-wrenching fear that Edward had learned of the deaths I had been involved with in Portsmouth, but

I contrived to answer him coolly enough while mentally preparing my defence if charged with murder. I replied: 'No, my lord, I am not configured to be a soldier or a fighter.'

To my relief, Edward's question was more rhetorical than inquisitive.

'I killed a man two days ago,' Edward said. I was not sure whether to reply but, before I could decide, Edward continued: 'The rebels were skulking like rats in the church at La Reole. We besieged them and finally forced them out into the open. They attacked and in the mêlée that ensued my knights became distracted and left me momentarily undefended. One of the rebels broke through and came for me. He wielded an axe but I was too fast for him. I struck off his arm with my sword and then split his skull.'

I looked at Edward's expression, trying to judge what reaction he expected from me. I could not tell and so decided on the always safe option of flattery. 'Well done, my lord! You gave the traitorous scum what he deserved.'

Edward looked back at me with an expression of relief and absolution. 'Yes, you are right, Hamo. I thought I would be shocked or upset when I killed my first man which, momentarily, I was. Does a prince commit murder when he kills a fellow human being in defence of his right? God clearly instructs us, within the Commandments, that we should not kill, but God, through the anointment of my father as king, has surely given me absolution from that Commandment. After all, God Himself, as the holy book tells us, has killed many times Himself, so I felt as if I was in the right, as if I was doing God's will. I am the lord of Gascony, appointed by my father, who is anointed by God. That rebel deserved to die for challenging my God-given authority.'

'Indeed, my lord,' I agreed, uneasy about where this conversation was leading.

'I ordered that the church be razed to the ground but my father later overrode my order.' The tone of Edward's voice was bitter and contemptuous.

This was the first time that Edward had said anything critical of his father in my presence and I decided that silence was the best response until I could understand why he was relating his sorrows to me.

Edward's Angevin temper suddenly exploded forth. 'By God, Hamo, I am becoming a man and I long to act as a man, and as I see fit in my own domain. I chafe at the bit like a bridled and spavined horse to be always controlled by my father. He countermanded my order and humiliated me in front of my men! What can I do, Hamo?'

This outburst marked a new balance in our relationship. Never before had Edward asked my advice or opinion, and certainly not in regard to the actions of the king. This was the first evidence of Edward's youthfully intense desire for independent action, a desire that, in the following years, would come close to causing his ruin.

Edward had ventured me into a dangerous moral and ethical quicksand and I had to reply circumspectly. 'Until you are the king yourself, my lord, perhaps there is very little you can do. As you have said, your father has been anointed by God so, if you refute his judgement then you refute God's judgement. I have reported to you how impressed your earls and knights have been by your demeanour in battle. Their love and loyalty towards you grows daily, as does mine, so I beg you to think not that you have been humiliated. We are both young men, my lord, with all the fire and impatience of young men but if there is one thing I have learned in my short life it is the value of patience and cool reflection. Be patient, my lord, be reflective, but be watchful and be prepared. Attempt the dispassionate opportunism of a Caesar and the calm nobility of an Arthur. I implore you not to ruin your inheritance and reputation with intemperate action.'

Edward sat down opposite me at the table, where the finely-carved ivory chess pieces were arrayed ready for our game. After some moments of pensive thought he leaned across and slapped me on the shoulder. 'By God, Hamo, you speak wisely. You make valid

points, especially about my father's God-given authority and the
need for patience. I must be patient.' He smiled warmly. 'I'm glad I
have found such a wise friend as you.'

I did not bother to point out to my lord and master that, actually,
I had found *him*. I was not sure what influence my advice would
have on Edward but I had already learned that invoking God and
the heroes of the past, especially King Arthur, was always a useful
ploy to convince him of anything. This conversation had moved our
friendship up to a new degree of warmth and confidence but, even
so, I was unprepared for Edward's next gesture of generosity.

I was expecting Edward, playing white, to move his first piece
to begin the game but he became lost in thought for several
moments. Then, his adolescent emotions still clearly affected by the
memory, he announced: 'The traitor Bartholomew Pecche owned
an estate at Coleby in Lincolnshire. He and his sons are now
banished and dispossessed so this estate has become Crown
property. I have spoken to my father about this estate. He cannot
ever know what service you rendered by unmasking the traitor but
he has allowed me to do what I like with the Coleby estate. It is
yours, Hamo.'

'Mine?' I gasped, genuinely taken by surprise. Despite the thrill
of this largesse I realised, given the circumstances by which the
estate had become available, that I had to react gravely and soberly
with no hint of gloating or ambition. 'My lord, I am but a humble
fool, a jester and entertainer. Perhaps it is not my place to be given
such an estate.'

'As we both know,' Edward replied with an ironic tone, 'your
talents mark you as very much more than a humble fool. My brother
enjoys your company and my mother is delighted by your
entertainment as well as your cure for sea sickness. You have already
brought me much valuable information, quite apart from exposing
the traitorous Pecche family. If they had betrayed our strategy to that
scum Gaston de Béarn then our campaign against the rebels would
have gone badly for us. You have given more valuable service to the

royal family than most of my sycophantic and time-serving knights and officials. But, I must say, you seem ungrateful for my gift to you.'

'No, no, my lord. I am simply surprised and overwhelmed by your generosity. I am deeply grateful.'

'Excellent! Of course, as your true nature and your services to me must remain a secret for however long is necessary, the fact of your ownership of the Coleby estate must remain a secret as well. It will be held in trust for you under my name but all the revenues from the estate will accrue to you.'

This was an astonishing demonstration of Edward's liking and affection for me. I said: 'My lord, I am forever in your debt.'

Edward's next gift was even more astonishing. He asked: 'We have become friends, haven't we, Hamo?'

'I am overjoyed to think so, my lord.'

'Then I have decided to trust you completely, Hamo. You have proved your usefulness and your love for me. As you have said, we are young men. We are on the threshold of life. We can travel the road of life together. Even princes, Hamo, need friendship and advice that they can rely upon. To be a prince is often a lonely occupation. I need a friend, of my own age, whom I can talk to as all other men are able to talk to each other, openly, frankly and honestly. I want you to be that friend.'

'I am honoured, my lord,' I replied, hardly daring to breathe in case my good fortune was suddenly snatched back.

'Good. In your capacity as my jester, in the time-honoured fashion, you have the licence to say to me, or anybody else, what you like in public. You can point out mistakes, wrong courses of action, inappropriate behaviour, and anything such as that without fear of sanction. Is that not so?'

'Yes, indeed, my lord, although we jesters are careful not to stretch that licence until it snaps!'

Edward smiled. When he did not have to publicly play the prince and when his temper was cool he was the most charming of companions. 'Well, Hamo, I hereby accord you the same privilege in private.'

'I'm not sure I understand, my lord,' I responded cautiously.

'Hamo, I give you *carte blanche* to advise me as you wish within the bounds of propriety and within the bounds of our respective stations in life. If you think I am acting foolishly, incorrectly or unwisely, I want you to tell me bluntly, without fear of punishment. Through your unusual ability to gather information and your proximity to me and the royal family, you will become privy to more secrets and become more aware of the political climate than perhaps even the royal council.'

Exciting as this proposal was, I feared a trap. I said: 'Is not the royal council you have just mentioned the suitable body to point out such indiscretions, my lord?'

'No, Hamo. Mostly they are much older sycophants seeking titles and estates. They trim their sails to my wind. I need a true friend to be brutally honest with me when necessary. You are the same age as me, you are very shrewd, and yet your low-born station ensures that you can never threaten my position or my interests. You are a good friend and the perfect candidate. Do you accept?'

'Of course, my lord. My most earnest desire, after serving God, is to serve you. You honour me beyond measure.'

'Excellent!' Edward exclaimed, and leant across the table to clap me on the shoulder again. He did not lean back but, conspiratorially, in a low voice, as if his mother might be listening at the door, he asked: 'Have you ever been with a girl, Hamo?'

I adopted the same conspiratorial tone and asked: 'You mean carnally, my lord?'

'Yes, carnally. I am to be married soon, Hamo, and I will no doubt receive instruction from some ancient bishop or whoever, but I want to know what to do, what it's like to know a woman.' Edward's excitement at this prospect was palpable.

'I'm sorry to fail my first test as your friend and advisor, but I have never had a woman. I bitterly regret that I cannot give you any advice.'

Despite Edward's *carte blanche* to be frank and honest with him I was very cautious about being so throughout all the years I served him. People claim that they value honest opinion but they never do, especially great lords, when it conflicts with their status, interests, advantages or their high opinion of themselves.

'Never fear,' Edward said, albeit crestfallen at my unhelpfulness in matters carnal. 'You can help me in another way. I am to be married in a few weeks time. I am excited about the prospect, Hamo. I am to marry Leonora, the half-sister of King Alphonso of Castile. I have been given good reports about her. They say she is beautiful and prudent. I don't care about the prudent, as long as she is beautiful. Have you heard any gossip about her, Hamo?'

'No, my lord, I haven't. She is unknown to your officials and retainers and so they are unable to pass any opinion about her.' My answer was truthful. I had not heard gossip, but I had heard many coarse and salacious jokes about the forthcoming nuptials.

Edward shifted in his seat excitedly. 'Will I like her, Hamo? More to the point, will she like me?'

I could not help chuckling and decided to put our new found intimacy to the test. I said: 'Have you ever looked at yourself in a mirror? You are fair of hair, fair of face, tall, strong-limbed, energetic, kindly, humorous, courageous, wealthy and the heir to the throne of England! Any woman in the world would be moonstruck not to like you or want to marry you! No, my lord, calm yourself. Leonora of Castile will adore you.'

'But will I make her happy in bed? Will she make me happy in bed? Will she give me children?'

'Have there been any reports that Leonora is less than fully and perfectly formed as a woman?'

'Not that I have been told.'

'And when you look at a pretty woman or a pretty girl, does your prick go hard at the thought of dallying with her.'

Edward looked away, pink with embarrassment. 'All the time,' he admitted.

'Then there is nothing to worry about! You will both be happy and have many children.' How percipient that prophecy was!

'When we arrive at Burgos, where I am to be married, I want you to find out what Leonora truly thinks about me. After we have been introduced to each other I will send you to entertain her and, using your ability to understand languages, listen to what she says about me to her ladies or her family. Will you do that?'

'Of course I will, but I think you fret too much over this, my lord. I am sure Leonora will regard you as the fine prince you are and accept you as the devoted husband you intend to be.'

'Even so, Hamo, I want to know.' Despite the newly bestowed cordiality, Edward's tone brooked no further argument.

'I am your loyal friend and servant in all things. But if Lady Leonora speaks in Castilian then I will not be able to understand her.'

Edward nodded thoughtfully. 'Well, if that is the case then it cannot be helped, but I have been told that Leonora is learned and has been well schooled and I surmise that she will speak in French as all civilised and educated royals should do.'

'I will attempt to learn and understand the basics of the Castilian language before we arrive in Burgos, my lord, and then, even if Lady Leonora does speak in her native tongue, I may be able to glean some idea of what she truly thinks of you.'

I had no idea how I could fulfil this promise but I did not want to disappoint Edward so early in this most fruitful relationship.

'Good!' Edward exclaimed. 'Pour me some wine and we will begin our game of chess. And promise me you will play properly and not attempt to lose to me. You no longer have to ingratiate yourself into my favour, I have freely given it to you.'

I smiled. 'I will do my utmost to defeat you, my lord.'

Two weeks later we set off on the journey to Castile for Lord Edward's knighting and marriage. To my surprise and disappointment Edward's mother and father did not accompany his numerous entourage. Such disappointment was because I had anticipated being allowed to travel in the royal wagon with Queen Eleanor and to lay on silk cushions strumming my harp rather than having to torture my arse by bouncing up and down on a horse.

The weather was fine and dry and the travelling party were in a gay and lighthearted mood as we moved under wide cloudless skies and cantered gently through the lush lands of Gascony.

I found the rolling countryside enchanting. It reminded me of the countryside of southern England, of Dorset, Hampshire and Devon, but with the addition of endless sweetly-smelling vineyards, the major source of Gascony's wealth. I could well understand the determination of King Henry, and preceding English kings, to keep possession of such a honeyed land, and the equal determination of the French kings to some day deprive England of possession.

Lord Edward was accompanied by as many nobles as could be mustered, together with a bodyguard of knights strong enough to defend Edward from all threats except a fully fledged army. This entourage of scores of fighting men, their colourful banners held aloft by their squires, was cheered by the Gascon peasants wherever we passed by. They were glad of any diversion to relieve the tedium of their lives.

The villages and hamlets we passed were in a more dilapidated state than those in England and the Gascon underlords, warned by the heralds of Edward's approach, could not afford the lavish hospitality bestowed on Edward by the much wealthier lords of England.

Despite my new-found intimacy with Lord Edward I had perforce to ride behind the supply carts with the other jesters, musicians, servants and minor court officials. I played the amiable idiot and unexpectedly found myself enjoying the journey, even when compelled by lack of accommodation to sleep under a wagon or, on odd occasion, out under the stars.

We were obliged to cross a mountain range known as the Pyrenees and we had to do so before the winter weather set in.

These Pyrenees were unlike any hills I had ever seen. They were huge grey peaks, topped with snow, and seemed to stretch across the sky endlessly. I found them frightening and overpowering but I had no choice but to ascend with the rest of the party.

We climbed upwards into blinding light reflected off the snow and crossed through a pass named Roncevaux where the revered French hero Roland, the champion of Charlemagne, had died fighting the Saracens almost five hundred years before. Edward stopped to pray at a stone erected to mark the place where Roland had been killed. I well remember Edward's tall frame kneeling to pay homage and pray for Roland's soul, inexpressibly moved to be close to one of the legendary heroes whom he so admired and aspired to be.

We descended into Spain. The land became drier and more arid but then the weather deteriorated and it began to rain heavily, which dampened our spirits as well as our clothing, and made for much harder going through mud-rutted tracks and across brown roiling waters.

After two days the rain stopped and the going became easier until, three weeks after we had left Bordeaux, we found the Arlanzón river and followed its sparkling waters until we arrived at the outskirts of the walled city of Burgos.

Edward's heralds had alerted Burgos to his imminent arrival on the previous day and the gates were open. We entered the city to another tumultuous cheering reception. Lord Edward and the most important members of his entourage were met and greeted outside the cathedral by a reception committee comprising a host of Castilian grandees and led by King Alphonso himself. This distinguished group proceeded into the cathedral to pray and give thanks for safe arrival.

We humble minions were provided with food and drink at long trestle tables set up outside the cathedral. After our noble superiors had finished their devotions we were all escorted outside of the city to the monastery of Las Huelgas. This monastery was how I imagine heaven will be, if God allows me a place there.

It was a place built with cool honey-coloured arched colonnades on all sides of a spacious central courtyard. Within this space grew lemon and orange trees, fountains played and created rainbows in the sunlight, and exotic birds sang in silver cages.

The sound of plainsong, beautifully sung by the monks, would drift across the courtyard to entrance the awakening dawn, the mellow afternoon sunlight, and the hushed twilight of evening.

I slept in the communal guest hall reserved for travellers. I overheard gossip that the bride, Leonora of Castile, had also arrived at the monastery with her entourage but I did not see her.

The next afternoon I overheard more excited gossip from servants and retainers. Lord Edward and Leonora of Castile were soon to meet each other for the first time. I expected to be summoned by Lord Edward shortly after that introduction.

I donned my best motley, a gay red and blue harlequin pattern accompanied by green leather boots and a vivid yellow cap, and checked that my harp was correctly tuned.

It was only a few moments after I had completed my preparations that Lord Edward's seneschal, Hugh FitzOtho, entered the servants quarters and ushered me to join him. He said: 'Lord Edward is sending you to play your harp for his bride-to-be. Keep your wits about you and try to behave like a normal person. This is a very high honour for you, so do your best.'

'Indeed I will, sir,' I replied.

FitzOtho examined my motley and approved it as clean and suitable enough to entertain a princess and then ordered me to follow him.

We walked along the shaded colonnades, accompanied by the soothing sound of splashing fountains, and arrived at the royal apartments. The guards stationed outside opened the door. FitzOtho led me to another door on the other side of a large antechamber. FitzOtho knocked on the door gently and respectfully.

After a few moments the door was opened by a stern elderly

duenna dressed all in black. FitzOtho indicated to me, standing behind him, and announced, in French: 'Lord Edward has sent his chief jester and court musician as a gift to entertain Lady Leonora. His name is Hamo. He is an excellent fool, harpist and tumbler but otherwise his wits are dull and he understands no language except English. He is completely trusted by Lord Edward. May he be admitted?'

The duenna held up a finger and replied, also in French: 'One moment, I will ask Lady Leonora if she wishes to be entertained. She is with her ladies.'

The duenna disappeared back into the room and we waited. I could hear much giggling and excited chattering inside the room. I was intrigued to meet Lord Edward's new bride. Gossip held that Leonora was a ravishing beauty but I was aware of how fawning courtiers exaggerated the virtues and attributes of royalty.

The duenna returned and, without the hint of a smile, said: 'Lady Leonora will receive Lord Edward's gift with great pleasure. Please convey her thanks.'

FitzOtho bowed and walked away down the hallway. The duenna ordered, in French: 'Come with me.'

I pretended I could not understand and simply stood there, shifting from foot to foot and smiling. She took me by the arm and pulled me into the room while muttering something under her breath about having enough to do without being obliged to look after some half-witted English clown. I adopted my most ingratiating smile.

A group of seven young ladies were seated around the windows on the other side of the wood-panelled room, windows which looked out on to a delightful formally arranged garden.

The young ladies squealed with delight at the sight of my brightly-coloured motley, but one of them commented: 'Ugh! It's the duende!'

This was said with an expression of disgust and I later learned that the duende was a monster of Castilian legend, an ugly troll who wears a big hat and attacks young girls in the forest. The other ladies giggled uneasily at this cruel analogy.

I humbly bowed to the assembled women. I could deduce which of them was Lady Leonora because of the richness of her apparel and the noticeably deferential demeanour of her companions.

The duenna announced: 'May I present Lord Edward's gift, my lady. His name is Hamo and he is skilled in the arts of music, singing, clowning, tumbling and even magic. He wishes to entertain you but he is slow-witted and does not speak or understand any language except heathen English and so you may talk freely in front of him.'

I hesitantly bowed again and gave them my brightest smile. They regarded me curiously and made several comments about me.

One said: 'He is sweet, and he has a lovely smile.'

Another said: 'Sweet! He is ugly, and he looks stupid.'

A third said: 'Look at those strange blue eyes! They look like the sky.'

The one who had called me a duende repeated her scornful opinion: 'An ugly little troll! The duende!'

I was well used to hearing such opinions but they were always more hurtful coming from the mouths of elegant and desirable girls of my own age.

I took a closer look at Lady Leonora, who had not yet spoken. Even before she had said a word I understood her nature because I recognised the expression on her face. I had already seen it many times on the faces of noble ladies forced into arranged marriages of state or in order to increase their husband's wealth and property.

It was a guarded, shrewd expression, with a hint of fiery determination, that announced: 'If I have to live this life that I have been thrust into without any choice then so be it, but I will make myself as comfortable and as wealthy as I can by any means that I can.'

Brother Godfrey now interrupts with doubts about my adolescent perspicacity. Yes, write that down, boy! At that age I had much more knowledge of the world than a sheltered and cloistered halfwit like you. You may not believe I could read such things into her lovely face without a word being spoken but I swear that I did, and the succeeding years proved me correct. Not that such a conclusion diminished my respect for Leonora. Exactly the opposite, in fact, and I came to adore her almost as well as Lord Edward adored her, despite my being much more aware of Leonora's true nature than Edward ever was. I can tell from your eager expression, my lusty young monk, that despite your vow of chastity you are eager to hear more about Princess Leonora and her delectable companions. Fear not, I will not inform your abbot of your secret titillation, but God will know. You do well to blush, boy!

Leonora was about fourteen years of age. Her head was uncovered and she was dressed in a blue silk gown trimmed with red and gold thread. Her long black wavy hair tumbled down her back. Her complexion was flawless and lighter than her companions. Her brown eyes looked at me coolly. She was little more than a child constrained to act like a lady, regally and with demure dignity, but there was a subtle playfulness in her expression. There was still an adolescent awkwardness in her demeanour but there was no doubt that, when she flowered into full womanhood, she would become heartbreakingly beautiful.

Thankfully for the true purpose of my visit, Leonora spoke in French. She asked her ladies: 'What shall we have him do?'

The one who considered me a duende said disgustedly: 'Feed him to the pigs. That's all such a monster is fit for.'

'Shush, Dolores,' Leonora replied, not at all upset by such a callous suggestion. 'This boy is well liked by my Lord Edward, and so shall he be by me.' To the duenna she instructed: 'Have him play his harp while we talk.'

The duenna mimed to me that I should play and pointed to the corner of the room. I shuffled about as if confused and then I made a sudden forward head-over-heels roll, holding my harp away from my body at the same time. This move, which always surprised and enchanted my audience, brought another squeal of delight from the young ladies, all except the one named Dolores. I ducked down and sat cross-legged under a long table at the side of the room.

I began to strum my harp in a soft, lyrical and unobtrusive manner and, as I hoped they would, the girls soon forgot all about my presence. I was in the shadows of the table and thus out of sight and out of mind. I could see them, however, and my eyes kept straying, not to Lady Leonora but to the girl named Dolores.

Dolores! The name means 'sorrows'. Was a woman ever more aptly named? She was slightly older than Leonora, about the same age as me, but once again I recognised a kindred spirit. Are ambitious and embittered men and women drawn to each other? Do they feel, in the depths of their soul, that their embittered nature makes them deserving of nothing more than an equally embittered partner? I do not know but, as I sat there strumming my harp, I already longed to possess Dolores.

She was shorter in stature than Leonora but her body was much more fully developed, almost chubby. I was entranced by how her breasts strained against the confinement of her laced bodice.

Her hair was shorter and much lighter in colour than Leonora's, a light brown colour. Her lips were thin, her nose tip-tilted, but it was her eyes that really fascinated me. They were almond-coloured eyes and slightly more slanted than normal, almost like the people from Cathay that I was to meet on my travels much later in life.

I fought to subdue this sudden overwhelming passion, which was unlike anything I had experienced before. Dolores enchanted me, a word I use advisedly, and she continued to do so. I felt intoxicated by her presence, even when she abused me, and, to this day, I know not the source of this irresistible attraction. Perhaps this was God's way of punishing me, or perhaps rewarding me, such was the dual nature of my relationship with my woman of the sorrows.

I forced myself to concentrate on the conversation of the women and, when I caught the end of one sentence, it shook me back into doing my duty and the true purpose of my presence.

One of the ladies-in-waiting was saying: 'He has legs that are very long. I hope, for your sake, that everything about Lord Edward is as long!'

The duenna tut-tutted and Leonora, making a dainty pretence of being shocked, replied: 'You are very naughty but yes, my Lord Edward is very tall. I shall always be looking up to him.'

'You will have to look up to him anyway,' Dolores said, with a hint of bitterness. 'We women are put on this earth for the purpose of looking up to men. At least you will one day have a king to look up to.'

I had already noticed that Dolores spoke to Leonora with considerably more freedom than any of the other women. I considered whether she could be Leonora's sister or some other blood relation. I desperately hoped not because I was already making plans to have her for my own. If Dolores was of royal or noble blood then it would be a hopeless cause.

Dolores went on speaking to Leonora: 'You are very beautiful, my lady, and Lord Edward is very handsome. What sort of match will I make? I will probably end up having to marry that stunted creature under the table!'

It was startling to hear Dolores suddenly musing on the very likelihood I was contemplating. It was poignant to hear her low opinion of me but, as is the case when passion seizes your heart, it made me more determined to persuade her of my virtues, if I ever had the opportunity.

'At least he would keep you amused,' Leonora replied, 'but do not concern yourself, Dolores, you are beautiful and will make as handsome a match as I have.'

'Not as handsome as Lord Edward,' Dolores said mournfully.

'Yes, I am lucky, but it is a pity about that eye.'

For a moment I could not understand what Leonora meant but then I realised it must have been a reference to Lord Edward's drooping left eyelid. I did not think it was unsightly but then I was well used to such a defect and what young woman does not yearn for perfection in her man?

Dolores almost snorted. 'My lady, Lord Edward is tall, broad shouldered, long limbed, fair of hair and face and, from what we have heard, courageous in battle, and his father has given him half of England! I would gladly take your place in his bed!'

The duenna again tut-tutted at this comment, which I also thought was unseemly. I did not think English ladies of nobility would talk so freely and openly, but Lady Leonora did not seem at all perturbed by Dolores's remark. She said, almost dreamily: 'King Alphonso thinks that Lord Edward's father is a simpleton, that is why my dear brother nearly took possession of Gascony away from the English.'

'Most of Europe thinks King Henry of England is a simpleton,' Dolores said.

'But what if Lord Edward is a simpleton?' Leonora asked anxiously.

'You have been assured that he is not, but even if he is, your job will be to have his babies and ensure his, and your, line of succession. But, while you are doing so, you can make a very comfortable life in England.'

'Yes, England,' Leonora said. 'I am frightened, Dolores. What is it like there? What are the people like? They say it is cold and wet and that the English do not like foreigners. What if I am unhappy? Will I know what to do?'

'Calm yourself, my lady,' the duenna interjected. 'You are going to England as the bride of a prince and will one day be a queen. Everything will be as you command it to be.'

'I will still need friends I can trust.'

'You shall have them,' the duenna said. 'Your ladies-in-waiting are going with you, to serve you in your new realm. Well, all except Dolores.'

I was so startled and disappointed by this news that I stopped strumming my harp and sat up straight, banging my head against the underside of the table. All the women looked down at me. I grinned idiotically, bobbed backwards and forwards in apology and then continued playing. They immediately forgot about me again.

Leonora asked plaintively: 'Oh, Dolores, won't you change your mind? You are my best friend, we have known each other since childhood. I want you with me.'

'You know I am promised to Lord Alcamanzar. I must stay here in Castile.'

'You just said you wished for a handsome man. Lord Alcamanzar is old, almost forty years old.'

'He is very rich.'

'Is that all that concerns you?'

'Yes, in a husband. I will take a handsome lover. Men are fickle but wealth is not and wealth should be what mostly concerns you, my lady.'

'Enough!' the duenna roared. 'You speak too freely, Dolores. Lady Leonora is well aware of what her duty is to be. You must apologise to her ladyship.'

Leonora herself did not appear to be offended.

'I'm am so sorry, my lady,' Dolores said, sarcastically and insincerely.

'It is nothing, my friend,' Leonora assured her, airily waving her hand. 'No, I am lucky. If I am obliged to marry for reasons of state then Lord Edward is as good a match as I could hope for. But I understand what you mean, Dolores. A woman, even a queen, must make certain of provision for herself in a most uncertain world, especially a foreigner like I am to be in England.'

I took full note of the tone of this conversation. I had already formed a notion to offer my services to Lady Leonora at the appropriate time.

I stayed with the women for a long time but their conversation turned to other court gossip and was of little further meaning or interest. I sang them a few songs and performed a few sleight-of-hand magic tricks until the time came for them to prepare for the evening meal. I was relieved when the duenna dismissed me.

Lord Edward summoned me to his chamber after the evening

meal and his evening devotions. His chamber was decorated with some sort of elaborate white stucco decoration and equipped with carved dark wood furniture, including his bed, and with a proper fireplace in which a cheerful log fire was blazing to ward off the October chill.

Edward, still attired in his formal princely surcoat of red and gold, was pacing up and down and was all eagerness. 'Well, Hamo, what did she say about me?'

I replied with the expurgated and elaborated version I had prepared. 'Lady Leonora could hardly restrain herself in praise of you, my lord. She is as happy as possible that you will soon be her husband. Naturally, she felt concerned before you arrived. She was worried that reports about your manly virtues were exaggerated but, as soon as she met you, all her doubts vanished and she is very happy. You have nothing to fear, my lord. Lady Leonora is yours, body and soul.'

Edward regarded me, wanting desperately to believe but sceptical that I might be exaggerating, which was exactly what I was doing. 'You speak truly, Hamo? You swear you do not simply tell me what I wish to hear?'

I contrived to look hurt by his question. 'My lord, have I not sworn by Almighty God to tell you the truth? I speak truly now.'

'Yes, yes, you are right, Hamo. This is a happy day, my friend. What did you think of Lady Leonora?'

'My lord, I think Lady Leonora is of a most wondrous beauty. She is soft spoken, dignified, and granted most bounteously of the womanly virtues. And yet... ' I pretended to hesitate and be uncertain whether I should continue.

'Come on, Hamo. Remember that you must speak honestly with me. Finish what you were saying.'

'Well, my lord, comely as Lady Leonora is, my attention was taken by another.'

'What do you mean? Another woman?'

'Yes, my lord. If I may speak frankly, as man to man, one of Lady

Leonora's attendants awoke a passion in my breast that I have never felt before.'

Edward roared with laughter and stopped pacing the room in order slap me on the back. 'Who is she, Hamo? What is her name?'

'Her name is Dolores. She is Lady Leonora's best friend.'

'Then surely she will be coming back to England with my bride.'

'I'm afraid not, my lord. She is bethrothed to a Spanish nobleman and will be staying in Castile to marry him.' I pretended to look distressed.

Lord Edward actually put his arm around my shoulders and reassured me. 'Don't distress yourself, my friend. Whoever has become betrothed can become unbetrothed by the will of princes. If this girl is my wife's best friend then she must come to England with us. I know it will be very strange and daunting for Lady Leonora to arrive in a new country with strange faces all around. She must have her best friend with her. You leave this to me, Hamo.'

'You are most kind and understanding, my lord.'

'I have something else for you, Hamo,' Edward said playfully.

'For me?'

Edward opened an ornately carved wooden cabinet and took out a glass flagon. He held it up for me to see and announced: 'As we are in Spain I have obtained some of the Spanish eau-de-vie that we both enjoy and which cured my sea sickness. Come, Hamo, let us have a drink and celebrate while we play chess and talk some more about my new bride.'

NOVEMBER 1254

As a lowly jester, albeit a secret friend of Lord Edward, I was not worthy to be invited to attend his marriage ceremony, which was conducted in the church of Las Huelgas monastery.

A few days later Edward and his new bride, escorted by hundreds of nobles, knights and armed soldiers, set off on the return journey over those forbidding Pyrenees mountains and back into his province of Gascony. I was frequently summoned to travel in the comfort of the royal wagon with Leonora and her ladies-in-waiting to alleviate the tedium of their journey with songs and harp and clowning.

The wilful and desirable Dolores had, by royal command of Lord Edward, been obliged to sever her bethrothal to her rich Spanish lord and accompany Lady Leonora to England. I considered that she had been saved from a life of indolent boredom in some Castilian backwater with a husband more than twice her age.

I was already considering ways by which to ingratiate myself into Lady Leonora's confidence as I had done with Lord Edward. I had perforce to be extremely circumspect and it was impossible to find an opportunity to be alone with Leonora.

All the Spanish women of the court, who otherwise found my antics amusing, assumed I was a dull fellow who could not understand a word they were saying, and thus had spoken freely and without restraint while I was present. How would Leonora, and the other ladies, react if they became aware that I had been able to understand every word they had uttered? It was a conundrum impossible to solve but I was confident that I could, in the right auspicious circumstances, persuade Leonora of the value of my talents and services, as I had persuaded Edward.

Oh, what now, monk? Did not your fellow brothers at Tournai teach you not to interrupt your elders and betters? You think it strange that, having ingratiated myself so securely into Lord Edward's favour, I should be so intent on ingratiating myself in a similar fashion with Lady Leonora? The answer is that Lord Edward, being immensely rich and the greatest land owner in England, cared nought for enriching himself further. He was an upright and pious character who placed duty and honour before wealth. To attain the riches and estates I craved I considered that Lady Leonora would be a much more willing accomplice than Lord Edward. Also, if I was to one day win the hand of Dolores then I had to let her know that I was more, much more, than a dullard jester. And that was hardly possible without Lady Leonora having the same knowledge. Let us get on, boy…

The more I observed and listened to Leonora the more I was convinced that hidden beneath that beautiful and refined royal exterior was a steely core of self-seeking greed. She fascinated me, and I adored her, but I harboured no illusions about her true character. Her well concealed impulse for self-preservation only added to her allure.

She was inclined to petulance and irritation directed towards underlings but her punishments were never cruel or arbitrary. Often I sensed a secretive humorous enjoyment in her dealings with the lesser mortals surrounding her, playing with them as a sleek cat toys with a frightened mouse.

Leonora was very happy with her new husband and talked about him in ecstatic, albeit discreet, terms. I had little opportunity to converse with Edward on this return journey but it was obvious that he was equally happy with his new wife.

Wherever the royal party stopped to spend the night the young couple retreated to their private quarters as soon as was seemly and the sounds of their frenzied lovemaking became a source of merry gossip amongst their servants and retainers. They were in the first flush of a lifelong love affair and already completely devoted to each other.

I perceived Dolores to be a vital element in my plan to ingratiate myself with Leonora, quite apart from my raging desire to win her love. Dolores was the object of my constant fantasies, but she was not happy. Throughout the long journey she scarcely bothered to be civil to anyone, including her friend and mistress Lady Leonora. Her rank bad temper and her open contempt for me only inflamed my ardour until I could hardly bear it, such can be the sickness of the human heart.

I would oft times look at her face when she was in repose and was not aware that I was observing her. At those times her expression was serene and quite beautiful. Then she would look up and catch me, then her expression would turn to sour lemons. Her flashing almond eyes and heaving bosom occupied all my night thoughts and most of my day dreams. I was utterly determined that she would one day be my wife.

1 2 5 5

E dward, thanks to his father's absence, was temporarily free to administer Gascony as he saw fit. His abiding problem was a sheer lack of funds. The public finances of Gascony were in a parlous state and so, as rulers are wont to do, Edward decided to add to the groaning burden of taxation borne by his Gascon subjects and imposed a new tax with the vindication that it was to celebrate his elevation to the knighthood.

His father the king, with equal tender concern for his wealth bloated subjects, had earlier imposed a new tax to pay for his intended holy crusade, so the consequence of this grievous two-pronged taxation was inevitable and Gascony exploded into pitchfork waving revolt again.

The new uprising meant that we were stuck in Gascony and I saw even less of Lord Edward because he was away spending the fruits of his new taxation on the campaign to suppress the rebellion caused by the new taxation but, thankfully, he ordered that I remain in Bordeaux with Lady Leonora and keep her happily distracted with my foolish antics rather than accompanying him on his stirring military exploits.

Despite my comfortable life I found that frustration was gnawing at my innards. Bordeaux and Gascony, for all their sun-warmed and scented attractions, were dull backwaters. I yearned to return to England, to be near the king and the royal court where the real power and influence resided. I had never been to London and I longed to see what the great city was like.

I desperately wanted to find the identity of my real father and to begin the climb up the social hierarchy to wealth and, perhaps, a noble title. I was becoming mind-numbingly bored with entertaining Spanish women.

Dolores, despite my attempts to ingratiate myself into her affections, ignored my existence. Lady Leonora simply took me for granted and yet, for all my brain-racking ingenuity, I could not conceive of a safe and plausible way to reveal to her my secret talents and what an inestimable help I could be to her.

If she discovered that I had been able to understand everything that she had been saying and thinking ever since we met, then female fury would surely cause her to have me removed from her presence, or perhaps mete out an even more severe punishment.

But then, thanks to the invocation of God and to the virility of my young liege lord and master, I stumbled upon the perfect opportunity to reveal myself to Leonora which was born, literally, out of tragedy.

Thanks to the whispered and concerned gossip of her ladies-in-waiting I became aware that Lady Leonora was with child, perhaps even before Edward himself knew. The child had been conceived soon after their marriage, perhaps as early as their ecstatic wedding night itself.

At the end of May something went amiss with the pregnancy, perhaps because Leonora was too young and not fully formed as a woman. The child, a girl, was born prematurely and lived for only a few hours.

Lord Edward was not present to witness the birth and death of his first child. Lady Leonora's blood-chilling and hair-clutching grief was enough to inspire pity in the hardest of hearts.

I had developed a conspiratorial and teasing brotherly affection for Leonora, quite unlike the raging lust for Dolores which stalked my daydreams. I was certain that Leonora and I would become firm friends if only fate would allow us to display our true natures to each other. I did my best to alleviate her grievous sorrow with my clowning and my soothing music but with little success.

I learnt from overhearing the royal physicians that intimate relations between Leonora and her husband had become temporarily unfeasible owing to her delicate physical condition. Edward was a lusty youth and the fevered serpent of jealousy stirred in Lady Leonora's breast and gave me a God-given and unexpected opportunity to reveal my true nature to her.

An extensive walled garden had been created just outside of the grounds of Chateau St. Pierre where unusual and exotic fruit and vegetables were grown for the royal table. It was guarded and completely secure from the restless populace. It was replete with scented wild flowers and murmuring breeze-blown shady trees.

There was a soft grassy area equipped with a finely carpentered wooden bench with arm rests and a high back. Embroidered cushions were strewn on the bench and a canopy could be erected if the sun became hot enough to mar Leonora's unspoilt complexion.

This part of the garden was intended for the benefit of Lady Leonora, a private nook to take her ease, but was also intended as a place where the newborn child would play, and so this garden had a precious meaning for Leonora.

One fine cloudless day in the middle of July, I was summoned to accompany Leonora and Dolores to the garden and play soothingly on my harp while they sat and enjoyed the sunshine. The warm air was scented with honeysuckle and lavender and rosemary. Birds sang gaily in the apple and plum trees. Guards accompanied us but remained a respectful distance away and out of earshot.

This was a most unusual situation for me, to be alone with Lady Leonora and Dolores without any of the other ladies-in-waiting or assorted flunkies being in attendance. I considered that this could be an ideal opportunity to confidentially ingratiate myself with the two women and I listened intently to what they were talking about. They were confident that I could not understand their conversation in the French language and thus they spoke without restraint.

As soon as the two women had settled down on to the bench

Leonora began to weep quietly but attempting, without success, to maintain her regal dignity.

Dolores gently begged her: 'Please don't distress yourself so, my lady. It is God's will that the child was taken. How can we poor mortals fathom God's purpose? All we can do is accept His will throughout whatever tribulations He burdens us with.'

That statement provided me with the inkling of a strategy.

'I know, I know,' Leonora sniffed, and withdrew a lace kerchief from the voluminous sleeve of her elegant green and gold gown. 'I am beginning to accept His will but that is not why I feel so distressed today.'

'Then why, madam? What is the cause?'

Leonora hesitated, unwilling to diminish her royal status by displaying human frailty, even to her childhood friend. At last she admitted: 'I think my husband looks to another woman while I am unable to please him.'

'Another woman?' Dolores repeated. 'Surely not? Lord Edward adores you and your condition has nearly righted itself, so the doctors tell you. What other woman do you mean?'

'Emilia de Clare, wife of the Earl of Gloucester.'

This admission was the perfect opportunity to effect the strategy that had formed in my mind, or perhaps that God had placed in my mind. This was another once-in-a-lifetime opportunity that had to be seized. I had to take the risk if the truly desirable connection between Leonora and myself was ever to be established.

I was sitting cross-legged on the grass, a few yards away from the two women. I let my harp fall to the ground and, clutching my head in both hands, I rolled forward to lay on my side. I made myself groan piteously and my limbs to shake and tremble. After this feigned seizure I lay as still as death with my eyes closed.

I heard Lady Leonora say, without much concern and a trace of irritation in her voice: 'Dolores, go and see what is wrong with Hamo.'

'He probably drank too much wine last night, as usual.'

A moment later I felt Dolores's hand shaking me by my shoulder.

Then I heard Lady Leonora's voice again, closer this time, asking: 'Is he all right?'

I opened my eyes to see both women looking down at me, Leonora looking concerned, Dolores looking annoyed. I sat up and rubbed my face with the palms of my hand and then clutched my head again, as if still in pain.

Deliberately speaking in French I said: 'Please forgive me for interrupting your conversation, my lady. I don't know what happened.'

The two women stared at me, both open-mouthed in astonishment. Dolores, forgetting all about protocol, clutched Leonora's arm and gasped: 'He spoke in French. The little duende spoke in French.'

I looked at Dolores as if I was bewildered by her statement and said: 'But I could not have done. I do not understand the French language.'

Leonora said excitedly, but in a low voice: 'He is speaking French and what he says makes sense. He is talking like one of us instead of a dull peasant.'

'My lady,' I said to Leonora, feigning dazed befuddlement, 'it seems that my wits are clear as they have never been before.'

'What happened to you just now, Hamo?' Leonora asked, her tone kindly and genuinely concerned.

The guards had tentatively approached to ascertain what was happening and whether their protection was needed.

I said to Leonora: 'Please, my lady, send away the guards. I have a message for you and no-one else must hear it.'

'A message?' Leonora repeated. 'A message from who?'

'A message from God, my lady. And from someone else… no, it cannot be possible.' I clutched my head and rocked backwards and forwards and wailed keenly.

'Compose yourself, Hamo,' I heard Leonora say. 'Who else is this message from?'

'I tremble to say so, my lady, but the message is from your daughter.'

Lady Leonora gasped in shock and stepped back. Dolores, speechless for once, grew pale and looked at me with bewildered incomprehension.

The captain of the guards had warily approached Leonora and asked if assistance was needed. Leonora, distractedly, told him: 'No, the fool is acting out mummery for our amusement. All is well. Return to your stations.'

The captain bowed and ushered his men away.

'Hamo,' Leonora said firmly, 'come over here and tell us what has happened to you.'

The two women returned to their bench and I followed them and settled cross-legged on the grass in front of them. If anyone now observed us it would appear as if I was simply telling a story or singing a song.

'Well?' Leonora asked, unable to restrain her eagerness.

'My lady, I was playing my harp when I felt a blinding light in my head. It was not painful. It was wonderful. I heard a voice say to me that I was being granted my wits and the power of tongues in order to be of service to you. I have been told by God to be your protector, to be your devoted servant, but to serve you in ways that no-one must know about.'

Leonora considered my statement for several moments. I could see that she was torn between wanting to believe me and yet disbelief that such a transformation could be possible.

Finally she said: 'I don't understand. What about Dolores? You have said that no-one must know but now she already knows because you have told her.'

'Madam, Dolores is your best friend and is utterly faithful to you. God commands that we are both to serve you.'

Dolores said: 'This is not possible.'

Leonora said: 'Shush, Dolores. I believe what Hamo is saying. How else can it be explained that this fool, this witless buffoon who could not speak French, or even string two sensible words together in English, apart from those he learned by rote to entertain us, is now speaking French with fluency. I am prepared to believe that God has entered his mind and given him such ability.'

'No, my lady!' Dolores protested. 'He is tricking us. Perhaps he has been able to speak French and understand what we have been saying all the time. The fool is trying to make fools of us!'

Leonora regarded me carefully. She was considering whether Dolores could be correct. It was now the moment to reinforce my supposedly God-given credentials. I switched languages to Latin and said: 'God wills that I serve you and protect you, my lady.'

Once again the women gasped in surprise. 'What was that?' Dolores asked. 'What is he speaking now?' She clearly did not understand Latin, which exactly suited my purpose.

Lady Leonora had received a good education befitting a princess and understood my Latin perfectly. She told Dolores: 'Hamo speaks in Latin. Now I am sure that God must have entered his mind. Only priests, monks and nobles are taught Latin, not humble jesters.'

Dolores refused to concede. 'Surely it is not impossible that the little ape could have known Latin. Perhaps he trained as a monk before entering your service.'

Leonora was wavering again, accepting the possibility suggested by doubting Dolores.

I made my expression dreamy, as if in a light trance, and continued in Latin: 'I have a message from Matilda, my lady.'

Leonora's eyes widened in surprise, tears began to form, and her pale hands trembled.

Dolores noticed and started to ask: 'What did he say, my lady? The little monkey is… '

'Silence!' Leonora roared in a commanding tone and Dolores, astonished, immediately kept her counsel. Leonora ordered: 'Hamo, give me the message from Matilda.'

I intoned dreamily: 'Matilda is in Heaven with the Lord. She sends her love to you, her mother, and to her dear father. She wishes with all her heart that she could have spent more time on earth with you but she is at the side of God and is very happy.'

Lady Leonora was now weeping copiously and I felt pangs of guilt at my manipulation of her emotions.

Dolores put her arm around her mistress's shoulders to comfort her and eventually Leonora managed to control herself.

'What did he say?' Dolores asked gently.

'He gave me a message from Matilda,' Leonora replied, dabbing at her eyes.

'Matilda? Who is Matilda?'

'Lord Edward and I had decided to name our daughter Matilda. Only he and I knew of our decision. And, of course, God. There is no possibility that Hamo could have known that name unless God had told him.'

In fact, Edward had mentioned the name during a game of chess.

Leonora continued, almost in ecstasy: 'God has entered Hamo's soul and corrected his wits and given him the gift of tongues to serve me.' She held out her hands. 'Come towards me, Hamo.'

I stood up and gently took Leonora's painfully thin white fingers. I kissed them tenderly. I said: 'As from this moment no-one must know of what has happened here and what gifts have been granted to me by God. If you or Dolores divulge this to anyone, including Lord Edward, I will lose my wits again, be of no use to you, and unable to bring you messages from Matilda.'

'I understand,' Lady Leonora nodded. 'I willingly accept the will of God.'

'He has ordained that Dolores and I serve you together.'

'How do you mean, Hamo. As man and wife?'

'Yes, my lady. With your consent and approval.'

'If it is God's will that you and Dolores be man and wife in order to serve me, then so be it.'

'Thank you, my lady.' Switching back to French so that Dolores could understand, I said to Leonora: 'Forgive me for encroaching on a delicate matter, my lady, but when God honoured me with His presence, He told me you were concerned about a possible relationship between Emilia de Clare and Lord Edward.'

Leonora nodded reluctantly and whispered: 'Yes.'

'Your concerns are groundless, my lady. Lord Edward loves you and is utterly devoted to you but, like most men, he may be vulnerable to a pretty face, especially one who lusts after power and the favour of a great man. My first service to you will be to remove Emilia de Clare from the company of your husband and then you can rest easy and recover your strength and your spirits in peace of mind.'

'Thank you, Hamo,' Leonora replied.

Dolores, however, was not convinced. 'Do you mean to say, Hamo Pauncefoot, that you will now return to clowning around as a fool, that we can tell no-one of what has happened here, but that you can still control the fate of the wife of an earl? How will you do that? The Earl of Gloucester is a most powerful lord. What effect can a humble jester have on his affairs or that of his wife?'

'It is not me that is ordering these affairs but God working within me.'

'You are right, Hamo,' Leonora said. She turned to Dolores and ordered: 'Do as God has required us to do. Hold your tongue, tell no-one of what has happened here today.' [7]

Fortunately for me, Lord Edward returned from campaigning the very next day. I had a quiet word in his ear, quite simply to the effect that I had overheard Leonora telling Dolores that she was jealous of Edward's relationship with Emilia de Clare. Edward, completely innocent of any intention to be unfaithful, was anxious to appease and reassure his young bride, and Emilia de Clare soon found herself travelling on a cog back to England, an accomplishment which securely cemented my place in the life of Lady Leonora.

Leonora was most impressed by this evidence of God working through me and relieving her of a threat to her marital bliss. It assuaged my guilt at my manipulative actions had, in all truth, greatly comforted and aided Leonora's recovery from the loss of her child.

I was delighted when, two months later, King Henry decreed that his new daughter-in-law travel to England, without her husband, to be received in London. And who should Lady Leonora choose to accompany her to this strange new land? Her faithful fool, friend and God-given protector, Hamo Pauncefoot, of course!

September 1255

We sailed from Bordeaux and straight into the maw of a heaving grey autumn sea lashed with steely rain. Lady Leonora, although sore afraid, was but little troubled by sea sickness. Dolores, however, was greenly racked with retching throughout the voyage and prayed for salvation more earnestly than I had known her to beseech God for anything. I offered her my cure for sea sickness but she refused, claiming that I was attempting to poison her or cast a spell over her. Eventually she accepted the cure. My sole reward was a brief smile and a hastily muttered thank you.

After an arduous and terrifying voyage of several days we found harbour at Dover in early October and, with many thanks offered to heaven for our delivery, sought rest, recuperation and refuge within the massive walls of the castle.

From Dover we set off for London in the royal wagon shielded by an escort of scores of knights honored to be doing service to their new princess.

We rested overnight in the Cistercian monastery at Ladywell. Here Lady Leonora was greeted by the Lord Mayor of London and informed that a lavish civic reception had been prepared for her entry into the capital.

I was in a high state of excitement, eager to see the sights of the great city for the first time, to begin finding out how the administration of the land was conducted, and what advantages and opportunities I could seize at court.

Lady Leonora, although excited to be in her new realm, was

fretting about whether the Londoners would like her or not. I sang soothing songs and assured her that her youthful beauty was sure to win them over.

On the appointed day we set off from the monastery at noon. It was, thankfully, a dry and windless autumn day, albeit chilly, but Lady Leonora, riding on horseback, refused to cover herself with furs, being anxious to appear as elegant and regal as possible for her first appearance before the citizens of London. She was dressed, in the latest Castilian fashion, in an intricately embroidered blue and gold loose-fitting gown with very long sleeves. On her head she wore a tall conical hat decorated with delicate silk and what looked, to a simple male such as me, like padded ear muffs.

The heralds and the advance guard of knights and nobles rode in the van, then Leonora with the main escort, followed by Dolores and the other ladies of the Castilian court, with me and my fellow fools bringing up the rear while clowning around and throwing sweetmeats and other presents to the assembled populace to sweeten their opinion of Leonora.

Many cheering and bowing serfs lined our route as we approached Southwark but when we rode through the city gate towards London Bridge we were almost overwhelmed by the clamorous greeting of a huge throng of citizens. The city streets had been decorated with gay bunting, with flags and banners hanging from private dwellings as well as the public buildings.

We crossed London Bridge and progressed through the winding streets towards St. Paul's cathedral. When we had passed the cathedral and were riding nearer to the palace at Westminster, through the more sophisticated environs of Fleet Street, the Temples and down the Strand, the cheers became intermingled with laughter and jeers, especially from the female onlookers. I could see many Londoners pointing at Leonora and her Castilian ladies and shouting derisive comments. I could not see Lady Leonora's reaction but I soon found out what it was when she summoned me to her chamber soon after we had arrived at the palace of Westminster.

Leonora was pacing up and down the spacious and newly-decorated chamber, which was hung with fine tapestries and furnished with a tester bed, a huge wardrobe, and carved oak furniture comfortably softened with embroidered cushions. A log fire was burning in the hearth to take the autumn chill off the room.

Despite the luxury of her surroundings, Leonora was close to tears. Dolores was trying to calm her down but having little success. Leonora's lower lip trembled as she said to me plaintively: 'The Londoners were laughing at me, Hamo. They hate me already. What have I ever done to them? Why were they laughing at me?'

I had already found out the reason for the laughter and was ready with a soothing reply. 'Please do not distress yourself, madam. The Londoners were not laughing at you. They were laughing at the manner in which you and your ladies are attired.'

Leonora stopped pacing and looked at me, mystified. She looked down at her gown and then looked at Dolores's green and white gown, which was similar in style albeit less decorated and made of inferior material. 'Explain yourself, Hamo,' Leonora demanded, her female vanity pricked. 'What is wrong with the way we are dressed?'

'Nothing wrong, my lady, but you are dressed in the latest Castilian fashions, and very beautiful you both look.' Dolores snorted contemptuously. I ignored her and continued: 'I am told by English ladies who know of such things that your future mother-in-law, Queen Eleanor, prefers much simpler fashions, in her native French style, which has become the accepted style of the court.'

'Simpler?' Leonora repeated. 'In what way simpler? Explain what that means!'

'It is difficult for me to explain with propriety, my lady. Apparently, the fashion at the moment is for tight lacing which holds the dress much closer to the... er, curves of the body.' Leonora continued to regard me with lips pursed in disapproval. Unnerved by her withering gaze, I blathered on: 'And the head is covered in a wimple, held in place by a band. Such tall and highly-decorated hats as you are wearing are not known in England. The Londoners are not accustomed to these fashions and so to them you appear to be dressed… oddly, even outlandishly.'

'Outlandishly?' Leonora said. 'How dare they treat their princess in such an insulting manner?'

When I had entered Lady Leonora's chamber I had felt a strange substance under my feet, which was now distracting me as I shifted about. I looked down and found I was standing on some sort of brightly coloured surface. I later found out that it was something called a carpet, of which I had heard but never seen. They were manufactured in Spain and the Levant but were, up until Leonora's arrival, unknown in England. I was to learn that Lady Leonora's use of something so gratuitously luxurious and un-English as this carpet caused sneering derision and merriment amongst the populace when it became the subject of general gossip.

Leonora became even more annoyed by my distracted manner and snapped at me: 'Answer me, fool! Why do these Londoners treat a princess so disrespectfully?'

I diagnosed that the balm of more soothing words should be applied to Leonora's sore festering temper. 'My lady, the English people are simply unused to your Castilian fashions. Within weeks all the ladies of the court, English and Spanish, and all of the high-born ladies in England will be slavishly copying the way you dress. The common people adore you already. During our progress through the city I heard many of them praise your beauty and how it is a welcome adornment to English life.' [8]

Dolores said: 'Your hearing must be keener than mine, Master Pauncefoot, because I heard someone denounce us, in French, as "strange Spanish bitches".'

Leonora had turned her back to us so I gave Dolores a warning look and held a finger to my mouth to ask her to hold her tongue but, as usual, she ignored me.

Leonora, disturbed anew by Dolores's crass comment, turned back to confront me. 'What say you to that, Master Pauncefoot? A fine greeting for a princess to be welcomed as a strange Spanish bitch.'

Those offensive words which seemed acceptable from the mouth of Dolores seemed the vilest of obscenities from the pouting pink mouth of Lady Leonora.

'My lady, there will always be dissenters in any society but I'm sure they are very few. You must understand that the people of London, and the people of England, have become afraid of the influx of foreigners into their city and their land. You will win all of them over to your favour in time.'

My attempt at soothing words was ill-received and was flung straight back into my face by Leonora's furiously spitting tongue. 'Foreigner!?' she exclaimed. 'How dare you!'

'Madam, it is not I who… '

'Shut up! Why should they call me foreigner? I am the wife of their future king. I am the daughter-in-law of their present king. I am English by marriage. And why should they be afraid of me?'

'You must understand, madam, that… '

'Must? Must, little man? Do not abuse my trust by telling me I "must" do anything.' Leonora's dark brown eyes blazed with indignation.

Dolores was delighting in my discomfiture, knowing that if I fell out of favour with Leonora then she would be released from the threat of marriage to me.

Through long humiliating years of experience I was well practised in the art of controlling my temper and hiding my true feelings so I simply hung my head, as if in shame, until the storm gradually passed.

Leonora took a deep breath and sat down on one of the wooden armchairs. First, however, she picked up one of the cushions, which were embroidered with the royal arms of England and Castile, and hurled it at my head. But then, with a hint of a conciliatory tone in her voice, she asked: 'Tell me what I "must" understand, Hamo. Why are the people afraid of me?'

'Forgive my earlier temerity, madam. My God-given desire, my only true desire, is to be your faithful servant and counsellor as wise as I can be within my limited wits.'

Leonora nodded her forgiveness and I continued, choosing my words carefully: 'The political situation in England has, for many years now, been aggravated by courtiers and nobles who have been invited here from outside of England by our liege lord King Henry and by his queen, Eleanor of Provence. It is a complicated situation to explain, my lady, and I... '

'Too complicated for a mere woman to understand, is that what you mean, Hamo?'

'Not at all, madam. I was... '

'Well, that is the response I always receive when I enquire about such things. Even my own husband, whom I love dearly, tells me not to worry my pretty little head about such matters.'

I frantically considered what to say next. Lady Leonora was still seeking a confrontation to relieve her adolescent fears and frustrations. Reluctant to embark on the murky and dangerous waters of court politics, I again attempted to deflect Leonora's enquiry. 'May I suggest, madam, that your husband, despite his reluctance, is the fitting person to explain such matters to you, not I?'

'I thought that God had sent you to assist me and protect me, Hamo, so why not you? My husband is not here to explain these things. Why not you?'

'Such matters involve the king and queen, madam. I am a humble jester. I tremble to comment upon or criticise my ordained sovereign.'

'But if God sent you, Hamo, then you will have to tell me the truth, not anodyne lies that some court flunkey, or even my dear husband, would tell me simply to appease me. Tell me, Hamo. Now!'

Lady Leonora's tone brooked no further argument. I must admit to being impressed by her new-found forcefulness, albeit born out of fear of the future. Such a refusal to be brow-beaten would serve her well.

'Very well, my lady,' I began but, to my relief, there was a knock on the door of the chamber just as I said it. I quickly picked up my harp and began to play. Leonora called out for whoever it was to enter and the door opened to admit several ladies-in-waiting.

'What is it?' Leonora asked irritably.

The ladies hesitated when they realised their mistress was in a foul mood and were reluctant to speak up. One of them found the courage to say: 'It is time to prepare you for the feast, madam.'

'Am I then to be the main course?' Leonora asked with a smile, but her jest fell on stony ground when none of the ladies dared to laugh.

In my role as jester I squealed: 'The Lady Leonora is the tastiest dish I have ever seen!'

My jest won a modest ripple of laughter from the ladies-in-waiting but Leonora herself merely glared at me. To the ladies she ordered: 'Come back when I call for you.'

The courageous one warned: 'Madam, you must not keep the king and queen waiting.'

Leonora banged the arm of the chair and shouted: 'Do not presume to tell me my duty! Go away!'

The ladies-in-waiting, chastened, shuffled back out of the door and closed it silently behind them. Leonora sighed wearily and said to me: 'I must attend this feast in my honour, even though I am not at all hungry. I am to meet the king and queen for the first time. I hope they approve of their son's new wife. They should do because they arranged the marriage. Dolores, when the festivities are over and my duties are done, I want you to bring Hamo here to my chamber. He will explain to me the political situation in England. We will talk alone.'

Dolores was wide-eyed with surprise. She was thinking more of the threat I posed to her privileged position rather than any impropriety when she protested: 'But, my lady, it would be most improper to receive a man alone in your chamber without a duenna!'

'Oh, shut up, Dolores. I am married now. And, besides, it is not a man, it is Hamo.'

Dolores smiled contentedly when she saw my pained expression caused by Leonora's crass remark.

Leonora said: 'Now, you two leave me. Give me a few minutes of peace to myself and then send my ladies back.'

I bowed and Dolores curtseyed and we murmured our respects to Leonora, who looked heart-wrenchingly frail and pensive, as we left the chamber and closed the door behind us.

The large antechamber outside was deserted except for two knights guarding the entrance on the other side. Both the guards looked to check who was leaving Leonora's chamber but both were out of earshot and I realised that this was the first time Dolores and I had been alone together for many days and an ideal opportunity to declare my love for her.

'You look beautiful, Dolores. I am stupid with love for you. Cannot you find a kind thought or word for me.'

Her eyes blazed in anger as she replied: 'You might have my mistress wrapped around your little finger but you will never have me!'

'God has sent me to Lady Leonora.'

'God!' Dolores spat. 'Greed has sent you to Lady Leonora. I don't believe a word of this God business. What can a fool like you do for a princess such as Lady Leonora?'

'The same as I can do for you.'

'I was to marry a rich man in Castile. I could have had a comfortable life with all the luxuries I desire and servants to do all the work and to kick when I am in a bad temper.'

'Then the poor brutes have had a lucky escape.' I took Dolores by the shoulders and said earnestly: 'I love you, and I will give you wealth, titles, lands and luxuries. I will do the same for Lady Leonora, far more than she possesses now.'

Dolores looked at me coldly and said. 'Take your hands off me.'

I had been used to insults all my life yet when Dolores spoke such words to me they pierced my heart like a crossbow bolt. I reluctantly took my hands away from her warm smooth shoulders.

Dolores asked: 'When do you begin to perform these miracles? In the meantime I am stuck here with no money of my own in this cold, misty, alien land whose people call me a Spanish bitch.'

'You speak fairly. It is time for me to perform miracles and reward you as befits my future wife. Now you had better summon the other ladies-in-waiting. We do not want to disobey our mistress, Lady Leonora, or keep the king and queen waiting. Be sure to fetch me when Lady Leonora needs me later.'

Dolores looked disarmed by my mild response. She nodded, her almond eyes flashed, and she turned and left me. I watched her walk away. I had never desired her more and, later that day, I would begin to perform miracles and to prove to her my abilities and my intentions.

It was long after dark when Dolores came to summon me. I was dozing on my straw bed in the small annexe of the palace that I, and three other favoured servants, had been allotted as sleeping quarters.

Dolores, by the light of her candle, inspected the bare stone walls of my tiny unadorned home and pronounced scornfully: 'This is too good for you. I expected to find you in the kennels where you belong. Come, bring your harp. Lady Leonora is ready for you.'

I stood up, shaking fatigue from my head, and followed Dolores through the corridors of the palace, attracting many curious glances as we went. We came to a deserted stairway where we were hidden from prying eyes. I said: 'Stop for a moment. I have a gift for you.'

Dolores turned around. 'A gift?' she asked warily. 'What sort of gift?'

From under my motley I withdrew a blue velvet bag tied with silver lace. I handed it to Dolores.

'What is it?' she asked, not taking it.

'Open it and look.'

Her curiosity overcame her reluctance to accept anything from me. She put down her candle on one of the steps, took the bag and untied the knotted lace. She slowly took out the exquisite string of pearls I had purchased from a Genoese merchant in Bordeaux, at a very favourable price, in exchange for ensuring some lucrative contracts were awarded to him.

Dolores held up the necklace. The flickering light from a torch in a wall sconce made the lustre of the perfect pearls fire and dance with a golden aura. Dolores, greedy to possess them but trying not to show it, breathed a small exclamation of surprise. She thoughtfully examined the pearls but then briskly put them back in the bag. 'I don't want them.'

'Why not?'

'Because I know what you will want in exchange.'

'I want nothing in exchange, I swear. They are yours to do what you like with. Wear them, hide them, sell them, whatever you like. There will be plenty more in the future.'

Still Dolores hesitated but then, as I hoped it would, greed for such rare and beautiful pearls overcame her antipathy towards accepting gifts from me. 'Thank you,' she said brusquely, and then turned to pick up her candle. She made to carry on up the steps, but then suddenly stopped and turned around. 'Are you going to tell my mistress about this gift?'

'No, of course not. Listen, I know that I can never win you with this face and this body but I will devote my life, out of love, to give you wealth and jewels and a high position in the nobility of this cold, unfriendly country such as you cannot possibly conceive of at this time. Perhaps I can one day win your heart that way.'

'Fine promises from a fool sleeping on straw in a bare chamber. You will never win my heart.'

But she kept the pearls.

We arrived at Lady Leonora's chamber and Dolores entered alone to ensure that Leonora was ready to receive me. After a few moments Dolores ushered me into the room. The evening was chill and Lady Leonora was taking her ease in an armchair in front of a crackling fire.

Dolores quietly left the room and Lady Leonora bade me to sit at her feet. I assumed a comfortable cross-legged position and looked up at Leonora. She was drinking wine from a golden goblet. She did not offer me any.

To test her mood I said: 'You look tired, my lady.' It had been a long and testing day for such a young girl.

Fortunately her mood was benign. She smiled and replied: 'Well, it has been a strange day, but at least the king and queen seem pleased with me, even if the people are not.'

'That is good,' I nodded, and taking advantage of the unusual intimacy of the evening, I dared to ask: 'What did *you* think of *them?*'

Leonora did not reply, perhaps reluctant to discuss her distinguished in-laws with a mere fool, albeit a fool supposedly sent by God.

I said: 'Forgive me for speaking out of turn, my lady, but if I am to be your friend and counsellor there has to be straightforward honesty and plain speaking between us. I beg you to understand that I can never betray your trust and confidence because if anyone in any exalted position of power ever discovers my true nature, then I am finished.'

Still Leonora did not give me leave to say more so I went on regardless. 'Please listen to me, my lady, if not for your sake but for that of Lord Edward. You are now bound to him in marriage and your future security and happiness depends on his success as a man and as a monarch. Lord Edward grows more impressive in both regards, almost daily. King Henry and his queen love each other but that does not prevent them from being engaged in a power struggle, not least for the ear and the soul of your husband. You would be wise to be very cautious.'

Leonora took a sip of wine and then said: 'Very well, explain yourself. I give you permission to speak freely. Whatever you say to me about the king or queen, or even my husband, will remain confided in myself and in God.'

'Thank you, my lady, and please believe me that I speak only out of concern for your best interests and those of Lord Edward. King Henry is a simple man, a poor soldier, and is easily led by the nose. He is bleeding this country, almost unto death, with burdensome taxation to pay for his foolish schemes.'

'Schemes such as what?'

'Such as his laudable but misguided plan to go on crusade. For such a poor general to lead a crusade would be to court disaster, as his ill-led campaigns against the Welsh prove. Such as his acceptance of the pope's proposal to install Edward's younger brother, Lord Edmund, on the throne of Sicily.'

'Why is that such a bad thing, to wish a throne for Lord Edmund?'

'Such a proposal is not only fraught with danger and sure to skew the balance of power in Europe, it is most impractical. Before the pope suggested Lord Edmund as king of Sicily he had offered the throne to King Henry's brother, Earl Richard of Cornwall. Now, Richard is a much shrewder man than Henry. It is said that when Richard heard of the pope's proposal that he should become king of Sicily, he dismissed the notion by commenting: *"You might as well say, 'I make you a present of the Moon – step up to the sky and take it down'."* And to achieve the impossible objective of buying this kingdom, King Henry has imposed an insufferable burden of taxation on nobles, church and commoners alike.'

Lady Leonora was looking uncomfortable but I was determined to make her understand the situation that she had married into, so I pressed on relentlessly: 'On top of all I have described, the land has been racked by famine. The burden on the common people is almost too much for them to bear. There is deep unrest, and also, which is much more threatening to the king's authority, deep unrest among the barons and other powerful lords.'

'Why should Henry worry about a few barons?' Leonora asked, in a petulant tone. 'He is the king!'

'Because the barons, especially the lords of the Marches on the borders of Wales, are in command of armies almost as large as the royal army. The Marcher lords are independent of the king's authority and are literally a law unto themselves. King Henry depends upon their support, and so will Lord Edward when it his time to ascend to the throne. If all the barons collude against the king, even the king and the royal army can be overwhelmed.'

'Very well,' Leonora said. 'I understand that the poor common people are suffering and that the king has to pander to the might of the barons, but why is there such unrest amongst the barons? They are rich and well-fed. Why are they so aggrieved with the king?'

'King Henry's mother, Isabella of Angoulême, abandoned Henry and his siblings when they were children. She married again, to Hugh of Lusignan, and bore him nine more children. About ten years ago, Henry – despite having been abandoned by his mother and also being the simple pious trusting soul that he is – welcomed these cousins, the so-called Lusignans, from Poitou into England and promoted them to positions of power and bestowed lavish gifts of money and land upon them. Such is his misguided family feeling that he can refuse them nothing, an attitude which, of course, they exploit to the fullest advantage. This favouritism naturally enrages English nobles who think that such favours should be bestowed on true-born English lords, not foreign interlopers.'

'Foreign interlopers like me?' Leonora looked at me archly. I was relieved that the wine had smoothed her temper.

I nodded. 'That is part of the reason you received a poor reception from some members of the crowd earlier today. If King Henry's favouritism towards so-called "foreigners" was all that troubled the nobles then the situation might be more tranquil, but Queen Eleanor is also playing the same game.'

'She is a beautiful woman,' Leonora said, 'but she frightens me. She seems so comfortable within herself, so knowing, so experienced. When she talked to me I felt like a little girl again, as if I was being chided and reprimanded by my tutor.'

'You would do well to be wary of her. She is indeed beautiful, and much more intelligent and forceful than her husband. When she married Henry, she also brought over to England many of her family and supporters from Savoy, the so-called Savoyards. These men have also been granted wealth and positions of power in England. They, and Queen Eleanor herself, have seized lands and titles that English-born nobles think should be reserved for them. Queen Eleanor cares not a jot what the nobles think, still less what the common people think. That is why, madam, when the crowd saw you and your entourage arriving today they assumed that it was a new influx of foreigners arriving to cause trouble, impose new taxes and, as far as the lords are concerned, deprive them of more lands and titles that they consider as rightfully theirs.'

Leonora said wearily: 'So I am to be blamed for what has been happening in England for many years, something I had no knowledge of, a situation I was obliged to marry into, and something I cannot control?'

'That is the way of the world, madam. You are blameless and yet you are blamed. But you have one great advantage on your side.'

'What is that, Hamo?'

'Your husband is Lord Edward.'

To my surprise, Lady Leonora looked at me despondently. 'We have come to love each other but, when the time comes to take the throne, will Edward's judgement be as misguided as his father's?'

'No, your ladyship,' I replied firmly. 'Your husband is still little more than a boy and yet he is more of a man than his father ever was. Have no fear, in my God-given subtle guise as court jester I have overheard talk amongst the nobles and the military and even the clerics. All are impressed by Lord Edward, despite his occasionally capricious temper, and believe he will be a much stronger and wiser king than the one we have now.'

Leonora smiled sweetly. 'Thank you for your advice and encouragement, Hamo. God has been kind to send you to me. In the absence of my husband, I find you a comfort.'

I was reassured and comforted myself to hear such praise. I went on: 'The trouble in Gascony which Lord Edward is now attempting to quell is a perfect example of the king's foolishness. He sent his brother-in-law as his royal lieutenant to administer Gascony but this man, despite being pious and a good soldier, attempted to rule with a rod of iron. His harsh regime caused the current unrest, which has been going on for years. King Henry was forced to dismiss him from this post, the two men argued furiously, and now the two men are at loggerheads. King Henry has made a dangerous enemy.'

'What is the name of this enemy?' Lady Leonora asked, now growing sleepy from the warmth and the wine and the exertions of the day.

'His name, my lady, is Simon de Montfort, Earl of Leicester.'

'I will mark it well. Thank you for your company and your advice, Hamo.'

Leonora could no longer keep her eyes open and I seized the opportunity to gaze at her beauty. The firelight illuminated her raven black hair and peach smooth skin. She looked so young. I felt a surge of affection for her, as if she were the sister I never had. I would do my best to protect her, as I had pledged to protect Lord Edward, because they had become my family. We were all three of a similar age and, if we guarded and watched over each other then surely no harm would ever befall us.

I gently took the goblet from her hand and whispered: 'I will send Dolores in to attend you.'

Leonora nodded dreamily.

I stood up and left the chamber.

Dolores was waiting outside the door. I had no doubt that she had tried to eavesdrop on the conversation. She was wearing the string of pearls that I had given her. I asked: 'What will you say if Lady Leonora asks you where the pearls came from?'

'I will say they are a gift from my suitor.'

'You mean me?'

'No, of course not,' Dolores said hastily. 'I mean a parting gift from my suitor in Castile.' She brushed past me and went into Leonora's chamber, closing the door firmly behind her.

Was I imagining or was her attitude towards me a tad softer than it had been before?

NOVEMBER 1255

Lord Edward returned to England from Gascony at the end of November. The citizens of London crowded into the streets to greet the prince with tumultuous joy. I also ventured out into the street to watch Edward and his retinue approaching. It was a magnificent sight.

Edward, a tall, elegant and handsome figure mounted on a richly caparisoned white charger, was accompanied by some two hundred mounted knights with their mounted squires holding aloft the banner of each knight. It was a jubilant and thrilling spectacle. I had no doubt that the reason Edward had orchestrated this stirring display was to impress his father with his rapidly maturing authority, intellect and influence.

As was becoming my habit I studied the banners of each lord, looking for a rampant lion emblem, intent on identifying my natural father. If I could prove to Dolores that my real father was of noble birth then surely she would regard my suit more favourably. There were three or four promising banners and I attempted to memorise the identity of each squire for possible later interrogation about his master.

I went back inside the great hall of Westminster Palace to witness the formal reunion of Edward with Leonora, and with the rest of the royal family. Edward retained his dignity but Leonora, charmingly, could not restrain her joy and affection at his return, no doubt as thrilled as everyone else by the magnificent pomp of his arrival.

I turned to Dolores, who was standing beside me, and said softly: 'Perhaps you will greet me in such tender fashion one day.'

Dolores snorted with contempt and replied: 'I would greet you with such tender caresses but only with a dagger in my hand.'

I could not reply as we were now being overheard by other onlookers. My every advance towards Dolores was rejected, most cruelly, and yet I found it well nigh impossible to express how much she enchanted me and how much, I truly believed, we could be happy together. I myself could not understand my passionate feelings towards her, so how much more difficult it was to make her understand.

Now, here at the end of my long life, the troubadours sing much more of courtly love than they did in those days, and unrequited passion is more understood and acceptable. Back in those days I floundered in the sea of my own inexplicable longings.

1256

During the next few months I became dismally aware that my influence over Lord Edward was waning. He was beginning to surround himself with a new group of friends and courtiers, powerful and wealthy lords, or men of consummate talent. They were also older men who now looked on Lord Edward as their equal, not simply a boy, albeit the son of a king.

Whereas Edward had once found friendship and counsel in me, a youth of the same age, he was now seeking the advice of men immensely more experienced in the ways of the world and the Byzantine politics of England than I was.

They were men such as Edward's uncle, Earl Richard of Cornwall; and Richard's son, Henry of Almain; and Queen Eleanor's uncle, Peter of Savoy.

Although we remained friends and chess companions, Edward more and more frequently consorted with such powerful figures. He would venture forth with the younger and more hot-headed members of this circle. They made themselves drunk and caused trouble in a way unseemly for a prince, behaviour that disturbed many folk.

To compound my dismal concerns I pryed out the secret that Dolores was willingly giving her favours to a knight. This overheard discovery thrust through my innards like a hot bodkin. The identity of this knight twisted that gut-searing bodkin back and forth with frenzied jealousy and anger. He was Stephen Bauzan, the arrogant bastard who had escorted me, trembling in fear, to Blanquefort Castle to witness the downfall of Bartholomew Pecche and his sons.

With a supreme effort of will I kept my face and my temper in check and did not make Dolores, or Bauzan, aware that I had found out about their furtive trysts. This sleep-shattering knowledge haunted me yet made me even more determined to somehow persuade Dolores of my love and my profound intention to be a devoted and faithful husband.

Yet another concern was that I was doing little to enrich or endow Lady Leonora with either gold or lands, and doing precious little else for her except clowning and singing frolicsome French ballads and playing the harp. As with her husband, I sensed that Leonora was wearying of me and that my influence was waning.

I decided that I needed more capital to further some schemes that were forming in my mind, based on the knowledge I had already gleaned of the opportunities for enrichment offered by courtly life.

I requested, and was granted, leave of absence. I journeyed, with much trepidation, to my detested home town of Portsmouth.

I took repast and overnight lodgings in the monastery, which was located at a safe distance from the town and harbour. I had no desire to visit the town or the hated St. Nicholas Inn and I did not want to risk being recognised in case I might be apprehended for my involvement in the deaths of Dick Bailey and Peter Pauncefoot.

In the middle of the night, wearing a simple woollen habit and cowl borrowed from one of the monks, I walked towards the town, taking every caution not to be seen, and to my mother's grave. By the coppery light of the spring moon I dug into the earth covering my mother's coffin and, to my relief, found that the cache of silver pennies was still intact.

I told my mother how well her son had risen, now being the friend of a prince and princess, and thanked her for my life. I offered up a brief prayer for her soul and said farewell to her forever.

I hurried away from that graveyard like a wraith, clutching my ill-gotten gains to my chest, and departed from Portsmouth, hoping fervently that I would never again have to visit the benighted place ever again.

MAY 1256

Soon after I had returned to court from my mission to Portsmouth, I was chagrined to be ordered to accompany Lord Edward and Lady Leonora on a grand tour of this damp and chilly island of Britain. I use those words advisedly because, when we set off for Nottinghamshire, it was snowing lightly even though it was the end of May.

At least I had an inestimable advantage over the rest of the servants and attendants of being allowed to travel in Lady Leonora's royal wagon for much of the journey instead of sitting for interminable shivering hours on the back of a horse.

Also, my secretly privileged position with the royal couple ensured that I was usually found a cosy nook indoors to sleep when we stopped for the night at various monasteries or castles, instead of having to sleep in the open air sheltered by a wagon, or even sheltered by nothing as was the lot of many members of the inferior entourage.

I decided to employ the long journey to press my suit for the hand of Dolores. She would consent to marry me only if ordered to do so by Lady Leonora and on pain of losing her highly privileged position with her illustrious mistress if she did not, so my task was to ensure that Lady Leonora so ordered.

Four days into the journey the royal wagon had to be halted while a collapsed river bridge was repaired. The snow had cleared and it was a blessedly fine and sunny day.

Leonora and I had been unaccompanied in the royal wagon and my mistress decided that we should take the air in a nearby meadow.

Leonora was wearing a grey and gold linen travelling gown and, heedless of the effect of the sun on her complexion, she took off her wimple and shook out her long black hair, and turned her face to the sun as we made our way through the grass.

I was still alone with Lady Leonora and, observing that she was in a playful mood, excited by the adventure of the journey, I decided to broach the subject of marriage with Dolores. The birds chirruped gaily among the elms, busy insects buzzed and fluttered around us, disturbed by our progress, and the spring flowers released their delicate scents as we crushed them underfoot.

I turned to Lady Leonora and asked: 'May I speak to you about Dolores, my lady.'

I was reassured that I had chosen my moment perfectly when Leonora looked at me archly and replied in a teasing tone: 'Of course, Hamo. Are you still of a mind to take her as your wife?'

'Yes, my lady. As God instructed me to do.'

'Ah, yes, God,' Leonora said enigmatically, and stooped to pick wild flowers. Having assembled her pretty posy, she went on: 'If you marry Dolores then God will be happy and you will be happy but Dolores will be most unhappy. And so shall I be. Perhaps.'

Puzzled, I said: 'I know Dolores thinks nothing of me but I truly love her and will strive to change her opinion and be a dutiful husband. But why should you be unhappy, my lady?'

Leonora playfully brushed her posy against my cheek. 'Why, Hamo, God sent you to protect me and help me to prosper in this strange land but, so far, you have done precious little for me. If I compel my best friend to marry you against her will, what will be my reward for such service?'

It would have been lamely useless to plead that I had had little chance to do anything for Leonora. I had given her several precious gifts of gold and jewellery. I considered pointing this out but a princess is showered with such gifts, albeit not usually from a lowly jester.

What Lady Leonora craved was lands and estates of her own.

They represented security in an alien and often hostile country. I was mildly shocked by this fresh evidence of the depth of Leonora's self-seeking nature and, for once, I did not know how to reply.

The ladies-in-waiting were approaching to attend Leonora and she dismissed me by stating bluntly, with a hint of steel in her voice: 'Make it worthwhile, my little friend, and Dolores will be yours. Otherwise… '

The unspoken threat left trailing in the May air warned me that I had to rapidly find some means to endow Lady Leonora and reassure her of my supposedly God-given largesse.

Two days later someone mentioned that we were passing the county of Lincolnshire. That fact gave me an idea and I resolved to seek an opportunity to approach Lord Edward in confidence.

JUNE 1256

The ultimate destination of this royal tour was Scotland. The king of Scotland, Alexander, was married to Lord Edward's younger sister Margaret. The two siblings had not seen each other for many years and Edward, and Lady Leonora, were excited by the prospect of meeting their Scottish royal counterparts. They were all of about the same age, not yet twenty, and Edward spoke in warm terms of his beloved sister and of his respect for her husband.

Edward told me all this during an evening chess game at Norham Castle in Northumberland. Edward had conceived a notion to play the game in the open air. A light drizzle had threatened to deny him his notion but Edward ordered a canopy to be erected, on a grassy knoll outside the castle walls, to keep us dry while we played.

I was concerned that such a public game would cause gossip and raise questions about my true nature as well as the nature of my relationship with Edward but, as Edward himself rightly pointed out, it was already common knowledge amongst the servants and retainers that we two battled over the chess board and none of them seemed to find this curious. They could hardly challenge Edward about the matter even if they did.

Norham Castle was just south of the Scottish border and stood on a ford of the River Tweed. I was to come to know this castle, with its massive square keep and towering walls, very well during the later melancholy years of Edward's reign.

Despite the drizzle the low evening sun kept breaking through the thin clouds to illuminate the river sparkling in the distance. The next morning we would be travelling into Scotland for the first time. Edward was in high spirits and frequently stopped the game in order to peer dreamily towards the border.

I decided that the companionable occasion and Edward's mellow mood were eminently suitable for me to broach my plan. This was the first time I was going to attempt to play Edward off against his wife in such a direct manner and I had to make my approach with tact and delicacy.

I said: 'My lord, may I speak to you about the estate of Coleby in Lincolnshire.'

I was taking the risk that Edward would not be upset at this reminder of the fate of his old tutor Batholomew Pecche and his two sons. He looked at me warily but simply asked: 'What is on your mind?'

'My lord, God has blessed me abundantly to be in your service. He has doubly blessed me to be of service to Lady Leonora.'

'She speaks well of you, Hamo. Your clowning and soothing music has been of much comfort to her since arriving in England.'

'Thank you, my lord. I am utterly devoted to Lady Leonora. To be admitted to the presence of her charm and beauty is all that I desire in reward for my poor services as a fool. I was... '

'Come, come, Hamo,' Edward interrupted. 'There are no secrets between my wife and I. I am only too aware of your devious machinations.'

Edward's statement transfixed me with horror. I had to employ all my self-control to conceal my fear that Edward had discovered I was playing the same game with both him and his wife. Surely Edward had not told Leonora of my true nature? Surely Leonora had not betrayed, as she thought, the will of God?

Edward fixed me with a piercing glance and, as my heart pounded with fear, he said: 'You are a manifest rogue, Hamo.'

I pretended hurt bewilderment and replied: 'My lord, I don't know what you mean?'

'I know what reward you desire from my wife. You desire the hand, and the body, of that delectable Spanish girl Dolores, don't you?'

I grinned sheepishly, as if discomfited but, in truth, intensely relieved. 'Your wisdom allows you to see into my heart, my lord. Indeed, I must admit to being besotted by her.'

'Little wisdom needed on my part, Hamo, since I arranged that Dolores should abandon her elderly Spanish suitor and come to England with Lady Leonora. She does not like you, Hamo. Oh, she is oftimes amused by your antics but she thinks you are the simpleton you pretend to be. It would be cruelty unbefitting a prince to force her to marry you. And if you did, how could you keep the secret of your true nature from her? If she found out what valuable secret tasks you perform for me, that would be tantamount to betraying my trust.'

I had considered that one day Edward would employ this argument against the marriage and I was ready with my reply. 'I have become adept throughout my life at hiding my true nature. If I marry Dolores I could act not as idiotically as she now perceives, as if being my wife was balm to my addled wits, and she would never even guess of the most valued friendship between you and I, my lord.' I was desperate that Edward accept my argument but tried not to betray such desperation.

Edward gazed out at the sunset shedding its red glow over the river. He took an age to move his next chess piece and then said: 'I believe you, Hamo, and I would hardly be a Christian or merciful lord if I denied you the right to be with the woman you love. But what has all this to do with the estate at Coleby? Do you wish to marry and leave my service to live there?'

'No, no, my lord. My greatest desire is to remain by your side for the rest of my life. My respect for you is matched only by my love for Lady Leonora, and to serve you both in any way I can is my sole ambition. I tremble at the thought of showing ingratitude or incurring your displeasure, my lord, and I am deeply grateful that you awarded the Coleby estate to me but, with your permission, I wish to pass the estate on to Lady Leonora.'

Edward stared at me in surprise and, for a moment, I thought I had overplayed my hand. He said: 'You confuse me, Hamo. Why do you wish Lady Leonora to have this estate?'

'Simply as an expression of my loyalty and affection for her ladyship. I have never even visited this estate and my place is by your side, and hers. I am a humble man. I have little opportunity to enjoy such an estate. I would like to think that Lady Leonora could use Coleby as a country retreat or haven whenever she needs it. I'm sure it would please Lady Leonora to know she has lands to call her own.'

Edward stood up, ignoring the game of chess, and began to pace up and down the damp grass. I could not tell whether he was excited, agitated or angry.

Eventually he cried: 'By God, Hamo, you are right! My mother the queen has acquired many estates and that has given her much comfort and, being a proud woman, made her feel less of a vassal to the king. But wait! How can I tell Lady Leonora that you are the owner of this estate? As far as she is concerned you are merely a half-witted jester in my service. What would you be doing with an estate such as this?'

'My lord, I seek no such credit. My only reward will be that Lady Leonora is happy and comforted to be given her own estate. She need know nothing about my ownership or, indeed, the unfortunate circumstances by which it came into my possession. If you grant my request to give the Coleby estate to Lady Leonora, then I beg you tell her that it is your gift without my name being mentioned.'

Edward resumed his chair and said excitedly: 'By heaven, you shame me, Hamo. What a loyal friend you are, not only to think of my wife in such an unselfish manner but to show me my duty as a loving husband. I *will* give the estate to Lady Leonora, and I will always bear in mind your selfless generosity in this matter.'

We returned to our chess game but my mind was in a turmoil. I now had to gain an audience with Lady Leonora before Edward had a chance to bestow the gift of the estate. I had made a huge sacrifice and it was vital that Lady Leonora gave me the credit. I waited until we had made a few more moves and then said: 'I will have to ask your permission to withdraw, my lord. I ate too much pheasant at the meal tonight and I am in urgent need of the latrine.'

Edward was not happy and grumbled: 'Can you not wait? I am about to defeat you.'

'My need has become most urgent, my lord.'

'Oh, very well. Be as quick as you can. I will wait here. Go then, Hamo, before you start farting and frightening the geese.'

I hurried back through the castle gate and into the Great Tower. I had decided to risk all by gaining an audience with Lady Leonora before Edward arrived at their chamber to retire for the night.

I pushed my way through the crowded great hall and climbed the steps up towards the royal chamber. The guards knew me well and did not attempt to stop me.

There was no wooden door to Leonora's chamber in this primitive Norham Castle but a heavy curtain had been hung across the entrance. I called out Dolores's name and shook the curtain. To my intense relief, her head popped around the side of the curtain. 'What do you want?' she whispered.

'I must see Lady Leonora alone, at once.'

'Impossible! My mistress has just retired to bed.'

'Nevertheless, I must see her. Believe me, Dolores, if you prevent me from seeing her now she will not forgive you when she finds out why I am here. Now please hurry.'

Dolores considered for a moment and then said irritably: 'Oh, all right. I will go to her ladyship and ask if she will admit you to her bedchamber. Wait here.'

Dolores seemed to take an age and I feared that Lord Edward might march around the corner at any moment. It would take some imaginative falsehoods to explain what I was doing here.

Eventually Dolores returned and beckoned me through. There were two other ladies-in-waiting in the chamber and they regarded me curiously as I went through to a sleeping alcove that had also been curtained off for privacy. Dolores stuck her head through the curtains, whispered something to Leonora, and then beckoned me in.

I entered to find Lady Leonora sitting up in her bed. A fur stole had been placed around her shoulders for modesty but she still looked enchanting, her long black hair tumbling down onto her pillow. Dolores did not leave us so I said to Leonora: 'My lady, I must speak to you privately,' and looked pointedly at Dolores.

Leonora shooed Dolores away and said, with a smile: 'Go, Dolores, I trust Hamo with my virtue.'

As soon as Dolores had left I began speaking in a whisper and without ceremony: 'My lady, you asked what gift I could give you in exchange for the hand of Dolores. God, through me, has arranged that you be given ownership of an estate in Lincolnshire. Lord Edward is to give you this as a gift from a loving husband but the estate came into his possession in a manner which was personally painful to him. I beg you not to mention my involvement in this matter and not to enquire how this estate came into your husband's possession. And please do not betray the fact that you already know that you are to be given this estate.'

Leonora's face registered confusion and pleasure at the same time. 'I don't understand, Hamo. How did you arrange such a gift?'

'My lady, there is no time to explain at present. Please accept this as God's will. Just know that this is my gift to you but Lord Edward need not know how this came about. I must leave now before he finds me here.' Not waiting for her permission to withdraw I ducked out of the alcove and hurried out of the chamber.

I made for the steps, ran down to the ground floor and out into the great hall to find Lord Edward striding towards me as the servants and courtiers bowed in his wake.

'Hamo!' he exclaimed. 'I thought you were visiting the latrines?'

'I became lost in this unfamiliar castle, my lord. I am not sure where I am.'

Edward laughed and pointed back to the main entrance to the great hall. 'Go back out there. The servants latrines are outside. Hurry man, before you shit yourself.'

I scuttled away with Edward's amused laughter ringing behind me. It had been too close for comfort.

The next day the wagons and horses of the English royal caravan splashed and heaved across the River Tweed and lumbered slowly into Scotland.

At our next overnight halt, at Dunbar Castle, I was summoned to entertain Lady Leonora and her ladies in the great hall.

Leonora indicated that I should sit near her, at her feet, so that she could converse with me without being overheard. As I began gently strumming my harp she asked gaily: 'Are you a wizard, Hamo?'

'No, madam.'

'A sorcerer then, like Merlin?'

'By no means, madam, simply a humble jester.'

Leonora acknowledged the respectful greetings of friends and courtiers as they passed by but no-one stopped to interrupt us. She said: 'Lord Edward gave me the gift of this estate in Lincolnshire last night. He said it was a gift of love to celebrate our journey to meet his beloved sister and our dear cousin, the king of Scotland. How did you arrange this?'

As if singing to Leonora, I replied: 'I swear by Almighty God, who has given me the insight to order such things, that I did nothing illegal or immoral to arrange this gift. Apart from that, madam, please accept it as a token of my devotion, and that of your husband.'

'And to sweeten my decision about your marriage to Dolores?'

'If you so will it, my lady.'

'Hamo, sing with a light heart. I have told Dolores that she must marry you. She is not happy but she will have to become accustomed to the idea. After all, princesses such as I are told who we must marry. I have been fortunate to have been given a husband like Lord Edward. Dolores will have to accept the situation. You have been of inestimable value to me since coming to England, Hamo, and this is your reward. Stay with me, Hamo.'

'Forever, my lady. Now that Dolores is to become bethrothed to me, may I request that you forbid her to grant her favours to the knight Stephen Bauzan.'

Leonora's eyebrows rose in surprise. 'Dolores is making sport with someone else?'

'Yes, my lady. I am sorry for having to apprise you of this affair in such a manner. I assumed that Dolores, as one of your senior ladies-in-waiting, had a duty to make you aware of this relationship.'

Leonora said: 'No, I did not know what game Dolores was playing. And she my best friend! Don't worry, Hamo, I will order Dolores to stay away from this knight, whoever he is. What did you say his name is?'

'Stephen Bauzan. He is a coward and two-faced bully, and not worthy of the favours of your best friend.'

Leonora inclined her head in agreement and said: 'Then I will order such dalliance to cease.'

'Thank you, my lady. There is one other thing that concerns me about Dolores.'

'Speak up then, Hamo.'

'I'm sore afraid that Dolores finds the thought of marriage to me so unacceptable that she will run away to avoid it.'

Lady Leonora chuckled lightly. 'That is what she threatened to do when I told her she must marry you. I tried to persuade her of your many virtues and I informed her that if she absconded she would be contravening God's will, she would be committing treasonous ingratitude against me, and if she took such a path then she would be excommunicated and I would make sure that she lost all position in the world and would not be able to marry any man of wealth or title anywhere in Europe. The material comforts of life are more important to Dolores than any man and she has acquiesced to my demands.'

'Thank you, my lady. I will devote my life to making Dolores happy.'

'When we return to Westminster in August there is a great feast planned. I think that such an occasion would be an ideal opportunity for your nuptials. Does that meet with your approval?'

'Certainly, madam. An excellent idea. You are most kind.'

I carried on singing with a happy heart.

Later that evening I contrived to meet Dolores at a place where we were unobserved and unaccompanied. She was coming from the kitchens carrying a tray laden with wine and sweetmeats for her mistress.

'What do you want?' she said.

'Lady Leonora informs me that we are to be married at Westminster in August.'

I expected a savage tempered response but Dolores's expression did not change and she replied: 'I have been so informed as well.'

'I am to be your husband. I know that grieves and disappoints you but I swear by Almighty God that I will strive to make your life as happy as I can. I have loved you since I first set eyes on you, even though you called me a… what was it?'

'A duende?'

'Yes, a duende. As your bethrothed I must demand that you no longer consort with Stephen Bauzan.'

Dolores's eyes widened in surprise. 'I did not know that you knew about him.'

'There is very little that goes on around court of which I am not aware.'

'I will not give him up. He is a real man, unlike you.'

'It is Lady Leonora's command that you give him up. If you dare disobey me, you cannot disobey her.'

Dolores was shocked by my revelation. 'My mistress knows?'

'Yes.'

'Then I have no choice but to comply.'

'I expect you to prepare yourself to become a virtuous and dutiful wife, just as I will strive to become a loving and protective husband. Have faith in me. Your future will be of greater happiness and prosperity than you can yet conceive.'

'That I very much doubt.'

Dolores shoved past me and disappeared up a stairway. I really did want to make Dolores happy despite her dismissive and contemptuous attitude. My feelings for her had awoken as adolescent lust and infatuation but had now matured into a feeling that was quite alien to my lonely and self-centred nature, a genuine desire to place the happiness of someone else above my own. It was a strange sensation. Somehow I had to find a way to convince Dolores that my intentions were genuine.

After the tour of Scotland the court returned to Westminster and, when the banns of my marriage to Dolores became public knowledge, everyone was astounded. They, of course, considered me a happy idiot, albeit talented at my duties as a fool and musician. They regarded Dolores as a desirable, intelligent and wilful girl and most of them were aware that she had been rolling in the hay with Stephen Bauzan. No-one could understand why Dolores had agreed to marry me, especially when she was so clearly unhappy at the prospect.

I perforce overheard the gossip of the knights and courtiers. I was inured to overhearing derogatory comments about myself, and even lascivious comments about Dolores, but to remain wearing my placid dolt expression when hearing some of the sarcastic comments about our forthcoming marriage took all my self-control.

Dolores's paramour, Stephen Bauzan, confronted me angrily one day and demanded to know by what means I had won her hand in marriage. Was it sorcery or black magic? Dearly as I would have loved to have strangled this arrogant gentleman, I had to remain in character and invented some reply about how much I amused Dolores, which only served to make Bauzan more angry.

I even noticed Queen Eleanor regarding Dolores with perplexed pity when someone mentioned to her that we were to be married on the day of the great feast. King Henry, seeing himself as the spiritual reincarnation of Saint Edward the Confessor, was not at all concerned with such earthy, and earthly, court gossip.

August 1256

The great feast at Westminster had been arranged, after a long delay, to officially and publicly celebrate Edward's marriage and knighthood.

Amid such pomp and circumstance, the marriage of Hamo Pauncefoot to Dolores Guzman in the unfinished St. Stephen's Chapel of Westminster Palace was an ignored sideshow.

Dolores had no parents or family. Her mother and father had been carried off by plague in the year before I met her. That is partly the reason why she had allowed herself to become bethrothed to Lord Alcamanzar and why Lady Leonora was so concerned for her welfare. Dolores had been a spoiled and now orphaned only child.

It would not have been seemly for Lord Edward and Lady Leonora to attend the marriage of a pair of humble lackeys, so the ceremony was witnessed by just a few ladies-in-waiting and fellow fools and servants.

After the ceremony, however, we were allowed to join the nobility at the feast. Dolores eased her sullen regrets by drinking too much wine. I was careful not to do so. I did not want my carefully nurtured mask to slip and I did not want the drink to impair the enjoyment of the carnal delights that awaited me that night.

Later in the proceedings Lord Edward's seneschal tapped me on the shoulder and ordered that Dolores and I should follow him. I helped Dolores to her feet and supported her by the arm as she staggered away from the banqueting table. We followed the seneschal to the door of a private chamber where he bade us to enter.

I followed Dolores into the room and was mightily surprised to find Lord Edward and Lady Leonora chatting happily to each other. They both turned to smile at us. I bowed and Dolores curtsied, unsteadily, which brought a broader smile to Edward's face, but then he bade us to stop our obeisance, insisting on no formal courtship on this happy day. He personally handed us silver goblets of his best wine.

I had to remain in simpleton pose and Dolores could not quite shake off her thunderous expression, but Lord Edward deferred to Lady Leonora to make the speech, in French, while he translated into English for my supposed benefit.

Leonora stepped forward and kissed Dolores on the cheek with the words: 'My dearest friend,' and then she kissed me on the cheek, a most pleasant experience, with the words: 'Our most skilful and faithful fool.'

Then the royal couple toasted our health and bid us a long and happy life together.

Lady Leonora spoke again: 'My husband and I thank you for the excellent services that both of you have performed for us, Hamo as chief jester and Dolores as my most faithful lady-in-waiting and dear friend. Accordingly, it pleases me to inform you that, as your wedding gift from us, you have been allotted your own chambers here at Westminster and at Windsor. Our seneschal will now show you to your new quarters. It is the most fervent wish of Lord Edward and I that you remain close to us, continue to serve us faithfully, and that you begin your married life in comfort.'

Of all the possible rewards I had hoped to be given by Edward and Leonora, I had not expected this signal honour! To be granted such private apartments in both royal palaces, even though it was no more than a single chamber in each palace, was a privilege usually accorded only to other royals, nobles and senior officials. It was a much more valuable reward than even a whole estate like Coleby in a backwater such as Lincolnshire. For a jester and a lady-in-waiting to be accorded such a privilege was unprecedented.

I was inwardly overjoyed but outwardly had to stay in simpleton character to bob up and down and say: 'Thank you, thank you.'

Dolores curtsied and said thank you but even this astonishing wedding gift could not compensate for having to marry me and it failed to put a smile on her face.

We withdrew from the royal presence and the seneschal escorted us to our new chamber. It was situated well away from the royal chambers and was sparsely decorated and furnished but I was delighted. I had planned to take Dolores to an inn to begin our married life but this was much better because our royal patrons had included a tester bed in their largesse.

We were obliged to return to the feast in the great hall but, as soon as was seemly, I took Dolores away and took her back to our chamber. She had deliberately made herself very drunk, knowing full well what was in store for her.

I was now tremendously excited at the prospect of having the woman who had inflamed my dreams every night since I had first met her. I still think every day of the moment when I first beheld Dolores's naked beauty in that chamber at Westminster. I could not believe that God had fashioned such wondrous shapes, such lustrous softness.

She submitted to my will but afterwards she wept softly as she lay beside me. I was overwhelmed with tenderness for my new bride. This was an alien emotion for me. I did not know what to say to Dolores. I was not sure how to behave. I desperately wanted to be the man she wanted me to be, but God had not allowed it.

All I remember is that I blurted out: 'I'm sorry.'

Dolores stopped crying but did not reply. Soon afterwards she fell asleep. I lay awake for many hours.

Brother Godfrey's eyes shine brightly at my description of marital lust... no, don't bother to deny it, boy. You probably already suffer the torment of unrequited lust and will do so all your life until old age quenches the fire. You will regret your vow of chastity every day if you are anything like a normal man, and why God enjoins such a savage denial in order to praise Him is beyond my wits. The fact that He created something as wondrously beautiful as Dolores is the best reason I know to praise Him. No-one in my life caused me as much pain and yet, by simply looking at her, such joy.

During that autumn of 1256 I was well contented with my lot in life. I was modestly wealthy, I had made myself a friend and confidante of the heir to the throne and his wife, I was living in my own chamber within their palaces, and I now possesed an exotic and comely Spanish wife. Apart from the nagging curiosity about the identity of my real father, I was untroubled. The dreams I had dreamed as a boy at the St. Nicholas Inn had come to fruition.

Lord Edward, however, was not so contented. He still chafed at his father's political control over him. But he and Leonora were blissfully happy together, and England seemed more at ease than for many a long year.

I looked forward to several years of relative ease. The near future looked settled and very rosy. How could I know that, within a few short months, England would be spiralling down into chaos and that foul death would stalk the land.

The trouble began when Death sent his emissary sweeping out of the west, out of Wales, and his name was Llewelyn.

November 1256

I well remember the day news arrived. The court was at Windsor, which pleased me because the royal apartments, to where I was often summoned to entertain, were probably the most luxuriously appointed rooms in England.

I was playing the harp while Queen Eleanor was working on her embroidery and Lady Leonora was weaving a tapestry, an occupation she enjoyed for many long hours at a stretch.

Edward was playing tables with his brother Edmund and they were cheerfully mocking each other's skill in a most charming and affectionate way. King Henry was also present. He was studying plans for the new abbey he was building at Westminster.

Edward's seneschal, Hugh FitzOtho, entered the apartments, bowed to the royal family and announced: 'Lord Edward, a messenger has arrived from Wales and wishes to speak with you urgently.'

'Very well. Let him come in,' Edward replied nonchalantly, not suspecting any untoward news.

A few moments later the messenger was ushered into the royal presence. His clothes were stained with mud and sweat from his journey. He said: 'Lord Edward, I regret that I bring grave news from Wales. A Welsh army under the command of Llewelyn ap Gruffyd has crossed the River Conwy and seized all your lands. Only your castles at Dyserth and Deganwy are holding out against this invasion.'

Both Lord Edward and the king looked stunned. Edward was the first to recover his wits and asked: 'When did this happen?'

'At the beginning of this month, my lord. This attack was

completely unprovoked and completely unexpected. I have been riding without cease for days to bring you this news without delay.'

King Henry said mildly: 'I thought Prince Llewelyn was our friend. This is very disappointing news.'

Lord Edward exploded with anger. 'Disappointing, father! It is more than disappointing! It is ungrateful and treasonous! By God, if the Welsh believe they can seize my lands with impunity I will hunt them down to extinction!'

'Calm yourself, my son. Perhaps we can resolve this problem by negotiation. After all, as you have said, Llewelyn surely cannot believe that he can steal our lands with impunity. He is probably looking for concessions.'

Edward snorted in disgust. 'Father, we should summon the royal council and decide what to do about this unwarranted invasion.'

King Henry rolled up the parchment plans for his new abbey and rose reluctantly from his chair. He said: 'Come, my son, we will have to start making plans as soon as possible.' To the messenger he ordered: 'You will accompany us and give as much information as you can to the royal council.'

The three men quit the apartments.

Queen Eleanor calmly returned to her embroidery but Lady Leonora had ceased her tapestry work and was in a state of some agitation. She asked: 'Does this mean that my Edward will have to go and fight this Welsh prince?'

The queen replied: 'Knowing my hot-tempered warrior of a son, I would say it is a certainty! But have no fear, daughter, this man Llewelyn may have scored an initial triumph but no Welsh lord can stand against an English army. Have no fear, daughter, Lord Edward will easily deal with this upstart barbarian. My husband had the same problems against another Llewelyn, the one the Welsh call "the great", and even Henry was able to dismantle the empire that Llewelyn the Great attempted to create.'

I inwardly smiled at Queen Eleanor's implied disrespect for her husband's military prowess.

1 2 5 7

Despite the queen's maternal confidence in her aggressive son, the war against Llewelyn did not go well, but it was not Lord Edward's fault.

One day in the Spring of 1257, while I was alone with Edward in his chamber at Westminster, he threw aside any semblance of protocol and began fuming against his father.

Edward was striding up and down and then stopped to ask me: 'Do you remember when this Welsh upstart began his campaign, Hamo? My father's response was to write a letter to Llewelyn expressing his surprise and disappointment! I'll warrant the Welshman was trembling in his boots at that attack! Even the weather has been on Llewelyn's side. It has rained constantly all winter. It is next to impossible to even get an army into Wales, let alone move it around. I had no choice but to beg my father for more money to fight Llewelyn. Do you know what he answered, Hamo?'

'No, my lord,' I replied, not willing to say too much when Edward was in this sort of belligerent mood.

'The king said to me: "What is it to me? Wales is your land by my gift. I am concerned with other business".' Edward slammed the palm of his hand on the table in anger and disgust. 'By God, that man is so contradictory. He grants me Gascony but then, when it suits his purpose, forbids me from ruling as I see fit. He grants me these lands in Wales and now, when it suits his purpose not to become involved, tells me that it is no concern of his how I rule my domains! Llewelyn grows stronger every day and more and more

Welsh lords flock to his banner. He is no longer known as the "lord of Snowdon" but is styling himself "prince of Wales"! But I think he has made a vital strategic mistake, Hamo. Llewelyn has moved south and is attacking the lands of the Marcher lords. I will have to seek their help if I am to defeat Llewelyn.'

'I tremble at the thought of what those men will seek in return, my lord. They are a law unto themselves, and perhaps the king will not be pleased if you seek their help.'

'What choice do I have, Hamo? My father has abandoned me and I do not have the resources myself. The Marcher lords are the only ones strong enough and wealthy enough to deal with this threat. But I do have one other alternative. There is a Welsh lord named Rhys Fychan who detests Llewelyn and is willing to lead a resistance movement within Wales. If I can cajole the Welsh into fighting each other then we might be able to achieve our objectives without shedding English blood or spending English money. I am sending Stephen Bauzan to Carmarthen, with an army, to put this Welsh lord back on his throne.'

I forgot myself for a moment and could not help exclaiming: 'Stephen Bauzan!'

Edward looked at me. 'Yes, Stephen Bauzan. Why did you bark when hearing his name?'

'Er... forgive me, my lord, but I remember him from Gascony. He escorted me to and from that unfortunate business in Blanquefort.'

I did not mention that he was also the bastard who had taken my wife's maidenhead before we were married, and I fervently hoped Edward was not aware of that scandal.

To deflect Edward's annoyance I said: 'He would seem to me an excellent choice. He is a strong and capable leader.'

'Yes, he served me well in Gascony. The weather has cleared and I am sending Bauzan to lead this counter offensive at the end of May. Llewelyn, the *prince of Wales*, has had things his own way for far too long.'

Edward spat out the phrase 'prince of Wales' with utter contempt.

The news that shocked the country arrived in June when the court was at Westminster. I had been practising some new acrobatic tricks and was taking an afternoon nap in my chamber in preparation for that evening's entertainment duties. I was awoken by a lady-in-waiting shaking me by the shoulder. She said urgently: 'Lady Leonora summons you to attend her immediately.'

'What for? What is going on?'

'Your wife has been taken ill.'

We hurried to Leonora's chamber. Dolores was actually laying on Leonora's bed. She was weeping uncontrollably while other ladies-in-waiting attempted to calm her and cool her by fanning her with fire screens.

I looked on in astonishment and asked Leonora: 'What ails her?'

She whispered: 'Come over here, Hamo, so we can talk.'

I followed Leonora to the other side of the chamber where the embrasures looked down on the River Thames. She said: 'Dolores was present earlier when the dreadful news from Wales was reported to me.'

'Forgive me, madam, but I have not heard any news.'

'It seems that an entire English army has been massacred at a place named Towy Valley. This army was led by the knight Stephen Bauzan. When Dolores heard that he had been killed and then mutilated in a most grievous way, she collapsed with the most piteous moans. We have not been able to calm or console her since. We thought that you might be able to calm her.'

'My lady, you well know that Bauzan was Dolores's paramour before our marriage. I very much doubt that she would welcome my ministrations at this time.'

Leonora nodded thoughtfully. 'You are probably right, Hamo. I will send for the physicians. Go back to your duties, Hamo. I will take care of Dolores.'

I bowed and said: 'Thank you, my lady.'

Instead of returning to any duties, I quit the palace and ran, for miles, along the bank of the Thames. I was jubilant, cock-a-hoop, at the news of Bauzan's death. Surely this was a sign from God! The removal of the man I most hated in the world and who was the most grievous threat to my marriage was a wondrous gift.

I now write this paragraph in my own hand, as well as my failing eyesight will allow, because my amanuensis, Brother Godfrey, has laid down the quill and subjected me to an account of the full horror that his Christian conscience feels towards my jubilation at the death of Bauzan. He has departed, in high dudgeon, to pray for the salvation of my soul. It transpires that his grandfather was killed at this battle of Cadfan where Bauzan died. This same tender Christian who I have heard exonerate Richard the Lionhearted for the massacre of over 3,000 Saracen hostages, or commend the massacre of heathen Jews at York on behalf of his lord Jesus Christ, now casts me as the Devil himself for celebrating the death of the man who cuckolded me. I will have to explain that I was jubilant at the death of Bauzan alone but, like all other true born Englishmen, was deeply melancholy at the fate of the hundreds of my fellow countrymen who died with him. Perhaps this will persuade Brother Godfrey, who has never suffered and thus can not possibly understand the bitter gall of being cuckolded and insulted by an arrogant knave, to return.

The massacre of an entire English army meant that King Henry could no longer avoid becoming directly involved in the Welsh insurrection. He ordered the royal feudal host to muster at Chester in August with the intention that he himself, together with Lord Edward, would lead the English army into Wales.

Edward foresaw little need for a jester during this foray into the wilds of Wales so, most fortunately, I was allowed to remain at Windsor with the royal women.

King Henry, in his usual inimitable style, made a debacle of the invasion. He ordered the army to advance before adequate supplies had arrived. He had gambled that they would arrive by sea from Ireland but after a week it became obvious that they would not be forthcoming and so King Henry ordered a retreat back to Chester. The English were mercilessly harassed all the way home by Welsh skirmishers. I could well imagine Lord Edward's intense frustration at his father's ill-considered tactics.

I saw little of Lord Edward after his return from this humiliating debacle in Wales. Such was the volatile political situation that he had little time or opportunity to play chess with me, and little use for my counsel either.

Once again I became aware that I was losing influence over Edward. When we were adolescents Edward had perceived me as an entertaining companion and someone with much more experience of real life. Now Edward was a man, well over six feet tall, handsome, energetic, charismatic and shrewd. He was surrounding himself with men who could exert much more power, in a military sense, and much more influence, in a political sense, than ever I could.

He was aligning himself with King Henry's half-brothers, the brutal and hated Lusignan faction. Paradoxically he was also forming alliances with the Marcher lords, who hated the Lusignans for the influence they exerted over the king.

Queen Eleanor, who naturally sided with her Savoyard relatives, was becoming alarmed by Edward's increasing independence and his alliances with the Lusignans.

One of Edward's new political friends was Robert Burnell. He had proved himself a very able administrator with shrewd political and diplomatic gifts. He was from a wealthy Shropshire family, a family that had given their name to the town of Acton Burnell, where the family seat was located.

Robert Burnell had been working as a clerk in the chancery but his energy, intelligence and administrative ability had brought him to the attention of Lord Edward, who had taken Burnell into his personal service as a clerk and secretary.

As soon as Burnell had arrived in Edward's inner circle he began to take an interest in my wife. Burnell was a well-made man, tall and handsome, expensively yet modestly dressed, with a fine head of chestnut hair, a glib tongue, a charming and easeful manner, and a mind as sharp as a Saracen blade.

He was well-educated, spoke and wrote in English, French and Latin, and thus could easily converse with Dolores in the French tongue. I could not but help noticing the lustful way in which he regarded Dolores whenever he looked at her. He, unaware of my own linguistic ability, spoke to his clerical colleagues in Latin about his passion for Dolores.

I, of course, could do nothing except keep my counsel, bear his impertinence, and consider means to thwart him in any way possible. Worse yet, I could see that Dolores was willing to reciprocate Burnell's interest. I regarded Burnell as a threat who could rob me of my wife's affection, limited as such affection was, and also some of my influence over Lord Edward.

My concerns about Robert Burnell, however, shrank into insignificance when, quite by chance and after several goblets of good Bordeaux wine, I suffered the revenge of Bacchus, incurred the severe displeasure of my liege lord Edward, but identified the illustrious nobleman who was my natural father.

Early in the spring I was ordered to accompany Lord Edward and a party of about thirty knights and noblemen on a journey to Wallingford in Berkshire. Edward was to visit his uncle, Earl Richard of Cornwall, at Wallingford Castle. I had been instructed that I was to provide the entertainment during the evening meal, which was to be attended by a small group of Earl Richard's closest friends and supporters.

When we arrived in Wallingford, at noon, the majority of

Edward's party remained at the Benedictine Holy Trinity Priory for rest and refreshment while Edward, with his seneschal and a small escort of knights, rode off to visit his uncle for a private meeting at the castle.

Edward's party remaining at the priory were mostly Lusignan knights and nobles, the pampered relatives and supporters of King Henry, who were also cultivating Lord Edward's friendship and patronage. The abbot and his fellow monks made us welcome in the refectory and we were given food and ample flagons of good Bordeaux wine.

We all became a little too refreshed on the wine. Drunken gossip began to circulate around the refectory table that the wealthy Benedictine monks had a strongbox, stuffed with gold and silver, hidden somewhere within the priory. The Lusignans decided to go in search of this strongbox. The monks protested vehemently but there was nothing they could do to stop the drunken ransacking. Several monks were beaten up for attempting to prevent the search or for refusing to confide where the strongbox was kept.

Fuelled by further copious amounts of wine, the situation spiralled out of control and the priory was wrecked in an orgy of drunken violence and destruction. Initially, I declined to take part, because I knew how angrily Lord Edward would react when he heard of such desecration. Eventually, goaded and threatened by the Lusignans and fearing it would be more dangerous to refuse, I joined in.

The Lusignans found it highly amusing to see the idiot jester joining in their antics, especially when they laughingly watched me kicking the defenceless abbot while he rolled around on the floor begging for mercy. I did my best to kick the poor man as lightly as I dared, and then only in parts of his anatomy that would not cause him serious problems.

I had no illusions about the Lusignans. They were my friends for the moment but I was well aware that they could easily turn on me as the target for their next "entertainment".

I became more drunk that I have ever been in my life, before or since. My forthcoming duty to provide entertainment in the evening was blotted out in a fog of wine, and the last thing I remember before I passed out was staggering around the physic garden while roaring an obscene song and pissing on the rhubarb.

I awoke to find myself laying on a pile of straw. I blearily prised my eyes apart to see that I was in a stable. It was a long and low wooden building with a sloping roof supported by stout oak beams and housed some dozen or so horses. The horses snuffled and kicked on their stalls as if disturbed by my presence. A door at the end of the stable was open and outside was oppressive darkness.

I was shivering with cold because I was soaking wet. I could not decide whether someone had thrown a pale of water over me, or if I had pissed myself, or whether one of the horses had pissed on me. I was still very drunk, my head throbbed mercilessly and my mouth was as dry as the Persian desert.

There was just enough moonlight for me to notice a long wooden horse trough outside the stable door. I shakily got to my feet. I staggered out into the cold and starry night and saw that the stable was built within the walls of a castle, which had to be Wallingford Castle.

To my ecstasy the horse trough was filled with blessedly cold water. I plunged my head into the water and then drank several handfuls, not caring what the horses might have drooled in there before me.

Then I heard the music of viol and harp floating across the night air. I looked up to see a group of men, most carrying torches, approaching across the courtyard from the great hall. Leading the group was the unmistakeably tall figure of Lord Edward.

Afraid that my legs would buckle, I leaned against the trough as Edward came near. He stopped and looked down at me. In a dangerously menacing and sibilant tone he announced: 'I will have you whipped for this, Hamo. I will have you flayed within an inch of your life. You have neglected your duty and embarrassed me in front of my uncle.'

I felt so ill that I was indifferent to Edward's threats and would, at that moment, have welcomed death as a relief. All I could manage as a reply was to sink to my knees, groan, and then vomit copiously on to the muddy ground.

Lord Edward took a torch from his seneschal and then bent over to lift me up, roughly, by my arm. 'Stand up in my presence, fool. Get back inside the stable.' Turning to his seneschal, Edward ordered: 'Leave us, all of you. I will deal with this ungrateful wretch personally. Express my apologies to Earl Richard and tell him I shall return when I have meted out sufficient punishment.'

I stumbled back inside the stable, the horses whinnying and shuffling restlessly at all the disturbance, with my drink addled wits desperately trying to think of excuses for my behaviour. I decided that my only escape was to blame everything on the Lusignans, which was true anyway, and pray that Edward accepted my excuse.

Edward followed me into the stable. Now that I was closer to Edward's face I could tell from his expression that his anger was half-feigned and that he was relishing my discomfiture, although I dare not admit that knowledge. My head swimming with drunkenness, I slurred: 'May I know where I am, my lord?'

'You are in the stables of Wallingford Castle. With the beasts. Where you belong.'

'How did I get here?'

'You were carried here on a wagon. You and many other members of your drunken gang. The monks despatched a messenger to the castle and my uncle was obliged to send some of his men to quell the riot at the priory. I ordered you to be put in here because I want to talk to you alone, to tell me what happened, how this shambles was instigated. In this secret game we are playing I cannot be seen to treat you any differently from any other of my servants who had disobeyed me so flagrantly, so everyone must assume that I am punishing you personally.'

I felt my legs buckling again and, unable to stop myself, I fell down arse-first on to the straw-covered floor.

'Stand up!' Edward barked.

'My legs will not support me,' I groaned. 'I cannot stand up, my lord.'

'By God, you try my patience sorely, Hamo Pauncefoot. I remember the agony of such sickness from when we were at sea and I am mindful that you cured me. I am also mindful of the many other services you have performed for me, which is why you do not find yourself stripped to the waist and tied to the whipping post, but my tolerance is not endless. Now tell me what happened at the priory.'

'My lord, the monks gave us wine and someone said there was a chest full of treasure and some of your men began to look for it and I tried to stop them but I only succeeded in making them angry and they forced me to drink more wine until I did not know what I was doing and... '

'Stop, stop, Hamo,' Edward ordered, losing patience with my rambling. 'I believe you. I know these relatives of mine. They are not men to be disobeyed when in their cups. I accept that they forced you to become drunk against your will. I know you are a God-fearing person and would not have voluntarily become involved in such blasphemous conduct. Was this strongbox found?'

'No, my lord,' I said, fighting back waves of nausea caused by simply thinking about drinking wine. 'I might have passed out before it was found, but I do not think it was found.'

'That, at least, is a blessing and God be praised. Now give me the names of those who instigated this... '

Before Edward could finish his sentence I had rolled on to my side and was bringing up yellow bile into the straw. From behind Edward a voice said: 'So this is the jester you have been bragging about, nephew. A tumbler who cannot stand up, even before his betters. Or does the sight of his betters make him sick!'

The speaker stepped into the light of Edward's torch. He was a tall man, even when compared to lofty Edward, but more stockily built. A powerful man, in every sense of the word and, at this time, at the very pinnacle of his power. Lord Edward, who had seemed like a man, now looked like a callow youth compared to his uncle. I could see the family resemblance to King Henry although this brother was more handsome, more determined and radiated an easy but unchallengable authority. This was Richard, Earl of Cornwall, King of the Romans.

Even in my befuddled and intoxicated state I remembered to revert to my fawning imbecile persona and I attempted to stand up by hauling myself up one of the oak beams supporting the roof.

Much earlier in my career at court I had seen Richard of Cornwall briefly from a distance, but never at close quarters. For several years since then he had been away from England travelling in such places as Germany and Italy in pursuit of his ambition to be elected *Romanorum Rex*, King of the Romans, the heir apparent to the title of Holy Roman Emperor. This immensely wealthy and influential man was plainly amused by my discomfiture.

I, however, was transfixed by the armorial bearing displayed on Richard's surcoat, a surcoat tailored from the finest gold silk and edged with a black silk border. His coat-of-arms, emblazoned across his chest, depicted a huge red and black eagle, wings spread, with a shield hanging from ropes that were clutched in the eagle's beak. This shield was bordered in black and decorated with golden orbs. Within the shield was a red lion, rampant, with claws extended and a pointed tail.

A lion rampant! With its claws held out and a pointed tail!

My befuddled mind returned to the St. Nicholas Inn and Peter Pauncefoot telling me about my real father, the man who had deflowered my mother on that fateful night. I was desperately trying to remember what else Peter Pauncefoot had told me about this nobleman. Then, without thinking, I looked up at Earl Richard and blurted out: 'Do you have a big cock with a birthmark on it?'

After a momentary stunned silence, Edward cuffed me around

the ear so hard that I fell back into the straw and into my own vomit.

But Earl Richard was laughing, accepting my question as the humorous licence allowed to jesters. 'You are right, Edward! He is indeed an impertinent fellow!' Richard looked down at me, his expression not unkindly.

Could it be? Could this man be my real father? The brother of the king of England, a king and earl in his own right, soon to become Holy Roman emperor, one of the wealthiest men in the realm, a man respected and influential throughout Europe?

Richard said to Edward: 'Come, nephew, let's return to the meal. We shall get precious little entertainment from this rogue tonight.'

'I will rejoin you in a while, uncle,' Edward answered. 'I wish to ask Pauncefoot a few more questions about the shameful riot at the priory.'

'Very well,' Richard said, and walked out of the stable, scattering the group of retainers and fawners who habitually followed such men as Earl Richard and who were gawping in to the stable to find out what was going on.

Edward shooed them all away and turned back to me. 'It is well for you that my uncle is a tolerant and kindly man, otherwise I might have had to punish you severely, even against my natural inclination. As it is, I can see that you are being punished enough by the consequences of your drunken disobedience. You will sleep here in the stable tonight.'

'But, my lord, could I not be allowed into the warm and...'

Edward held up his hand to silence me. 'If a stable was good enough for Our Lord then it is certainly good enough for a drunken rogue named Hamo Pauncefoot. I will deal with you further on the morrow.'

Before Edward could walk away I shifted on to my knees and held my hands together as if in prayer. I began: 'My lord, as you have said yourself I have performed many services for you. You have rewarded me amply as the generous prince you are. But I have never actively sought reward from you except to allow me to continue to serve you and Lady Leonora. I now ask for a reward. I beg you to answer me a question, truly, and I swear I will never ask you for anything again.'

Edward regarded me with narrowed eyes. 'God's breath, you are an impertinent scoundrel. But today is the first occasion you have disobeyed me and disappointed me. I accept that you were led astray by your companions, and they are not men who can be gainsayed by a mere jester. So, mindful of your past service and of the affection with which I, and Lady Leonora, regard you, then ask your question, Hamo, and I will answer it truly.'

I shook my head to try and clear my wits and asked: 'My lord, is your uncle Richard married to a lady named Marshal who was once the wife of an earl?'

Edward regarded me with puzzlement. 'That is a strange question, Hamo. Not what I expected at all. The answer is no, he is married to Sanchia of Provence.'

I sank down on to the vomit-covered straw, my dreams shattered.

Edward stepped away but then stopped in the doorway and turned back to me. 'But as I recall, however, my uncle was once married to Isabel Marshal, who was the widow of the Earl of Gloucester. She died in childbirth soon after I was born, so I know little about her. What is the purpose of your question, Hamo? Have you overheard anything that might affect affairs of state?'

'No, my lord. I was desperate to find out if Earl Richard might have known someone who was once very dear to me.'

'Who? Man or woman? Noble or common?'

'A woman, my lord.'

'Did you love her, Hamo?

'I would have grown to love her. I hope she might have grown to love me. She was merely a common serving wench. Forgive me for asking such a question, my lord. It is unthinkable that a great man such as Earl Richard would consort with such a lowly woman.'

To my surprise, Lord Edward chuckled. 'On the contrary,

Hamo. My uncle is a lusty man and enjoys consorting with women of whatever station in life, whenever he can. He has fathered seven legitimate children and at least three or four illegitimate children. He would consider a common serving wench, if pleasing to the eye, certainly worthy of his attention.' Edward suddenly realised that his admiration for his manly uncle had loosened his tongue. He said severely: 'You will sleep in here tonight, without food or drink. And thank God for my mercy. It will not be repeated if you ever disappoint me like this again.'

'I am so sorry, my lord,' I mumbled, but Edward had swept out of the stable, leaving me to darkness and my wet, stinking bed.

But I had never been happier in my life. I knew that I had to be the son, albeit illegitimate, of Richard of Cornwall. I was related to King Henry himself, and to Lord Edward. The only drawback, a seemingly insurmountable one, was that none of them could ever know, unless I could prove such a relationship.

I resolved that when my mind was free of the clouds of wine I would have to give deep thought to how I could prove my noble ancestry. Everything Peter Pauncefoot had told me about my real father had been confirmed by this night's encounter, confirmed from the mouth of Prince Edward himself. All the facts fitted. There could be no other possibility. I was the natural son of Richard, Earl of Cornwall, King of the Romans.

I lay down and let sleep take me, warmed on my soggy and vomit-soaked bed by knowledge of my noble origin. [9]

APRIL 1258

AWestminster parliament had been decreed to assemble at Easter in the year 1258. It was convened in order to discuss all the problems besetting the nation. Being a lowly jester I had never attended any of these parliaments, an omission that concerned me not a jot because they consisted of hours of boring debates.

This day I happened to be walking past Westminster Hall on my way back to my chamber in the palace. I noticed a large group of nobles gathered outside the doors of the hall. I recognised them as some of the most powerful earls in England. They were conversing earnestly and appeared nervous and restless. It was plain that they were planning something. I decided to stop and find out what was occurring.

I unobstrusively crept into Westminster Hall and looked around. King Henry was seated on his throne at the far end on the dais above the assembly. Beneath him, ranged along either side of the hall, were rows of benches where those officially attending the parliament were seated. At the end by the doors through which I had furtively insinuated myself was a standing throng of spectators.

King Henry was waiting for the answer to his demand for a new tax. Lord Edward was sitting at Henry's right hand side. I could not see much past the stone columns or over the heads of the throng so I slowly pushed my way forwards.

A few moments after I found a clear vantage point, the tall wooden doors at the main entrance of the hall burst open and the host of nobles shoved their way through the standing throng. They walked purposefully between the rows of benches and up to the dais where King Henry and Prince Edward were seated on their thrones. This insolent gang of intruders were all wearing chain mail but they had left their weapons outside.

I could see that this threatening cabal was headed by the three most powerful earls in the land. They were Richard de Clare, Earl of Gloucester; Simon de Montfort, Earl of Leicester; and Roger Bigod, Earl of Norfolk.

King Henry watched their approach and, unlike his son who looked angered by the intrusion, was visibly unnerved. He asked tremulously: 'What is this, my lords? Am I your captive?'

'No, my lord, no,' Roger Bigod hastily replied, glancing warily at the enraged Lord Edward. 'What we have come to seek is the removal of the wretched and intolerable Lusignans and an oath that you will in future listen to the good counsel of the lords gathered here before you.'

It was the enraged Lord Edward who answered. He slammed his hand down on the arm of his throne and stood up. His full height of six feet two inches was intimidating, even to those powerful earls. He roared: 'By God, gentlemen, you overstep the mark to burst in here and make demands of your rightful sovereign. Take yourselves away!'

The earls hesitated and might, indeed, have turned away but the king, with his usual ineptitude, said mildly: 'I will answer them, Edward. It seems that we have no choice. Please sit down.'

'Father, you do not have to answer to anybody except God,' Edward insisted.

'I will hear what they have to say, my son. Please sit down.'

Lord Edward reluctantly resumed his throne.

Emboldened by the king's timidity, Roger Bigod asked him: 'Are you prepared to swear on the holy gospels to accept our counsel?'

'And if I choose not to... '

'Then you make enemies of all of us,' Bigod replied firmly.

Henry hesitated for a few moments and then, to Edward's evident disgust, replied: 'Very well.'

After a long and uncomfortable interlude a bible was found and King Henry swore as requested. Then Bigod said: 'We wish Lord Edward to swear this oath as well.'

Edward glared at him and said, with steely resolve: 'I will not bind myself with such an oath.'

Simon de Montfort, Earl of Leicester, an arrogant and forthright man, said defiantly: 'You must, my lord, or you will lose everything.'

Edward answered, barely able to control his temper: 'You may be my godfather and my uncle, Earl Simon, but do not seek to threaten me or *you* will one day lose everything, beginning with your head.'

Henry turned to his son and said: 'I command you to swear this oath, Edward.'

'Father, you should not have sworn the oath. You are now in their power and if I swear the oath then so shall I be.'

'It seems we are in their power already, my son. Swear the oath.'

Lord Edward swore the oath most reluctantly and grudgingly. Then he turned away in disgust and took no futher part in proceedings.

Even though the three earls were wealthy men and fearsome warriors, a firm stand by King Henry following his son's example would almost certainly have persuaded them to withdraw. [10]

Having faced down the king, however, the earls launched into a list of demands, the main one being that a council of twenty four men be appointed to undertake the reform of the realm. They conceded that King Henry could select half of the members of this council and, with abject stupidity, he later nominated some of his Lusignan relatives, thus making a mockery of the very problem which most concerned the nobles.

After more heated argument the parliamentary session descended into chaos and broke up with nothing agreed save that the parties concerned should meet again at Oxford in one month's time.

I later learned that Lord Edward had not been scheduled to

attend parliament that day, which is precisely why the plotters had chosen that particular day, but Edward had decided, at the last minute, to support his father and learn more about parliamentary procedures.

His strong response to the demands of the earls might have made them withdraw if Henry had supported him. As it was, the power of the Lusignans was severely damaged by this momentous confrontation but at the cost of the country descending into ever-increasing chaos.

Both factions went their separate ways to prepare for civil war. City gates all over the country were kept locked and strongly guarded. The earls made sure that seaports were closed for fear that King Henry might bring foreign mercenaries over from Europe to fight his cause.

Everyone expected the civil war to begin at any moment and, on top of Llewelyn's astonishingly successful conquest of Wales, the prospects for England looked bleak.

JUNE 1258

To general surprise and relief, civil war did not erupt, apart from one or two minor skirmishes, and parliament convened at Oxford in June as planned. My services were not required at Oxford and I remained at Windsor with Queen Eleanor, Lady Leonora and Lord Edmund.

Edward returned from this parliament and, two days later, summoned me to his chamber for a game of chess. I was gratified by this proof that he still desired my company.

We commenced the game but between virtually every move I looked up to find Edward staring into space and lost in thought. I was beginning to manouevre him into a position where I could beat him easily.

I was curious to learn what had occurred at this Oxford parliament to cause Edward such excessive distraction. I took a risk and commented: 'Forgive me for saying so, my lord, but your mind does not seem to be on our game. I will soon be able to defeat you easily.'

Edward grunted sardonically. 'Why should the fate that you mete out be any different? It seems that the whole country is now able to defeat me easily.'

'I don't understand, my lord?'

'Isn't there any gossip among the servants about what happened in Oxford? Aren't they sneering about how they now serve rollicking nancy men, ragged-arsed puppets and two emasculated eunuchs as their anointed king and prince?'

I had overheard Queen Eleanor in conversation with Lady

Leonora about what had occurred at Oxford. Queen Eleanor, despite her tacit support for the earls and overt support of the Savoyard faction, was not pleased by the thought of her husband's powers being stripped away but, to Lord Edward, I pretended ignorance. 'I have not heard any details, except comments that it went badly for your father.'

'Badly you say!' Edward exclaimed, his face contorted with bitterness. 'If things remain as they are then I will be a mere clerk when I take the throne. I will be nothing more than a cypher, a wax seal, a signatory to the will of other men!'

'But how can this be, my lord? Your father has been anointed by God as the rightful ruler of this realm?'

'God must be sleeping, Hamo. Or otherwise engaged. Almost everyone at this wretched Oxford parliament spoke against my father. Lords to lepers say that his rule is unjust and oppressive.'

'A grievous calumny,' I lied. 'King Henry is a good and pious man.'

'Yes, he is, Hamo, and I love him dearly. But he is a weak man and he has allowed himself to be neutered.'

I dare not make any comment about such an astoundingly frank admission from Edward, so I kept silent.

He continued: 'The country is now governed by a new royal council. They will be making the major decisions. All the royal castles are to be put in the keeping of what these usurpers call "reliable Englishmen". That is a direct move against my Lusignan half-uncles who support me and the king. Of course, they opposed this move. My godfather, Simon de Montfort, the Earl of Leicester, said to them: "Make no mistake about it, either you lose your castles or you lose your head". By God, that man frightens me. He is driven by steely arrogance and unbending religious zeal.'

'But surely you still have the freedom to act, my lord? Surely you, on behalf of your father, can resist the new oppression and regain what has been lost.'

'No, Hamo. I have been shackled as well. I was compelled to take an oath to abide by these so-called Provisions of Oxford. And a four man council has been appointed to control my actions. Control my actions! As if I were no more than a ploughman or a pot girl or dairy maid.' Edward suddenly swept all the chess pieces from the board and rose angrily from his chair. 'By God, I will not accept this humiliating situation for long. I will find new friends, new alliances, new ways to combat these arrogant earls.' He looked at me but he was seeing through me, beyond to his enemies ranged throughout the land. Eventually he said: 'Go, Hamo. I cannot think on chess tonight.'

I quit Lord Edward's chamber feeling deeply concerned, not just for the country or for Edward's bruised sensibilities but for my own privileged position with Edward. Of what use were my covert skills, my conveyance of court gossip, when momentous events were happening elsewhere and while the important decisions were being taken elsewhere by power brokers who were not King Henry and Prince Edward?

I had to think of a scheme to help restore Edward's rights and further ingratiate myself into his confidence, affections and – most importantly – usefulness, before all my influence and future prospects dissipated like morning mist over the marshes.

Such was Edward's deep chagrin at this time that, in later years when he assumed the throne, all his prickly assertion of royal rights and careful husbandry of royal privileges stemmed from the humiliation that he and his father had suffered at this Oxford parliament. [11]

Within the next few days the Lusignans, now fearing for their lives, fled from the country. Lord Edward's main supporters were now exiled, there appeared to be nothing he could do to reverse the balance of power, and the royal cause looked bleak indeed.

Having been deprived of the support of the formidable Lusignans, the only option left to Lord Edward was to secretly set about building new alliances and covertly connive to regain the support of those nobles who had deserted him.

These nobles knew that Edward would one day be king and that he would be a much more formidable opponent than his father was. If the earls earned the undying enmity of Edward and Edward came to the throne with unencumbered authority, the earls knew that their situation would be very desolate indeed.

I was able to kindle a small measure of good favour from Edward by my necessarily limited involvement in building these new alliances but it was scarce enough to make him consider me indispensable.

Then, most unexpectedly, I was presented with a God-given opportunity when the court encamped at Winchester.

JULY 1258

Lord Edward arranged to pay an informal visit to Richard de Clare, Earl of Gloucester, and Richard's younger brother William, at Winchester Castle. Richard de Clare was one of the earls who had favoured ridding England of the Lusignans but now he considered that the baronial reforms had achieved their objectives and should be halted, particularly as his own corrupt dealings were perilously close to coming under legal scrutiny. Edward, therefore, considered Richard de Clare to be a prospective new ally in the restoration of royal dominance.

Edward was to take breakfast with the two de Clare brothers, followed by a day of stag hunting and falconry, with minstrels and jesting as entertainment at the evening feast.

In the morning I accompanied Lord Edward's retinue to Winchester Castle. The Earl of Gloucester's steward was a knight named Walter de Scoteny. He was a tall, well-dressed and saturnine man with irregular rotted teeth, a large nose, and excessively hairy arms.

I had visited Winchester Castle before and this man de Scoteny had had the temerity to cuff me about the head after I had inadvertently jostled him while playing the fool in the kitchens. He considered me an easy and weak target. He had also made unwanted advances towards Dolores, as he did towards any woman he considered susceptible. De Scoteny was a cruel and furtive man, and the servants hated him.

As soon as we arrived at Winchester Castle I made my way to the kitchens. Here amongst the iron pans and skillets, the steaming

162

cauldrons and the tantalising aromas of meat and spices, I began to amuse the cooks and kitchen maids with my antics. They remembered me fondly from my previous visits and were delighted to again be afforded free entertainment as a relief from their mundane tasks. My aim was also to glean any gossip that might be of use to myself or to Lord Edward.

I asked, like the simpleton they assumed me to be, what the great lords were having for breakfast and was told that they were having a simple meal of sop *(white bread dipped in wine or ale).*

As an honoured royal guest, Lord Edward was being served with a gold goblet and platter while the two de Clares were being served with silver platters and goblets. I pretended to stare and drool over this precious ware, gurgling my idiotic delight, and then, in pretended excitement, I accidentally swept an earthenware pitcher of wine onto the rush-covered floor while waving my arms.

A few moments later, before the mess had been cleaned up, De Scoteny entered the kitchens. I ducked down and hid behind a table, as if in fear of him. He angrily berated the kitchen servants for wasting wine and making a mess and then pompously announced that the lords were ready for breakfast and that he was claiming the honour of serving them himself. He ordered all the servants to leave the kitchen. He did not know that I was watching him.

De Scoteny withdrew a small phial of liquid from inside his fancy doublet. He removed the wooden plug and carefully sniffed the contents. Then, after looking around to make sure that the kitchen was deserted, he sprinkled a few drops of liquid into each of the goblets. He then took a large earthenware jar from a shelf behind him and placed the phial within the jar and put the jar back on the shelf. He then picked up the large copper charger on which the breakfast items had been arranged and, balancing his precious burden carefully, walked out of the kitchen.

I asked myself what it could be that de Scoteny had sprinkled in my lord's goblet. Could it be a digestif or a spice to liven the taste of the simple sop? I went to the shelf and had to stand on a stool to reach the jar. I took it down and withdrew the phial of liquid. I sniffed the contents.

I let the jar drop and smash on the stone floor and leapt off the stool.

I ran through the two long corridors that led to the great hall, unceremoniously shoving aside anyone who got in my way.

The lords were seated informally below the salt on either side of one of the long tables. No-one else was seated at the table. Two mangy dogs snuffled about in the sleeping straw and there were a few servants going about their business but they were keeping well away from their lords and masters so as not to disturb them.

The early morning sunlight of a fine day streamed in through the high windows and illuminated the colourful banners that hung from the grey stone walls. Minstrels up in the gallery were playing soft airs on the lute to entertain the royal guest.

De Scoteny had placed the breakfast items in front of Edward and the two de Clare brothers. He was obsequiously backing away from their presence as I ran into the hall.

The two de Clare brothers were already eating the sop with relish and taking swigs of wine in between mouthfuls. Lord Edward was explaining something, accompanied by much gesticulating with his hands, and had touched neither the bread or wine.

Edward then raised the golden goblet to his lips. I shouted: 'No, my lord, no!' Edward looked up wide-eyed with surprise as I jumped on to a bench, vaulted across the table and forcefully dashed the goblet from his hand as I tumbled to the floor on the other side. The goblet bounced away on the flagstones.

Edward stared at me with eye-blazing anger at such a flagrant breach of protocol, but then had to turn his attention to the de Clare brothers. They were already beginning to feel the effects of the poison. They were clutching at their throats and shouting that their mouths were on fire. In their agony they drank more of the wine to cool their mouths, which was the worst thing they could have done.

'My lords,' I shouted, 'the wine is poisoned. Drink no more!'

Servants were approaching the table to find out what commotion was affecting their noble masters. I turned to them and said loudly: 'Fetch ale for your masters, as quickly as you can.'

The servants, unwilling to be instructed by a mere jester, looked at Edward to confirm my order. Edward told them emphatically: 'Do as he says.'

Edward had stood up from the table and was watching, with blank incomprehension, the agonies of the ailing de Clare brothers. The younger brother, William de Clare, had collapsed on to the rush-strewn flagstones and was copiously vomiting green bile, his body seized with convulsions. The earl himself was frantically clutching at his mouth and throat, his skin already of a waxy pallor.

The servants returned with jugs of ale at the same time that armed soldiers began entering the hall. I told the servants to make the de Clare brothers drink the ale. I had no idea whether the ale would alleviate their symptoms but it was the only remedy I could think of that might dilute the effects of the poison.

Lord Edward pulled me to one side and whispered: 'Hamo, what in God's name is happening here?'

'My lord, I was hiding in the kitchen when I saw the earl's steward, that man de Scoteny, put poison in your breakfast goblets.'

'De Scoteny?' Edward repeated, turning around distracted as the earl himself, Richard de Clare, collapsed on to the floor. The servants were carrying out the writhing body of William de Clare and someone was literally screaming for a doctor to be fetched with all speed.

Edward, stupefied and temporarily dull witted, said: 'De Scoteny has served the earl for many years. Why should he poison his master now? Why should he want to poison me?'

'Think, my lord!' I urged. 'These are evil times and there are great matters at stake, as you well know. De Scoteny is an evil and furtive man. He is probably in the pay of your enemies. You must be very careful.'

Edward nodded, then turned to the soldiers and ordered: 'Find Walter de Scoteny and arrest him!' Then he asked me: 'What was the poison, Hamo?'

'Wolfsbane, my lord. I recognised the noxious smell. I am mightily relieved that you had not drank it but heartsick that I was too slow to prevent the earl and his brother from drinking it.'

'Do not chide yourself, Hamo. You have once again performed a great service. You have saved my life. Let us hope that the doctors can save the life of the poor earl and his brother.'

The earl himself, Richard de Clare, eventually recovered although his hair, fingernails and toe-nails had fallen out. The physicians credited me with saving his life by making him drink copious ale to dilute the poison. The earl's brother William died in agony some six hours later. His death surprised and shocked me but I was told that William had been considerably debilitated following a hunting accident and had not had the strength to recover from the poison.

Walter de Scoteny was found guilty of poisoning his master and was drawn and hanged. By leaving the phial of poison concealed within a jar in the kitchens he could have accused any one of the many innocent kitchen servants of committing such a ghastly crime. I thank God that I was there to witness de Scoteny's evil intent. [12]

De Scoteny had owned a small estate and charmingly rustic manor house near Winchester which, at Lord Edward's instigation and with Earl Richard's full approval, was awarded to me in recognition of my courageous and timely intervention. Unlike the Coleby estate, this estate was awarded to me openly.

The royal family showed their gratitude with gifts. King Henry, in his usual pious and po-faced fashion, gave me a large silver jewelled crucifix to thank God for helping me to save his son's life. Queen Eleanor gave me an ornate gold chain studded with jewels.

Lady Leonora, no doubt in collusion with Dolores, arranged that our apartments at Westminster and Windsor Castle were refurbished with the finest furniture, wall hangings, carpets and other decorations.

Best of all, and what thrilled me immensely as the culmination of so many hopes and dreams, was a service of thanksgiving in the Chapel of St. Edward the Confessor at Windsor Castle. After the service Lord Edward dubbed me a knight, an almost unprecedented honour for a man from my background, especially one whom everyone regarded as a simpleton.

This accolade caused much rancour, with the tough military knights from noble backgrounds finding it offensive that a mere jester should be awarded their title, even if he had saved the life of their liege lord Edward. They sulked and whined about my knighthood in my presence, thinking I could not understand, but I graciously forgave them and basked in the knowledge of Lord Edward's favour, and the secret knowledge that I was the son of Earl Richard of Cornwall. These disgruntled knights, strong as they were, could not oppose the will of Lord Edward.

I was now Sir Hamo Pauncefoot. Even Dolores was impressed by my abrupt rise in favour and preened that she was now a Lady in her own right and that we possessed our own estate in Hampshire.

Until the novelty wore off, she showed me more wifely deference than she had ever displayed before which, of course, is not saying much. I could not help but remark that our conversations were more cordial and she seemed more at ease in my company. Even our marital relations in bed seemed to elicit a more enthusiastic response from Dolores, now that she was sleeping with a 'Sir'.

1259

The sinister and agonised death of the Earl of Gloucester's brother wrought a new, albeit wary, closeness between Edward and the earl who had narrowly escaped the same fate. A few months later the two men made a formal but secret alliance. This was but one measure by which Edward was covertly building up military alliances ready to fight back against the barons who had humiliatingly stripped his father of power.

I was able to reinforce my newly won favour with Edward by employing my secret knowledge of languages. Throughout the year of 1259 Edward took part in as many tournaments as he could accommodate, both in England and in France.

This brutal and frenetic schedule lulled Edward's guardian council into believing that Edward had accepted his political impotence and had decided to pass the time in the activity that most young English noblemen enjoyed, drawing blood with hunks of whetted steel, while the reality was that we were recruiting allies among the knights and barons who also participated in these tournaments. [13]

I was able to move freely amongst these men, respected and accepted as a fellow knight, Lord Edward's jester and the man who had saved his life, but otherwise unconsidered as any threat.

None of them suspected that I could understand every word they were saying. Thus I discovered, without possibility of their dissembling, which of these nobles were genuinely sympathetic to Edward's cause and those who opposed him. Employing jester's licence I could provoke candid comments with my jokes and antics and reaped a rich harvest of potential recruits whom Edward could then approach discreetly with the strong possibilty of winning their pledge of support.

Throughout these months I became aware of a new seriousness and self-belief in Edward's manner, despite the occasional drunken high jinks at some of the tournaments. Edward the boy had been replaced by the twenty-year-old man, fully formed in mind and limb, and fully prepared to accept his duties as husband, prince and future king.

The forced diminution of royal authority and the incessant demands throughout the country for reform of the myriad corrupt abuses taking place at every level of English society had given Edward a new sensibility of the duties and responsibilities that would fall on his head along with the crown. He took a deep interest in the work of reform being initiated by the ruling council of barons, despite the bitter fact that it was they who had deprived his father of his authority.

At the same time as Edward was recruiting support, the cohesion of the ruling baronial council was beginning to disintegrate. Disagreement had erupted about how far and how fast reforms should be introduced.

The more honest and idealistic barons desired to press ahead with far-reaching legal reforms. Most of the other earls and barons found reforming zeal beginning to clash with their own self-interest. It was perfectly acceptable to stamp out corruption perpetrated by the lower orders but when inquiries began into corruption that was feathering their own well-cushioned nests, the earls began to fly away like timid sparrows. Such craven reluctance could not be disguised for very long.

The common people became aware that the revolutionary council had rightly curbed the abuses committed by King Henry, and were inquiring into abuses committed by sheriffs and other officials throughout the shires, but they were doing very little to curb their own abuses and excesses.

This climate of hostile opinion, raised to fever pitch by the cunning propaganda of the increasingly influential Robert Burnell, rattled the earls into taking swift action by passing a new set of legal reforms known as the Provisions of Westminster.

I had been shown another warning of Master Burnell's moral perfidy when I had unexpectedly returned to Westminster from Edward's continental tournaments and encountered Burnell walking down the corridor that led to my private chamber.

Burnell had regarded me coolly and smoothly, briefly nodding his head in acknowledgement of my knighted rank, but had said nothing. I perforce had to play the respectful jester and bowed in return as he passed me.

I hurried into my chamber to find Dolores, who gasped in astonishment to see me standing there. She was fully dressed but red-faced and flustered. 'Husband!' she exclaimed, seeking to disarm me with a display of wifely concern. 'I did not expect to see you back so soon. Are you hungry? Do you require refreshment?'

'What was Burnell doing here?' I asked, ignoring her attempt to distract me.

Dolores, her cheeks burning, hesitated and then replied: 'He came to tell me that you had returned to England and we would soon be reunited.'

'Liar! Burnell did not know I was back in England and, even if he did, a man of his stature does not play messenger boy for ladies-in-waiting unless there is some reward for him. It grieves me to think what reward you have just given him.'

'I have to attend Lady Leonora,' Dolores muttered, attempting to walk past me.

I grabbed her by the shoulders and questioned her angrily but her temper took hold and she spat back her contempt for me and denied that anything was going on between her and Burnell. I pushed her away in disgust and stumbled out of the chamber.

I knew Dolores was lying. I felt heartsick and viciously betrayed.

I had not won her love and accepted that I probably never would but our relationship had become cordial enough. Our lovemaking, passionate on my part, tolerated but sometimes responsive on hers, seemed to have achieved a level of satisfaction I once thought nigh on impossible. Evidently I was wrong.

I eased my torment by making my way to the kitchens to get drunk with the servants, despite my knighted status and royal paternity, and to sleep in warm straw, haunted by dreams of Dolores and Burnell, their limbs entwined in ecstasy.

A few days after the autumn parliament had ended, Lord Edward ordered me to accompany him on a journey to the castle at Dover. I had respectfully begun to ask the purpose of our journey so that I could properly prepare myself for the performance of my duties. Edward, with uncharacteristic brusqueness, cut me off in mid-sentence and warned me to keep my counsel and not tell anyone where we were going, not even Lady Leonora or Dolores.

Such unusual secretiveness sent my mind into a ferment of speculation but, despite my wildest imaginings, I did not foresee the extraordinary and dangerous purpose of our mission.

We arrived at Dover Castle without receiving any of the usual ceremony that would normally greet the prince. Edward ordered me wait in the great hall, to take only a light repast, and not to partake of any wine or ale whatsoever.

I waited for several hours. Growing bored, I took a nap on the straw beside the warmth of the blazing fire.

I was awoken, with a shake of the shoulder, by one of Edward's trusted knights. I realised it must be the middle of the night because everyone in the great hall, including the dogs, was asleep. The knight asked that I follow him and led me, by torchlight, out of the castle.

We began walking down the hill towards the slumbering port of Dover, the moonlight casting eerie shadows over the town and glimmering on the restless sea.

We walked about a mile until we arrived at a large inn situated on the outskirts of the town. The knight opened the door of the inn, which disturbed the landlord who was sleeping on his straw bed just inside the door. The landlord looked up at the knight. The two men nodded to each other but nothing was said.

The knight led me through the inn, out through the back door and then into a separate annexe built at the back of the inn. We entered a large room filled with benches and stools, but which was now deserted. At the back of the room was another door. The knight tapped three times on this door and a voice ordered us to enter.

The knight ushered me through and I went in to find Lord Edward sitting at a kitchen table. He was surrounded by pots and pans and all the other accoutrements of a working kitchen. I was perplexed as to why Edward had chosen such an odd venue for whatever was going to take place. The room was lit by several candles and rushlights.

Edward, who usually eschewed elaborate finery, was dressed in chain mail over which he wore a surcoat embroidered with his coat-of-arms. Despite the martial ceremony of his dress, Edward was bare headed and unarmed, which served to arouse my curiosity even more.

Lord Edward, not inviting me to sit, began promptly: 'Hamo, I am about to entrust you with a very important duty that must remain completely secret between the two of us. I am about to receive a visitor and we are going to talk about affairs of state. If it becomes known that I have met this man in secret I could find myself in high disfavour with my father.' Edward pointed to a corner of the kitchen where a large side cupboard, long and low and made of oak, was placed against the wall. 'Over there is a pot cupboard. I want you to conceal yourself in that cupboard and make absolutely sure that you make no noise or betray your presence in any way. I want you to witness and remember what my visitor has to say to me. He is a formidable man, Hamo. If he finds out he is being eavesdropped then it will be dangerous, even for a prince like me. Do you think you will be able to do as I ask?'

'Certainly, my lord,' I replied. I felt uneasy but intensely curious to know who this visitor was and why Edward had chosen me to perform this work of spying, but I did not think his edgy mood would allow me to ask him any direct questions.

As if reading my thoughts, Edward continued: 'I have chosen you for this task because you are small enough to fit into that pot cupboard, you have no political influence or ambitions, you can understand any language my visitor chooses to speak, and I trust you implicitly. I have seen you remain still and silent for long periods of time but, however, if you feel for any reason that you cannot perform this task, you must tell me now. I will let you leave without any ill will on my part. It is a dangerous business I ask you to perform and you must be sure of your ability to perform it. What do you say?'

'May I be permitted to try concealing myself in this cupboard before I say for certain, my lord. If I can breathe and lay reasonably comfortably I can remain completely still and silent for at least three or four hours.'

Edward nodded and said: 'Try it now.'

I went over to the cupboard, swung open the double doors and manouvered myself into the cupboard so that I was lying down with my knees drawn up. I called out: 'Please close the doors, my lord.'

Edward carefully closed the doors. I could see a sliver of light between the iron hinges because the cupboard was crudely made. I pushed open the doors and climbed out again. 'All is well, my lord,' I said. 'I will be able to hear what is being said but I cannot see anything.' This last part was not true because I had been able to see Edward moving about the room, although it had been difficult to discern much detail.

'Good,' Edward said: 'My visitor will arrive at any moment. Get back in the cupboard and, in God's name, stay silent and undiscovered.'

I hesitated and dared to ask: 'May I be permitted to know the identity of this visitor? It may help me to prepare my mind to understand and recall the terms of your conversation.'

At first Edward appeared reluctant to tell me but then must have admitted to himself the common sense of my request. 'My visitor is Simon de Montfort, Earl of Leicester.'

My shocked expression actually made Edward smile.

'Yes, Hamo, you now see what a dangerous business this is. I do not know why my godfather wishes to see me or why he insists that we meet alone in absolute secrecy. That is why I want a witness. You have a retentive memory and you are a shrewd man, Hamo, and so is my Uncle Simon. He may be married to the king's sister but he is also bitterly opposed to the king. With the country in the sort of treasonous turmoil that now exists I must be very careful. This meeting could be useful for me and my father or it may be a trap and a prelude to more bloodshed. Take careful note of everything de Montfort says.' Edward looked down at my belted tunic and observed: 'I see you are not wearing your dagger.'

'No, my lord. I did not think it would be necessary.'

Edward turned to an array of carving knives hanging on the wall behind him. He selected a knife with a deer horn handle and a razor-sharp blade some eighteen inches long. He handed it to me and said: 'Take this into the cupboard with you.'

I could not restrain my reaction and replied without thinking: 'Surely you do not think that Earl Simon would seek to harm you, or even assassinate you?'

Edward regarded me coolly and chose to overlook my impertinent outburst. 'Tell me, Hamo, who is the only person who can ultimately thwart this lawless usurpation of the throne? Who is the one person whose removal would leave the king lost in the wilderness without hope? Yes, me, Hamo. Earl Simon is a relentless and unforgiving man, driven by his own righteousness and his own perceived role as God's instrument on earth. Kill me, and his path to the throne is swept clear. I know not why Uncle Simon wishes to see me but my death would be of benefit to him and to many others. Let us be prepared for the worst, Hamo. Now, no more questions and go and conceal yourself in the cupboard.'

I bowed and, clutching the carving knife, snuggled back into the cupboard and waited, intrigued and curious, for de Montfort to arrive. It was several long and tense moments before he was ushered into Edward's presence. Through the hinge gap I could see that de Montfort was wearing the robes of a monk, with a cowl covering his head, so that no-one could discern his identity. He threw back the cowl and I saw his face closely for the first time in my life, a face I came to hate bitterly.

His nose was long and straight, his stubble-covered chin square and wide, and his thick black hair hung down to his shoulders in straight lanks, his whole head appearing as square and solid as a castle keep. He was a tall and powerfully built man. Edward was taller but looked spindly compared to his war-like uncle.

De Montfort nodded his head rather than bowing to Edward and said: 'Thank you for agreeing to receive me, nephew.'

'Whatever your purpose and whatever the outcome, I entreat you to keep this encounter secret,' Edward replied.

'You have my word. I appreciate the risk you have taken by agreeing to this meeting.'

I could already sense that Edward was trying to take the initiative and not be intimidated by his much older and more experienced uncle. He said hesitantly: 'I hope we can find some mutual ground to resolve the grave differences that divide our family and our land.'

'I think we can,' de Montfort replied.

'Please sit down, uncle. Would you like some wine?'

'That would be most welcome. Thank you.'

Edward walked across to my pot cupboard and the sliver of light was temporarily blocked out while he poured wine into silver goblets. He went back to the table and sat down after handing de Montfort his goblet.

De Montfort waited for Edward to take a sip.

With a half-smile, Edward urged: 'Please drink, uncle. I swear by Almighty God that the wine is not poisoned.' Edward took a long draught to demonstrate that the wine was not fatal.

De Montfort had the grace to smile in return and took a sip of the wine. He said tentatively: 'I have no need to remind you, Edward, that I am married to your aunt. She loves you and has always been concerned for your welfare. I want to assure you that the differences between your father and I do not diminish the high regard I have for you. I have watched your maturity progress with admiration, Edward. You have grown into a fine man and a fine warrior. You have fashioned yourself into a formidable opponent for anyone.'

Edward nodded in acknowledgement.

De Montfort continued: 'You well know that your father and I had considerable disagreement about the administration of Gascony after he had appointed me as his royal lieutenant. All that is now in the past and Gascony has been granted to you. We are rid of the king's half-brothers, the Lusignans, who I strongly believe were a pernicious influence on the king and on you. I know that you accept that there is much in this land that needs reformation.'

'But not at the expense of my father's authority and dignity,' Edward said. 'He is the sovereign, anointed by God. Yes, there is a need for reform but I must support my father and his royal authority.'

De Montfort studied his goblet for a few moments, considering his next statement. 'Henry is a good and pious man but, God forgive me for saying so, he is too gullible. He gives too much away to men who have done little to deserve such favour. That was the trouble with the Lusignans. Your father allowed their flagrant abuses to continue for many years, unable to overcome his family feelings by controlling them in the way that it was seemly for a king to do. I must speak even more frankly and say that your mother, Queen Eleanor, now advocates the advancement of her Savoyard relatives in the same fashion. These factions and conflicting interests have done grave harm to the tranquility of the realm. True born Englishmen feel that their laws and rights have been trampled into the mud by gangs of foreigners.'

Edward laughed theatrically at this last remark. 'Do you forget, uncle, that you are a so-called foreigner yourself and that your secret unapproved marriage to my aunt enraged my father and caused my uncle Richard of Cornwall to rise up in revolt?'

'I do not forget,' de Montfort bristled, unused to being corrected by anyone. 'That is why I am well aware of what discontent such situations can incite. I did my utmost to serve the interests of your father while I was his lieutenant in Gascony but he cut the ground from under my feet. Now we have a mutual interest, Edward, and the king may be about to cut the ground from under your feet.'

'How so?' Edward growled.

'Let me be blunt, Edward. These negotiations currently being conducted with France, surely you cannot be happy with what is being proposed? One day, you will be king. Now Henry proposes to give away his ancestral claims to the lands of Normandy, Anjou, Poitou and Maine! What sort of shrivelled inheritance will you receive when you take the throne!? You know that my wife, your aunt, must give her quitclaim before these lands are given away to the French crown. For months, with my full support, she has been refusing to do that. If these lands are given away your kingly inheritance will be considerably diminished before you receive it. Your timely influence on the king might prevent this rash venture.'

Edward thought for a moment and then said: 'I admit that I am bitterly opposed to this treaty even though it has support, however reluctantly, from my father and from many others. True, it will protect my rights to rule Gascony but I fear too much will be given away. I may be prepared to join with anyone who can help me prevent this travesty. The king is being unduly influenced by the French king, who is a wily and devious man. Perhaps you and I together can counter the influence of the French king and dissuade my father from stripping me of my birthright. I am also willing to support some, if not all, of the much needed reforms proposed by the barons, but I will never do anything to diminish my father's security and authority.' [14]

De Montfort nodded thoughtfully. 'If you can find it in your heart to support me over this issue of the French lands, and also lend your support to some of the measures proposed by the reform movement, even if not all of them, I can promise you that I will use all my influence to unshackle you from the control of the council appointed to guide you.'

Edward looked sceptical. 'Promises are easily made and easily broken, uncle. I will need something more substantial before risking my father's wrath, and my integrity as heir to his throne.'

The two men talked for what must have been more than an hour. It was apparent that they would never be close friends but agreement was reached.

After de Montfort had left, Edward opened the cupboard doors and I climbed out. I was not very stiff but, in the hope of improving any possible reward for such service, I made more of my discomfort by stretching and groaning.

Edward poured me a goblet of wine and handed it to me. What a strange evening to be cramped in a cupboard listening to a conversation that affected the fate of the nation and then to be served wine by the heir to the throne from his own hand!

'Well done, Hamo,' Edward said. 'Do not mention this meeting to anyone, not ever, whatever results from this night. Do you understand?'

I bowed my head and replied: 'I swear by Almighty God I will never breathe a word, my lord.'

I had been astonished that Edward had indicated that he was willing to throw in his lot with de Montfort against his own father. Edward loved his father but was consumed with youthful impatience to be his own man, unfettered and uncontrolled. I sensed great danger but, to my eternal regret, I did not have the moral courage to try to dissuade Edward from such a perilous liaison.

We briefly discussed the implications of what de Montfort had proposed. I feared Edward's temper and brittle mood, thus I shamefully kept my counsel and agreed with everything. Then Edward dismissed me so that he could consider his next course of action while the events of the night were fresh in his mind.

MARCH 1261

Of the next few months I can relate little of interest or import as far as my life was concerned. Dolores and I, and even Lady Leonora, were buffeted by the conflicting gales of political upheaval, blown about as helpless as leaves in the wind. I was sent hither and thither, one day to entertain Lord Edward, the next day to support and comfort his wife during their separation.

I also became very ill with a malady that caused me to take to my bed for several weeks and afterwards left me feeble and debilitated. Dolores was a dutiful wife and was diligent in taking care of me. Our relationship became as warm and cordial as never before. Lady Leonora was equally diligent in ensuring that I was constantly attended by the most skilled physicians, and Lord Edward prayed daily for my recovery.

Thus I could do very little to influence our fates, and my memory of the entire period, now so long ago, is as confused as the events themselves.

Then, in March 1261, after I had fully recovered from illness, I heard news that caused me to rush to seek an audience with Lady Leonora. This was not difficult to accomplish because, by then, she was effectively imprisoned within the Tower of London.

Leonora was in her chamber, engaged in her tapestry work, accompanied by her ladies-in-waiting, including Dolores. I was ushered into her presence.

Her chamber had been made as comfortable as circumstances allowed, with wall hangings to hide the damp walls and many pieces of carved and painted furniture, including her tester bed. The floor was also covered with a Persian carpet that must have cost a king's ransom.

I remember to this day how the light from the window illuminated Leonora's face, still beautiful despite the strain of events, and the sheen of her black hair. She was wearing a becoming blue and gold silk gown. A gilded bird cruelly trapped in an ungilded cage.

'Hamo!' she greeted me cheerily. 'We are grateful to God to see you recovered. Have you come to sing us a new song?'

I guffawed stupidly for the benefit of her ladies and then whispered in her ear: 'My lady, I beg permission to speak to you alone. I have news of events that we may be able to turn to our advantage.'

I stepped back and Leonora, excited by my statement, ordered her ladies to quit the chamber, except for Dolores. After they had departed Leonora said urgently: 'Tell me what news, Hamo. Does it concern my husband?'

'Indeed it does, my lady. I have just learned that Lord Edward has returned to England, and that he is accompanied by Aymer de Valence.'

'Who is he?' Dolores asked.

I replied: 'Aymer de Valence is the most powerful lord of the Lusignan clan. It is with Lusignan support that Lord Edward hopes to consolidate his authority within England.'

'Why does Lord Edward need this man's support,' Dolores asked. 'Isn't the support of de Monfort enough?'

'An excellent question, my dear. I surmise that Lord Edward, ever since he pledged his support to de Montfort, foresees that that exalted gentleman might well betray him in an attempt to seize the throne. I perceive an opportunity here to encourage Lord Edward to return his allegiance to his rightful sovereign and turn back from the dangerous path he has been following for the past several months.'

'What dangerous path?' Dolores demanded.

'Surely you know what has been happening in England these few months gone? I would have thought that Master Burnell has kept you informed during my illness.'

Dolores's face reddened as Leonora looked at her curiously.

Dolores said: 'Politics is all fluff and blather. I cannot make head nor tail of what has been going on, or why we are incarcerated in this gloomy tower.'

'You will remember, my dear, that just over a year ago Lord Edward made a pact with Simon de Montfort. It also meant that Lord Edward was willing to wage war against the king.'

'Who?' Dolores asked. 'The French king?'

'No, no. Our king. His own father, King Henry. I can only surmise that Edward was seduced into such wrong-headed action by de Montfort's fanatical certainty. Many people, from paupers to princes, can be persuaded to follow a leader, even against their own conscience, however unscrupulous and plain wrong that leader may be, if the cause is unwaveringly stated with complete unbending moral certainty, especially when reinforced by the assurance that God's will is being carried out. While his father was away in France, Lord Edward staged a *coup d'état*. He overrode the ruling baronial council and, with the help of the Marcher lords and other supporters, he seized back all of his castles in England and placed trusted custodians in charge of each one, thus clamping a military stranglehold on the entire realm. For all intents and purposes, Lord Edward had deposed his own father.'

Dolores said to Leonora: 'I remember that horrible Christmas we spent at Bristol Castle, my lady. You said that you were afraid to approach Lord Edward because of his foul temper.'

'Yes,' Leonora said. 'Lord Edward was unable to control his guilt at his usurpation of his own father's authority. He prayed often for divine guidance. He paced and spat and snarled like a caged tiger. Even I was sore afraid.'

I said: 'My liege lord is basically an honourable, loyal and God-fearing prince. He is, let us not forget, still only twenty-one years of age. I fear that the Devil, by playing on Lord Edward's impatience to rule, may have used his youth to lead him astray.'

'A devil named de Montfort,' Leonora said bitterly.

I said: 'Thank God for Earl Richard of Cornwall. After months of upheaval, Earl Richard's strength and diplomacy restored his brother to the throne, persuaded the king and queen to forgive their rebellious son and put de Montfort on trial, but de Montfort has luckily avoided his fate.'

'Why is that?' Dolores asked.

'News arrived that Prince Llewelyn was marching to invade England. The parliament during which de Montfort was to be tried had to be abandoned so that the nobles could meet the threat.'

'So why has Earl Simon not been put back on trial?' Dolores asked.

'Because Lord Edward and Earl Simon made a deal with Richard de Clare, Earl of Gloucester. His wealth and military power makes him a man who cannot be ignored and he had been supporting the king but agreed to transfer his allegiance to Lord Edward and Earl Simon. No doubt he was well-rewarded in some way for betraying the king. During the October parliament at Westminster, the three men simply announced that they now controlled the government of the country. The king, despite retaining his throne and being assured that his position as the monarch was not being threatened, did not have the military authority to prevent this new coup. But what King Henry has done, most courageously, is to order us to retreat here behind the impregnable Tower of London, which is why we, together with the king's most loyal supporters, languish behind these stout stone and flint walls, safe but impotent.'

Leonora ceased her tapestry and, unable to contain herself any longer, ordered: 'Enough of this babble. Come then, Hamo, you have tortured us for long enough. What action do you propose?'

'My lady, the baronial reform movement is losing momentum and becoming less and less popular. The fact that Lord Edward has brought this man Aymer de Valence from Gascony indicates that he feels he needs the extra support of the Lusignans. Lord Edward loves his father and we have seen that he suffers the torment of the damned for having betrayed him and usurped his authority. He surely cannot trust de Montfort or de Clare. Now that my liege lord's intemperate ambition has cooled, he must be considering returning his allegiance to his beloved father, the rightful monarch. If this Aymer de Valence can be persuaded to transfer his allegiance, and by definition the allegiance of the entire Lusignan clan, from Lord Edward and back to the king, then Lord Edward would have to give serious thought to also giving his allegiance back to King Henry.'

Leonora nodded thoughtfully. 'How can de Valence be persuaded to transfer his support to the king?'

'The usual way, madam, by bribery. Offer to return all his lands that were seized when the Lusignans were expelled.'

'So you wish me to speak to the king and try to persuade him to return this man's lands?'

'No, madam,' I said. 'The king will be only too willing to return lands to his favoured Lusignan clan. It is Queen Eleanor, who hates the Lusignans, you must persuade. She must be made to see that, in this way, she will regain her son.'

'Then I will do my best. I am comforted by your wise advice, Hamo.'

'Thank you, my lady. With your permission I will now withdraw.'

Dolores said: 'May I also withdraw for a few minutes to speak with Hamo, my lady?'

'Yes, of course,' Leonora replied. 'Send the rest of my ladies back to my chamber.'

Dolores and I bowed and quit the chamber. As soon as we had left and were walking through the antechamber, Dolores rounded on me.

'Why did you see fit to embarrass me in front of my mistress?'

'In what way?'

'By accusing me of consorting with Robert Burnell. I am doing no such thing.'

'So you say, my dear,' I said equably, but inwardly unable to control the gnawing pangs of jealousy.

'Was I not an attentive wife during your recent illness? Did I not do everything in my power to return you to health?'

'Yes.'

'Was that the behaviour of a wife who was cuckolding you with another man?'

I shifted uncomfortably under her accusatory gaze but did not reply.

'Anyway, it makes no matter,' Dolores shrugged. 'You have probably just signed our death warrants.'

'What on earth do you mean, woman?'

'Do you really think that if Edward puts himself back in the hands of King Henry that Henry will let him live? Our security is in helping Edward destroy the king.'

'Shush, woman,' I commanded. 'Do not speak such treason in public, even in jest. You could not be more wrong! Henry could no more kill his beloved eldest son than he could kill himself. What Henry wants is for his strong and able son to return to his side, wholeheartedly, for the peace and future security of the realm. I am *frantic* for Edward to return his allegiance to the king. That is our true security. If the king is deposed and killed then there is no guarantee that Edward could keep the throne against such devious and formidable opponents as de Montfort and de Clare. If Edward falls then our hard won position in life will vanish. Our best interests lay in the maintenance of the *status quo*, with King Henry remaining as the anointed king and his son inheriting the throne, with all moral and legal weight, upon Henry's death. Your job is to support Leonora and help her to win Edward back to the rightful side.'

Dolores glared back at me. 'You damned ungrateful idiot,' she breathed. 'I just pray that you are right.'

Lady Leonora played her part well and King Henry, with the

support of Queen Eleanor, persuaded by Leonora at my behest, offered to return all Aymer de Valence's lands. De Valence accepted, changed sides and swore allegiance to the king.

We now waited to see if Lord Edward, having suddenly and unexpectedly lost his new Lusignan ally, would also return his allegiance to the king. But Edward still dithered. There was nothing further I could do to influence Edward's decision... or so I thought.

Then one day I was present, by great good fortune, at Windsor Castle when a king's messenger arrived back from Rome.

May 1261

The king's messengers were a tight-knit and intrepid body of men who shared amongst themselves, in strictest confidence, information which might benefit each other. I often used to visit them, pretending to be awe-struck by their manly exploits and strictly guarding my awareness of what they were sharing behind my mask as a buffoon, and sometimes learned information that I could turn to financial advantage.

On this day one of the messengers presented me with an almost priceless nugget of information and, as soon as I could without arousing suspicion, I bade them farewell and hurried to obtain an audience with Lord Edward.

I was dismayed to be told that Edward was away visiting his falconer. I found myself in a quandary whether to take horse and try to find Edward or wait until his return which, I was assured, would not be until late in the evening.

I fervently hoped that Edward really was visiting his falconer and had not used that excuse as a cover for some other clandestine meeting. I decided that it would be wiser to wait for Edward's return rather than to scurry off looking for him. I prayed that I would be in time to pass my information to Edward in order to prevent him making a disastrous move that could destroy everything.

I encamped in the stables courtyard, determined to catch Edward at the moment he returned, and ordered servants to bring me food and drink when needed. I did not abandon my station, ignoring all curious glances and impertinent questions. Once again my mask as an oddly-behaved dolt served to deflect too much inquiry about my unusual behaviour.

It was nearly midnight when my vigil was rewarded and Edward, preceded by squires and servants carrying torches and accompanied by a dozen or so of his high-spirited friends, trotted his favourite hunting horse, Ferrault, into the courtyard. I immediately went to greet him. I waved the grooms away and took hold of the rein of his horse. Edward looked down at me, not best pleased by my actions.

'What do you think you are doing, Hamo?' he demanded, in an irritated and distracted manner.

Conscious that Edward's companions might overhear, I whispered: 'My lord, you well know that I never trouble you with petty problems. I have become privy to some valuable information and I beg you to allow me to speak to you alone without delay.'

The grooms rushed back to help as Edward dismounted from his horse. He shooed them away again. 'Cannot this matter wait until tomorrow? I am tired and hungry after a long day in the field.'

'Tomorrow may be too late, my lord. My information may persuade you to make peace with your father.'

Edward, his curiosity inflamed by my statement, looked at me keenly. 'What are you talking about, Hamo? What information is this?' Becoming aware that his friends were waiting for their liege lord, Edward turned to them and said: 'Gentlemen, please go and take refreshment without me. I am trying to understand what this imbecile is saying. God enjoins us to be patience with the lame and infirm and it may take me some time to coax any sense out of him.' His friends laughed at Edward's sally and then went inside.

Edward took me by the arm and led me over to the courtyard gate. Servants with torches attempted to follow us but Edward bade them to leave us alone. They retreated but hovered waiting several yards away while Edward and I stood wreathed in the moonlight. He enjoined me: 'Speak quickly, Hamo! My stomach groans grievously for sustenance.'

'My lord, one of the king's messengers has this day returned from Rome. His holiness the pope has absolved your father from the oath he took at Oxford. The king now has papal dispensation to act as he wishes against the barons and, God forgive me, against you, my lord. It may be in your best interests to make your peace with the king voluntarily now, before this dispensation becomes public knowledge, and before he compels you to comply with his will.'

Edward looked stunned by this news. 'Are you certain of this, Hamo?'

'I overheard the royal messenger. He has carried back a document from the pope and is fully aware of its contents. The royal messengers blabber amongst themselves, my lord, and often know of such information before the recipients of these messages.'

Edward exclaimed: 'By God, Hamo, I have been in a quandary since that bastard de Valence defected to my father.' He began pacing up and down, ostensibly talking to me but in reality muttering to himself. 'I am burdened by debt and the king is the only one who can clear me of such debts. If your news is true, then returning allegiance to my father is the only sensible course of action. But it would mean betraying my loyal friends and supporters by returning to my father's camp. What is the honourable thing to do?'

Of course, Edward was not asking me that question but, in my frustration and exhaustion of waiting and in the face of Edward's obduracy, I temporarily forgot my position as a humble jester. I grabbed Edward's sleeve and hissed: 'You are a prince, my lord, and the future of this country is in your hands. Your loyalty is to your people and to your king. The honourable thing is to accept your royal obligations and return to your father's side.'

Edward's face reddened with anger. Forgetting the fact that he had once given me *carte blanche* to speak to him honestly and openly, the strain of recent events must have affected him and he roared: 'Do not presume to lecture me about my royal obligations, little man. I have raised you up high and I will just as swiftly cut you down again if you dare to speak to me thus. It seems that, once again, you have done me a great service but take care not to abuse your position.'

A show of servility was in order and so I hung my head and

murmured: 'Forgive me, my lord. It is my love for you and Lady Leonora, and for your mother and father, that prompted me to speak too boldly.'

Edward, mollified, grunted. 'I will think on what you have told me. I hope to God you are right about this papal dispensation.' Edward looked up at the waxen moon for a few moments and then mused: 'I am surprised by my father's deviousness. He has made a shrewd move. It is so shrewd that I see my mother's hand behind this. They have outwitted us all. Perhaps I did choose the wrong side in the first place.'

This time I kept silent.

Edward said: 'Thank you, Hamo. You may go.'

So, thanks to my intervention, Edward rejoined his father's side, making the change appear to be out of genuine filial love before it became *force majeure*.

Underhand betrayal was the reaction of most of the barons when Henry, free of the control of the usurping triumvirate now that Edward was back by his side, finally revealed his dispensation at the Winchester parliament a few weeks later. He made the announcement that the pope had absolved him from adhering to any of the Provisions of Oxford and promptly exacerbated the resentment by setting about dismantling all of the reforming work achieved by the baronial movement.

The black clouds of civil war now once again loured over the entire realm. Lord Edward was faced with the possiblity of having to wage war against men whom he had previously supported and who had supported him. He asked the king permission to withdraw to his lands in Gascony and the king consented.

While King Henry and Queen Eleanor remained in England, Edward, Lady Leonora and Dolores and I, together with a small band of Edward's loyal friends, crossed the water to France, far away from troubled England.

JULY 1261

In Gascony Lord Edward busied himself with the affairs of the duchy and appeared to lose interest in the volatile political situation back in England. I made it my business, however, to ascertain what was happening in England because Lady Leonora wished me to do so. Edward was, apparently, as taciturn with her about the situation as he was with me.

Our exile in Gascony also had the advantage of removing Dolores from the attentions of her paramour, Robert Burnell. I was unable to prove conclusively that Dolores was being unfaithful with Burnell but, in my own mind, I tortured myself with the certainty that she was.

The conflict between the king and the barons soured into a more bitter and menacing confrontation soon after Edward had exiled himself from England. The magnates had been stunned and enraged by King Henry's perceived duplicity in obtaining the papal dispensation that allowed him to abjure the Provisions of Oxford.

Simon de Montfort became the self-appointed figurehead of the festering opposition to the king's rule. He fomented opposition to the king's sheriffs in the counties and blatantly attempting to convene a parliament without royal authority. King Henry responded by recruiting foreign knights who were ready to journey to England to support the king's cause.

Civil war appeared inevitable and then, like a decisive strategem on a chessboard, one player moved and secured the king's position. Richard de Clare, Earl of Gloucester, defected to the king's side. With the support of this most powerful and wealthy magnate, King

Henry looked to have completely won back his authority. Opposition to his rule collapsed and Simon de Montfort was obliged to leave the country.

All this occurred while Lord Edward maintained his self-imposed exile and we spent several months in the relative peace of Gascony. The king made no attempt to recall his wayward son.

NOVEMBER 1262

T hen, at the end of November 1262, the news arrived at
Westminster that Prince Llewelyn and his Welsh army, with
surprising speed and ferocity, had overrun the Marches.
Emissaries were sent to Gascony to inform Lord Edward of the
Welsh invasion. I expected him to return to England immediately
but, cannily, he made no such move. Instead, he despatched me back
to Westminster to glean all the information I could, not about the
invasion but about the political climate in England.

King Henry, however, was not there.

It was another month, at Christmas-tide, before King Henry
and Queen Eleanor arrived back in England. Henry was in a
towering ill-humour. He had journeyed to Paris for negotiations
with France in order to once again settle the situation with Simon
de Montfort. Negotiations had come to nothing and, even worse,
the royal party had been visited by the plague. The king himself
had nearly been carried off and dozens of his friends, supporters
and retainers had died. To arrive back in London and hear news
that the Welsh were rampaging through the Marches, and had
made an incursion into Herefordshire, set Henry in to a fierce
dudgeon.

I happened to be in the council chamber at Westminster,
deliberately dressed in my full motley, when King Henry was raging
about the Welsh uprising to his advisers. Having enjoyed several
weeks of freedom with hardly any duties, I was in a sprightly mood.
Having enjoyed myself mocking some of the pompous aristocrats
gathered around the council table, I eventually found a suitable

opportunity to further Lord Edward's cause, as was my reason for insinuating myself into this meeting.

'What are we to do?' Henry flapped ineffectually, his usual stance when it came to military matters.

I leapt up from my cross-legged squat in the corner of the chamber and stood rigidly to attention. 'I am a fool,' I squawked, 'but a bigger fool allows the bravest knight in Christendom, the most noble prince in Europe, to languish in Gascony while his lands are being torched in Wales!'

'Sit down!' Henry ordered querulously.

'I cannot rest, sire, while my country and Lord Edward needs me!' I proceeded to march around the council chamber blowing an imaginary trumpet and making a fearful din.

Henry picked up a parchment document and then threw it down again in disgust. 'The buffoon is right,' he conceded. 'Where is my son? Has he been informed of this Welsh invasion?'

'Yes, sire,' someone murmured. 'Many weeks ago.'

'Then why hasn't he returned to help me?'

None of Henry's advisers dared to reply, which made him even angrier. 'This jester dares to speak while you remain silent. Order my scribe to attend,' he shouted. 'I will write to my son and command the ungrateful wretch to present himself here.'

I marched out of the chamber still blowing my imaginary trumpet.

1 2 6 3

Lord Edward arrived back in England in late February. He summoned me to his chamber to greet Lady Leonora. She entered the chamber followed by several scurrying and giggling ladies-in-waiting. She was wearing an elegant green and gold gown with a circlet of emeralds holding back her long black hair. She had put on some weight, which suited her very well, and the long restful sojourn in Gascony had performed miracles for her health and spirits. She looked dazzlingly beautiful. She was also carrying her new-born daughter.

She gave me her sweetest smile and I kissed her hand. 'My lady, you are more beautiful than ever,' I mumbled truthfully.

'Thank you, Hamo,' Leonora replied. 'I am well pleased to see you again.' Pulling back the soft woollen blanket which swaddled her child, she said: 'This is Princess Katherine.'

I looked at the grizzling and mewling red-faced child and made the appropriate idiotic cooing sounds of delight.

Edward said to his wife: 'I have instructed Hamo to remain here with you and Katherine while I am away on campaign against the Welsh.'

'I am well pleased, husband. I have missed Hamo's comforting silliness.' I bowed and shifted around on my feet as if stupidly embarrassed.

Leonora's praise gave me an unexpected frisson of pleasure. I was only too aware of Leonora's scheming and avaricious nature but she was a breathtakingly beautiful and charming woman and I was genuinely gratified to find her so well content with motherhood after losing her first child at such a young age.

I was soon to be spending much more time with Leonora and Princess Katherine because events conspired to force us back into incarceration in the Tower of London on the orders of King Henry.

JUNE 1263

Lord Edward returned to London and discovered that the citizens had turned against King Henry and that the royal family had retreated, once again, to the sanctuary of the Tower.

When Edward arrived to rejoin his family he was visibly shocked by the living conditions we were being compelled to endure. A few loyal troops remained to guard the gates of the Tower. Food and other supplies were almost exhausted.

Edward summoned me and I well remember him standing in the bleak and ill-furnished royal chamber. He was still wearing his chain mail but tenderly cradling his new-born daughter Katherine in his arms.

Despite carrying the infant he paced up and down and could scarcely control his anger. He commanded: 'Tell me what has been going on since I last saw you, Hamo. Speak freely and honestly. You are my most loyal and faithful friend, so speak without fear of my displeasure. If I display anger, it is not directed at you.'

'My lord, as you are no doubt aware, your father and your mother have become deeply unpopular since the king seized back untrammelled power from the barons at the behest of the pope.'

'Yes,' Edward agreed despondently. 'My father has reversed all the work of reform carried out after the Provisions of Oxford. This was stupid and unnecessary.'

'The king's actions have outraged many sections of society, not just the barons, and unrest has been erupting throughout the country. I have heard, my lord, that Simon de Montfort has returned to England to lead the rebellion. Is that true, my lord?'

'I regret to say that it is, Hamo. By the middle of May he had gathered an army at Oxford. When I heard this news I led my army south to secure the Channel ports and prevent the rebels bringing over reinforcements from Gascony or Ireland. But what has happened in London to cause my family to hide here in the Tower?'

'As far I understand it, my lord, London has supported the baronial reforms and the Provisions of Oxford.'

'Yes, that is true.'

'De Montfort sent an ultimatum to the rulers of the city. He demanded to know if they now stood for upholding the Provisions of Oxford or for supporting the king. The rulers of London decided to support de Montfort. The king and the rest of your family are now ostracised within their own capital city. None of the wealthy citizens of London will lend them a penny. The king wisely decided that the only course of action was to retreat here to the safety of the Tower.'

'These accursed Londoners!' Edward cried out. 'One day, I will make them pay dearly for their treason! You say that they have not allowed food or provisions to be delivered?'

'No, my lord. I have been making clandestine forays out of the Tower in disguise and bringing back as much food as I could carry concealed under a long woollen surcoat.'

'By God, Hamo, I am indebted to you for protecting the welfare of my wife and child.'

I shrugged modestly. 'I have done what I could, my lord. I managed to obtain some provisions with my own money but I wish I could have done more.'

'You have done much for my family, Hamo, and more than most of my retainers would have done. I am deeply grateful.'

I had begun to make another modestly demurring comment when, behind me, I heard someone entering the chamber. I resumed my idiot persona by cooing delightedly over Princess Katherine.

'Your daughter thrives, my son, but the country goes to rack and ruin,' announced Queen Eleanor, with a thunderous expression and totally ignoring my presence.

She was wearing a wimple held in place by a gold chaplet and a plain blue linen gown embroidered with small silver stars. Even in this simple garb she looked elegant and regally beautiful.

She began to pace up and down in an agitated manner. 'What are we going to do about it, Edward?'

Edward rocked his child up and down gently and replied, with a sibilant hint of sarcasm: 'Surely that is for your husband, the king, to decide.'

'Don't act the disingenuous loyal son with me, Edward. You know as well as I do that only firm action will extricate us from this mess. That turncoat de Montfort and his lackeys attack my estates everywhere. They blame me for placing all these so-called foreigners in positions of power.'

Edward replied, still in that dangerously mild and reasonable tone: 'De Montfort and his "lackeys" are not entirely wrong, mother, but what can I do? I join you and father here to discover that you have no food and drink, except what this gormless fool provides, no supplies, no soldiers and – worst of all – no money. What we need is money, mother, and lots of it. What am I to do? Ask foolish Hamo here to conjure showers of silver marks out of the air.'

I chortled merrily and mimed being a wizard by waving my arms around. Queen Eleanor regarded me contemptuously and then replied: 'I know where there is plenty of money, sufficient to subdue this insurrection.'

'Where?' Edward asked, suddenly alert.

'Where I keep my jewels, my son.'

Edward chuckled with derision. 'You mean the New Temple?'

'That is exactly what I mean. Not only could you repossess my jewellery but most of the wealthy citizens of London, those traitors who have turned against us, keep their riches in the tender care of the Templars. To seize their own money in order to fund their own subjugation would indeed be a gratifying course of action.'

Edward sighed with exasperation. 'The New Temple is the most secure and strongly guarded building in London, mother. It is guarded by a host of fanatically devoted Knights Templar. How do you propose that I break down those massive oak and iron doors and then fend off those knights while I spend hours loading their valuables on to a cart, or probably several carts, and spirit it all away to somewhere safe? Not to mention incurring the undying hostility of the Knights Templar in general, a body of men unhealthy to displease, even for a prince?'

'Those French knights who escorted you back to England would be sufficient to hold off the Templar knights. There are only fifteen or sixteen Templars guarding the church at any one time.'

'True, but breaking through those massive doors will still be nigh impossible.'

Queen Eleanor looked at her son in disgust. 'Perhaps you are not the man I judged you to be. Perhaps you take after your father too well. Perhaps you do not have the required courage or will to preserve our throne.'

Lord Edward looked as stung as if his mother had slapped him around the face.

I was familiar with the exterior of the New Temple building and I considered that it could be vulnerable in an unexpected way. Speaking in my most idiotic simpering manner I flapped my arms up and down and squawked: 'Birds fly into the Tower of London where our enemies cannot.'

Both the royals looked down at me. Queen Eleanor asked Edward: 'What does the fool mean?'

I could tell from his expression that Edward had understood my meaning instantly, but he said to his mother: 'I seems as if my fool is day dreaming and drawing circles in the air.'

Queen Eleanor looked at me, and then at her son, snorted with contempt and sneered: 'No wonder the realm slips through our fingers when you choose as your advisers drunkards, madmen and airhead dreamers such as this dolt. Your daughter in arms gurgles more sense. I will leave the three of you to play your childish games while I go to seek men who will act as men.'

I bowed low as Edward watched his mother quit the chamber. He was no longer seemed perturbed by his mother's sarcasm. He said to me: 'If I understand you aright, you mean that small birds can circumvent any number of guards and doors and gain entrance into the Tower by crawling through small orifices. We can do the same at the New Temple. We do not need to batter down the doors of the New Temple. If we can gain access in the same way, those doors can be opened from the inside.'

'That is exactly what I mean, my lord.' I explained my reasoning.

'Do you think you can do it, Hamo?'

I held out my arms to their fullest extent, flapped them up and down, and chirruped like a sparrow. 'Release me from my jesses, my lord, and I will soar or insinuate wherever you command.'

Edward laughed heartily. 'Come then, my new Strathbogie, let us prepare for your maiden flight!' [15]

Two days later, long after midnight on a warm and starry night, I watched as Lord Edward and thirty of his mounted French knights trotted slowly towards the New Temple. I was hidden by the shadow of a massive battering ram and the heavy open wagon upon which it was stored.

The moon-thrown shadows of the bulky church loomed over Edward and his men as they approached. The handful of citizens who were still abroad to witness this advance were summarily ordered to disperse and go home. None of these gawpers dared to challenge this command and the street was now completely deserted of onlookers. It was vital that no-one saw and gave warning to the Templars of the acrobatics I was about to perform.

Edward and ten of the knights dismounted and walked towards the main entrance of the Temple. The other knights remained mounted and positioned well back from the doors, ready to repel any surprise sortie by the Templars.

The main entrance was located in the old round church, double doors made from stout oak inches thick and strenghtened with iron staves half an inch thick. It would be nigh on impossible to batter down those doors, or to enter by the strongly barred main windows, but as I gazed up and studied, by moonlight, the small windows at the top of the church I became more than ever convinced they could be breached.

The building consisted of a round church with rectangular chancel attached to it. At the very top of the round church, just below the roof, was a ring of small windows. Each window was protected by a lattice of iron bars behind stained glass.

Lord Edward, wearing chain mail but carrying his helmet under his arm, walked up to the doors of New Temple. He drew his sword and rapped on the doors with the hilt of the sword. It took several long moments of rapping before a tiny observation hatch in one of the doors was opened and a voice asked: 'Who goes there? What do you want at this ungodly hour?'

'I am Prince Edward, first born son of King Henry and Queen Eleanor. I have come to retrieve my mother's jewellery. I have a warrant signed by the queen.' Edward thrust the parchment through the small aperture. 'Open up in the name of the queen.'

We had little expectation that the doors would actually be opened and, indeed, the parchment was thrust back through the aperture with the words: 'Come back tomorrow, my lord. I will not open this door tonight.'

Whoever was speaking had undoubtedly seen the heavily armed French knights accompanying Edward, and the array of mounted knights waiting to the rear.

Edward tried one more ploy. In a firm voice he cried: 'You dare to displease my mother, the queen? The Templars remain in England at the tolerance of my father, the king. Disobey this instruction and it will go hard for you and your entire order!'

'I will not open this door!' the voice shouted back, unperturbed by Edward's threat.

Edward stepped back, looked across at the wagon under which I was hidden, and shouted: 'Bring up the ram!'

This was my signal. I leapt out from the cover of the wagon and silently ran to the dark sanctuary of the shadows behind the chancel.

The wagon, drawn by four horses, trundled off towards the main doors. On the wagon was an enormous log of oak with carrying chains attached to it. It would take all ten pedestrian knights in unison to lift the battering ram and swing it against the oak doors of the church. It would take all night to actually batter down such doors and the use of a battering ram was merely a ploy to conceal the noise of my activities.

I carried a long coil of rope draped around my shoulders and a hammerhead axe stuck into my leather belt. Avoiding the stained glass windows at the end of the chancel I began climbing the wall. There was sufficient decorative stonework and drainage gargoyles to make my ascent easy although I soon found myself breathing hard.

I clambered on to the roof of the chancel just as the battering ram struck the doors of the church for the first time. The entire building vibrated with the impact. I gingerly made my way along the ridge tiles of the roof and nearly fell off as the impact from the second blow of the ram sent shivers throughout the stonework.

I reached the end of the chancel roof and studied the wide gap across to the sloping pinnacle of the round church roof. The only way to cross the gap was to jump and I frantically gazed through the moonlight to see a ledge or handhold that I could aim for and that was sufficiently strong to support my weight.

The impact of the third blow of the ram nearly knocked me off balance again. I was still considering how to accomplish the jump when, suddenly, the street below was full of running men. The Templar knights, wearing their distinctive white tabards bearing a red cross, had decided attack was the best defence. They must have sneaked out of the church by a side door and they now appeared around the corner armed with swords and shields.

Edward and his men carried swords but no shields. I could see Edward struggling to don his helmet as the two bodies of men clashed. I watched in fascination as the vicious street fight became more intense.

Edward and his men, caught by surprise, were being pushed back by the Templars. White sparks flew through the still night air as steel clashed with steel. Angry cries and the moans of wounded men floated up to my precarious perch. The mounted knights urged their steeds forward and, despite their courage and tenacity, I could see that the Templars were doomed to lose this encounter.

I recovered my sense of purpose. I had to act swiftly or all this bloodshed would be in vain. I could see there was a ridge of drainage tiles, intended to throw rainfall away from the roof, running all around the edge of the pinnacle of the church and above the small windows.

After trying to judge the amount of forward thrust needed for the leap, I launched myself over the gap and grabbed for the tiles. The coil of rope cushioned the impact to my chest as I hit the wall. I managed to grab on to the ridge of tiles, praying they would not give way, while frantically scrabbling with my feet to find a purchase. I found a crevice foothold at the instant my grip began to slip and, with intense relief, I carefully stepped down to a narrow ledge under one of the small windows.

Holding on to a shallow ridge of stonework with one hand I pulled out the hammerhead axe with my other hand and smashed the stained glass window. I had a short length of rope securely attached to my leather belt and I looped the other end of this rope through the bars of the church window. Secured by this rope I could now lean back and throw the noose of the long coil of rope over the pinnacle of the church roof. It was a much more difficult task than I had anticipated and soon I felt the sweat of effort and anxiety rolling down my back.

It took more than a dozen attempts as the noise from the fighting down in the street intensified. Eventually, with my heart now racing in panic, I saw the noose fly over the pinnacle. This rope now secured me completely and I could swing away from the wall and attack the lattice of thin iron bars with my axe. To my surprise this proved to be easy. The bars soon gave way under my pounding and allowed me to push back the twisted metal grille.

The window opening was narrower than I had anticipated. I began to wriggle my way into the aperture feet first but found that, whichever way I turned my body, my broad shoulders would not go through.

I wriggled out again and sat on the ledge with my feet dangling inside the church and my torso outside. I tried raising my arms above my head and scrunching up my shoulders. I decided it would work but, once through, I would be left dangling on the rope and would have to trust to luck that I could then find a foothold and free myself.

I wriggled my way through the opening but the jagged edge of the metal lattice caught my upper left arm and gouged a chunk of flesh out of my shoulder. I shrieked in pain and found myself hanging inside the pitch black church with blood pouring down my arm and dripping on to the floor below.

Fortunately for me, the builders of the church had inserted an arcade of niches a few feet below the windows. I managed to crawl into one, balancing precariously dozens of feet above the stone floor of the church, and untied the securing ropes. I could not retrieve the long rope to aid my descent but I still had the shorter rope to work with.

The darkness within the church below had the advantage of concealing my presence but the disadvantage of not allowing me to see anywhere to tie the end of the rope. I desperately felt around the stonework of the wall with my hand. I would simply have to begin climbing down and trust that I could find sufficient crevices and footholds to prevent me falling to certain death or serious injury.

Sweating and bleeding profusely, I began my descent. If anyone caught me descending I would have no chance to defend myself but, fortunately, this part of the round church was deserted. I managed to find enough crevices until my foot struck the pediment at the top of a thick column. I lowered myself down and examined the stonework of the column with my hand. It was ribbed and provided all the handholds I needed.

I clambered down like a squirrel down an oak tree and then, exuberant at my escape, jumped the final six feet or so. My exuberance cost me dear. I hit the stone floor and my ankle buckled beneath me. I collapsed on to the cold flagstones as searing pain shot through my foot. I cursed myself for my careless stupidity.

I slowly raised myself up and supported myself on the column until the pain subsided, but when I attempted to walk I found I was almost completely disabled and could move only with intense pain and difficulty.

On the other side of the church I could see the shimmering light of hand-held torches and candles shining through an archway and, well beyond the archway, the sound of voices talking and shouting.

I hobbled across the floor of the church towards the light and carefully peered around the corner of the arch. On the far side a group of ten men were gathered around the main doors. They were trying to listen and ascertain what was happening outside and animatedly discussing what action they should take.

Another violent shuddering crash rang throughout the church, which meant that Edward's men must have subdued the Templars and resumed work with the battering ram.

The Templars had made a tactical mistake. If the knights had stayed inside the church our plan would have been thwarted but we had calculated that they would be compelled to try to stop the doors being battered down, unaware that I would be attacking from within.

As I watched and listened to the group of men gathered around the doors it became obvious they were not knights or soldiers but merely clerks or servants. I doubted they would wish to die in order to protect the Templar riches.

Taking my courage in both hands I limped towards them and barked the order: 'Open those doors!'

Startled, the men looked around with blank astonishment to see a diminutive, sweaty and blood-soaked apparition hobbling towards them. One of their number, more courageous than the others, withdrew a dagger from his belt. I pulled the axe from my belt but as I did so my swollen ankle gave way and I stumbled to the floor.

The men moved menacingly towards me. I raised myself up to a sitting position, still clutching the axe, and shouted: 'You now have two choices. You can refuse to open those doors, in which case you will have to kill me and incur the severe displeasure of Lord Edward, the future king of England. Your knights have been defeated and taken prisoner. Lord Edward has resumed battering down the doors and he will not stop until they are down, in which case you will all be butchered. If, however, you open the doors, I will speak in your favour and you will be rewarded generously for your actions. Prince Edward intends to remove all the riches held in this place and all the blame will be placed on him. The Templars need never know that you voluntarily opened the doors. Use your heads, open those doors and save yourselves.'

The men looked at each other and, after a brief discussion, accepted that my reasoning made sense. One of them opened the aperture in the door and shouted: 'We are opening the doors. We claim sanctuary inside this church. We are not Templars, merely servants!'

I heard Edward's voice shouting back: 'This is Lord Edward. I hear your plea and sanctuary will be honoured. Open the doors and no harm will befall you.'

One of the servants was despatched to fetch the iron key with which to unlock the doors while the others drew back the six massive iron bolts that also secured the doors. The key man returned with the elaborate iron key, which was at least a foot long, and unlocked the doors. It took the strength of two men to draw back just one of the enormous oak doors.

Two of Edward's French knights, swords drawn, warily peeped through the doorway. They saw me sitting on the flagstones, soaked in blood, and turned around to say something to Lord Edward. The two knights entered the church and looked down at me. I saw the anger fire in their eyes and, without another word, one of them turned and drove his sword through the body of the nearest servant.

'No!' I shouted, but my plea went unheeded as the French knights poured into the church, their hot killing blood inflamed by the fighting outside, and butchered the rest of the servants.

The floor of the New Temple church was swimming with blood. This was the first time I had seen innocent men butchered with swords in cold blood. I felt sick to my stomach.

Lord Edward entered the church and asked: 'Where are you injured, Hamo?'

Despite my horror at the carnage I had witnessed, I decided to take advantage of a situation I had not caused and that was beyond retrieval. I replied: 'In my shoulder, my lord. I think I have broken my ankle. Those fellows refused to open the doors so I went at them with my axe but my foot gave way as I did so. I managed to fight them off but one of them drew a dagger and slashed my arm. They would have killed me except for your presence here, my lord.'

Edward looked down at me with a puzzled expression. 'Why, if they had disabled you, did they then decide to open the doors?'

It was a good question but I had learned well enough that flattery will disarm the wits of any royal personage, even one so lacking in personal vanity as Edward. 'I warned them it was Prince Edward who was seeking rightful access to the jewellery belonging to your mother and that your princely wrath and displeasure would be terrible if they killed me and refused you admittance.'

Edward knelt down beside me, his knee in my blood. 'Bless you, Hamo. I am more certain than ever that God has sent you to me. I will get you to a surgeon as speedily as I can.'

I smiled bravely, inwardly gratified at this latest evidence of the hold I had achieved over the future king. It made all the suffering I had endured this night worthwhile.

Edward's knights had found the chests of gold and jewels hidden within the New Temple and I could hear them smashing the strongboxes open with axes and sledgehammers.

Edward instructed four of his knights to lift me on to the wagon and escort me back to the safety of the Tower of London and then to find a surgeon to treat my wounds. I passed out as the knights lifted me up. [16]

I was only dimly aware of my journey back to the Tower of London. I was physically exhausted and passing in and out of consciousness.

I had been laid face up in the back of the wagon. I remember looking up and watching the passing jetties of the houses in the narrow streets, and the inky black summer sky filled with stars. I remember the intolerable rattle of the cartwheels on the cobbles and how the infernal noise roared through my aching head.

I must have passed out again or slept for several hours. I dreamt fitfully of lakes of blood, hammers smashing against wood and steel, and the screams of dying men.

When I awoke I was lying on a bed in a small and sparsely furnished chamber with whitewashed walls. I was wearing my breeks *(under drawers)* but was otherwise naked. I was covered with a woollen blanket and my head was supported by goose-feather pillows. Through a small window I could see it was daylight outside. The wound in my arm had been bandaged and wooden splints, tightly bandaged, were supporting my injured ankle.

I looked around gingerly, taking care not to move my throbbing head too quickly, and saw, to my surprise, that Dolores was sitting next to my bed and regarding me with an expression of tender concern. Such an expression gave me pause and persuaded me that I must still be dreaming, but Dolores helped me take a few sips of watered wine and dabbed a soothingly cool damp cloth on my forehead.

It was strange how Dolores seemed to regard me tenderly only when I was sick or injured. Perhaps it gratified some feminine need to nurture hidden deep within her soul.

The wine lubricated my voice and helped me to fully recover

my wits. Then I became aware of a furious noise emanating from somewhere outside. 'What is happening?' I croaked. 'Are we still in the Tower?'

Ignoring my questions, Dolores stood up briskly and said: 'I must fetch Lady Leonora.'

Several moments later Dolores returned with Lady Leonora and they stood on either side of my bed, both regarding me with smiles of tender concern.

Leonora took my hand and then bent down to kiss my forehead. 'God bless you, Hamo,' she whispered. 'Thanks to you my husband is now in possession of the funds he needs to defeat these infernal rebels. He will teach this traitor de Montfort a lesson with cold steel.'

I well knew that a warrior like de Montfort would not be so easy to subdue but, of course, I kept my counsel and modestly accepted the praise. 'Thank you, my lady,' I replied, pleased with the realisation that I had become a hero. 'May I ask if Lord Edward is here. Could I see him?'

'Lord Edward has left for Windsor where he is now gathering men and supplies with which to strike back at de Montfort.'

I made a loyally manful charade of struggling to rise from my bed. 'Then I must join him, my lady.'

Lady Leonora gently took my shoulders and eased me back on to my pillows. She smiled consolingly. 'Rest easy, Hamo. My husband has sent word that you are to remain here with us. He trusts you above all others to protect us.'

Even Dolores looked impressed by my noble effort to rejoin my liege lord and Lady Leonora's admission of the esteem which her husband now felt for me.

Dolores said: 'You must rest, husband. The doctor has examined you. The wound in your arm is clean and your foot is badly sprained but not broken. You should be able to walk again in a few days.'

I gave Lady Leonora a brave wan smile. 'Then I will be unable to entertain you and Princess Katherine with my acrobatics for a while, my lady.'

'Do not worry yourself on that score, Hamo.'

At that instant there was fearful crash as something was dashed against the wall of the Tower. Even through those thick walls the commotion outside was disconcertingly loud.

'What is going on outside?' I asked.

The two women looked at each other, mutually fearful and concerned for their safety. Lady Leonora said: 'The common people of London were not pleased by my husband's raid on the New Temple. They have taken to the streets and there is rioting all over the city. They even have the temerity to gather outside here at the Tower and attack us with rocks and stones.' Seeing the unfeigned look of concern on my face, Leonora continued: 'The captain of the Tower assures us that we are safe within these walls but we are trapped here. The peasants are demanding the renewal of the agreements that the king signed at Oxford, and the expulsion of all foreigners which, of course, includes Dolores and I.'

I mumbled some anodyne words of reassurance and then Leonora quit the chamber and Dolores followed her out. I heard them exchange words outside and then Dolores came back in. She said: 'My mistress has given me permission to stay with you and minister to your needs while you recover.'

'I could not find the words to comfort her.'

'She is sore afraid of what might happen to us. We are both "scheming foreigners" in this hateful country. She is worried for her new-born child, and for her future. Are you hungry? Would you like something to eat?'

'I need the privy first,' I said. Then, before I could bite my tongue, I asked: 'What is the reason for this new-found solicitous affection you have shown towards me over recent months?'

Dolores sat down next to me and took my hand. 'Perhaps it is because you are more of a man than I understood you to be.'

'Not convincing, my dear. More likely it is because our lord and master, Edward, is now so deeply in my debt that you anticipate more rewards and honours coming my way. Is that not so?'

'What if it is?' Dolores answered petulantly. 'These are hard and perilous times. Wealth and privilege and the protection they bring are not things to be regarded lightly.'

'And you have found that I am more adept at gaining wealth and privilege than you ever imagined possible?'

'Yes, I admit that is true. Also, my life here with you is more exciting and surprising than it would have been had I remained in Castile. I would have married my fat and wealthy aristocrat and I would have been bored senseless with my existence. I am a passionate woman.' She indicated to the window. 'Even all this commotion excites me, even as I tremble for my life. We are involved at the centre of momentous events. It is stimulating.'

She bent down and kissed me on the lips. It was the first time that Dolores had kissed me with true affection and passion. I found her kiss exciting beyond measure and I became aroused. Dolores noticed the stirring under the sheet and her hand strayed to caress me.

Still the bitter serpent of jealousy and cynicism would not let me accept my wife's gesture and I could not stop myself saying: 'Please do not toy with me, Dolores. Why this sudden desire for my flesh?'

Dolores replied. 'I am a woman like any other. When I see Lady Leonora cradling her baby daughter Katherine in her arms, I am surprised to find I become jealous. Something stirs inside me, an impulse so overwhelming that I cannot resist it. I want to have a baby and I want it to be legitimate. I want you to give me a baby.'

I could tell that Dolores was speaking the truth. It crossed my mind to confess to her that my real father was an exalted noble but swiftly realised I dare not. Such a confession might spark dangerous questions about my background

'Yes,' I agreed, 'I would like a son, a son who is well-formed and handsome.'

Having won her way, Dolores smiled at me indulgently, and began to unlace her bodice.

JULY 1263

We received reports that Lord Edward, by seizing Windsor Castle and raiding from that secure base, had attempted to provoke de Montfort into a battle or, at least, provoke an assault on the castle that could result in the rebels being defeated, but de Montfort was too canny to be lured into such a trap. He led his army into Kent where he seized all the Channel ports. Only the massive royalist stronghold of Dover Castle held out against his siege engines.

One day in July, it being a pleasantly warm afternoon, I was sitting cross-legged on the grass down by the quay and close to the protecting walls of the Tower. I was practising a new magic trick and attempting to learn, on the harp, a new *pastorela* to which an intinerant Gascon minstrel had introduced me.

I noticed a royal messenger emerge from the Tower and begin walking in my direction. He was wearing Lord Edward's distinctive livery. The messenger stopped in front of me and asked: 'Are you Pauncefoot?'

Needled by the man's peremptory and insulting tone, I replied mildly but with a firm reminder of my status: 'I am Sir Hamo Pauncefoot, Lord Edward's chief jester.'

Evidently unimpressed by my status, the messenger went on: 'Lord Edward commands that you join him at Windsor Castle with all possible speed.'

'Have you come to escort me?'

'No.'

'Has *anyone* come to escort me?'

'No. You must make your own way to Windsor without delay.'

I could not see any purpose in asking further questions, so I said: 'Tell Lord Edward I will do as he commands.'

The messenger nodded and walked away.

I threw down my harp on the lush soft grass and cursed. My liege lord had provided no escort and given no advice as to how I was to accomplish the feat of single-handedly joining him at Windsor.

Walking, in the guise of a peasant taking wares to market, would be the slowest but safest way, but I was still having difficulty in walking after injuring my ankle during the raid on the New Temple. To ride by horse would be to court danger, not least while attempting to avoid rebel patrols, and a wagon was even more impossible for the same reasons.

As I looked out over the gently feathering surface of the River Thames it became obvious that the safest and fastest route would be by water, to find a boat and row leisurely along the river, perhaps under cover of darkness or on the pretence of a fishing expedition or something similar. I could float as near as possible to Windsor Castle, find a sheltered place on the bank where I could disembark without being seen and slip past de Montfort's cordon. Such a plan was much easier to imagine than to actually accomplish.

I abandoned my music practice and went in search of a rowing boat. I found a skiff that suited my purpose and decided, as the weather was warm and clement, to make the journey that night under cover of darkness.

Early in the evening I was on the quay packing a fishing rod and other supplies into the skiff when Dolores came dashing out of the Tower and ran down to the stone steps where the boat was moored. 'Hamo, Hamo,' she cried, 'the queen wishes to see you immediately!'

Distracted by my tasks and making mental plans for my voyage, I asked irritably: 'Which queen?'

'Queen Eleanor, you fool! How many other queens are incarcerated with us in this frightful prison?'

'Why does she wish to see me?'

'How should I know?' Dolores replied, now thoroughly exasperated. 'The queen of England does not confide her thoughts to a lowly Spanish lady-in-waiting! She is with the king and she is not in a good humour. Hurry man!'

Fearing the worst, I followed Dolores to the royal chamber and was ushered into the royal presence. I removed my cap, bowed, and stood shifting nervously.

Queen Eleanor was pacing up and down the chamber while King Henry sat passively in an armchair by the window. He appeared to be deep in thought and less than happy with life.

'Pauncefoot!' the queen barked in English. 'I have heard that my son has ordered you to join him at Windsor and that you are making preparations to travel by boat.'

'Yes, my lady.'

'Good. I am coming with you.'

I was dumbfounded by the blatant insanity of the suggestion but I had perforce to remain in character as the eternally willing fool. 'Very well, my lady,' I replied happily, but glanced at the king in the hope of finding common sense from that direction.

Thankfully, the king, in no uncertain terms, said to his wife: 'Calm yourself, madam. What you are proposing is preposterous. It is far too dangerous. If you fall into the hands of de Montfort he will bargain with your life to compel us to abandon our sanctuary here in the Tower.'

I felt like applauding an excellent argument from that not always shrewd monarch.

'Unlike you,' the queen replied venomously, 'I cannot sit here and do nothing while the common mob insult us and de Montfort seizes the kingdom! I *will* join my son at Windsor. At least he is ready to fight for our freedom and your throne.' She pointed at me. 'Even this imbecile here is willing to fight, though he has not the wits to lace up his own shirt.'

I chortled merrily as if gratified by Queen Eleanor's insults, but then said: 'Forgive me for speaking without your leave, my lady, but I have only a small rowing boat, hardly big enough to carry me, let alone a fine lady like yourself.' I chortled again as if the whole situation was highly amusing.

'There you are,' King Henry said wearily, 'the fool speaks wisely. There is not room for you in his ark.'

'Then we will wait until morning and take the royal barge.'

I clapped my hands together with glee as if a picnic was being arranged. My glee was only half feigned because I assumed the queen's decision to take the royal barge had freed me to revert to my original plan.

The king made a contemptuous noise and said exactly what I wanted to explain. 'You would not get a hundred yards down the river in the royal barge! The mob, not to mention de Montfort's men, would spot you instantly. You would be in grievous peril.'

'Nonsense!' the queen cried. 'We will remain in the middle of the stream. I will take a few heavily armed guards with me, as well as my attendants, and this buffoon here will come with us. He has recently proved his strength and courage in a fight because he has not the wits to know how to be frightened.'

My spirits plummeted at once again being recruited into the queen's Argo. I looked pleadingly to the king to put a stop to this insane adventure but, as he usually did when confronted with a superior will, he caved in and simply said to his wife. 'Do it then, madam, if you are so intent, but mark my words, you will be the ruin of us all.'

The next day, at mid-morning, after saying farewell to Dolores and being presented with a letter from Lady Leonora to her husband, I found myself gliding along the River Thames in the royal barge. It was a long and sleek clinker built vessel, propelled by four oarsmen either side, with a round canopied shelter, made of wood and covered in embroidered velvet, at the stern. If that did not make our vessel conspicuous enough, it was also painted in vivid rainbow colours.

Queen Eleanor had ludicrously decided to dress herself as an ordinary woman, not considering that using the royal barge accompanied by eight fully-armed guards made our expedition as inconspicuous as a leper in a bagnio.

The London mob spotted us as soon as we had pushed off from the quay at the Tower. They commenced following our course up the river, congregating on both banks, hurling insults and any handy objects they could lay hands on. Many courageous souls embarked on boats to try to intercept us but the presence of the armed guards on board our barge dissuaded them from trying anything too daring.

It seemed possible we might accomplish our escape until we approached London Bridge. I had foreseen that this would be the most hazardous part of the journey but I was unprepared for the intensely hostile reception waiting for us. Even unmolested by the mob it was going to be dangerous to 'shoot' between one of the nineteen small arches under this miraculous structure. The London mob, warned of our coming, had invaded the bridge with astonishing alacrity.

The bridge was lined with shops, houses and taverns, some as tall as seven stories high and some that overhung the river itself. We could see people hanging out of every window, including St. Thomas Chapel. They were armed with rocks and stones, and even bows and arrows, ready to thwart our passage. The mob had even climbed down on to the 'starlings', huge prow-shaped blocks of masonry that supported the piers of the bridge, ready to clamber aboard or attack the royal barge as it shot the arches.

No-one on board the royal barge had the seniority or the courage to suggest to the queen that we must turn back so it was left, as usual, to the jester. 'My lady!' I cried, 'it is too dangerous to continue. Sore afraid as I am of failing to join Lord Edward, I would be more sore afraid of explaining to the king if any harm came to you!'

Inwardly I felt happy with the situation. Even Lord Edward could not blame me for failing to join him when I had been protecting his own mother, and this failure prevented my involvement in whatever madcap escapade Edward had summoned me to perform.

Queen Eleanor gazed at the mob waiting on London Bridge and baying for her blood. 'You are right, Pauncefoot. We must turn back.'

There was a cry from the stern of the barge. One of the guards was gesticulating frantically. We leaned out to see what he was pointing at. A flotilla of small vessels was now bearing down on us. They were manned by shouting peasants brandishing a variety of weapons, from swords and sickles to spears and barge poles.

We were now trapped between London Bridge and the armada moving up behind us. None of our pursuers, however, was carrying a longbow, but I had foreseen the need to fend off such pursuing vessels from a distance.

I clambered back to the stern and, almost shoving the queen to one side, retrieved a longbow and a sheaf of arrows that I had stored under the canopy to prevent them being damaged by water. The immense upper body strength I had built up in the sawpits of Portsmouth dockyards had been augmented by compulsory longbow practice during my youth.

I hastily strung the bow and selected an arrow. The pursuing boats were now only about fifty yards away. Supporting my body weight on the side of the canopy, and trying to balance to compensate for the unsteadiness of the barge, I drew back the arrow and aimed at the men in the nearest vessel. They saw what I was doing and frantically began to turn their rowing boat away.

I loosed the arrow and it flew with the savage hiss of an angry bee. The arrow struck an oarsman in the upper arm, causing him to drop his oar with a shriek of agony. The oar tipped up and fell into the Thames as the oarsman stood up and, with agonisingly futile movements, tried to pull the barbed arrow from out of his shoulder blade. As a demonstration of our aggressive capabilities, my shot had worked perfectly. The oarsmen in the pursuing boats ceased rowing, unwilling to face my longbow.

My feeling of reassurance was immediately shattered by the sound of an arrow buzzing past my head and falling into the water off the larboard bow of the barge. We had floated nearer to London Bridge and the mob, outraged by the injury I had inflicted on one of their own, had commenced firing arrows back at us. Fortunately we were still out of range of all but the most powerful longbows and they did not have an archer of sufficient strength and accuracy.

We were, however, still in mortal danger. I made a show of attempting to shield Queen Eleanor from the stray arrows with my own body. In desperation I abandoned my feigned idiotic demeanour and said to her anxiously: 'Madam, we must turn around and return to the Tower. We can fend off these boats behind us but to attempt to pass under the bridge will be fatal. We must go back.'

Queen Eleanor, her wits addled by shock and fear and also humiliation, did not notice or remark on my new-found common sense and replied: 'Yes, you are right, Pauncefoot. Oarsmen! Turn the barge around! We will return to the Tower!'

I looked around, trying to gauge from whence the nearest threat might come and then noticed, off to starboard on the bank of the river, armed soldiers running down to the river's edge within the grounds of a grand building situated about fifty yards further up the bank. The soldiers gathered on the landing stage and beckoned us to row towards them.

All protocol forgotten I tugged the sleeve of the queen's mantle and cried: 'Look over there, my lady! There are soldiers! Are they ours? Are they with us?'

The queen looked across to where I was pointing and exclaimed: 'Yes! That is the palace of the bishop of London. He must have seen what is happening and has sent his men to help us. They wear his livery and I know he is loyal to the king. We are saved.' To the oarsmen she commanded: 'Turn towards the bank, over there, as quickly as you can!'

The royal barge turned towards the shore with agonising

slowness. The flotilla behind us, already dissuaded by my longbow, saw what was happening and abandoned the chase. They had made their rebellious disapproving point and had no wish to tackle my longbow as well as armed and disciplined soldiers both on the shore and on the barge. So, with intense relief, we disembarked and took refuge in the bishop's palace.

The next day Queen Eleanor exchanged clothing with one of the bishop's washerwomen. With the bishop's soldiers escorting this washerwoman back to the Tower, with the London mob assuming she was the queen and hurling insults at her, the disguised real queen and I boarded a small rowing boat and simply joined the early morning water traffic on the Thames and, without anyone taking the slightest notice of us, slipped back into the Tower of London.

I bowed as Queen Eleanor, looking bedraggled and chastened by her experience, mumbled her thanks to me. I gurgled idiotically while inwardly calculating the handsome reward I would wheedle out of her devoted son for protecting this most foolish and troublesome queen. [17]

Two days after our abortive attempt to reach Windsor by way of the River Thames, Simon de Montfort led his army into London. King Henry was left with no alternative but to surrender to the rebels. He despatched orders for Dover Castle to surrender thus abandoning the port and any hope of importing military aid from abroad.

Only Lord Edward and his men held out against de Montfort but when Edward was informed that his parents had submitted and that the entire rebel army was marching on Windsor, with no possibility of any relieving army marching to his aid, he was compelled to agree to terms.

Simon de Montfort was now the ruler of England.

The royal family were allowed the comfort of house arrest in Westminster Palace instead of the Tower and, of course, they took their faithful jester and his wife with them. I had never known Lord Edward so desolate, angry and frustrated.

Soon after we had entered captivity at Westminster, he had summoned me to his chamber to berate me for disobeying his order to join him at Windsor.

He paced up and down while I explained the circumstances, exaggerating my courageous role in protecting his mother, and he accepted my reasons, with some mumbled noises of thanks and apology, but he was still morose and tetchy.

He said, as much to himself as to me: 'What to do now, Hamo? Where to turn?'

'My lord,' I replied, 'de Montfort has his own army, loyal to him, but it is not large and must perforce rely on the support of powerful magnates such as Clifford, Leybourne and Mortimer and their ilk. You must lure these magnates back to your side. I cannot envisage any other hope.'

Edward grunted. 'Yes, Hamo. Robert Burnell and I have been thinking along those very lines.'

For the next few weeks Edward stalked his political prey with all the subtle sleuth of a leopard. He feigned all smiles and swallowed proud spittle to remain on amiable terms with his uncle, Simon de Montfort, while slippery Robert Burnell oiled his furtive way into secret conclaves with de Montfort supporters who might, by guile or offer of coin or lush estate, be persuaded to transfer their allegiance back to Lord Edward and King Henry.

I do not exactly know what sneaky bribes were offered to those haughty magnates by the slippery tongue of Master Burnell but the kingly promises of future rank and ornament must have been abundant. With a few honourable exceptions these magnates were self-serving men, much more engaged by the lust for their own interests than they were for the true welfare of the realm.

I became frustrated because I could not take part in these political machinations but I had ample consolation in my wife's new-found affection for me. My life devolved into warming the marital bed with Dolores, in order to plant the seed of the child she now desperately desired, and to perform my duties as jester in order to laugh spark the dampened spirits of the royal family.

In September that latter duty was doubly required as Lord Edward was struck by two blows.

Messengers brought news that another of Prince Llewelyn's scorching campaigns in Wales had succeeded triumphantly. Edward's castles at Dyserth and Deganwy had fallen and Llewelyn now bestrode northern Wales with complete mastery.

A few days later, to compound Edward's misery, Lady Leonora, who was exiled in Windsor Castle and thus separated from her husband, sent news that their daughter Katherine had died. Croup had turned into pneumonia and the sobbing infant had died gasping for breath.

Over the succeeding years Edward and Leonora were to become inured to the early deaths of their children but Lady Leonora, at this time, racked with grief, uncertain about her future, and denied the loving presence of her husband, was plunged into a dark place of endless tears.

Then, in October, the gloomy prospect was suddenly warmed and illuminated by the sunlight of hope.

Simon de Montfort, protected by his soldiers and by gangs of armed London citizens, held a parliament in Westminster. Edward, claiming to want to comfort and console his bereaved and distraught wife, which was partly his true desire, asked de Montfort's permission to visit her at Windsor Castle. Edward also asked permission for his faithful jester and Lady Leonora's closest friend, Dolores, to accompany him, to further console Lady Leonora. His request was granted.

The next day King Henry, appearing to accept de Montfort's hegemony and control of the parliament, also asked permission to visit his distraught daughter-in-law because he could play no useful part in the proceedings. De Montfort, glad to be rid of such potential royal nuisances at parliament and not suspecting any double-dealing, readily agreed to the visit, and thus King Henry and Queen Eleanor joined us at Windsor.

Now it was revealed how adroitly Edward and Robert Burnell had organised the counter-coup. De Montfort could only watch in silent agony as virtually all of the powerful magnates abandoned the Westminster parliament and led their forces away to join the royal family at Windsor.

Not only had the magnates been tempted by the promise of rich rewards for their defection but they also yearned for the stability that only a strong king, anointed by God, could provide. The civil war had cost them huge amounts of money, they desperately desired a return to the old status quo and, as a bonus for the royal faction, Simon de Montfort's fanatical, self-righteous and didactic manner repelled them, and they were loathe to bend to his will.

Dolores and I remained safe and comfortable at Windsor Castle attempting to console Lady Leonora over the death of her daughter. Leonora's slim, pale and frail body, wasted by grief, became more ethereal until, in desperation, I lied that dead Katherine had spoken to me through God's will and fervently asked her mother to eat and drink and build strength to aid her husband in the forthcoming struggle. My compassionate lie, and the comforting arms of her dear friend Dolores, gradually brought Leonora back to sanity and, calmed and reassured, she took food and ceased her tears.

While life seeped back into Lady Leonora, King Henry and Lord Edward struck back at the rebels with unremitting ferocity.

In November, the cities of Oxford and Winchester fell to the resurgent royal army. By the next month, the vital port of Dover and even the capital itself, London, was in the iron grip of the royalist forces.

De Montfort, shocked and bewildered by this sudden change of fortune, was left to carry on the fight with his two sons, a handful of friends and a small army of fellow fanatics who still believed in the reforms promulgated by the Provisions of Oxford.

De Montfort now considered all-out attack to be his only course of action with any chance of success and launched a series of raids.

Now banners were raised and swords unsheathed all over England and the country swiftly degenerated into the long tormenting agony of full-blown civil war.

MAY 1264

Lord Edward was often away on campaign during the first few months of the year 1264 and we were sorely deprived of his company. This unfortunate but necessary absence of husbandly affection did not help his distraught wife to recover from her grief.

Then, one warm and cloudless day early in May, the swirling banners of Edward's army were sighted moving towards Windsor. Lady Leonora, unable to contain her excitement, rushed to greet her husband as soon as he had ridden into the castle grounds and dismounted.

The young couple embraced most touchingly and then Edward, who was hot, tired and battle-weary, took leave to divest himself of his chain mail and ordered his squires to refresh him by dousing his naked body with several pails of cold water.

After a feast of welcome in the great hall I was ordered to accompany the royal family to their private chamber to entertain them with soothing harp music while they took their ease.

Lady Leonora, still pale and thin but very beautiful, was attired resplendently in gold silk and snow white linen adorned with gold and jewels in honour of Edward's return home. She was touchingly content that he was home again and she could not help gazing at him adoringly.

Edward, wearing the red and gold royal surcoat, was making short work of a pitcher of wine, but Queen Eleanor, looking radiant in her blue and gold gown, was chafing to know how the campaign against de Montfort was progressing. Finally she could contain her impatience no longer and asked waspishly: 'Before your wits are completely befuddled by your Bordeaux imports, my son, tell me how our army is faring?'

Edward, relaxed and unruffled by his mother's barb, asked in return: 'You must have received reports, mother? You surely know the campaign is going well, thanks be to God.'

'Reports!' Queen Eleanor snorted. 'They are usually days, if not weeks out of date, and then usually censored as befits a woman's sensitive ears! Tell me the truth, Edward.'

Edward smiled, still unworried by his mother's aggressive restlessness. 'You must have been informed that we seized back considerable territory in the Midlands during March?'

'Yes, yes, but I have heard precious little since then.'

'You have not heard of what happened in Northampton last month?'

'No,' the queen replied, alert to Edward's smug tone. 'What happened there?'

Edward, with a self-satisfied smile, announced: 'We won a significant victory, mother. De Montfort's army was routed and we captured about eighty of his knights, including his son Simon.' The queen nodded in satisfaction and Edward continued: 'Then Uncle Simon attempted to besiege the castle at Rochester but my approach frightened him off and I pursued him back to London where he took refuge among those traitorous and benighted citizens who have so little respect for our station.'

The queen nodded vigorously in agreement and pointed at me as I sat cross-legged on the carpet. 'Those citizens would have certainly done for me if it was not for your fool down there. I sometimes suspect that yon jester is not such a fool as he would have us believe.'

I gurgled happily and tried not to betray discomfort at being the subject of the queen's shrewd royal gaze. Then Lady Leonora, bless her, deflected any suspicion by saying: 'Hamo certainly is dim witted, but God seems to brighten those wits when the situation necessitates, as He does with many poor folk who have been born to a low station and little learning.'

Edward raised his goblet towards me. 'Well said, dear wife, for Hamo has rendered us signal service over the years, like a faithful hound.'

Again I gurgled with feigned pleasure at the dubious compliment of being compared to a faithful dog, but Queen Eleanor had already lost interest in me and asked Edward: 'Where is the king now?'

'He is stationed outside the walls of London to prevent any move that Uncle Simon might make.'

Queen Eleanor nodded in approval. 'That is excellent. Now Simon is bottled up and cannot escape. We can starve him into submission, together with that recalcitrant London scum. My husband has done well.'

The queen's satisfaction with her husband's strategic prowess lasted barely two days. Once again we were gathered in the private royal chamber but this time accompanied by several favoured friends and relatives in a less formal setting. I was entertaining the assembly with acrobatics and magic tricks.

Edward was in a bullish and distracted mood, as were his companions. They all agreed that de Montfort was caught like a rat in a trap and it was only a matter of time before starvation would compel him to surrender.

Then a retainer entered the chamber and informed Edward that a messenger had arrived from the king and was seeking immediate audience with Edward. The messenger, wearing a blue surcoat with a badge bearing King Henry's coat-of-arms, was ushered in and bowed to the assembled royals and nobles, uncertain whether to continue.

'Speak,' Edward ordered. 'These are all trusted friends.'

Reassured, the messenger announced briskly: 'The king requests that you rejoin him with all possible speed, my lord.'

Edward smiled at his companions with satisfaction and said: 'Back to London, gentlemen.'

The messenger, uncomfortable at contradicting the prince, continued: 'No, my lord, the king is in Sussex.'

It was Queen Eleanor who recovered her wits most rapidly after this baffling announcement and asked the messenger: 'Sussex? What on earth is he doing in Sussex?'

The messenger was made even more uncomfortable by the concerned looks on the royal and noble faces. Edward reassured him: 'Speak truly and freely, man. No harm or blame will befall you. What is the king doing in Sussex?'

'The king considered the royal army would be better employed by subduing the rebels and safeguarding the ports in the south, my lord. The rebel army has left London and followed him. The king and his advisers are of the opinion that the rebels seek battle and the king has made a tactical withdrawal to the town of Lewes, where he requests you join him with all possible speed, my lord.'

The messenger was dismissed and Edward requested his companions to take their leave and prepare themselves for the ride to Lewes. Only his wife and mother remained, and me, disregarded, sitting cross-legged under a table.

Queen Eleanor could not resist commenting on her husband's hapless strategic decision. 'Why did he leave London to go to Sussex? He has let de Montfort spring the trap. All he had to do was wait patiently and de Montfort would have been forced to surrender!'

Edward, downcast, nodded and said wearily: 'What's done is done. No doubt Uncle Simon is seeking a decisive battle, which is now his only hope, even if it is a dangerous gamble.'

'Dangerous!' the queen scoffed. 'It is desperate! Given his depleted resources he cannot possibly prevail against our combined forces!'

Edward nodded again and then said: 'At least father has chosen a sensible course in withdrawing to Lewes. The castle is strong, and so are the town walls.'

Reviving his downcast spirits after another demonstration of his father's military ineptitude, Edward stood up and began pacing up and down the royal chamber like a caged beast. 'This is it,' he roared to no-one in particular. 'If de Montfort seeks a battle, by God, he'll get one. This time we'll finish him off for good.'

The royal women looked uncomfortable and did not reply. Edward asked them: 'What is the matter? Do you not think we will triumph, my father and I together.'

'Yes, of course,' Lady Leonora replied, 'but I fear for your safety.' She turned to me. 'Hamo, you must go with my husband.'

Shocked by this unexpected suggestion but unable to abandon my self-imposed mask to make rational objection, I blew an imaginary trumpet and replied idiotically: 'I will fight by my master's side and protect him from this monster de Monsterfort!'

'I do not expect you to fight, Hamo,' she replied, 'but simply to attend him and take care of his comforts.'

'But I want to fight, madam! There are many servants who can attend to my lord's comfort.' I hoped that Edward would intervene to quash this ridiculous idea. Instead he did the opposite.

'As ever, dear wife, you are solicitous for my comfort and welfare. It is an excellent suggestion.' To me, he said: 'You can soothe me and entertain me before and after we win this battle, Hamo. We might even find time for a game of chess. Perhaps your singing will also frighten away de Montfort's men!'

What could I do but join in the gentle laughter that greeted Edward's joke and simper happily at the thought of being decapitated by a broadsword if I happened to be in the wrong place at the wrong time?

So it was that, within two hours, I found myself dragged away from a comfortable domestic billet and most reluctantly joining Lord Edward's army advancing to this town named Lewes, which I had never heard of.

Looking back over all these years, however, it was a fortunate mercy that I did accompany Lord Edward.

Lord Edward led the mounted advance guard of his army into the Sussex town of Lewes two days before de Montfort's army arrived.

The May weather had been kind, the roads were dry and passable, allowing us to ride at the gallop most of the way, and our swift arrival had allowed us to take secure shelter behind the massive walls of Lewes Castle before de Montfort could intercept us or even be aware of our arrival.

We found that King Henry himself was encamped at St. Pancras Priory, about a mile to the south of Lewes Castle.

Like everyone else I was feeling bullish about the imminent battle. The combined royal army outnumbered de Montfort's depleted army by at least two to one.

A few hours after our arrival, once rest and refreshment had been taken, Lord Edward left the castle to visit his father for a council of war and ordered me to join his retinue. He did not inform me of what possible use I could be at a council of war. To my eternal humiliation, I was soon to find out.

The council of war, held in the refectory of the priory, consisted of King Henry, Lord Edward and his younger brother Lord Edmund, as well as several important magnates and Marcher lords. I was also excited to find that my father, Earl Richard of Cornwall, was in attendance together with his son, my half-brother, Henry of Almain.

To avoid offending the sensibilities of these august gentlemen with the presence of a mere jester I hid myself from view by sitting cross-legged at the other end of the long refectory table where I was able to listen to the proceedings.

It soon became apparent that King Henry, in his usual lily-livered fashion, was in favour of negotiating terms with de Montfort. Much more surprisingly, and to my filial disappointment, his militarily able and shrewd brother Richard of Cornwall agreed with him.

Edward, supported by the younger and more aggressive nobles, disagreed vehemently. Edward rose from the refectory table, unable to contain his furious energy, and I could glimpse his long legs pacing up and down the room. 'I beg you, father,' he pleaded, 'let us finish this troublesome Earl of Leicester once and for all. He now seeks battle because he knows that a decisive battle is his sole chance of emerging victorious. If he…'

'That is precisely why we should not give him a battle,' Richard of Cornwall interrupted. 'We should negotiate, delay, talk, bribe, do whatever it takes to undermine his strength and his cause. It will then soon collapse without any risk to ourselves.'

Edward responded: 'Your skill at negotiation and diplomacy is well known and well respected by all but I consider that negotiation will be the wrong tactic. If we allow Earl Simon to negotiate then we allow him time to regather his strength and support. Who knows how the situation may change if we delay? Who knows if some of our supporters might find it in their interest to change sides?'

Edward paused and I could well imagine him looking pointedly at some of the slippery and self-serving magnates gathered around the table, and also perhaps regretting his own role in supporting de Montfort against his own father.

He continued: 'Every advantage is now with us. We are secure behind the walls and castle of this town, we have ample supplies, de Montfort does not have the resources to besiege us, and he cannot launch a surprise attack. We outnumber de Montfort's army, and we are supported in this place by the cream of England's most skilful and courageous lords, most of them gathered around this table. Every advantage is now with us. For God's sake, and for your sake, father, let us strike down this quarrelsome earl once and for all.'

There were loud murmurs of approval for Edward's speech but King Henry was still not convinced, and neither was Earl Richard. He said to Edward: 'Forgive me for saying so, nephew, but you have never fought in a real battle. I do not doubt your courage, which you have proved time and time again at tourney and in skirmishes against the Gascon rebels, but a pitched battle is a different matter and, once it begins, it can quickly descend into chaos and much can go wrong. Why willingly hand de Montfort the opportunity to possibly defeat us?'

I could hear the exasperation in Edward's voice as he replied: 'I have the utmost respect for your opinion, uncle, but I think you are being over-cautious. I don't think we will ever have a better opportunity to finish this business decisively and forever.'

Edward stood two inches over six feet tall and, even from under my table, his dominating presence seemed to fill the room.

King Henry, who always preferred peaceful and inexpensive solutions, asked the council generally: 'What is your opinion, gentlemen? Should we negotiate or fight?'

The opinion was overwhelmingly in favour of Edward but Henry still did not acquiesce. Stalling for time while he marshalled new arguments for a peaceful settlement, he announced: 'De Montfort has sent emissaries to negotiate. We should at least listen to what they propose.'

'Out of simple courtesy,' Edward conceded irritably, 'but my mind is made up to fight, whatever terms are offered by these emissaries.'

King Henry answered firmly: 'I value your advice, as with all my advisers seated here, but I will decide whether we fight or not, my son.' He then ordered that the emissaries be brought in to the council chamber.

Edward was in a foul humour, having been mildly upbraided by his father in front of this array of formidable warriors, and the mood was tense, punctuated by tetchy and querulous comments, while we waited.

Several long moments later two men were ushered into the refectory. Their names and titles were announced and, judging by the strained tone of the perfunctory courtesies, they were two magnates who were known to most of the council members.

The two emissaries scarce had chance to state their case. After listening to their absurd proposals, which were plainly intended to buy time for de Montfort, Lord Edward lost his temper and roared: 'You can have peace, gentlemen, and your master and his army, if they present themselves to us with halters around their necks ready for hanging!'

The two emissaries, silenced by Edward's fearful outburst, looked to King Henry and asked him if that was to be the answer.

With surprising forcefulness the king supported his eldest son, although he could hardly disagree with Edward in front of de Montfort's emissaries. Henry barked: 'My son has given you the answer. Take that back to the Earl of Leicester with my compliments.'

The two men bowed low and bustled out of the room as quickly as they could.

Lord Edward, who now resumed pacing the room, was delighted and again presumed to speak before his father. 'Now, gentlemen, let us make what preparations we need, then get a good night's sleep and tomorrow the country will be ours again when this impudent upstart de Montfort is planted in the earth along with the spring grain.'

King Henry accepted Edward's summary, thanked his advisors and dismissed them, but Henry of Almain suggested to the king: 'Forgive me, sire, but should we send out patrols to observe what de Montfort is doing?'

Edward laughed and, standing behind his beloved cousin, ruffled his hair and teased him. 'What's the matter, Henry? Are you afraid that de Montfort might break into the priory tonight and steal your toys?'

The older men chuckled at this affectionate barb but Henry of Almain retained his dignity and composure and reiterated: 'Surely we should send out men to watch the enemy and warn us if de Montfort approaches during the night.'

Again the supposedly wiser heads chuckled, even Henry's father, Richard of Cornwall, who affectionately helped his son out of his embarrassment. 'In different circumstances your suggestion would be eminently sensible, Henry, but de Montfort will not dare approach the town tonight.'

At this moment I was seized by a terrible and consuming jealousy. Henry of Almain was Richard of Cornwall's son, and so was I, but I was made to hide under a table, like a dog, unknown and unappreciated by my father, while Henry of Almain, who was tall, intelligent, well-formed and honourable, enjoyed the open love and affection of our father and would one day inherit his titles and his wealth. I had to stop myself from crying out in anguish.

I had become dreamily rapt while bitterly ruminating on my lost inheritance when Edward's face appeared as he bent down to look under the table. 'Ah, Hamo,' he said in a jocular tone, 'I thought I might find you under there. Come out, little man! I am about to bestow a singular honour upon you.'

Enlivened and brought back to the present by Edward's statement, I expected that I was now, on the eve of battle, to be given my just rewards for my many services. I was excited by the prospect of the nature of this honour. What would it be? Perhaps one of de Montfort's estates after he had been killed on the morrow, or that of one of his supporters, or a title, or both estate and title!

Everyone else had quit the council chamber so Edward was able to speak freely to me. He regarded me with an amused twinkle in his eye. 'Your conduct and loyalty in recent weeks has pleased me greatly, Hamo. Therefore I am going to reward you with the greatest honour of which I can conceive.'

My excitement and expectation soared but I remained looking suitably humble as Edward continued: 'You, Hamo Pauncefoot, are tomorrow going to lead the attack on the rebel army.' Edward smiled broadly as he watched for my reaction.

My true reaction was to feel my bowels turning to water and my legs buckling under me. I clutched the refectory table for support and croaked: 'Forgive me, my lord, but I do not understand.'

'You will, Hamo, all in good time. Report to me in the morning. I will explain what I want you to do. In the meantime, make sure you rest well tonight.'

Little chance of that, I thought, as Edward swept out of the chamber and left me with black spiders of terror crawling inside my skull.

The prior, at the behest of Lord Edward, had granted me permission to make a bed in the warmth of the refectory rather than having to sleep with the snoring and grunting throng in the communal hall.

I helped myself to mouthfuls of the wine that had been left by the nobles but I could not dull the fear of what Lord Edward expected me to do on the morrow. Not only was I terrified of what he had vaguely suggested, I was annoyed that he had found his little tease so amusing, and I was becoming resentful that all the recent dangers I had braved for him had not yet resulted in any significant additional rewards whatsoever. Now he was threatening to place me in the front line of the gravest danger!

Exhausted after the long ride from Windsor and by the frightening events of the day, I finally drifted off to sleep well after midnight.

MAY 14TH, 1264

I was startled awake from my dream demons when the refectory door was flung open and crashed against the stone wall near my head. I had made my straw and woollen bed under a long oak side table spread with overhanging linen tablecloths, so whoever had entered so abruptly was not aware of my presence. I peeped out to see that it was King Henry, accompanied by Earl Richard of Cornwall, and another man I did not recognise but who was plainly nervous at finding himself in the presence of the king.

The man, who wore the apparel of a common soldier, was dirty and dishevelled, with wet straggly hair, and his surcoat was ripped and streaked with mud. The man's nervousness was understandable considering his disrespectful appearance and the vicious mood of the king.

Henry, who had thrown on an ermine-trimmed robe to cover his nightshirt, shouted out of the doorway: 'Where are my sons? Get them here now! And the rest of my council! They snore like hogs while my throne is in mortal danger! Get them in here now!'

I silently rolled back into the shadows under the table. I had observed that it was early morning with dawn beginning to break and pale shafts of light piercing through the narrow lancet windows. I needed a piss but I dare not reveal my presence while the king was in such a murderous passion.

Lords Edward and Edmund, Henry of Almain and other advisers, in various states of dress, entered the refectory. They appeared sleep-worn and bewildered by all the commotion.

When the council members had assembled, King Henry

announced: 'While we have been sleeping, de Montfort has duped us.' Turning to the nervous soldier, he barked: 'Tell them what has occurred.'

The soldier, in a tremulous voice, began: 'My lords, Simon de Montfort's army has seized the high ground to the west of the town. His army is already formed into battle array and is preparing to descend upon us.'

Henry of Almain asked: 'But how can this be? I sent some of my own men out into the hills to act as pickets and warn us of any approach?'

The nervous messenger bowed his head and replied: 'I am grieved to report, my lord, that most of those men became cold and hungry during the night and returned to the castle without permission. The few remaining pickets were killed as De Montfort used the darkness to move his men into position. I had to hide to save my life and I am the only picket to have returned with this warning. I wish to God I could have been swifter.'

Henry of Almain was about to speak again but Lord Edward interjected: 'Strike the quarrel about what went wrong. Now we must form our army into battle line with all possible speed. At least our men will be well rested while de Montfort's men must have had a sleepless night.'

'You are right, my son,' King Henry said. 'Go now and rouse the troops as swiftly as possible.' Edward strode out of the refectory, already barking out orders as he did so.

Richard of Cornwall asked the messenger: 'How is de Montfort's army arrayed? Did you see it?'

'Indeed, my lord,' the messenger replied, relieved at being able to report something useful. 'It is formed into three divisions of left, right and centre, and positioned on the slopes leading down to the town. Thus he has secured the high ground.'

'Where are his mounted knights stationed?' Richard asked. He was much the most experienced military leader present and the others were looking to him for sage counsel.

'They lead each division, my lord, with the infantry in line behind them.'

To his brother, King Henry, Richard suggested: 'It would be safest and swiftest to simply match their formation, sire. We have no time for clever strategies.'

The messenger boldy interjected: 'De Montfort keeps a reserve division at the top of Offham Down, my lords. It is arrayed the same way as the leading divisions, with mounted knights at the forefront.'

Richard of Cornwall nodded and said to the messenger: 'You have performed good service and will be well rewarded.' He turned to King Henry and said: 'I recommend that we do not need to keep a reserve, sire. We outnumber de Montfort's army and, thanks to this man, we have been warned of his deployment in time. I recommend we strike our enemy as soon as possible and with all possible force.'

'I accept your wisdom, brother,' King Henry nodded. 'Please find Edward and apprise him of our intentions.'

The refectory now emptied of noble personages as rapidly as it had filled up. I crawled out from under the table and, trying not to be noticed, made my way out to the jakes.

All this commotion was a promising opportunity to avoid whatever dangerous plan Lord Edward had in mind for me. I would lurk in the jakes and hope Edward forgot all about me while he rode off to tackle de Montfort.

My ploy lasted a mere few moments before one of Edward's servants entered the jakes and brazenly climbed up to look over the top of the line of enclosed cubicles that were reserved for nobles and high-ranking clerics. 'Ah, there you are, you idiot,' he sneered. 'You should not be stinking up these perfumed lordly shit-holes with your peasant turds. Lord Edward wants you up at the castle right away, although God knows why he wants a simpleton like you by his side at such a battle as will be fought this day. There is a horse waiting for you outside.'

'Very good,' I said, cursing the fate that had led me to this situation but well knowing I could not avoid the summons.

The town of Lewes was bustling with early morning activity and excitement in anticipation of the battle as I rode through the narrow undulating streets to the castle. The air was soft and bright with a welcome hint of warmth.

Since being so rudely awakened I had not broken my fast and so I took a few moments to halt at a market stall to buy cheese, bread and a flagon of wine to fortify myself against whatever ordeal the day would present.

When I arrived at the castle I was ordered to report to the field, about half a mile distant, where Lord Edward was forming his division into line of battle. I trotted down the lane towards the battlefield accompanied by the incongruous sound of chirruping birds, the scents of wood-sorrel and wild radish, and the confident greetings of marching soldiers and wagon masters leading their rumbling wagons to their allotted stations.

The hedgerows parted and there before me was the right wing of the royal army in magnificent array on a lush green field brightened by a host of meadow buttercups and oxeye daisies.

The final contingent of mounted knights were entering the field and joining their colleagues forward of the infantry. Scores of colourful banners, borne by the squires, flew above the knights. The early morning sunlight glinted off lances, swords, helmets and buckles in dancing waves as the knights moved into position.

Behind the knights the foot soldiers waited patiently, cheerful yet disciplined. Many of them recognised me and engaged me in good-natured banter as I slowly trotted on to the meadow. I smiled and snorted and simpered foolishly but did not reply.

Away to the left I could see Richard of Cornwall's division forming in similar fashion and, out of sight beyond Richard's division, was King Henry with his division.

Arrayed on the slopes in front of us, having seized the high ground with their daring night manoeuvre, was the left division of Simon de Montfort's army. They bore white crosses on their surcoats as their recognition mark. I was reassured that their army appeared to be much smaller than ours but I was still anxiously perplexed as to why Edward had ordered me to appear on this battlefield.

I was directed to the front of the division where Lord Edward, wearing a surcoat bearing the royal arms and mounted on Lyard, his magnificent black destrier, was ordering his men into line.

I trotted past Edward's noble and faithful knights and supporters and presented myself to the prince. After the initial shock of being outmanoeuvred by de Montfort, Edward appeared to be supremely confident about the outcome of the battle. 'Good morning, Hamo,' he greeted me cheerily. 'Are you ready to lead us into the fray?'

Shifting uncomfortably in the saddle I replied: 'Forgive me, my lord, but I still do not understand what is required of me?'

Edward smiled broadly. 'Why, Hamo, you are to be my Taillefer.' He ignored my look of bafflement and went on by pointing to the enemy. 'Yonder on that hill are de Montfort's mounted knights. Beyond them are de Montfort's infantry. Do you know of what his infantry is comprised, Hamo?'

'No, my lord.'

Edward's expression became thunderously serious. 'They are Londoners, Hamo. When the battle commences we will smash the mounted horsemen first and then I am going to take my revenge on the citizens of that traitorous city.'

I decided not to point out the fact that Edward himself had once been in league with de Montfort, so I simply answered: 'What do you wish me to do, my lord?'

Edward looked at me with the fire of hatred in his eyes. 'I want to treat de Montfort and his army of Londoners with the contempt such cowards deserve while, at the same time, raising the spirits of my own men who have been roused from their beds so abruptly to risk their lives with me.' Suddenly smiling he continued: 'As I have said, you are going to be my Taillefer.'

'Command me to do anything, my lord,' I said, 'but I do not understand what you mean by "taillefer"?'

Edward chuckled. 'I did not think you would, Hamo, so let me explain. When, two hundred years ago, my glorious predecessor, Duke William of Normandy, took possession of England at the battle of Senlac Hill, his faithful jester Ivo Taillefer requested that the duke give him the honour of being the first man to engage the English line. I cannot help but notice that you do not request the same honour of me today, Hamo!'

I knew, or at least hoped, Edward was teasing me and so contrived my expression to make me appear even more uncomfortable than I actually was, a reaction which delighted Edward.

'Fear not, Hamo,' he cried, 'I am merely making sport with you.' He pointed across to the end of the battle line where a wagon was standing. 'Go to that wagon, Hamo. My servants are waiting for you. They have your finest motley with them and one or two other things. Go quickly now, don your motley, and come back and lead my men into battle.'

'But, my lord,' I protested desperately, 'you know I am not a trained fighting man like yourself. How can I lead the attack?'

Again Edward grinned. 'Do not fear, Hamo. All will be explained to you.'

'Sire, what happened to Duke William's jester, this Taillefer you told me of.'

Edward, in high good humour, replied: 'Why, he rode in front of the English line juggling his sword in the air and hurling insults. Then he charged and drove his lance through the first Englishman, drew his sword and defied them all until they killed him.'

'Is that what you wish me to do, my lord?' I said, ready to turn my horse and make an escape if Edward said yes.

'No, Hamo, my faithful friend. You are too valuable for me to throw away your life. When the real advance takes place you will be left far behind. Go quickly now and know that you have my full permission to insult me in any way you wish. Go now.'

Exceedingly reassured I trotted off to the servants waiting at the wagon. A few minutes later, after finishing off my flagon of wine, I was dressed in my jester's motley, complete with cap and bells, drunkenly mounted on a braying ass, a wooden toy shield slung on my left arm, which was also holding the reins, and waving a wooden toy sword around in the air with my right hand.

I began to parade up and down in front of the line of mounted knights shouting: 'I am Prince Edward and I come to lead you to glory!'

'Show us the way, sire!' one of the knights shouted back.

'I don't know the way, good sirs! I haven't got my daddy here to hold my hand!'

I warily glanced across at Edward to see how this jibe had been received but he seemed to be enjoying this display as much as his men.

'Good sirs,' I shouted, 'I don't know how I got here! Prince Llewelyn chased me out of Wales and I had to steal my mother's jewellery to pay you all. My uncle de Montfort waits up on those hills to spank my bottom. Are you going to let him?'

'No, sire,' the knights shouted in unison.

Then Edward spoke up in a loud theatrical voice: 'Tell us, sire, those men waiting up there on the hill, from whence they come?'

I realised instantly what Edward wanted me to say. 'Why, you impudent knave, they are from the great city of London.'

'And are they going to win the day?' Edward bellowed.

'Of course not, you impertinent rogue.' I lifted my arse out of the saddle. 'I fart in their direction. That will see them off, the vile, pig-shagging, ugly, stupid bunch of peasants.'

The assembled nobles found my fart jibe hilarious. Encouraged by the success of my performance, and given false courage by the copious amount of wine I had consumed for breakfast, I shouted:

1: The Making of a King

'Are we going to let those cock-sucking London turd-eaters defeat us?'

'No!' was the concerted roar from knights and foot soldiers alike.

'Then follow your prince to victory,' I shouted, and in a fit of half-inebriated stupidity I rode off, swaying in the saddle and brandishing my toy sword, towards de Montfort's line of mounted knights waiting a mere quarter of a mile away.

I was clearly visible to the enemy as I drunkenly lurched towards them. They watched me impassively as, given stomach by the delighted shouts of laughter and encouragement from the royal army behind me, I waved my toy sword above my head and hurled scatalogical insults at the Montfortian host.

Then, to my utter horror, their line of knights began to move towards me. I cursed my show-off stupidity as my courage instantly drained away. I desperately tried to turn my recalcitrant donkey around but the cursed animal, transfixed and terrified by its approaching fellow equines, would not budge.

From behind me I heard Lord Edward's voice shouting the order to advance and then heard the thundering hooves of the royal chargers as de Montfort's men, now themselves charging at full speed, lowered their lances.

In a moment of mind-numbing terror, which instantly sobered me, I realised that I was going to be caught in the middle as the two lines of armoured knights clashed. My mind conjured haunting visions of my mangled body lying spreadeagled on the Sussex turf.

At last I managed to wrench the donkey's head around and, by ferociously slapping its rump with my wooden sword, forced the benighted animal to begin trotting back in the direction of safety, but it was too late.

Our knights swept past me, lances lowered and screaming defiance. I caught a glimpse of Lord Edward as he galloped past, shouting exultantly, tall and imposing in the saddle of his charger Lyard.

One of the royal chargers barged into my donkey and sent me flying backwards on to the ground. I landed on my back on the soft turf. I was badly winded but otherwise unhurt.

The two armies collided not more than twenty yards from where I lay on the grass fighting to regain my breath. The sounds of lances splintering on shields, the clash of steel upon steel, and the screams of wounded and dying men drowned my senses with a deafening cacophony.

The Montfortian knights had been smashed by the royalist charge. Dead and dying horses lay everywhere. Edward and his knights were pursuing those enemy who were still mounted up the hill and the opposing infantry lines had already broken in panic at the terrifying advance of our heavily armed horsemen. I looked around to see our infantry moving at a steady disciplined pace towards me up the hill to mop up the surviving enemy.

In the meantime, however, I was laying on the grass with no chain mail and only a wooden sword to defend myself. Dozens of dismounted knights were now fighting hand-to-hand merely yards from where I lay. I was transfixed and numbed by the sight of heads and limbs being severed by broadswords and battleaxes. The fighting was so close that blood from these terrible wounds was spattering my motley.

I scrambled back and tried to conceal myself behind the broken-necked body of my donkey. A Montfortian knight noticed my movement and, perhaps remembering the insults I had hurled, came towards me. He was wearing his helmet but I could see through the slit that his eyes were blazing with killing frenzy. His only weapon was a shattered lance but its jagged shards were well capable of doing for me.

My only weapons were my size, speed and strength. With agility born of panic I leapt to my feet and charged. I ducked under the scything lance and caught the knight around his legs. He toppled backwards, roaring with anger, and slapped the broken lance down upon my back time and time again but it did me no harm. The helmet that was meant to protect the knight now became my weapon. I grabbed the edges and wrenched it around with all my strength. I could not snap his neck but I had stopped him breathing and he struggled fiercely as his face turned purple and spittle drooled from his mouth. Then he fell silent and limp.

Bile filled my mouth and my breakfast rose from my gorge to join the slick of blood trickling down the hill of this hellish place.

I looked up to see my doom approaching. Another Montfortian knight, this time helmetless, had witnessed what I had done to his comrade and was charging towards me swinging a deadly ball mace. The great black iron ball, studded with spikes, swung around and around on its chain with an angry whooshing sound.

I was completely defenceless. All I could think to do was fall backwards and try to kick at the knight's legs. The ploy failed and the knight stood astride me and raised the mace to bring it down upon my head.

I heard a sound like the crack of a whip and a crossbow bolt embedded itself into the knight's throat. Blood spurted from his wound and he fell backwards gurgling and clutching at his throat.

I felt hands lifting me up as our infantry swarmed past me and on up the hill. The last of the dismounted Montfortian knights ran from the field.

I stood among the carnage, blood-stained and trembling with shock, scarcely believing that I was still alive.

My horror at having to witness this gory shambles was replaced by a another horror. What if Lord Edward was killed? Not only would I lose my friend and protector but most of my fortune and future would disappear with one blow of a sword.

I had often considered such a prospect but being so shockingly apprised of the appalling nature of warfare made me realise that even a formidable warrior such as Lord Edward could find himself done down, in an instant, by sword or axe or mace.

I looked up the hill to see if I could locate Edward. To my relief he was still mounted, his tall frame rising above every other knight on the field, and he was charging backwards and forwards striking down his enemies with furious abandon. I could hear him shouting orders for his men to regroup around him, which most of them were doing.

All resistance from de Montfort's knights had been broken and now Lord Edward, brandishing his sword and filled with pitiless blood lust, was determined to take his revenge on the Londoners who made up the bulk of the opposing infantry.

I looked across the field to ascertain what was happening to Richard of Cornwall's division. I was anxious that Earl Richard himself was not killed and thus deprive me of any possibility of claiming my true birth right.

The two sides were advancing upon each other but had not yet clashed, although the royal faction must have been hugely encouraged by Lord Edward's success on our field.

I was not trained in the arts of war but I fully expected Edward to halt his advance and turn his knights against the flank of de Montfort's division now opposing his uncle Richard. Such an immediate flanking manoeuvre would surely bring victory sooner, especially if King Henry was having success with his division. De Montfort would have been obliged to deploy his reserve division from Offham Down but with the royal army having numerical superiority by at least two to one, and with such warriors as Lord Edward and his friends joining up with Richard of Cornwall, the outcome of the battle would surely not be in doubt. But Edward simply kept leading his men forward, slaughtering as he went, until he was out of my sight.

I became seized with the fear that Edward and his men were being lured into a trap, perhaps to be ambushed by archers or the like, or at the mercy of some other devious ploy dreamed up by de Montfort.

I decided to follow Edward and do what I could to protect him and perhaps even persuade him to turn back and engage the flank of the enemy attacking Richard of Cornwall's division. I reasoned that my motley would save me from being taken seriously as any sort of threat by de Montfort's men and, judging by the carnage which lay before me, any of de Montfort's surviving infantry would have sheer survival on their mind rather than taking revenge on a humble jester who was plainly a innocent harmless imbecile.

I picked up a discarded sword, stuck a discarded axe in my belt, managed to grab a loose horse, mounted, and began trotting the melancholy path of destruction that would lead to Lord Edward.

Some victims were still alive, grievously injured, moaning and dying, some with limbs missing, and some with head severed from body, eyes sightlessly looking up to the scudding white clouds.

I followed the chain of corpses along the Downs until I was heart weary and sickened by this continual vision of death. For mile after mile there was no sight of Lord Edward or his men. I was certain I could not be taking the wrong direction but I considered whether Edward might have already turned his men back towards the battlefield by another route in order to support his father and uncle, yet the corpses kept on littering the grass.

At last I found Edward and his supporters, all dismounted, about three miles from where the battle had begun. They were gathered around a wagon. This wagon was Simon de Montfort's personal wagon and, as it was known he had recently suffered a broken leg, the royalists had hoped de Montfort himself might be hiding inside. They had broken in and slaughtered six or seven innocent unfortunates who had been sheltering inside after sensibly fleeing the carnage.

Edward and his men were swigging from flagons of wine found inside the wagon. Edward saw me cantering towards him and hailed me. 'Hamo! I am overjoyed to see you alive! And I see you have found yourself a better steed!'

As the other knights and nobles, now laughing at Edward's remark, were also observing my approach, I was obliged to don my idiot mask. I simpered stupidly and waved. 'A glorious fight and a glorious victory, my lord.'

'Indeed it is, Hamo,' Edward said. 'Did you see those cowardly Londoners break before our lances?'

One of the knights handed me a flagon of wine. I drank from it greedily, suddenly realising I had a raging thirst and being more than ready to blot out the ghastly sights I had witnessed with the balm of Bacchus.

'It was magnificent, sire,' I cried. Then, trying to pound some common sense into these laughing and celebrating high-born fools, I asked Lord Edward: 'Will you now return to help your glorious father finish off this rebellious scum?'

'Indeed so, my faithful Taillefer. You can lead us back to the battle where I will have high delight in helping my father and uncle to complete the destruction of de Montfort's army. Come, gentlemen, let us away!'

Edward and his retinue remounted, gathered behind him, and we set off at a gentle gallop along the rolling hills and through the lush warming grass back towards the town of Lewes. The men were in high spirits and were laughing and bantering with each other as we rode.

Gradually, however, the laughter faded as we came upon foot soldiers fleeing in panic and it became apparent they were not de Montfort's men but ours.

Nearing the battlefield we came upon a knight who was well known to Edward. This knight was sitting in the grass. He was white with exhaustion and blood was coursing down his arm. He was trying to staunch the flow of blood with his hand. Edward called down to him. 'Sir Geoffrey! What has happened here?'

Sir Geoffrey, who appeared much older than most knights, looked up at Edward with watery and accusing eyes. With stinging contempt and no regard for Lord Edward's rank, he replied: 'Where did you go, you cowardly whelp!? If you had returned to support us then the day would have been ours. Now it has ended in disaster. God curse you, sir.'

Edward was so shocked by this news that all considerations of royal etiquette were quite forgotten. 'You mean de Montfort has triumphed?'

'That, thanks to your hot-headed stupidity, is exactly what I mean.'

I had never seen Edward look so bewildered and crestfallen. He asked: 'What of my father? What has happened to him?'

'He fled the field, as did your uncle, both beaten.'

'Where are they?'

'I have no idea. We flew in all directions. This is a black day, and all that is said about you has proved true.'

This time Edward's royal sensibility was not prepared to overlook such aggressive and disrespectful hostility. 'What do they say about me, Sir Geoffrey?' he asked menacingly.

Sir Geoffrey replied more cautiously, knowing, in his grief and humiliation, that he had overstepped the boundary. 'No-one doubts your courage, sire, but your prickly hot-headed temper and your lust for revenge will make you unfit to be a king. If you are to become a great king, which I believe you can be, then you must learn wisdom and self-control. Help me get to my horse, damn you.'

Edward was distraught and chastened at the realisation of his disastrous tactical blunder. If Sir Geoffrey had physically struck him around the face he could not have looked more pained.

Before Edward could say any more there was a warning cry from behind us. A band of de Montfort's knights, wearing their distinctive white crosses, were galloping down on us from the east. Sir Geoffrey looked up and shouted: 'Save yourself! Flee and seek safety, Edward. Do not fight them, save yourself for the resistance!'

John de Warenne, Earl of Surrey, shouted across: 'Sir Geoffrey is right, my lord! We will hold them off! Retire to Lewes and find your father, if he still lives.'

Edward, and certainly me, did not need any second bidding. Splitting our forces, more than half remaining behind to delay de Montfort's knights, the rest of us galloped as fast as we could towards the protection of the town, the castle and St. Pancras Priory.

I was mightily relieved to have escaped de Montfort's raiding party. The custom of war was that princes and nobles were captured for ransom but humble foot soldiers, and jesters, were wont to be slaughtered without mercy.

We reached the town without further alarms and soon discovered that King Henry was still alive and had taken refuge in St. Pancras Priory. The remains of his army had gathered inside and around the priory to protect him. De Montfort did not have enough men to launch a full scale assault on the priory so, for the time being, the king was safe.

When we arrived Edward was told that the king was in the refectory, surrounded by armed soldiers, partaking of a meal. It seemed a lifetime ago since my meagre breakfast and, to my rumbling stomach and despite the horrors I had witnessed, the refectory seemed an excellent place to be.

We followed Lord Edward through the gloomy cloisters to the refectory. The rest of us stopped respectfully at the doorway as Edward went in.

The king, still clad in soiled and stained chain mail beneath his resplendent surcoat, was sitting at the top table. Edward approached his father and then dropped to one knee to kiss his hand. Edward was expecting a severe rebuke from the king but Henry said mildly: 'Thank God you are safe, Edward.'

'And thank God for His mercy in preserving your life, father,' Edward murmured uncomfortably.

King Henry, although trying to maintain his regal composure, looked ghastly. His face and eyes were hollow and his skin of a parchment pallor. He regarded Edward pensively for a few moments and then asked: 'Why did you abandon us, Edward?'

Edward answered, and it was one of the few occasions I ever witnessed him truly nervous and embarrassed. He said: 'We defeated de Montfort's knights handily enough, father, and then we pursued his infantry to destruction. We thought you and Uncle Richard would easily deal with de Montfort's other divisions.'

King Henry looked affectionately at his son and offered the only rebuke for the day's fiasco I ever heard the king offer to Edward. He simply said: 'That was unwise of you, my son.' Seeing Edward was close to tears, the king said: 'Come, join me and eat something. It will restore your strength and your spirits.' He looked across at the group of nobles, and me, gathered in the doorway and asked Edward: 'What is your jester doing here? This is no time for amusement.'

Edward replied: 'He fought by my side today, father. He conducted himself bravely. He has performed many services for me in this crisis. If you remember, he helped to protect the queen when she was threatened by the London mob during that abortive journey down the Thames.'

King Henry nodded, and in a loud voice called: 'Join us then, master jester. And the rest of you gentlemen. Join us in food and refreshment.'

And that is how I came to be sitting at the same table as the king of England, on the day of his most shameful humiliation, and next to his first-born son whose rash folly had almost certainly cost Henry his throne. I realised that I was wearing my blood-spattered motley and, for a moment, thought that the king might be offended. I looked around and saw that the clothing of all the men at the table was spattered with blood.

The priory servants rushed forward with plates of food and pitchers of wine to succour their distinguished guests.

Edward asked the king: 'Tell me father, what news of Uncle Richard, and brother Edmund and cousin Henry?'

'All safe, but Richard has been captured by de Montfort. He had taken refuge in the windmill but they winkled him out. He will make a useful bargaining chip for my victorious brother-in-law.' King Henry appeared overwhelmed with weariness.

I had been eager for news of my father and was mightily relieved to hear he had been captured and was still alive. He would have to pay a high ransom but I had little doubt that Earl Richard would soon be restored to the bosom of his family.

For a few moments the two royals chewed away in silence, while I hummed to myself like the dolt I was supposed to be. Then Edward asked: 'Where do we go from here, father?'

Henry, with a slight catch in his voice, answered: 'It is in God's hands now, my son. It appears that God has deserted me and I must wait for His verdict on my reign.'

King Henry finished his meal and we stood up and bowed as he quit the refectory. For the time being, Edward and I were out of earshot of everyone else in the room. I whispered: 'I beg your permission to speak freely, my lord.'

'Not if you are going to chide me for my hot-headed stupidity, Hamo,' Edward replied, with a wan and exhausted smile.

'I would not presume to do so, sire. You have naturally been shocked and chagrined by this day's events but permit me to remind you that you are still in a strong position. You have lost this day's battle but you have not yet lost the war. You still have your powerful allies, the Marcher lords. Your army is virtually intact and remains more numerous than de Montfort's. And, for the time being, we are safe within the walls of this priory. I venture that you will agree that your position is not lost and, indeed, is stronger than events have made seem plausible.'

Edward grunted sceptically. 'I realise you seek to cheer me, Hamo, but I'll wager de Montfort is preparing to storm the priory at this very moment.'

'But de Montfort is a devout man, my lord. Fanatically devout. To storm this priory with all the attendant risks of killing holy men, not to mention the king and yourself, would not find favour with the country at large.'

'Your argument is well made, Hamo. Yes, the earl is too shrewd to make that mistake.'

'He has captured your Uncle Richard and holds him hostage. I suspect de Montfort will seek to negotiate rather than shed more blood. And I can surmise who he will send to negotiate on his behalf.'

Edward looked at me keenly. 'Gilbert the Red,' he breathed.

I leaned forward to whisper but held my tongue as a group of knights passed our table and bowed in respect to Edward.

Now that Edward had grasped my meaning I wanted to spur him into action before all was lost. We were talking of Gilbert de Clare, Earl of Gloucester, known as Gilbert the Red because of his ginger hair and his fiery temper. He was immensely wealthy, courageous and ruthless, and controlled the most powerful private army in the land.

I urged: 'De Clare has serious grievances against your father over his inheritance but I suggest you try to persuade your father that de Clare is the key. Win him back into our camp, my lord, and most of de Montfort's power and influence vanishes overnight. Promise him anything, my lord, I beg you.'

My words of encouragement, like a bowl of hot potage on a cold day, infused fresh energy and confidence into Lord Edward. 'By God, Hamo, you do good service to remind me there are still many attacking moves to be made on the chess board of England.'

Edward's speech was interrupted by a royal retainer who approached the table and bowed. The retainer said: 'The king requests you join him in his chamber immediately. An emissary has arrived from the enemy camp to negotiate terms.'

'Who is this emissary?' Edward demanded.

'It is the Earl of Gloucester, my lord.'

Edward glanced at me and smiled as he rose from the table.

The negotiations lasted all day. Messengers went back and forth and, in the late afternoon, de Montfort himself arrived to approve and finalise the agreements being made. I, of course, could not be present at these negotiations but I soon found out what had been agreed from the mouth of Lord Edward himself.

He summoned me to his chamber late that evening and immediately launched into an explanation of what had been agreed. He paced up and down the chamber and it was apparent he was as much talking to himself, to make clear his own thoughts, as he was to me.

'My father has been compelled to accept the full implementation of the Provisions of Oxford, that damnable process that has so sorely troubled us. The king will be allowed to live at Westminster and will still be king in name but he will be controlled by a council of de Montfort's men.'

Edward stopped pacing and stood deep in thought, his face suffused with anger at the humiliation of his father's confinement.

I said: 'May I ask, sire, what has been agreed about the Lords of the Marches?'

'Umm?' Edward responded and, for a moment, I thought he had not understood my question, but then he smiled and said: 'Even de Montfort does not have the resources to keep those gentlemen in check. They have been allowed to return to their lands. They have made promises and taken sacred oaths promising they will not interfere to aid the king.'

I was seized with hope and optimism. 'I cannot believe de Montfort agreed to let such men loose. It is a grave mistake on his part. Knowing many of them are your friends, my lord, I hope you will forgive me for saying that the Lords of the March will not let the mere taking of an oath interfere in the preservation of their own interests. You can surely persuade them their best interests are to regroup and come back to your aid and restore the king to his rightful power?'

Edward smiled as if he found my enthusiasm endearing. 'My dear Hamo, it is not quite that simple. Uncle Simon is not so careless. To ensure the good behaviour of my Marcher friends, I am to be held hostage. As from now, I am effectively a prisoner. De Montfort already holds my uncle, Richard of Cornwall. Now he will hold me, and my cousin, Henry of Almain. If my Marcher friends move against de Montfort, or if my father does not keep to this bargain, our lives will be forfeit.'

I had been perplexed as to why Edward had summoned me, a

useful but lowly jester, to explain what had been agreed that day. Now I could sense why he had done so and what he was going to ask me.

Surely enough, he asked: 'I am to be separated from my beloved wife and family and go into captivity. I am asking you to come with me, Hamo. I know this will mean you being separated from your own wife and I will not order you to do this, but I believe your skills could be very useful to me in the weeks ahead, not to mention your entertainment, but if you do not wish to accompany me I will not hold it against you.'

Edward looked at me to judge my reaction. Although I was extremely reluctant to make myself a captive, there were two reasons I agreed to do so.

Firstly, I hoped it would mean I would be in close company with our fellow hostage, Earl Richard of Cornwall, and could possibly find evidence or proof to convince him I was his natural son.

Secondly, I realised Edward would hold it against me if I did not comply, as exalted personages are apt to do when their inferiors fail to acquiesce to their wishes, so I quickly decided that a flamboyant show of loyalty was the order of the day.

I dropped to one knee and kissed Lord Edward's hand. 'My lord, I have sworn that my life is yours to do with as you will. I will follow you into Hell if you wish me to.'

Edward took me by my shoulders, raised me up and then embraced me, his tall body towering over my short frame. 'God bless you, Hamo. Go and rest now. We are to be taken to Dover Castle in the morning.' Edward was putting a brave face on this prospect but I could see in his face that he had been deeply humiliated by the day's events and my gesture of loyalty had pleased him more than it would usually have done.

Early the next day, after the warming sun had risen to disperse a ghostly low lying mist, we began the melancholy and humbling journey, under close escort, to Dover Castle. After a few restive and frustrating days at Dover we were transferred to Richard of Cornwall's castle at Wallingford in Berkshire where, to my inexpressible joy, my father was allowed to join us.

Earl Richard had spent enormous sums of money on fortifying and adorning Wallingford Castle, inside and out, and this was his favourite home so, despite his confinement, he was pleased to be allowed back and reasonably content with his lot.

I was equally pleased to be closely confined with my father. My affection and admiration for his kindness, dignified behaviour and manly bearing increased immeasurably during the months we spent together at Wallingford. He would often tease me about my drunken humiliation subsequent to wrecking Wallingford priory with my Lusignan 'friends'.

Occasionally he would summon me to oppose him over the chessboard. He could not match the skill of his nephew Lord Edward and, despite my best attempts to lose, I often defeated him.

He once commented, puzzled by his defeat, as were many of my opponents on and off the chessboard, why someone who was such a dolt in most respects could summon the wits to best him at such a subtle game. I, of course, had to remain in the character of a simpleton while in his presence but I ached to openly express my affection for him and dreamed that one day fate would allow me to do so.

Simon de Montfort had interpreted no sinister motive in the request that I accompany Edward into captivity. De Montfort accepted that I was simply a dull-witted jester whom Edward required to entertain him through the long tedious months of captivity.

Tedious they certainly were for the royal hostages but I have to admit that, for me, it was one of the most satisfying and enjoyable periods of my life. I was living with my father, Wallingford Castle was comfortable, food and drink was plentiful and, while the royal hostages griped and chafed at their confinement, I sought companionship and entertainment with the servants, who were not aware of my knighted status.

There were drawbacks. I truly missed the charming company of Lady Leonora, and I passionately missed Dolores. Our frequent attempts to conceive a child had cemented our relationship with a new warmth and affection, and she now seemed satisfied with me as her husband. Our separation convinced me even further that I loved her beyond all reason. I tortured myself that such enforced separation might have driven her into the arms of another man, particularly the shrewd, ruthless and charismatic Robert Burnell.

Using unguarded windows, clambering down rough stone walls, and using concealed routes through the kitchens and store rooms, I found that, during hours of darkness, I could exit and re-enter the castle with only a small risk of being detected.

Twice I was arrested but pretended I was merely lost and, baying at the full moon, persuaded the guards I was demented by that celestial body and, after mocking my mental incapacity, they laughingly released me.

I accomplished a midnight mission to deliver a letter to Edward's loyal supporters and was able to establish a regular conduit of written information to keep Edward and the other royal hostages fully informed of the political situation in the country.

1265

During the early months of 1265, encouraging news began filtering through that de Montfort's regime was collapsing from the inside. He was an arrogant autocrat and he had lavished the spoils of war on his two equally arrogant and over-bearing sons.

Word reached us that the populace, common and noble, were becoming uneasy at the imprisonment of the heir to the throne. They were well aware that Edward was a courageous, wily, formidable and highly tempered man who would one day become a formidable king. He would remember, with princely abundance, those who had supported him and, with implacable retribution, those who had turned against him. Most of Edward's Marcher lord friends already felt this unease.

Then information arrived that Gilbert de Clare, Earl of Gloucester, the most powerful lord of all, was becoming unhappy at the way affairs were being governed, particularly as de Montfort had rewarded his own sons with so much but with so little to himself, the earl who had fought at his side against the king at the battle of Lewes.

De Montfort was no fool and decided he must take action to quell the unrest caused by Edward's captivity. In March, Lord Edward was informed that he was to be taken to Westminster Palace and reunited with his father, King Henry.

Edward was in a high state of excitement when he informed me of this new development. Edward had been allowed to leave the castle, closely guarded, to pursue his favourite pastime of falconry.

He ordered me to stay close by him as we watched the sleek brown birds swoop and soar over the River Thames sparkling below us in the spring sunshine.

Out of earshot of the guards and his retinue, we pretended to be talking about the hawks by gesturing towards them at frequent intervals.

Edward said softly: 'This is our opportunity, Hamo. It is now essential that I contact Earl Gilbert and win him back to our cause. We will all be together at Westminster but de Montfort will never allow me to talk to Earl Gilbert.'

'I could deliver a letter to him,' I suggested.

'Perhaps, but Gilbert would suspect a trap or a forgery. And a letter, if captured by de Montfort, would offer proof of my duplicity and would be used against me. It is too dangerous.'

'I could speak to him, my lord.'

'No, Hamo. I cannot allow you to reveal your true capabilities. Besides, Earl Gilbert would not accept the word of a servant, a jester.'

'You did me the honour of making me a knight,' I reminded Edward.

'It would make no difference to the earl. He would not respect such a person of short stature and lack of military prowess.'

Edward's thoughtless reference to my physical shortcomings cut me to the quick, but he was correct to think that Gilbert the Red would have naught but contempt for me. I swallowed my humiliation and suggested: 'Then send someone who is accepted as honest and trustworthy by both of you.'

'I have been thinking deeply on that, but everyone I truly trust is captured, and everyone Gilbert would trust is also captured or being watched. There is no-one I can think of who could carry out this task without the risk of betraying me and with the assurance to Earl Gilbert that the deal being offered is genuine.'

'There is one person, my lord.'

'Who do you mean, Hamo?'

'Lady Leonora, my lord.'

'Lady Leonora? My wife?'

'Yes. De Montfort would not envisage anything sinister or underhand about the earl wishing to pay his respects to Lady Leonora. She could meet with Earl Gilbert, state your case and offer him your assurances. He would surely trust your own wife and would not feel threatened by meeting her. I could deliver a letter to her and explain what you wish to offer to Earl Gilbert.'

'But my wife has no skill or interest in these matters,' Edward objected.

I almost laughed at the man's naïvety. I had no doubt that Lady Leonora was shrewd and strong enough to deal with Gilbert the Red.

Edward, after long moments of thought, found enthusiasm for my suggestion and cried: 'By God, Hamo, it's worth a try!'

And so we were escorted back to Westminster Palace where Edward was allowed a brief reunion with Lady Leonora, a reunion accompanied and closely observed by de Montfort's men.

I was allowed a private reunion with Dolores. She seemed well pleased to see me again but I was once more disappointed that she did not display the passion towards me that I had always dreamed of, and I again tortured myself with the worry that Robert Burnell may have been paying court to her while I had been in captivity. For the time being, however, I kept my counsel because I had more pressing problems to solve.

MARCH 1265

Lord Edward was formally reunited with his father at a grand ceremony held in Westminster Hall. This touching reunion was nothing much more than a masquerade and it became apparent that Edward would have little more freedom of action than while confined in Wallingford Castle.

It was vital that the royal faction found some means of extricating themselves from this situation before de Montfort became too powerful, perhaps powerful enough to formally depose King Henry and set himself upon the throne of England.

Lady Leonora was unable to escape her vigilant guards so I took it upon myself to arrange the crucial meeting with Gilbert the Red. Lord Edward had insisted that such a meeting should take place in total secrecy to avoid compromising Leonora and possibly instigating reprisals from de Montfort.

In my role as court jester I had free access to most areas of Westminster Palace, but I could not, without raising suspicion, contrive access to Earl Gilbert and speak to him secretly and privately as was desperately necessary. I decided the only way to meet him face-to-face was to sneak into his chamber and wait in his garderobe *(a primitive lavatory, usually situated within a small chamber of a castle)*.

I requested Lady Leonora to make herself ready to meet Earl Gilbert at a moment's notice and I managed to sidle into Earl Gilbert's chamber while the guards were distracted by flirtatious antics performed, too well for my comfort, by Dolores.

The garderobe was given privacy by a heavy curtain and was

positioned around a corner off the main chamber. It was narrow and dank but, unless anyone else used the earl's facilities, which was most unlikely, I was confident I would remain undiscovered. My most pressing fear was that the earl would take fright and impale me with his dagger or break my neck before I had chance to explain my presence.

I had to wait a long time before I heard Earl Gilbert and some of his supporters entering the chamber. Not long after their arrival I heard the garderobe curtain being drawn back and Earl Gilbert appeared round the corner preparing his attire to relieve himself. He saw me sitting on the wooden bench over the garderobe and reeled backwards in shock, uttering a cry as he did so.

As he reached for the dagger in his belt I held my arms up to show I was unarmed and started jabbering as fast as I could. 'My lord, I wish you no harm. Please do not cry out. I bring a message from Lord Edward and beg you to hear it.'

Earl Gilbert stared at me, his florid face blazing even redder than usual. One of his acolytes outside the garderobe shouted: 'Are you alright, my lord? We thought we heard a cry!'

Gilbert was silent for a moment, still staring at me, but then shouted back in reply: 'Yes, do not worry, I caught my arm on the wall.' Turning back to me, he said: 'You are Lord Edward's jester, are you not?'

'Yes, my lord. I am a man of slow wits and I beg pardon for this strange intrusion. Lord Edward knows that you are not allowed to speak to him but begs that you speak to his wife, Lady Leonora, on a matter of urgent concern, as soon as possible.' I pretended to stumble over these difficult words.

While Earl Gilbert was pondering what to do, I said: 'Lady Leonora waits for you in her private chamber. If you agree to see her no-one else will know about this meeting, you have her solemn word and that of Lord Edward.'

'Very well,' Earl Gilbert said, suddenly brisk with action. 'Wait here. I will dismiss my men and then I will meet with Lady Leonora.'

I nodded vigorously, simpering like an idiot, as he quit the garderobe. I could not hear what excuse he gave to his companions but a short time later he reappeared and ordered: 'Wait in my chamber while I take a piss as I had intended. Then we will visit Lady Leonora.'

Thanks to more flirtatious distractions by Dolores, Earl Gilbert and I were able to slip into Leonora's chamber unnoticed by her guards.

Lady Leonora was sitting by her fire screen. She looked pale but elegant in a simple white gown trimmed with gold. She appeared calm.

Earl Gilbert drew up a stool and sat down opposite her. He did not look pleased when I sat myself down, cross-legged, at the entrance to the chamber.

Speaking in French, Gilbert asked Leonora: 'Is this fool staying to overhear what we are discussing?'

Leonora replied: 'We will be speaking in French, which the jester does not understand, even if he had the wits to comprehend what I wish to tell you. He will guard the entrance against unexpected visitors. I should inform you that, as such imbeciles often are, he is completely devoted to Lord Edward and myself. It comforts me to have him with us. He is stupid and witless but possessed of surprising speed and strength. I assure you, Lord Gilbert, that he would not be afraid to break your neck if you tried to harm me, even allowing for your fearsome reputation.'

I had never loved Leonora more than I did at that instant when I saw the expression on Earl Gilbert's face as he turned to regard me with new respect. I returned his look with one of blank bovine incomprehension.

Turning back to Leonora, Earl Gilbert sighed. 'There is no need to fear me, madam. I know you must resent me as a prime cause of your husband's troubles but I do have honour, despite what many people think of me, and I would not sink so low as to assault a royal princess in the sanctuary of her own chamber. Let me remind you that you requested this meeting, Lady Leonora. What do you have to say to me?'

Leonora, her hands resting calmly on her lap, began: 'I speak on behalf of my husband and my father-in-law, King Henry, the rightful ruler of this realm, and with their full awareness and authority. You are aware that my husband has been made to give possession of his lands in England to de Montfort. It is surely apparent to you that Earl Simon seeks to place himself on the throne of England and, for his own protection, to… get rid of the king and my husband.'

'My lady!' Earl Gilbert protested. 'I assure you that Earl Simon has no such intention. Our concern is reform of the realm under the terms of the Provisions of Oxford and to stop the abuses heaped upon the land by the influx of the king's pampered foreign relatives. Earl Simon does not seek the throne for himself!'

Leonora replied in a deceptively mild tone. 'Let me remind you that Simon de Montfort once served as the king's royal lieutenant in Gascony.'

'Indeed he did. What of it?'

'How much concern did Earl Simon display for the rights and legal protection of the people when he ruled in Gascony?'

Earl Gilbert looked uncomfortable and did not answer.

Leonora continued: 'Your silence is eloquent, my lord. Simon de Montfort ruled that land with a rod of iron and showed not a whit of conscience or desire for reform. His law was made of steel, his reform his own ambition. Why does Earl Simon now display tender concern for such matters in England? Do you truly believe that de Montfort does not seek the throne for himself?'

Earl Gilbert grunted and said: 'It is possible.'

'Then consider that possibility, my lord, and consider it hard. Lord Edward asks you to be aware that he still has many active and powerful supporters. De Montfort made the Marcher lords promise to go into exile in Ireland but, out of loyalty to Lord Edward, they are refusing to comply. A new war is inevitable, sooner or later, even if Edward and the king are incarcerated as they are now. Edward is fully aware of the grievances you harbour against the king. They can be redressed. Your support for de Montfort has perilously endangered my husband's future throne, but all that can be forgiven and forgotten. Lord Edward wants you to understand that if you now move to his side, his gratitude when he becomes king will be bountiful. If, however, you continue to support de Montfort and your campaign is lost, Edward will move heaven and earth to hunt you down and destroy you. Your lands, your titles, your wealth, and that of all your future generations will be stripped from you. Your only estate in this world will be six feet of soil.'

Leonora's dark Spanish eyes flashed as she flayed into the earl, who sat like a naughty schoolboy, surprised and struck dumb by Leonora's eloquent vehemence.

Earl Gilbert cleared his throat and replied: 'You make your case strongly, Lady Leonora. You are a credit to your husband.'

Leonora did not acknowledge the compliment but urgently implored him: 'Move to our side, Lord Gilbert, to the side anointed by God and sanctified by law. King Henry will remember your action with gratitude, as my husband certainly will. You were friends once and can be again. Think you that if de Montfort seizes the crown he will sufficiently reward you after his two ravenous sons have taken their spoils? And do you think that if he usurps the throne and becomes king he will allow a rival such as yourself to remain so dangerously strong? If you move to our side then de Montfort is finished and your victory is also certain. Remain with de Montfort and your likely reward is disgrace and death.'

Earl Gilbert nodded soberly and replied: 'You have given me much to think about, my lady. Allow me to retire and consider what you have said.'

Lady Leonora nodded back in acquiescence. 'Think hard and long, Earl Gilbert. My husband will not seek your favour again, even if it means death or the loss of his throne.'

I leapt to my feet and bobbed up and down respectfully as Earl Gilbert rose. Dolores and I staged an argument to divert the attention of the guards while Earl Gilbert slipped out of the chamber and disappeared down the steps.

I went back in to Lady Leonora's chamber. She asked me: 'Well, Hamo, do you think we have succeeded?'

'I am not sure, my lady, but no-one could have been more eloquent and persuasive. I can see that when Lord Edward takes the throne he will have a consort fit to grace the realm as his queen. You have skilfully performed a difficult service for the king, your husband and for England.'

Leonora nodded in appreciation. 'I hope you are correct, Hamo. That man, with his blazing hair, frightens me.'

'Not as much, my lady, as I venture you just frightened him.'

Leonora smiled wearily. 'Please find Dolores and send her to me. I am quite exhausted by this confrontation and wish to retire for the night.'

I bowed and went to summon Dolores. My mind was in a ferment. Had Leonora said enough to convince the formidable Gilbert the Red? No-one could have performed the task any better. I recalled the conversation in my mind over and over again but could not decide if the persuasion had worked. My fate, the fate of the royal family and of England itself, now hung on Earl Gilbert's decision.

The next day, watched with amazement and utter consternation by Simon de Montfort, Earl Gilbert led his men away from Westminster Palace, out of London, and took route back towards his estates in Herefordshire. Lord Edward and the rest of the royal family were jubilant.

De Montfort, who had not received the slightest indication of defection from the formidable earl, was visibly shaken by this unexpected development. Gilbert the Red's shift of allegiance had delivered a devastating blow to de Montfort's ambitions of ultimate and permanent victory.

De Montfort was initially unsure how to respond to Earl

Gilbert's betrayal but eventually decided to follow him westward in the hope of persuading the earl to change his mind or engineer a rapprochement.

King Henry, Lord Edward and Lady Leonora were bundled into the royal wagon to travel slowly towards the west of England, and Marcher territory, surrounded by the whole of de Montfort's army to preclude any possibility of their escape.

Dolores was allowed to travel with Lady Leonora and I was occasionally allowed to enter the wagon to entertain the royal hostages. For most of the journey, however, I rode with the servants and retainers. It was early in the Maytime and the trees and hedgerows were decked out in green, the weather pleasant and the roads dry.

De Montfort and his advance guard rode fast and far ahead in search of Earl Gilbert and the faint possibility of rebuilding the alliance. Our prison convoy was nearly in sight of the city of Hereford when de Montfort unexpectedly reappeared among us.

Lord Edward and I were strolling in a meadow, stretching our stiffened limbs and taking our ease away from our arse-numbing saddles. Edward was simply dressed in a white linen shirt under a blue tunic, his long fair hair tumbling to his shoulders and, in some unusual manner that I cannot explain, he appeared to be enjoying the lack of responsibility and the informality of his enforced captivity.

We had strolled so far that the royal wagon was now out of sight. We were surrounded by a cordon of guards but they were keeping well away at a distance respectful to such an exalted personage as Prince Edward.

On a sudden we saw de Montfort, unaccompanied, riding towards us through the meadow on a dapple grey horse. He was wearing a surcoat, emblazoned with his arms, but no chain mail.

As de Montfort rode closer Edward watched him warily while I adopted my fawning idiot demeanour. I asked permission to take my leave but Edward snapped: 'Stay close, Hamo, and listen.'

Simon de Montfort, visibly angry, dismounted and strode

towards Edward, who greeted him with a cheerily ironic comment. 'Good day, uncle! This is an unexpected pleasure!'

De Montfort, bristling with bruised pride, his hateful square face scowling, looked at me and said to Edward: 'Send your fool away, nephew, I would speak to you alone.'

'You may speak freely, uncle,' Edward replied. 'Hamo does not understand French and he is too slow-witted to comprehend what we are saying even if he did.'

I sat down cross-legged on the grass, plucked a clover and examined it as if entranced by my discovery. De Montfort paced up and down restlessly and then burst out: 'Congratulations, Edward. You have outflanked me.'

'I'm sure I don't know what you mean,' Edward responded, pretending ignorance but with an unmistakeable frisson of satisfaction in his tone.

'What promises you must have made to the Earl of Gloucester to persuade him to desert me! And how you or your father communicated those promises when you have both been under constant watch, night and day, then God only knows.'

I thought to myself: you were duped by the unconsidered fool sitting humming at your feet, you arrogant turd.

Edward, thankfully not looking down at me, observed: 'Yes, God does know, uncle. The same God who anointed my father as king and will one day anoint me. I hope you pray to Him for mercy for you may not receive it from me.'

Even de Montfort, aggressive and formidable as he was, flinched under Edward's towering gaze and sibilant lisp, so full of menace and hatred.

De Montfort moderated his belligerent attitude and continued: 'You know full well that an army loyal to your father has just disembarked in Pembrokeshire, in territory controlled by Earl Gilbert. You have won Gilbert back to your side and now you have conjured up another army to march against me, together with your other Marcher friends.'

I was aware that Edward had hoped for, but had not yet been apprised of, this crucial development. His face betrayed no triumph or emotion. 'If that is so,' he replied softly, 'then it is my father's doing.'

'Bah,' spat de Montfort. 'More like Queen Eleanor's doing. She has more temper for such work than Henry does.'

'Well, you seem to have been caught in a neat trap, uncle. What do you expect of me?'

De Montfort stopped pacing and stood face to face with his nephew. He was almost as tall as Edward and the two of them radiated power as they stood their ground and locked horns.

De Montfort said: 'You were once sympathetic to what we were trying to achieve with the Provisions of Oxford. You know there is much in this realm that needs reforming but your father is bitterly opposed to these much needed reforms. It is not too late for a rapprochement between Henry and I. You now have sufficient forces to possibly defeat me but there is no need for further bloodshed. If Henry would agree, genuinely, to such reforms, perhaps moderated in some form, he could resume the throne with the country at ease. I would need some token of good faith and some guarantee of my future security, but the situation is not beyond repair. What say you?'

I looked up at Edward and his face bore the expression I had often seen when he brought down a stag or when one of his falcons stooped on its prey.

Edward, however, spoke coolly. 'What you say may be true and feasible, but why are you talking to me about all this? You should be talking to the king.'

'No, Edward,' de Montfort replied firmly. 'You are the key. You have the loyalty of your Marcher friends. You have sympathy with our reforming causes, whether you now deny that fact or not. You are the future king. You know that Henry's mind, after long years on the throne, is stuck in the mud like a broken wagon. You can broker a peace, some sort of agreement between us.'

'There has been much bad blood, uncle, imaginary and real. Your supporters have humiliated my father, imprisoned me, threatened my mother, slaughtered many of my friends and abused the sanctity of the throne.'

'Your hands are not so clean in all of this, nephew. You supported me once. And what of my sons, my family? They have suffered as well. That is why I ask you to help me resolve this conflict before there is more suffering.'

Edward nodded, as if in acquiescence. 'What do you wish me to do?'

'Talk to your father. I have to keep you in Hereford Castle for the time being but I will allow you visitors. Invite your Marcher friends to visit you. Persuade them away from any rash folly. If you can control the situation and win me guarantees then perhaps I can step aside and let Henry rule, unfettered, once again.'

Edward nodded again. 'Very well. After all that has occurred you are still my uncle and my godfather. I have no further wish for bloodshed. I will do as you ask but I cannot foretell or guarantee how others might react, especially my mother.'

'Very well. I trust God to bless your endeavours, Edward, for all our sakes.' De Montfort thrust out his hand. Edward hesitated for a moment and then shook it. De Montfort turned, remounted his horse, and trotted away.

Edward looked down at me. We were both grinning broadly.

'Well, my little Puck,' Edward chuckled, 'it is only a matter of time before I have that gentleman's head impaled on a spike above London Bridge. Uncle and godfather, my arse! Devil more like, and like the Devil he shall one day receive his just desserts. Come along, Hamo, we have much to do.'

MAY 1265

De Montfort installed the royal family in Hereford Castle, a most impressive structure, almost as large as Windsor Castle, overlooking the River Wye. The castle was defended by moats and towering ramparts such as to make any prospect of a siege impossible to contemplate without massive resources such as siege towers, mangonels and trebuchets.

De Montfort was true to his word and Edward was permitted to receive visitors. All visitors were searched for weapons and secret documents before they were admitted to Edward's presence and de Montfort, or one of his senior officers, listened to what was being discussed.

Edward displayed every appearance of complying with de Montfort's desire for a negotiated peace and the rebellious earl was well content with Edward's co-operation. What de Montfort did not know was that I was slipping out of the castle and delivering letters to Edward's Marcher friends who were lodging at a nearby monastery. These letters assured them of Edward's real intentions and requested them to connive in the charade when talking with Edward while under the auspices of de Montfort and his watchers.

I well remember my encounter with the Marcher lord Roger Mortimer. The only method I could contrive to contact Mortimer without being observed was to follow him into the communal jakes of the monastery.

He was a big, burly, lumbering man and, on this day, was wearing a thick brown leather surcoat, having been out practising his military skills. He somehow sensed I was following him and, as we entered the otherwise deserted jakes, he quickly turned around, seized me around the throat with his left hand, and with his right hand drew his dagger and held it to my neck with the point pricking my gooseflesh. His surly unshaven face and beady eyes were so close that I could smell his sour breath.

'Don't kill me, sir,' I blubbed hoarsely, genuinely terrified and hardly able to speak. 'I bring a letter from Lord Edward.'

Instead of letting me go, Mortimer tightened his grip. 'Who are you?' he hissed.

'My name is Sir Hamo Pauncefoot, my lord. I am Lord Edward's jester.'

'Jester?' Mortimer repeated. 'Yes, I know you. I have seen you at Lord Edward's feasts.' He released his grip and I stumbled backwards choking.

After recovering my breath and my poise I bowed and took Edward's letter out of my tunic and offered it to Mortimer. He looked at the letter warily, as if it might be poisoned. He did not take it. 'Why does Lord Edward send his jester on this errand? I know what you are. You are an imbecile.'

'Indeed I am, my lord, that is why no-one takes any notice of me. But I am nimble and acrobatic and I am able to enter and leave the castle when others cannot.'

Mortimer accepted my explanation and took the letter. He read it and his eyes widened with excitement. He looked at me and said: 'Tell Lord Edward I will be ready. Will you be able to remember that?'

'Yes sir, I think so, sir. You will be ready.'

'Then off you go back to the castle and do not get caught.'

I bowed, bobbed up and down once or twice and then ran out of the jakes.

The plan was put into effect three days later. Edward, on the night before, had asked de Montfort if he might be allowed out of the castle on the morrow to exercise his horses. De Montfort, well pleased with

Lord Edward's apparent efforts in brokering a truce, gave permission but ordered a strong and numerous guard for the prince.

The next day, after taking breakfast, I accompanied Edward out to the courtyard of Hereford Castle where grooms were preparing the horses. I was to ride out with Edward, on a pony and dressed in my motley, ostensibly to provide entertainment but with the real intention of disarming any suspicions about the true purpose of the excursion. To further disarm suspicions, Edward was dressed simply and casually in a plain grey tunic, albeit with a gold pendant around his neck.

While Edward was inspecting his horses we were left alone for a few moments. He murmured: 'Are you ready, Hamo? Are you certain you know what to do?'

I whispered in reply: 'Yes, my lord. Fear not, soon we will be free!' I was excited at the prospect of escaping the confines of the castle.

'Not we, but I. You are to stay here, Hamo.'

'But, my lord, you will need me!' I protested.

'Not as much as the king and Lady Leonora, not to mention your wife, will need you here to protect them. You cannot aid me in the sacred duty I have to perform.' I opened my mouth to protest further but Edward snapped: 'Enough, Hamo! Do as I tell you!'

One of the grooms returned and I could plead no more, even if I thought such pleading might succeed. Edward was right. There was little I could do to help him once he was free but I might be able to enhance my reputation by doing service to the remaining royal hostages.

We rode out of the castle and on to a meadow, known as Widemarsh Common, that sloped gently down to a wood about half a mile away. The warm air was scented with wild flowers, birds twittered gaily, and the billowing white clouds held no threat of rain.

The mounted armed guards formed in a wide circle around the edges of the meadow to allow plenty of space for exercising the horses but also prevent any possibility of escape.

My appearance caused merriment amongst the guards and I performed every antic I could conceive in order to distract them.

Edward made an elaborate display of testing each steed in turn and galloping them up and down Widemarsh Common until the horses were almost exhausted.

Gradually I worked my way down the meadow and closer to the wood. The mounted guards, and the guards on the castle walls, were losing interest in my antics.

Edward mounted his last horse, which had not been ridden to exhaustion, and suddenly spurred on towards the woods. He swooped past me and shouted: 'Now, Hamo, now!'

I was carrying an inflated pig's bladder on a long stick. I waved it furiously in the air as if idiotically excited by Edward's sudden charge.

Almost immediately I heard the thunder of hooves and charging out of the wood came about thirty knights, summoned by my signal, all heavily armed with lances and shields, aiming directly for the nearest cordon of de Montfort's guards.

Taken completely by surprise, the guards attempted to form into a defensive line but it was too late. I caught a glimpse of Roger Mortimer as he galloped past me at the head of his men.

Edward had almost reached the safety of the woods, where Mortimer's men were waiting to escort him, but he reined in and turned around to shout exultantly: 'Lordlings, I bid you good day! Greet my father well and tell him I hope to see him soon when I release him from captivity.' [18]

Edward disappeared into the wood as the two opposing groups of mounted men clashed. As the lances of Mortimer's men scythed into de Montfort's guards it was plain that the fight would not last long. The guards, despite being armed with swords and protected by chain mail, could do nothing against Mortimer's heavily armed shock troops.

Most of the guards were thrown from their mounts by the

impact of the lances. The others had the good sense to turn their mounts towards the castle and retreat. A few brave souls tried to stem the advance but they were cut down.

Mortimer called to his men to withdraw as soon as he saw that Edward was safely away. As swiftly as Mortimer's men had appeared they thundered back and disappeared into the wood.

My pony had been badly frightened by all this commotion. It bucked, threw me off, and ran away, but no-one was laughing at my discomfiture any longer.

I trudged back towards Hereford Castle as de Montfort's men ventured out to retrieve the bodies of their comrades and any weapons that had been left behind.

I had walked back over the moat and through the barbican when De Montfort's guards seized me by the arms and dragged me into the great hall.

Simon de Montfort himself was pacing up and down, in a towering rage, surrounded by apprehensive knights and retainers. My captors threw me down on to the straw in front of de Montfort. His brutish square face and burning eyes gazed down at me. 'What do you know of this escapade?' he snapped.

'Men rode out of the wood, sir,' I mumbled. 'They were dressed in such fine armour with pretty coloured surcoats. They rode… '

'Shut up! I know what happened. What part did you take in arranging this escape?'

'Me, sir? I am a simple jester. I don't know anything.'

De Montfort regarded me with a keen mixture of contempt and wariness. 'A simple jester, eh? A simple jester who seems to be constantly in the company of his master, especially when Edward is playing his tricks on me.'

'He is kind to me,' I simpered. 'I perform acrobatic tricks and play the harp for him. Would you like me to play for you, sir?'

De Montfort suddenly spoke in French to catch me out. 'Quel est votre nom?' he asked.

He had simply asked what my name was but I had been used to

defending myself against such ploys all my life and I was not about to be caught out. I just bobbed up and down nodding and replied in English: 'I don't understand, sir.'

De Montfort regarded me for several more moments. Then he pronounced: 'I don't trust you. I don't like you. Stay out of my way and don't give me cause to see you again. Take him away.'

I was roughly dragged out of the great hall, expecting to be executed but, to my intense relief, I was allowed to rejoin Lady Leonora and Dolores. I ordered Dolores to fetch me wine, and lots of it.

Having daringly escaped captivity, Lord Edward rode to Ludlow, accompanied by Roger Mortimer and his army, where they joined forces with Gilbert de Clare. The three men formed a new alliance, thus persuading most of the Marcher lords, and many other significant magnates, to join the coalition against de Montfort.

Those of us who remained in the thrall of de Montfort were made to follow his army. Dolores and I were allowed to travel with King Henry and Lady Leonora in the royal wagon.

I remember long hours uncomfortably rocking from side to side as we creaked from camp to camp. De Montfort had decided to move east, where there was more support for his reforms, and hoped to gather reinforcements.

Edward and his new allies, however, were determined not to let de Montfort escape. They deployed swiftly to destroy every bridge and boat that would allow de Montfort to lead his army across the River Severn. De Montfort was now trapped behind the barrier of the river and his only option was to keep his army, and his royal hostages, interminably moving around in western England and southern Wales in the hope that his desperate situation might improve and a saviour appear.

That putative saviour was his son Simon and the excitement in de Montfort's camp was palpable when a messenger arrived with the news that young Simon and his reinforcements had arrived at Kenilworth Castle.

JULY 1265

This messenger arrived when de Montfort, his senior supporters and the royal captives were installed in a monastery. We were surrounded by de Montfort's army, which was camped outside to forestall any possible assault to rescue the king.

I feared that if de Montfort's position became too precarious he might execute the king and perhaps Lady Leonora, but even de Montfort would be aware that such barbaric acts might buy him a little time but would cause utter revulsion throughout the land, not to mention the undying hatred of Lord Edward. I did not communicate such fears to Lady Leonora, whose life in this troubled country of England had already been tragically filled with the woe of lost children and civil war, and leavened only by the love of her husband.

I was in the refectory of the monastery playing the fool and hoping to overhear any snippets of information I could use to my advantage. After reporting to de Montfort the messenger had been sent to the refectory to take food and that is where I overheard information of the purest gold.

The messenger was sitting at the table with two of his fellow knights. He was chewing on a chicken leg and greedily guzzling wine. He was repeating the good news he had earlier communicated to de Montfort. The knights were talking in French and taking no notice of me as I sat cross-legged on the straw covered floor humming quietly to myself.

The messenger was saying: '... our approach forced Edward and his army to retreat to Worcester. That move caught the haughty prince by surprise.'

One of his companions grunted and said: 'Don't underestimate Lord Edward. He lost his head at the battle of Lewes but he won't make that mistake again. I have fought against him, and with him, in tournaments. There is no more courageous man in the land, although young Simon will be safe behind the walls of Kenilworth, even from Lord Edward.'

It was the messenger's turn to grunt sceptically. 'Young Simon thinks he is safe enough from attack without bothering to hide in the castle. He and his men are enjoying the delights of the town, the beds, the baths, the ale houses and the women. It's fortunate that Edward does not know of this insouciance or Simon would not feel so secure while he is tupping the local whores!'

I was casually making my way out of the refectory, as if unconcerned about anything, to seek out Lady Leonora even while the three men were still laughing at the messenger's scabrous comment.

Leonora was in the spacious and well-appointed chamber that, out of respect for her rank, had been allotted to her. The two guards stationed outside the door were used to my comings and goings and allowed me entry without demure. Leonora was accompanied by Dolores and two other ladies-in-waiting. The women were sewing and chatting but looking intensely bored with life.

I whispered my request to Dolores who, in turn, whispered to Lady Leonora. The two other ladies-in-waiting were dismissed and the three of us remaining moved to the window as if interested in something occurring outside. Here we could not be overheard by the guards outside.

Quietly, I informed Leonora: 'My lady, I have just overheard reliable information that Lord Edward is encamped at Worcester and that young Simon de Montfort and his army have arrived at Kenilworth but are encamped *outside* the walls of the castle and at the mercy of a surprise attack. If such information could be conveyed to Lord Edward before the enemy moves again he could descend on them like the wolf upon the fold and destroy de Montfort's reinforcements before they are able to join up with the main army.'

Leonora, boredom now replaced by hushed excitement, responded: 'Then we must get word to Lord Edward, but how can we do so?'

'It is up to me, my lady,' I replied nobly. 'I must perform this service for Lord Edward.'

Brother Godfrey has stopped writing and is now regarding me cynically. He doubts the veracity of my account, and of my courage and devotion to Lord Edward. He has reason. As much as I admired Edward, my motives were also self-serving. I readily volunteered for such dangerous work because my stock with Edward, already high, would increase enormously if I could deliver such vital tactical information to him. My future safety and security was dependent on preserving Edward as heir to the throne, and so it was essential that Edward should be victorious against de Montfort. I was willing to take the risk. Now, cynical monk, take up your quill again. Where was I… ?

'Bless you, Hamo,' Lady Leonora said, with all sincerity, her expression betraying true admiration for my devotion. 'But how can you get away from here? De Montfort's men surround the monastery. Even a mouse could not slip through.'

'I know, and Earl Simon does not like me or trust me. Alas, my lady, I cannot, at the moment, think of a way of getting out.'

Leonora replied briskly: 'Then we must all think hard on this matter. We must find a way of warning my husband.'

We ruminated and discussed ideas for a long time. Whenever Leonora's other ladies-in-waiting requested entry, or any other visitor, they were preremptorily shooed away. We could not think of any viable plan until, by good fortune, the baby woke and began to cry. Lord Edward had performed his husbandly duty well and Lady Leonora was caring for their infant daughter Joan, who had been born in the January.

I suggested to Lady Leonora: 'Would you be prepared to act unwell, my lady, or to pretend that the infant is unwell? You could then claim you need a certain medicine from an apothecary. Perhaps de Montfort would allow me out into Hereford to obtain it, then I could make my escape from there. Despite this current conflict I think Earl Simon is fond of you and would not wish any harm to come to you or your child by refusing such treatment.'

Leonora seized on my suggestion eagerly. 'I think you are right, Hamo. I would certainly be willing to pretend to be ill, or to pretend Joan is ill. It is the least I can do to aid my dear husband in this struggle.'

Dolores interjected by saying to me: 'De Montfort will not let you out of this camp alone. He will send an escort with you, possibly several men. How could you hope to escape them?'

'You make a sensible point,' I replied, 'but it is a chance we will have to take. I may be able to make my escape, even if I am surrounded. My advantage is that I am a little man whom everyone regards as a brainless idiot. Perhaps Earl Simon will not think it is necessary to send a whole squadron to escort one small and weak minded jester. Besides, it is the only plan I can think of!'

'What drug shall we ask for?' Lady Leonora said.

'Whatever it is we must be sure that the monks do not have it here in the monastery,' Dolores suggested.

'An eminently sensible point, my dear. Have you any suggestions?'

Leonora and Dolores discussed possibilities and then Dolores remembered something. 'In Castile we used an extract made from a plant of the mint family. It is known as skullcap tincture. It is used to treat women who are suffering from migraine or from the pain of menstruation. I doubt whether an all male monastery such as this would have a use for such a medicine.'

'An excellent suggestion,' I said. 'I will visit the apothecary here to find out if he has this skullcap tincture. In the meantime, may I suggest that your ladyship take to your bed, in case the apothecary reports my request, while Dolores summons Earl Simon.'

Leonora eagerly consented to our plan. She laid down on her bed, which was installed in one corner of the chamber, while I informed the guards that she was feeling unwell. They greeted my news indifferently and allowed me to go off and find the monk in charge of the herbal remedies.

The apothecary, thankfully, did not have any skullcap tincture so I returned to Lady Leonora's chamber just as de Montfort arrived. I followed him into the chamber but he stopped and looked round at me. 'What are you doing here, you idiot?'

I opened my mouth to reply but Dolores answered for me. 'He is my husband,' she said firmly, 'and he has been to find out whether this monastery has a drug that my mistress needs. Well, Hamo?'

'No, madam, there is none here in the monastery.' I bobbed up and down, slobbered a bit and wiped my nose with the sleeve of my woollen tunic.

De Montfort looked at me with disgust and then looked at Dolores. 'I pity you to have chosen a husband such as him. You must be more of a freak than he is.'

I saw Dolores's temper flaring in her eyes but I put my fingers to my lips to warn her to mind her tongue. This was no time to stiffen de Montfort's intransigent and obstructive arrogance.

He looked down at Lady Leonora, who was laying, well covered by blankets, in her narrow bed, and said gently: 'I regret to find you unwell, my lady. What do you require?'

Dolores answered for her. 'My mistress requires skullcap tincture.'

'And what is that?'

'It is a remedy for severe headaches and for… women's pains. It is the only remedy that is safe for my mistress in her condition.'

'Are you a doctor?' de Montfort asked sarcastically.

'No, my lord, but I am a woman, and I know what my mistress needs. These monks here do not have it but we can certainly find this drug in a town like Hereford.'

'What are you suggesting?'

'We are suggesting that my husband here is allowed out to obtain this drug.'

De Montfort looked at me again with that arrogant and dismissive gaze. He turned back to Dolores and said: 'None of you will be allowed to leave this monastery. Especially him.' He nodded his head derisively in my direction. 'If Lady Leonora needs this drug then I will send one of my trusted men to obtain it.'

Our plan looked to have been immediately dashed on the rocks and I could not think of any further argument, even if I could have abandoned my pose as a simpleton, but Dolores could. She attacked de Montfort verbally with all the Castilian passion she could muster. 'Why you cruel and unfeeling monster!' she cried. 'I have seen you praying and you call yourself a Christian! Not only do you make my dear mistress trundle around this God forsaken country with her new-born babe in arms, you would now have her condition and her malady the gossip of your whole army by sending some nonentity on such a mission. And how would he know what to look for or to ask for? I have instructed my husband on exactly what he needs to obtain. He is a trusted servant to my lady and he it must be who undertakes her care!'

De Montfort was completely taken aback as Dolores, breathing heavily, glared at him. He was simply not used to being talked to in that manner, especially by underlings, but he appeared amused by my wife's caustic assault and it was sufficient for him to overlook the obvious flaws in her argument. 'Very well, calm yourself, madam. Your husband shall go, but he shall go with an escort.'

'Perhaps you should send your entire army to guard one small simpleton?' Dolores said.

'No, madam,' Earl Simon replied, 'I shall need my whole army here to protect myself from you!'

De Montfort ordered me to accompany him and so I did not have time to congratulate Dolores for her superbly judged outburst.

Within the hour I found myself riding out of de Montfort's camp and down the road to Hereford escorted by two of de Montfort's knights. They had been given orders to kill me without mercy if I tried to escape. I, of course, was unarmed while they were armed with swords and daggers, but I was exultant that our ploy had succeeded thus far.

De Montfort had wildly underestimated me. If there had been any more than two escorts then my plan could not have been implemented. Now I knew exactly what performance I needed to give.

It was the first day of August and it was the middle of the afternoon. I had been given a pony so that I could not out-gallop my escorts but, for my mission to succeed, I needed one of their horses. The sun was hot and the air clammy. I was dressed in a light woollen tunic but my escorts were encumbered with chain mail and weapons.

As we trotted along I kept up a torrent of inane and inconsequential banter as if I was a moron whose only thought was to enjoy the ride. I waited until we had ridden a mile or so and saw that the guards were beginning to sweat profusely. Then, from my saddle bag, I produced a flask and took a long swig and smacked my lips in a display of satisfied contentment. As I had intended, the two guards looked longingly at the flask.

'What have you got in there? Water?' one of them asked.

I giggled inanely. 'No, sirs, this is a drink called eau-de-vie. It comes from Spain. My wife is Spanish, you know, and gave this to me. It is a spirit that soothes the thirst and makes you merry at the same time.' I burst into a drinking song and pretended to sway drunkenly back and forth. Then I took another long swig.

The escort on my left took the bait. 'Let me try some of that.'

I pretended to hide the flask under my arm. 'No,' I replied petulantly. 'Get some of your own.'

'I'm thirsty,' the escort protested. 'I didn't bring anything to drink!'

'Not my fault,' I replied in a childish and petulant tone.

'Give me a drink or I'll break your arm, you little turd!'

I stuck out my lower lip like a chastened child and handed over the flask. The guard took two long draughts and then offered the flask to his companion on my right. 'No thanks,' he said. 'I don't want to put my mouth anywhere near where that monster has put his.'

That reply was a setback to my plan but I would have to improvise when the time came. That time came after we had ridden another two miles or so.

'We'll have to stop,' the guard on my left announced.

'Why?' his colleague asked in an irritated tone.

'I have to take a shit.'

'Can't you wait until we get to town?'

'I can't wait another minute,' the knight replied. He reined in his horse, dismounted and hobbled off out of sight into the shrubbery while already loosening his underwear. I had paid the apothecary at the monastery well to provide me with the fastest acting laxative that he possessed. I had only pretended to drink the doctored eau-de-vie.

His companion sighed and ordered me: 'Pull up. Let's dismount for a while. And don't try to run away or I'll hack you down.'

I walked around to the side where the knight was dismounting. I could not afford to engage either of my guards in swordplay. Strong as I was, I was not trained in that skill as they were. I would have to act swiftly and decisively.

We were hidden from view by the horses and the escort made my task easier by throwing back the chain mail hood covering his head. I grabbed him in a headlock and, with a fearful wrench, snapped his neck, but he contrived to utter a gargled cry before he died.

I lowered him to the ground. His eyes had popped out of their sockets to turn his face into a grotesque deformed mask. Bubbles of spittle fell from his mouth as the last of life drained out of him.

I removed his sword and dagger and buckled them around my waist. The other guard, warned by his colleague's dying cry that something was amiss, hobbled out of the bushes with shit running down his legs and desperately trying to pull up his drawers.

I ducked under the stomach of the horse. As the guard hobbled around the hind quarters I rose up behind him. I drove my dagger into the nape of the guard's soft neck where it was unprotected by chain mail. He sank to his knees clutching the wound with both hands. Blood from a severed artery spurted out from in between his fingers.

I grabbed him around the head and sliced the dagger across his throat to finish the job. I released him and he slumped forward, making rasping and gurgling sounds as he took his last breaths. He was soon stone dead.

Pausing only to cross myself and ask for God's forgiveness for having to kill two innocent men, I wiped the blood off my hands and clothing with handfuls of dry grass, selected the fittest looking horse and rode away from the scene of my brutal but necessary crime as swiftly as I could.

Although it was only some twenty miles from Hereford to Worcester, and I was travelling in daylight and in dry weather, it took me several hours to locate Lord Edward's army. It was twilight by the time I was first stopped by the pickets and, fortunately, one of the soldiers recognised me as Lord Edward's jester. I was escorted to where Edward had made his temporary headquarters in the requisitioned house of a wealthy Worcester merchant.

Edward was astonished to see me being ushered into his presence. He was sitting drinking at a long table, wearing his royal surcoat to emphasise his authority, and all around him were seated most of the great nobles of the realm, men such as Leybourne, Clifford, Roger Mortimer and Gilbert the Red. They regarded me and my blood-stained tunic with curiosity as I entered. I could see that most of them were drunk but fortunately not too drunk. In fact, the amount they had already consumed had made them perfectly ready for the night's adventures.

'Hamo!' Lord Edward cried, 'what are you doing here? How did you get here?'

I moved closer to Edward and whispered in his ear. 'I must speak with you in private, my lord. I have news of the utmost urgency.'

Edward turned to the assembled magnates and announced: 'Stay and finish your wine, gentlemen. Do not get up. I have to speak with my fool here. He brings tidings from Lady Leonora.'

Edward followed me out of the room and outside of the house into the moonlight. As soon as we were out of earshot, he asked frantically: 'Speak quickly, Hamo. Are my wife and daughter ill?'

'Calm yourself, sire, both are well. I have brought news of de Montfort's son and his army.'

'But I know of this, Hamo. They are in Kenilworth Castle.'

'No, my lord, they are at Kenilworth but camped in the town, *outside* the castle!'

Edward cried: 'God's blood! *Outside* the castle you say?'

'Yes, my lord.'

'All of them? Even young Simon himself?'

'Yes, my lord. Simon disports himself with the whores of the town while his army makes free in the taverns and whorehouses.'

'But how do you know this?'

'A messenger arrived for Earl Simon. I overheard this messenger telling his friends this news after he had reported to the earl.'

'Could this be a ploy to lure us into a trap?'

'No, my lord. These men took no notice of me. They were speaking in French and they certainly do not know that I can understand the French tongue.'

'But how did you escape, Hamo? Your clothing is stained with blood. How did you get here?'

I exaggerated the courage and resourcefulness I had employed to make my escape and Edward was suitably impressed with my exploits but was still hesitant about the truth of the news I had imparted.

I desperately wanted him to act upon this information. I wanted this damnable war finished so that I could return to a life of ease. Ignoring protocol I urged Edward: 'They are naked to your swords, my lord! Descend on them tonight and you can destroy these reinforcements before young Simon can join up with his father.' I pointed back to the house. 'All the men you need are sitting in that room.'

Still Edward hesitated, fearful of chancing everything on one bold stroke. 'I know, I know,' he said, 'but to gamble all on one throw! I dare not risk another Lewes.'

Gambling that my exploit had raised my licence with Edward to the fullest measure, I spoke to him bluntly. 'Strike them now, my lord! Lady Leonora risked the wrath of de Montfort and I have risked my life to bring you this news. If I had any doubts I would not have done so. I urge you to act now. If I am wrong then hang me in the morning.'

Edward looked at me, princely pride stung by my tone but manly pride in his military prowess stirred by my words. 'If this night's attack fails then I might just hang you on the morrow. But you are right, Hamo. I must take this chance. Do you want to come with us?'

'I would like to, my lord, but I am afraid I would be of little help and might possibly slow you down. I have not eaten or drank since this morning. I have been in the saddle for six hours and my arse feels like a leper's tongue.'

Thankfully, Edward laughed. 'You are right, Hamo. Stay here and eat and rest. I will gather our men and we will ride to punish young master de Montfort for his carelessness.'

Edward went back into the house to explain his plan to the assembled magnates. Being half drunk they were already fired up for the night's action and, within the hour, Edward's raiding party were thundering through the streets of Worcester on their way to Kenilworth.

I made my way to the kitchen and found some good beef and bread and wine. Then I found a comfortable corner to make a bed but sleep came fitfully. I was certain that my information was reliable but what if young Simon moved his men back into Kenilworth castle before Edward arrived? Or what if I had unwittingly been manipulated to lure Edward into a trap? If Edward's expedition turned into a disaster then I would certainly be used as the scapegoat.

Despite my fears I eventually managed to doze off, exhausted by the day's events.

The raiding party returned early the next afternoon. I watched as they returned. They were exhausted but in a jubilant mood. The surprise attack had succeeded and several high-ranking nobles had been captured for ransom.

Edward, forgetting my role as an idiot in the exultation of his success, summoned me to the room where he and his supporters were liberally refreshing themselves after their night's exertions. 'Hamo!' he cried when he saw me enter the room. 'You were right. We caught them with their hose down, literally.'

The magnates laughed at Edward's remark and again regarded me curiously, even more so when Edward actually put his arm around my shoulder. He had to stoop quite low to do so.

I decided I had to remind him of how doltish I was supposed to be and, clapping my hands together and slobbering, I danced a little jig and cried: 'Wonderful, sire, wonderful.'

It sobered Edward a little and he said: 'You and Lady Leonora have served our cause well. I am most grateful, Hamo.'

'How many did you kill?' I asked, making dagger-like thrusts with my hand.

'We killed dozens, Hamo,' Edward replied. 'Dozens and dozens, but there are still many left. We could not kill them all.'

'Did you kill young Simon?' I asked, making an ugly face, much to the amusement of the magnates.

'He's a bloodthirsty little brute, isn't he?' Gilbert the Red commented.

'Aye,' Mortimer answered, 'almost as much as you, Gilbert!'

When the laughter had subsided, Edward told me: 'Simon eluded us. Lucky for him he was with some local trollope when we attacked. He had to jump out of a window and the last we saw of him he was stark naked and rowing for his life across the castle moat! Unfortunately, we couldn't find another boat to go after him.' [19]

I clapped my hands with delight and joined in the general laughter. I listened to the conversation until, about an hour later, news arrived that served to dampen the hilarity.

Simon de Montfort had somehow been given warning of the night's raid and had taken advantage of Edward's absence to cross the River Severn with his army. They were now camped only a few miles south of Worcester.

After a hurried council of war Edward decided that it would be folly to attack immediately as everyone was exhausted from lack of sleep. They would rest the men and engage de Montfort on the morrow but, once again, events overtook their decision.

De Montfort received the news of Edward's victory over his son at Kenilworth and decided to move his army again under the cover of darkness. He thought he could move unobserved but Edward, learning the harsh lesson delivered at the battle of Lewes, had sent out scouts to observe de Montfort's movements.

On August 4th, 1265, we had followed Simon de Montfort's army to another town. Even to this day, even after a long lifetime, I cannot hear the name without a shudder of horror… the name of Evesham.

AUGUST 4TH, 1265

The new day dawned, thundrous sultry and overcast, sun livid yellow behind louring grey clouds. Scouts rode in to report that de Montfort's army had halted outside Evesham to take breakfast. Edward, after swift consultation with his most trusted military advisers, decided this was an ideal opportunity to catch de Montfort by surprise. He ordered that our army be fed while he held a council of war with his commanders.

This council was convened in a shabby and rundown wayside inn that had been commandeered as a temporary headquarters. I had spent the night in the cellar of the inn, just as I used to sleep in the cellar back at the hated St. Nicholas Inn, albeit this time accompanied by seven or eight fellow shelter seekers.

I was sorely troubled by night demons about my detestable childhood. I awoke sweaty and slack-mouthed with thirst and unaccountably despondent.

When I heard about the coming battle I decided to wheedle my way in to the council of war. I badly wanted to to know what was being planned and discussed.

The council members convened at the rough wooden tables normally used by wayfarers taking meals. I contrived to conceal myself under an unused table at the side of the room.

The pale morning sunlight, often broken by cloud, streamed through narrow windows and made patterns on peeling plaster as the council, grim and hard faced with thoughts of imminent death, glory or disfigurement, took their places.

Edward allowed Gilbert de Clare, as his second-in-command,

to address the assembled warriors first. De Clare, face blazing with lust for action, briefly explained the location and disposition of de Montfort's army. Then he picked up a parchment and read out a dozen names. I recognised most of them as among the most skilful and renowned fighters in the royal army. 'These men,' Earl Gilbert announced, 'have been selected for the specific purpose of seeking out Simon de Montfort on the battlefield and killing him.'

Roger Mortimer, always a man with an eye to making money and well in favour because of his part in the release of Edward from Hereford Castle, spoke up and asked: 'What if we find an opportunity to capture de Montfort? His ransom will bring a high price.'

Lord Edward rose from his chair. His six feet two inch frame towered over the stocky Gilbert de Clare. Edward was already wearing chain mail beneath his surcoat emblazoned with the royal arms. His impressive intervention imposed immediate silence on the gathering.

I could tell from his manner and expression that his Angevin blood was hot and that now was his time for vengeance and redemption.

'Gentlemen,' he announced firmly, 'the rules of chivalry are today suspended. There will be no quarter, no surrender accepted, no ransom considered. Today we finish with this troublesome Earl of Leicester and the anguish he has brought upon my family and upon this land. The only escape that de Montfort and his army will have this day is death.'

Edward sat down again. His unexpected and uncompromising announcement caused a stunned silence amongst the assembled commanders.

Gilbert de Clare broke the silence by saying: 'De Montfort is camped about three miles from here. As far as we can tell, he is unaware that we know where he is. We will have the element of surprise but, in the final few minutes of our attack, he will inevitably see our advance, so it must be as swift as possible.'

While de Clare was continuing his briefing I conceived of a ploy to retain the element of surprise over de Montfort until the last moments of our attack. I considered how I should relay this idea to Lord Edward. If I waited I might not find a chance to talk to him in private before the battle. I decided I must make my suggestion immediately, even if it was deemed to be dishonourable or against the rules of warfare.

I crawled out from under my table, stood up, went over to Lord Edward and tugged at his surcoat as if I were a nervous toddler.

Edward looked round, highly irritated by whoever was disturbing him. 'What?' he snapped.

I leant forward and whispered in his ear. As I described my idea I was relieved to see a broad smile cross Edward's face. When I had finished he stood up and announced: 'Gentlemen, we have a volunteer to lead the attack this morning, just as he did at Lewes, my trusty fool Sir Hamo Pauncefoot here!' He ushered me to move up and stand beside him.

There was a sprinkling of uncertain laughter, most of the magnates being amazed at the licence with which they had seen me approach and talk to Lord Edward.

'Not only that,' Edward continued, 'but he volunteers to ride at the head of my army carrying the banner of de Montfort that we captured at Kenilworth.' Edward turned to me and, to my discomfiture, announced: 'So you shall, Hamo!'

Although I perforce had to grin and simper with delight, inside I was horrified. This was not what I had suggested at all! Had Lord Edward misunderstood me?

There were a few murmurs of discontent at the idea of a mere jester leading the royal army into battle but Edward silenced them by saying: 'Out of the mouths of babes and fools, gentlemen! Hamo has given me an idea. We captured many banners during our adventure at Kenilworth. Those at the forefront of our advance will carry those banners and it will fool de Montfort into thinking that it is his son Simon come to reinforce him. It may give us more opportunity to take them by surprise. Are there any objections to this plan?'

As conveyed by the sibilant hint of disdain in his voice for anyone who might have dared to object, Edward did not receive any objections. 'So be it. Sir Hamo Pauncefoot will lead us into battle.'

I reeled away from Edward's presence cursing myself for making the suggestion. Edward had evidently interpreted my suggestion as a desire to volunteer to lead the army, but that had not been my intention at all!

I was confident of the outcome of the day's conflict, we outnumbered de Montfort by about three to one and Edward would surely make no more hot-headed mistakes as he had made at Lewes, but what good would victory be to me if I was laying face down in a muddy field and in a pool of my own blood?

Anyway, that is how, later that morning, I came to be riding by the side of Lord Edward as he led the advance of the royal army. At least I had been given a strong chestnut destrier to ride instead of a pony as at the battle of Lewes. I was carrying the banner of the de Montfort clan and cursing myself as a fool for speaking so rashly.

But, as we learned much later, my ruse had worked. De Montfort, observing our advance from the top of a church tower, had delayed preparing his troops because he initially believed that our army was reinforcements led by his son Simon. A lookout with keener eyes than de Montfort had turned to him and said: 'We are all dead men, for it is not your son, as you believed.' [20]

The town of Evesham is situated in a loop of the River Avon and the only approach by land is from the north. That is the way we approached on that fateful day, down the road from Worcester, and thanks to my deception we made full use of the element of surprise and seized the vital high ground.

Our army was arrayed in three divisions in echelon formation at the top of a place known as Greenhill. We looked down a gentle slope at de Montfort's army below us. They were trapped between us and the river.

There was an intact bridge over the river by which de Montfort might have retreated but we could still have swooped down and decimated his army and retreat was not in de Montfort's arrogant nature. Retreat would have certainly meant the ruin of his reputation and the end of his campaign but pitched battle offered the possibility of another victory as at Lewes. At that battle, de Montfort's army had worn white crosses as distinguishing marks. Here at Evesham our royal troops were distinguished by a red cross.

The sky was rapidly darkening as black thunderclouds piled up and filled the air with the steely smell of rain. I was literally quaking with terror at the prospect of having to lead the advance.

I looked at Edward, seated on his black destrier Lyard, towering over me. He looked regal but also serene as he held his helmet under his arm and surveyed the enemy below him. How do such men find such courage? Is it bred into them by virtue of their royal blood? Or does the fact of possessing royal blood instil the obligation to be fearless?

In a fit of trust and honest affection for my liege lord I said: 'Sire, I am sore afraid.'

Edward, as usual, had been teasing. He turned to me with a sweet smile full of kindness and camaraderie and said: 'Go to the rear, Hamo. You have led us here and given us an advantage because of your excellent suggestion. I do not expect you to fight. You are not a warrior. Go to the rear and keep close company with the men earmarked to kill de Montfort. You will be safe with them. Say a prayer for me, Hamo, and watch over me if you can, but if God wills that I do not survive this day, then Lady Leonora will need the consolation of your drollery. It may be God's intention to allow Earl Simon to rule England, in which case my life will be forfeit. God may punish me for the sin of betraying my father. I place myself in the Lord's hands. He has blessed me by giving me a wife whom I love beyond all measure, and a staunch friend in you, always at my side and always faithful to me and Lady Leonora, for which I thank you with all my heart. If the Lord cares to take my life then carry my love to my wife, Hamo, and tell her I shall spend eternity ever grateful for her love and companionship.'

'I will, my lord,' I promised, and wheeled my horse around and retreated to the rear.

Through the mist of the years I cannot say for certain whether it was the first of the rain or my own tears that coursed down my cheeks as I took leave of Edward.

As if ordered by nature to suit the day, the sky had suddenly darkened and a huge clap of thunder heralded a torrential downpour.

My retreat to the rear was greeted with many ironic cheers and jeers from the waiting infantry, but I did not care.

As I reached the rear of our lines, de Montfort unexpectedly made the first move. I heard the warning cries from our own men as fat droplets of rain began to descend in a driving torrent.

I heard the distant pounding of horses hooves and turned around to see De Montfort's knights charging up Greenhill towards our lines. It was an almost suicidal act of desperation to seize the initiative, and it almost succeeded.

At first our stationary front line buckled under the impact of the charge. Through the rain I could just make out Lord Edward rallying his men for a counter attack. The charge up the hill in increasingly muddy conditions had exhausted de Montfort's horses and, as the charge lost momentum, our mounted knights simply rode around their flanks to close off their retreat while our infantry began their advance down Greenhill.

The slaughter began. It all seemed too easy. Those enemy knights who could not battle their way back down the hill were dragged from the saddle and hacked to death. The agonised and tormented screams of the dead and dying haunt my mind to this day. I moved forward through the carnage with the group of knights detailed to kill de Montfort but keeping close company behind them.

Prince Llewelyn had sent a detachment of Welsh infantry to aid de Montfort's cause but as we advanced the Welsh sensibly decided they wanted no part of this English slaughter and took to their heels towards the river bridge. With them went de Montfort's last faint hope of victory.

Our flanks began to move forward to surround de Montfort's infantry. Many of the enemy stood their ground but many others, seeing that they were about to be surrounded and trapped, followed the Welsh and fled from the battlefield.

The rain was becoming heavier as we advanced and torrents of water mixed with blood were now pouring down the slick grass of Greenhill. The infantry battle looked, through the downpour, as if it was being fought by grey silhouettes punctuated by vivid red spurts of blood.

The death squad moved closer to the centre of the battlefield and I could see Lord Edward, in the thick of the fray, trying to reach de Montfort, whose position was marked by his banner. The death squad had also noted his position and were walking their mounts towards him in echelon formation, fighting as they went.

I was trotting behind closely, watching carefully for any wounded enemy who might still be trying to make a fight of it. The downpour was now so fierce that it was difficult to see more than a few feet in any direction. Ghostly figures were running through the sheets of water, screaming, crying out, clutching gaping wounds, imploring God for an end to their ordeal.

Intent on looking from side to side in order to protect myself from stray attackers, and blinded by rainwater inside my helmet, I suddenly found that, without realising, I had closed up with the death squad.

I took off my helmet to ascertain my position and could see de Montfort, surrounded by his loyal guard, only about fifty yards away. Lord Edward was about fifty yards off to the left, trying to reach de Montfort. He was slashing and stabbing with his sword from the commanding height of his horse. The enemy were gradually backing off from his formidable presence.

The loyal knights guarding de Montfort had noted the advance of the death squad and, surmising its menacing purpose, were changing formation in a last desperate effort to protect their leader. A group of them wheeled their horses around and broke away to charge at the death squad. Their impact caused our men to break formation.

As my comrades were forced apart and backwards I suddenly found myself, helmetless, at the forefront of our group. I struggled to don the awkward metal can but, before I could do so, Simon de Montfort himself was wheeling his mount towards me and raising his great sword above his head to finish me off.

I dropped the helmet in the mud and, although I carried a sword and a small buckler to protect myself, I was no match for de Montfort and I accepted that I was about to die. I was transfixed, unable to move, by the sight of his falling sword driving through the rain drops to cleave my head open.

At the last moment I raised my buckler in a vain attempt to ward off the blow and at that instant a lance appeared by the side of my head and drove straight under de Montfort's arm and into his chest. His deflected sword blow glanced off my buckler as blood spurted from his savage death wound.

Roger Mortimer, who had landed the death blow, accidentally knocked me off my horse as he had passed, desperately trying to control his terrified bucking mount.

Ecstatically relieved to be saved from death, I now found myself scrabbling in the muddy earth. My horse had bolted. I still held my sword and buckler but I found myself in the midst of a scene from hell.

The ground was sodden and I still remember the smell of hot blood mingling with warm rain. I looked up. De Montfort's bodyguard, seeing their leader slain, were trying to escape certain death.

Our death squad, driven insane by blood lust, were hacking at de Montfort's body with swords and axes. The body jerked like a marionette as the blows fell and his limbs were parted from his body.

After witnessing this ghastly spectacle I could not keep down the bile and vomited in the mud. The sudden realisation of the true horror of my surroundings caused my head to roar as if filled with angry voices and a strange sensation of unreality, as if all was a dream, numbed my mind.

I began to panic. I stood up and started running I know not where, slashing left and right with my sword at friend and foe alike. All around me were dead and dying men and haunted figures staggering or running through the rain, some clutching at terrible wounds, all shocked into crazed numbness by the slaughter all around.

I was trying to find an escape route away from the carnage when another panicked knight, dressed in Montfortian colours, came staggering towards me. He was wide-eyed with terror and shouting to no-one in particular: 'I am Henry of Winchester, your king! Do not kill me!'

Instead of ignoring his ravings, as others were doing, I recognised that it was, indeed, King Henry. De Montfort must have forced him to be present at the battle dressed in de Montfort's colours.

I grabbed King Henry by the arm and looked around frantically to find Lord Edward. As the fray parted for a moment I saw him about twenty yards away. He was no longer wielding his sword and looked as if he was simply observing the closing stages of the battle.

'Sire!' I shouted to the king over the din of battle. 'Follow me. Lord Edward is yonder and you will be safe.'

The king stumbled as he moved closer to my side. I held him by the arm and supported him as I guided him towards where Edward was directing the final massacre.

I managed to ward off two or three half-hearted attacks from wounded and crazed de Montfortians but soon Edward was within hearing. 'Lord Edward!' I shouted. 'Lord Edward, here is your father!'

He did not hear me for a few moments but as we stumbled towards him he looked round and saw us approaching. After looking around swiftly to make sure their was no imminent danger Edward ordered some of his knights to guard him while he dismounted. He took off his helmet and ran forward to meet us.

The king and his son fell into each other's arms. Edward said: 'The day is ours, father. De Montfort is dead. Praise God!' To me Edward said: 'Thank you, old friend, for my father's life. I will find horses for you both and we will take the king to safety.' [21]

I was only too eager to escape that dread armageddon. The battle was almost over, the outcome not in doubt, and Edward ordered Gilbert de Clare to take command of the mopping up.

Edward gathered a bodyguard of twenty or so knights. No doubt anticipating future rewards, these knights were overjoyed that the king had been found alive and were honoured to be given the task of escorting him to a safe haven.

We quit the battlefield and set out on horseback towards Evesham. The way was littered with the bodies of de Montfort's army, most of them hacked and mutilated in a most terrible manner.

We arrived at the abbey church and Edward decided that here we should rest and take sanctuary in order to let the king recover his shattered wits. When we opened the door, however, we realised it had been turned into a charnel house. The walls, the statues, even the cross and the high altar itself, were covered in blood. Bodies were strewn everywhere and the floor was swimming with blood.

Edward gazed at this awful sight and murmured: 'May God forgive me for this murder at Evesham, for battle it was none.'

We journeyed on, away from that house of death, and soon arrived at the monastery of St. Egwin, who is the patron saint of Evesham. Here we were given shelter and succour by the monks, well pleased to perform such service for the victorious king and his illustrious son, again in anticipation of future rewards and favours.

Edward took wine but refused food. He ordered me to stay in

the refectory with the king while he went to pray in the monastery chapel.

The king was in the grip of inner demons, wide-eyed with shock and babbling in a most alarming manner. After a few sips of wine, however, he calmed down somewhat and asked: 'Where is my son? Where is Edward?'

As the concerned knights and monks of St. Egwin looked on anxiously, I replied soothingly: 'Sire, he is in the chapel giving thanks for your victory.'

King Henry looked at me, wild-eyed, as if he had never seen me before. 'Who are you?'

'Sire, I am Sir Hamo Pauncefoot, Lord Edward's jester.'

'Jester? What need of a jester do we have? Fetch my son! I want to see my son!'

The king became agitated beyond any persuasion so I left him in the care of the monks and went to fetch Lord Edward.

I entered the quiet sanctuary of the chapel to find Edward, still wearing his mud-caked and blood-stained chain mail, kneeling in front of the altar. His shoulders were shaking and I feared that he might be having some kind of fit.

I said, quietly and respectfully: 'Forgive me for interrupting, my lord, but the king is asking for you.'

Edward did not look around and it was several moments before he answered: 'I will go to him shortly, Hamo.'

'The king is much distressed and sore in need of your comfort.'

'And who is to comfort me?' Edward asked. He turned to face me and I was shocked to see tears coursing down his face. 'Yes, Hamo, today you see that I am merely a man like any other. The things I have witnessed this day grieve me sorely.'

'But you are victorious, my lord. You have saved the kingdom.'

' "What profit a man to gain a kingdom but lose his soul", Hamo? Simon de Montfort was my uncle and my godfather. His son, Henry de Montfort, was my friend. I watched them both being hacked to death on that battlefield. Many of my friends fought against me. I saw many of them die. And then to have to follow that ghastly trail of death to this place. I am culpable, Hamo. All this was my fault.'

I had never seen Lord Edward so upset and bereft of self-control. I was nonplussed as to what to say, and replied lamely. 'You did what you had to do, my lord, as befits the gallant prince that you are.'

Edward looked at me, his body wracked with sobs, as if pleading for my understanding. 'No, Hamo. I acted foolishly at the battle of Lewes. If I had not done so, we would have won the battle and the war and all of this slaughter would not have been necessary. In my wrath and need for vengeance I gave the order that no quarter was to be given this day, no prisoners to be taken for ransom. If I had not given that order then all today's bloodshed might not have been necessary. Well, I am sick to my heart, Hamo. As the aftermath of all this carnage I have sworn to God that in future I will act with mercy and temperance. I know what men say of me, they compare me to the shifty and cruel leopard, but all that is over. You see before you a changed man and a more sober prince. I am naked and penitent before God.'

Edward bowed his head for a long moment and gradually regained control of his emotions. He looked up at me and then smiled to show the coming threat was not to be taken seriously. 'If you ever tell anyone that you have witnessed me so distraught or ever speak of this conversation to anyone, I will have you flogged. Come, old friend, let us go to comfort the king.'

Brother Godfrey's eyes shine with excitement. You are excited by my account, aren't you, boy. No, don't deny it, my tonsured friend! You lust for adventure. Your cloistered life bores an energetic young man like you. You secretly yearn to be involved in momentous events like Evesham. Let me tell you that you are wrong to yearn so. Such slaughter haunts my dreams to this day. Anyway, you have probably been taught your history. You know what happened next. Our victory at Evesham had been so complete that the baronial cause, as led by de Montfort, collapsed. King Henry was, once again, the undisputed sole ruler of England. His son Edward, my friend and liege lord, to a far greater degree than before, was now the second most powerful person in the land and, in many ways, more influential than his father, who was diminished in mind and spirit by the torrid events of his reign. [22]

OCTOBER 1265

At the end of October Dolores and I were residing in our chamber at Westminster Palace. One day I said to her, with deliberate casualness: 'Don your riding habit, woman. It's a fine day for a ride through the city.'

Dolores looked at me curiously, then pouted with exasperation and asked off-handedly: 'Why should I want to ride through this stinking sewer that surrounds us?'

'Do not argue, woman. Prepare yourself.'

Dolores eventually acquiesced, albeit with considerable irritation. Her mood brightened, and her curiosity deepened, when we went outside to the palace courtyard and found we had an escort of twelve heavily armed soldiers for our excursion.

'Where are we going?' Dolores asked, but I told her to be silent and patient.

It was a pleasant and sunny day, despite a fresh breeze, and it took us only a short time, trotting through narrow and sullen streets, to reach our destination.

We stopped outside a grand house. It was a cruck framed house with wattle and daub infill, constructed on three stories, and with three high gables on the frontage and an ornately thatched roof.

'What do you think of this house?' I asked Dolores.

Dolores studied it for a few moments and replied: 'It is very grand. It is beautiful.'

'None grander or more beautiful in London.' I dismounted and offered my hand for Dolores to dismount. As she did so I told her: 'This house is ours, my dear.'

'Ours? What do you mean?'

'I mean that this is our house, given to me by Lord Edward as a reward for my services to him. It belonged to a wealthy merchant who used to be the Lord Mayor of London until he made the mistake of siding with Simon de Montfort. Now he is a pauper and in prison and this house is all ours, complete with servants.'

I had never seen Dolores look so happy, and it thrilled my heart that at last I could give a gift that she truly desired.

Her eyes shone as we toured the grand reception rooms, the upstairs bedrooms, the enormous kitchen complete with subservient staff, and the elegant walled garden that stretched about one hundred yards down to the River Thames.

To be the mistress of such a house would make Lady Dolores Pauncefoot the envy of London. Just before we left, when we were alone, she embraced me and kissed me on the lips. She whispered: 'You have done well, husband.'

The return of peace allowed me to take stock of my life. I was now approaching thirty years of age. I was knighted, wealthy and I owned an estate in Hampshire and the grandest house, apart from royal palaces, in London.

Best of all, Dolores was now well content with me as a husband. She did not love me and never would but I loved her, and that was something beyond my understanding, a condition I was unable to change.

I was still popular with the royal family as a singer and harpist but demands for my services as a jester and acrobat were diminishing, but I was not worried about that. The sudden easy living meant that I was putting on weight through too much eating and drinking. Fresh young fools were performing acrobatics that I could no longer manage and they were cognisant of the new songs and new jokes. They looked up to me, however, and respected my close relationship with Lord Edward. My position with the royal family was secure.

My only real gnawing regret was to know that I was the son of Earl Richard of Cornwall but unable to prove it or to publicly claim such knowledge. I had accepted there was no means by which I could prove my birthright. The secret knowledge of my blue blood was satisfying but, at some time, I wanted the world to know the truth, and that is part of the reason for committing my life story to this parchment.

Dolores was delighted with our grand new residence and often entertained Lady Leonora while Edward was away fighting against the last pockets of baronial resistance. When I was at home I would often overhear Leonora and Dolores talking in Castilian and giggling together. I had never bothered to learn Castilian and I could not understand what they were saying.

It was balm to Lady Leonora to escape the strictures of court life in the informal atmosphere of our home. She had, once again, suffered the loss of a child, Princess Joan having died soon after the battle of Evesham.

But Leonora was pregnant again, a situation that pleased me because Lord Edward insisted that I stay in London and guard Leonora's welfare while he was away. I was delighted not to be invited on more military campaigns.

Edward was eventually able to spend some time with Lady Leonora at Windsor Castle. Leonora, to great rejoicing, had given birth to a son, who was named John.

Over the past few months, Lord Edward, with a wise policy of clemency combined with irresistible force and his formidable reputation as a warrior and military leader, had mopped up the last elements of disaffected baronial rebels.

The only major military problem remaining was Wales but there was nothing to be done to retrieve that situation. Prince Llewelyn still held northern Wales and England, in its weakened and chaotic state, could do nothing about it. The English people had been sickened and exhausted by the years of conflict and were loathe to contemplate new wars. Accordingly, King Henry and Lord Edward had travelled to the Welsh border and granted Llewelyn a permanent truce.

England was now truly at peace.

I looked forward to many years of pleasant living without the fear of being hacked to bits by a sword. Lord Edward, in his usual inimitable way, made an announcement that shattered all my hopes.

DECEMBER 1267

I was unconcerned by Lord Edward's announcement when I first heard it. The royal family were gathered at Windsor Castle for the Christmas celebrations. It was St. Stephen's Day of 1267 and the family, after attending worship in the chapel, were resting in their luxurious apartment.

I was present to entertain the ladies with my harp and songs, and to amuse young John, the royal infant, who was now about eighteen months old.

It was a pleasant domestic scene. There was a hard frost outside but we had a log fire inside to keep us warm and servants to bring us food and drink whenever we wanted anything.

After a time Lord Edward dismissed the servants, leaving the royal family in privacy, apart from me, and then he stood up, looking unusually nervous. He cleared his throat. Everyone stopped what they were doing and looked at Edward. He announced to the family in general: 'I have been thinking about my future and I have made a decision for which I need my father's permission and blessing.'

King Henry, who was sitting playing chess with his youngest son Lord Edmund, looked up at his tall eldest son with an expression of surprise. The queen and Lady Leonora also looked at Edward expectantly while the infant John gurgled happily and crawled around the carpet. Lord Edward stood in the middle of this carpet, looking very handsome, regal and manly in a gold surcoat, with his thumbs stuck into his red leather belt.

King Henry asked: 'What do you wish to ask me, my son?'

'Father, your enemies have been defeated. The kingdom is yours again. You no longer need me here. I wish to serve God and do my duty by going on crusade to the Holy Land.'

King Henry could not disguise his dismay. Lord Edmund, however, smiled broadly and, like an eager puppy, said: 'What an excellent notion! Let me go with you, brother. We could have many adventures together.'

'Hush,' King Henry ordered his youngest son. To Edward he said, quietly: 'Your desire to serve God is laudable. But you are wrong to say I do not need you here. I am growing older. One day you will be king. Your conduct during the recent conflicts have proved you are a son to be proud of, a man with the courage of a lion and the guile of a fox, a truly worthy king to rule this realm. I have never been a military man, Edward. While you are at my side, no enemy dare threaten the throne. If you are not here, the country could descend into rebellion again.'

Edward bowed his head thoughtfully but then said: 'Your praise warms my heart, father, but your enemies have been driven into the dust. You have nothing to fear, and you have able friends and advisers like Uncle Richard.'

Queen Eleanor looked appalled by her son's proposal and spoke up. 'The king is right, Edward. You are needed here in England. Whether you are aware of it or not, whether you like it or not, you are the most feared and respected man in the realm. Your duty is to your family and your future subjects. God can wait.'

Both King Henry and Lord Edward looked irritated by Queen Eleanor's blunt speech. It had inferred that her husband was no longer the most important man in the land despite being the king.

Edward seized on this statement and turned it to his advantage. 'If your estimation of my reputation is true, mother, than who better than me to lead the English contingent. God needs the best warriors to fight for his cause. King Louis of France himself has taken the cross and at this very minute prepares to free the Holy Land from the infidel. How can I stay here twiddling my thumbs while he fights for God?'

King Henry made a gesture of irritation. 'You certainly will not be twiddling your thumbs. There is much work to be done in rebuilding the administration and our authority after the rebellion.'

'All tedious talking and writing, father. I cannot… '

'All part of a king's duties,' Henry interrupted sharply. 'Do not dismiss such duties. They are as vital as the ability to fight.'

'I beg your pardon, father,' Edward said contritely. 'I did not mean to belittle such tasks, but only to point out that you can perform them much more ably than I, and that I am not really needed here.'

The king brooded for a few moments and then said: 'Even if I allowed you to go on crusade, from where would the money be obtained to finance such a venture? You know as well as I do that it takes a huge amount of money to conduct a successful crusade. The country is still in chaos and the people bear a heavy burden of taxation already.'

'The pope will provide most of the funds, surely?' Edward said.

'The papacy is in chaos! The cardinals cannot agree on who should be the next pope since the last one died. It will take months, possibly years, to obtain funds from that direction.'

Edward looked defeated but then rallied and found another line of argument. I was losing interest in all this tooing and froing and was playing happily with little John on the carpet. I was not at all worried about Edward's proposal. I knew that Edward would not invite me to participate in this crusade so his announcement did not concern me.

The argument ended with King Henry firmly denying his son permission to go on crusade and that seemed to be the end of the matter. Edward refused to give up, however, and over the next few months he gradually won permission to take the cross.

King Henry eventually accepted the argument that the outside distraction of a crusade would help in reuniting the country. Edward would take with him most of the powerful magnates in the land, even those who had fought for de Montfort, and they would all be united in God's cause, with the common people at home supporting their holy mission.

A new pope was eventually elected and, having been apprised of Lord Edward's fighting qualities, readily gave permission for him to lead the English contingent.

J U N E   1 2 6 8

In June of the year 1268, a parliament was assembled at Northampton. It was held at Northampton because that town was the site of the Church of the Holy Sepulchre, which had been built in imitation of the original Church of the Holy Sepulchre in Jerusalem.

It was in this church, in the grandest of ceremonies, that Edward, Edmund, Henry of Almain, and a host of the most wealthy and powerful nobles in the land would pledge themselves to free the Holy Land from the infidels.

The day before the ceremony Edward seemed to be at a loose end and, late in the morning, summoned me for a game of chess. The table and chairs had been set up outside the walls of Northampton Castle and it was pleasant to sit in the mild June sunshine and partake of a battle of wits with my master.

Lord Edward was also in a mild and benevolent mood. We were out of earshot of the guards and retainers so the two of us could talk freely. 'Well, Hamo,' he said, 'tomorrow I pledge my future to the Lord and prepare to do His work. I am well pleased with my decision. I am, at last, to atone for my sins.'

I was somewhat startled by that last sentence, and I blurted out: 'Sins, my lord? What sins?'

Edward looked at me and replied: 'You, of all people, should know. You were the only witness to my distress after the slaughter of Evesham.' He held up his hand as I began to speak. 'I know what you will say to reassure me, that I saved the kingdom and so on, but the bloodshed still haunts me, Hamo. I should not have given the order for no quarter.'

'If you had not done so then the rebellion and the bloodshed might have carried on for much longer.'

'Perhaps. Anyway, I now must make amends to God for my decision. I hope He will forgive me. We will serve the Lord well, Hamo, and have many adventures in the East.'

Stupidly, I did not realise the import of what Edward had just said and compounded my stupidity by saying: 'I wish I were going with you, my lord.'

Edward paused while holding a chess piece in mid-move and answered: 'But of course you are coming with me, Hamo. Tomorrow you are to take the cross with the other servants and laymen after we royals and nobles have performed our ceremony.'

I really thought Edward was teasing me, as was his habit, and I chuckled. Edward, with that threatening sibilant hiss of a voice, challenged me: 'What are you laughing about? Do you dare to mock me?'

'Of course not, my lord,' I answered hastily. 'I thought you were making a jest at my expense. What possible use could a fool such as I be when you fight the Saracens? I will stay here to take care of Lady Leonora and your sons John and Henry.'

Lady Leonora had given birth to their second son, Henry, only about a month before.

Edward looked at me with an expression of severe disapproval. 'Lady Leonora is coming on crusade with me, and so are you.'

To say I was shocked would be a gross understatement. 'But, my lord,' I protested impertinently, 'to expose any woman, let alone your own wife, to the horrors and privations of a military campaign, is iniquitous.'

Edward regarded me coolly. 'I will be the judge of what is iniquitous in regard to my own wife. Anyway, you talk nonsense. The queen of France is to accompany her husband on crusade. Lady Leonora is a pious and devout woman and would not countenance allowing me to face all the dangers alone. She insists on accompanying me and I would not have expected anything less.'

As soon as Edward dismissed me I went in search of Dolores. I found her leaving Lady Leonora's chamber and beckoned her down to the stairway where we could not be overheard.

'Did you know that Lady Leonora plans to go on crusade with her husband?' I hissed.

'Yes, of course,' Dolores replied, puzzled. 'What of it?'

'Why didn't you tell me, woman?'

'Why should I? Why are you interested?'

'Because I have been ordered to go on crusade to help and entertain her ladyship! Are you going with Leonora?'

'No. I am to stay here in England and take care of the children.'

'Well, this is a pretty kettle of fish,' I exploded. 'I am to be dragged off to some eastern hellhole while you remain here. You are Lady Leonora's best friend. Cannot you talk her out of going on this crusade?'

'No,' Dolores glared. 'Leonora wants to go with her husband and Lord Edward expects her to go. I have no influence in this matter.'

I was desolate. My relationship with Dolores had finally achieved a mutual warmth and satisfaction that I once thought would be impossible, even though we had been unable to conceive the child that Dolores desperately wished for. Now I was to be parted from her, probably for many years.

Even worse news was to follow. Not only was Dolores remaining in England but so was Robert Burnell. He had established himself as Edward's most influential adviser and a member of the royal council. He also continued to cast lustful glances at Dolores. She swore that their was nothing going on between them, and I accepted her word, but I was still desperately uneasy.

Most of what I can remember of the next few months is Edward's obsession with his damnable crusade. He was searching everywhere for funds while I was constantly praying that he would not be able to find them. My prayers were not answered.

AUGUST 1270

Early in the month of August 1270 I was obliged to pack my belongings, take leave of my comfortable house in London and travel to Dover to join the crusading army. Dolores was given permission to accompany me to Dover to bid me farewell.

Edward had appointed a committee headed by Earl Richard of Cornwall, and including Robert Burnell, to supervise his affairs and to act as guardians to his children while he was away.

The entire crusading army, together with squires, attendants and servants, numbered well over a thousand souls. It was a fine sight to behold, the tented camp, with gay pennants flying, spread along the high cliffs above Dover, and the harbour crammed with ships to transport the army to Bordeaux.

I remember to this day my parting words to Dolores. I said: 'I go to serve God with our liege lord Edward and your mistress Lady Leonora. Remember that God sees all we do and remember your duty as a wife and as a protector of the royal children. Also remember that I love you and I have strived to be a good husband. I beg you not to do anything to shame or embarrass me, or our royal patrons, and try to think of me with affection until I return. If I do not return then all my wealth and property are yours. Do you swear before God to be a faithful wife and not dishonour me?'

Dolores responded: 'You well know that I do not love you. That I cannot love you. But you have proved yourself a good provider and a brave and faithful husband. I will think of you with affection and I so promise as you ask.' Then she leaned forward and kissed me on both cheeks.

I turned on my heels and embarked on the royal cog. When I looked back from the rail of the ship I could no longer see Dolores. The dockside was crowded with hundreds of soldiers. I searched the throng for a last sight of my wife but she had left me.

After the army had disembarked in Bordeaux Edward decided that, as we were weeks behind schedule, we would push on directly for the Mediterranean coast port where we were to rendezvous with the French contingent.

Driven by Edward's unflagging energy, the army travelled six hundred miles through France in little over a month and we reached the port of Aigues Mortes at the end of September.

SEPTEMBER 1270

At Aigues Mortes I was relieved to be allowed to stay in the royal chambers in the secure castle built by the French king Louis specifically for his crusading journey.

It was in these chambers, where I was entertaining Lady Leonora and her ladies-in-waiting while they settled in, that Lord Edward entered in a thunderous rage and informed us of the first disaster of this ill-fated expedition.

Ignoring my presence, and that of the ladies-in-waiting, he immediately launched into a tirade. 'King Louis,' he spat out contemptuously, 'has left without us!'

Edward proceeded to march up and down uttering fearful imprecations against the French monarch and swiped a pitcher of wine off the table. The vessel burst and the contents spilled over the rush-covered floor.

Even Lady Leonora, as much as she loved her husband, was intimidated by his rage. 'But husband,' she said timorously, 'you expected as much. We have arrived weeks later than the appointed departure time.'

I, sitting cross-legged on the floor, had rolled myself into a ball with my hands over my head and made myself rock backwards and forwards in mock terror.

Edward looked down at my antics, about to scold me for my disrespect, when he suddenly realised the fear encased in his wife's tone, and the awestruck expressions of fear on the faces of the other women. Being a basically kind and considerate man, he took control of himself and softened his tone. 'It is true that I expected Louis might leave without us, but he has not sailed for the Holy Land, he has been persuaded to sail for North Africa. He is going empire building.' Edward pronounced the last sentence with a withering sneer.

'North Africa?' Leonora repeated. 'Why should Louis go there? Surely his bounden royal and Christian duty is to free the Holy City from the infidels?'

Edward dismissed the ladies-in-waiting. I stood up to leave but Edward barked: 'Not you! Sit down!'

I deliberately fell backwards on to my behind with an elaborate show of haste and was rewarded with a giggle from Lady Leonora.

Edward could not stop himself from pacing up and down the chamber in his usual restless fashion. 'A snake named Charles is behind this change of plan,' he roared. 'A snake named Charles of Anjou, king of Sicily.'

'King Louis's young brother?' Leonora said. 'What is his involvement in all this?'

'Charles seized the throne of Sicily and now seeks to extend his empire into North Africa. His brother Louis conveniently arrives with a ready-made army and Charles has persuaded him to sail to Tunis in order to depose the ageing emir and add Tunis to his domains. My God!' Edward shouted, becoming intensely agitated again, 'when I think of the trouble I have gone to, the expense I have incurred, and the arguments I have had with my father, simply to be allowed to serve God in this most Christian and sacred duty of defeating the infidels, only to see our French allies diverted to serve an ignoble selfish jaunt, I could strangle Charles, and King Louis, with my bare hands!'

I had no doubt whatsoever that Lord Edward would be more than capable of doing just that. Leonora and I were silent as Edward, breathing heavily, tried to control his temper.

I began thinking of my warm bed, with Dolores beside me, and my comfortable house back in London and fervently hoped that this treacherous blow would mark the end of this crusading madness. I was to be disappointed.

Leonora finally spoke up and asked: 'What is to be done now, my lord? Are we to return home?'

Edward grunted. 'No,' he replied firmly. 'I have no choice but to follow King Louis and his army to Tunis. I may be able to persuade him to abandon his heathen mission and set his face towards Jerusalem where it belongs.'

A few days after first arriving in Aigues Mortes, therefore, the whole army embarked and set sail for Tunis.

OCTOBER 1270

The voyage from France was uneventful, apart from having to suffer Lord Edward's ill-tempered moods, but I will never forget our first sighting of the port of Tunis. We had sailed along the coast, past towering blue mountains, and then, after rounding a headland, the port came into view.

The ships of the French fleet were anchored in seemingly random and confused fashion in the large harbour. The seamen of my home town of Portsmouth would have been appalled by this lubberly display.

Beyond the azure water, the gleaming white and sombre ochre buildings of the city nestled under a brilliant azure sky. Smoke from several huge fires was rising over the city and the reason was obvious: an overpowering stench of death hung in the still air. We assumed that the French must have launched an attack on the city.

As our ships slowly moved closer over the mirror-calm blue water, a barge, flying the French royal standard, rowed out to meet us from their flagship. Our ships hove to and anchored as the French barge, its long sweeps making it appear like some enormous water insect, approached our royal cog.

Edward usually eschewed elaborate dress but he had swiftly donned a red and gold surcoat, embroidered with the royal arms of England, when he saw who was in the barge. It was Charles of Anjou himself, together with the son of King Louis, a young prince named Philip.

I was standing with a group of common seamen watching this

spectacle when, to my surprise, Lord Edward looked around and beckoned me forward into his presence. 'Hamo,' he whispered, 'arm yourself with a dagger, but conceal it well. I do not trust these men and, until I know what has occurred in this city, I want you to mark well any attempt on my life. Stay close outside the door after I have taken these gentlemen down to my cabin.'

The young French prince, Philip, who I judged to be no more than twenty years of age, *(he was, in fact, 25)* looked as pale and drawn as a spectre. He was dressed plainly, but with an elaborate gold chain around his neck, and I judged him, from his pale eyes and thin facial features, to be weak and indecisive. Compared to the robust and dominant figure of Lord Edward, who was only a few years older, Philip looked like a lost little boy.

Charles of Anjou, in complete contrast to Philip, radiated confidence and brutality. He was over forty years of age and at the height of his power and influence. Although not as tall as Lord Edward (very few men were!) he was darkly strong-featured, square-jawed, stockily built, and impressive in his surcoat emblazoned with his arms of gold fleurs-de-lis on a blue field.

Henry of Almain accompanied them down to the royal cabin to act as Edward's advisor.

The captain of the royal cog, together with his officers and distinguished passengers, watched curiously and disdainfully from a few feet away as I stood outside the cabin door.

I concentrated to block out all distractions and listened intently as Charles of Anjou began to speak: 'I have grave news, Lord Edward. A virulent plague struck soon after we had arrived and were investing the city. It destroyed any chance of defeating this infidel emir but, worse than that, it carried off our dear king and brother Louis. Young Philip here is now the king of France. He has also lost his younger brother. He grieves deeply.'

The discomfort in Charles's voice was evident, even from outside the door, as he conveyed this momentous news.

Edward said to the new King Philip: 'I fervently wish I could greet your accession in happier circumstances, sire, but I pray to understand what we are doing in this God forsaken hellhole? Our duty to God was to go to the Holy Land, not to depose this ancient emir from his city.'

Charles responded: 'We could have done both, Edward, if this dreadful plague had not intervened. I had received reports that the emir was amenable to conversion to Christianity. Surely it is doing God's work to depose or convert the emir and place his lands within the Christian domain of Sicily. Then we could have journeyed to the Holy Land to complete our task.'

Henry of Almain asked Charles: 'How many men have you lost, sire?'

'Hundreds,' Charles replied bluntly. 'And this pestilence has not yet done with us. That is why we rowed out to meet you, to prevent you and your army from suffering the same fate.'

'So you have neither gained Tunis as a prize or preserved an army in any condition to go on crusade?' Edward commented brutally.

In a reply calculated to infuriate Edward, Charles of Anjou replied: 'You did not join us at Aigues Mortes in time, Lord Edward. If we had successfully seized Tunis and you had then arrived, I have no doubt that you would have claimed your share of the spoils.'

'If I had arrived at Aigues Mortes in time,' Edward said, 'I would certainly have dissuaded King Louis from pandering to your foolish and self-seeking whim.'

Henry of Almain defused the vicious argument brewing by saying: 'Gentlemen, what is done is done and nothing can be gained by arguing whys and wherefores. You are all Christian princes and warriors for Christ. Let us consider what can be done to serve His purpose and rescue this venture? King Philip, what do you think we should do, sire?'

In a timid whisper that I could barely hear, King Philip of France, shocked out of his wits by fear and grief, replied: 'I don't know. I don't know.' Clearly the decisions would have to be made without his blessing or opinion.

'How secure is your fleet and your army?' Edward asked. 'What is to prevent this emir sending out his army to destroy us?'

It was Charles who answered: 'Have no fear, Edward. His army and his city suffer as grievously as we do and they are in no fit state to take advantage. It is a stalemate and I have already negotiated terms for our safe withdrawal. All that we have to do now is to decide where to proceed next.'

'That decision is clear,' Edward said. 'We must continue to the Holy Land, as soon as possible.'

'I agree,' Charles said. 'But my army… forgive me, King Philip's army, is in sore need of rest and recuperation. May I suggest that we all sail for the safety of my kingdom in Sicily and there replenish our ships and salve our battered souls.'

'And will you then follow us to the Holy Land yourself, Charles?' Edward asked, with unmistakeable sarcasm.

'I will try, but I have many administrative duties that need attending to in my kingdom.'

'Duties not pressing enough to have kept you from pursuing this impious escapade,' Edward said. 'Will you at least provide us with supplies?'

'Yes, of course,' Charles agreed.

'And men?'

'Perhaps, but I am sore pressed keeping control of my lands with the few men at my disposal. You, Lord Edward, should appreciate that problem.'

Once again Henry of Almain intervened to prevent more angry exchanges. To Edward he said: 'Whether or not our beloved cousin Charles can provide men to bolster our campaign, it seems eminently sensible to take advantage of his offer of rest and replenishment. It will make our chances of eventual success in the Holy Land more assured.'

Despite Edward's restless eagerness to get to grips with the infidel, he was too accomplished a military leader not to accept the common sense of improving preparations and for a period of rest and reflection before pressing on.

So it was decided, with the new king of France, Philip, taking no part in the decision, that both fleets would set sail, as soon as possible, for the haven of Christian Sicily. It was agreed that the French fleet, being far worse in condition, would make the shortest voyage, to Trapani, a port on the western tip of Sicily, while the English fleet would sail for the more prosperous and secure port of Palermo.

Thus we settled into our winter quarters in Palermo, a prosperous, pleasant and cultured city. A stay in such a favoured place was a prospect I viewed with more equanimity than that of being trapped in some dusty baking hellhole in the Levant.

Palermo is set on a crescent-shaped bay and enclosed by hazy blue mountains to the south. The city was once ruled by the Arabs, which is apparent from its architecture, including our quarters, the castle known as El Zisa. The Arabs had also constructed underground water storage chambers known as kanats, so both water and food were plentiful.

Despite the comfort of our surroundings I was still anxious to remove myself from this insanely ill-starred expedition and return to England. Lady Leonora was much too loyal to her dear husband to ever admit it, but I sensed that she felt the same way.

Lord Edward, however, and his increasingly influential cousin Henry of Almain, recovered their buoyant optimism and, after seemingly endless sessions of prayer, were fired with a new zeal for their crusading mission.

I was well aware that Lord Edward was listening more to the shrewd and sensible counsel of Henry than he was to the advice of a humble minstrel like me but there was nothing I could do to change that situation and I was secretly proud that Henry of Almain was my half-brother. I was also jealous of Henry's open and affectionate relationship with my liege lord. Then God or fate took a hand, which led to lethal consequences that haunt me to this day.

I was idly exploring the harbour in Palermo, buying fish and appreciating the delights of the local women, when a small sailing vessel arrived bearing momentous news. The gossip spread like the plague throughout the crowded dockside. The French fleet, while attempting to put into the port of Trapani, had been caught in a mighty squall and had been smashed to pieces along the west coast of Sicily.

Not only had the French lost many more men and horses, in addition to their losses suffered while besieging Tunis, but most of their treasure and supplies had been taken by the waves.

Young King Philip, already traumatised by the loss of his father and younger brother, and by the unexpectedly sudden burden of being the king of the great and complex nation of France, had decided to abandon the crusade and had already taken what remained of his battered army over to the mainland of Italy and was making a doleful and humiliating progress back to Paris.

It was fortunate that I heard this news before Lord Edward did because when, later that day, he summoned me for a game of chess, I had had time to conceive of a strategy that might succeed in either extricating myself or Henry of Almain from this forlorn expedition. If I could not get myself to a place of safety then I wanted Henry to be safe so that if, one day, I could prove that I was his half-brother and that Richard of Cornwall was my true father then I could take my place by his side openly and without subterfuge.

It was necessary to feign ignorance of the fateful news while Edward explained to me what had happened as we sat together over the chessboard in his royal chamber at the El Zisa, warmed from a chilly Sicilian evening by a fire burning in an ornate brass brazier.

I shook my head as if deeply grieved. 'That is calamitous news, my lord. One would almost think that God is doing His best to prevent this holy crusade.'

I waited impatiently for Edward's reply while he considered his next move. Eventually he said: 'God does, indeed, move in mysterious ways, Hamo, but in this situation His intention is, I believe, abundantly clear.'

'He wishes you to abandon the crusade?' I ventured hopefully.

'No, Hamo, quite the opposite. He wishes this crusade to continue but led by myself and not by that snake Charles of Anjou and his foolish French relatives. God has sent his wrath by punishing them with a storm and sending them home. This crusade continues, my friend, but led by me.'

Disappointed, but not surprised, that the crusade was not going to be abandoned, I prepared my next ploy with a serving of flattery. 'After freeing your father from the evil thrall of the barons back home, my lord, I believe there is no prince in Christendom more able to lead God's army.'

'I think you are correct,' Edward said smugly.

'May I ask, sire, what manner of man is the new French king Philip?'

'It ill behoves me to tittle-tattle about my fellow princes to a mere jester, Hamo.' I was relieved to see that Edward said this with an ironic and mocking smile. He asked: 'Tell me what you think of him?'

Carefully considering my words, I replied: 'As you say, my lord, I am but a mere jester, but I have heard say that King Philip is a weak and timid man, indecisive and easily lead. But who am I to pass judgement on great men?'

Edward, still smiling, replied: 'You have summed him up admirably, Hamo. King Philip is like a cushion. He bears the imprint of the last person to have sat on him.'

I chuckled dutifully at my master's joke, and then said: 'So he poses no threat to your future realm, my lord?'

Edward, suddenly wary, asked: 'In what way do you mean, Hamo?'

'Oh, I was merely thinking, my lord, that you are here accompanied by the flower of English knighthood and nobility while King Philip of France returns near to your lands in Gascony with his army, albeit a considerably weakened army. Perhaps a more formidable king would seek to take advantage of such a situation by casting covetous eyes on your rich provinces or even, dare I suggest it, England itself.'

As I suspected, my comments made Edward pensive. 'I have considered that possibility, Hamo, but, as you say, Philip is not man enough to take advantage of the situation, even if his army was intact.'

'Well, my lord, as I listened to your conversation outside the cabin door in Tunis harbour, I could not help remarking that King Charles of Sicily, the ruler of a far smaller kingdom than France, was doing all the talking for the king of France.'

Edward looked at me keenly. 'Yes, he was. And there is certainly no love lost between that avaricious and ambitious man King Charles and myself. Are you suggesting that Charles might persuade Philip to make an attack on my lands, now that he has been thwarted at Tunis?'

'You said yourself, my lord, that Charles is a snake. Who knows where he might bite next? Might it be a wise decision to temporarily abandon this crusade and return to make sure that your domains are safe from these devious men?'

'No, Hamo, that is not a possibility. I cannot abandon God's work simply on suspicion of a threat against either Gascony or England. My father and my uncle are perfectly capable of ensuring the safety of my lands while I am away.'

Pressing my argument in a way I knew would infuriate my master, I continued: 'The Welsh renegade Llewelyn still waits to the west to threaten England. If the French and the Welsh moved against your lands, a two-pronged attack from both sides simultaneously would be difficult for even the king or for your Uncle Richard to handle.'

As I had expected, Edward abandoned the chess board and sat back in his chair with an exasperated expression. 'Well, Hamo, when did my loyal fool become a student of the commentaries of Caesar or the strategy of Hannibal?'

I suspected that Edward was needled because, in his crusading zeal, he had not given suffcient consideration to these possibilties.

'Forgive me, my lord, if I speak too boldly but surely the king and the royal council should at least be made aware of the situation. If you need someone you can trust to take a warning message back to England, I am ready to serve you.'

Edward, duped by my apparent willingness to sacrifice myself, replied: 'God bless you, Hamo. I know I could trust you but what would Lady Leonora and I do for entertainment if I sent you back to England? And, alas, you are supposed to be an imbecile in the eyes of others. But you are correct that someone must return, and it will have to be someone I can trust implicitly and who has the stature and authority to fully explain what has occurred here to my father and the royal council.'

I had known that Edward would not, indeed could not, select me for this mission so, as carefully as I played my next chess move, I played my next suggestion. 'I can think of only one man of sufficient nobility, shrewdness, skill, courage and loyalty to be given this task.'

'My cousin Henry,' Edward said, before I could.

'Indeed, my lord. He is sufficiently respected to be able to ascertain what the French court are planning, if anything, while he travels through France, and then advise your father and the royal council back in England.'

Edward drummed his fingers on the table. 'He would be most upset to be deprived of the chance to fight for God in the East.'

'But he would be doing God's work in protecting your realm and ensuring that you can do your Christian duty by leading this crusade without any worry about the security of your lands.'

To my relief, Edward nodded in agreement. 'You are correct, faithful friend. Cousin Henry must follow the French army home.'

So Henry of Almain reluctantly said farewell to the crusade and those of us who remained spent a pleasant enough winter in Palermo. Early in the spring of 1271, with our ships and men refreshed and replenished, we set sail for the Holy Land.

MAY 1271

It was the month of May when the English fleet gained landfall at our destination, the great crusader port and citadel of Acre. Borne in by hot winds and welcomed by cheering crowds and the smell of exotic fruits and spices, the fleet dropped anchor. The harbour was situated next to a spit of land and was protected by a massive tower, known as the Tower of the Flies, which had been constructed at the very end of the spit.

We were greeted with joy by the inhabitants of the city. It seemed as if the entire population had bustled down to the harbour to help unload the ships, bring us refreshments, and offer all sorts of goods and services. We soon discovered the reason for their jubilation. A few weeks earlier, the most formidable crusader castle in the Holy Land, Crac des Chevaliers, had fallen to the infidel hordes, which sent a frisson of terror and apprehension through the citizens of Acre. If a great fortress like Crac des Chevaliers could fall, then perhaps even the mighty walls of Acre were not impregnable.

When I was allowed ashore, grateful to be relieved of a swaying deck, I immediately made a tour of the city and was mightily impressed by the strength of Acre's fortifications and the city's extensive facilities. There were also many churches and hospitals run by the Knights Hospitaler and Knights Templar. The residential area, known as the Montmusard, was surrounded by its own double wall and, best of all, the palace of the crusader kings, where I would be based with Lord Edward and Lady Leonora, was protected by the most massive fortifications I had ever seen.

All in all, the city was a lot safer, more comfortable and

1: The Making of a King

prosperous than I had dared hope, being the largest city in the crusader kingdom of Outremer.

Within the palace, I was allotted my own sleeping niche situated within the apartments occupied by Lord Edward and Lady Leonora. My living condition was nowhere near as comfortable as my own homes in England but it was much more tolerable than I had been fearing.

Having examined the seemingly impregnable walls of the city for myself, I was not concerned when Edward's spies brought news that the formidable Mamluk leader, a man named Baibars, had received news of the arrival of the English crusading army and had abandoned his siege of the city of Tripoli in order to move on Acre.

Brother Godfrey now once again interrupts me and displays his youthful ignorance by asking me what 'Mamluk' means. Well, boy, the Mamluks were an army of former slaves, drawn from many countries, that were used by the Muslim sultans because their low-born status could not threaten such a ruler. What's that you say? You think they do not sound very formidable? I made the same assumption, so pick up your quill, listen carefully, and learn…

This man Baibars had defeated the crusaders in several battles. Gossip told that Baibars was a former slave, that he was seven feet tall, dark-skinned, and with piercing blue eyes. I dismissed all this gossip as superstitious nonsense and, secure in the belief that a former slave could be no match for a formidable royal warrior like Lord Edward and certainly no threat to the massive fortifications of Acre, I continued unconcerned to enjoy the life of this warm and vibrant eastern city.

Even when news came that a nearby fortress, known as Montfort, had fallen to the advancing Mamluk army, I was not concerned.

But then, one day towards the end of June, I witnessed a sight which terrified me more than any other sight I have ever seen in my long life.

JUNE 1271

L ord Edward had decided to make a formal and detailed inspection tour of the defensive walls to ensure they were being sufficiently manned and to bolster the morale of his men. He had dressed himself in his most splendid surcoat and chain mail and had ordered his senior commanders, and many other august personages, to accompany him on his inspection.

Lady Leonora, bored with her confinement within the palace, insisted on accompanying him, albeit at a discreet and respectful distance behind the military group. I was ordered to accompany Leonora and protect her from the sun by the use of a device, common among the Spanish, called a parasol. This device consisted of a large square of fabric stretched and secured over a light wooden frame. I was supposed to hold this parasol over Lady Leonora's head.

Much to the amused delight of hundreds of citizens who were watching Edward's progression around the walls, it was proving a difficult task for me to position this parasol correctly, as Leonora was taller than I was, and she was snappily chiding me for my incompetence.

We were walking along the top of the outermost defensive wall, which overlooked a vast empty plain stretching out to the shimmering horizon, when Lady Leonora suddenly stopped walking. Edward, in company with his many commanders and advisers, was well ahead of us and had not noticed that we had ceased following him.

Lady Leonora was in a capricious and delicate condition having miscarried of a daughter a few weeks before during the arduous journey to the Holy Land. Fearful for her welfare, I looked at her taut and pale features and asked: 'What ails you, my lady?'

Leonora held a finger to her lips to instruct me to stay silent, which we remained for several moments. Then she asked: 'Did you hear that, Hamo?'

Perplexed by her question, I replied: 'I heard nothing untoward, my lady. What can you hear?'

Leonora stood pensively for a long moment and then said: 'It sounds like a host of voices, far, far away in the distance, like a heavenly choir or a great sea of voices rolling towards us.'

Debating to myself whether Leonora had been touched by the sun or was experiencing a religious ecstasy, I looked anxiously ahead for Lord Edward.

Then, faintly, I heard what Leonora had heard.

It sounded like a communal wail of anguish or triumph, I could not tell which, emanating from thousands of voices. I again looked along the wall towards Edward and saw that he and his retinue had evidently heard the same thing because they had stopped and were standing, without speaking, and looking out towards the horizon.

Leonora and I looked out over the vast undulating plain, treeless apart from scattered small bushes and scrub. Very gradually, it appeared as if the line of the horizon was turning black. This black line advanced and became broader and, through the shimmering heat, the line appeared to dance and wriggle like a monstrous black snake covering the horizon. Towering plumes of dust were forming above this black snake.

The snake increased in width and was moving forwards, like a black wave moving in slow motion towards us. The sound of voices was increasing in volume.

Then banners became visible, thousands of them, filling the sky above the advancing tide of men, for men is what they were. The hideous black snake was the army of Sultan Baibars arriving at the walls of Acre.

The advance guard of the Mamluk army became visible as a line of chargers, horses of different colours, ridden by men wearing elaborate armour and carrying brightly coloured banners which bore all manner of arcane symbols. You may call me a liar, but I have never seen so many men in one place, before or since, and I estimate that Baibar's army must have numbered at least fifty thousand men.

Edward had become anxious for the safety of his wife, even though it would take the enemy at least another half an hour to reach the walls of Acre. He strode towards us and, looking at his pale and shocked face, I could tell that he was thinking exactly what I was thinking. What could Edward's army of a mere few hundred knights achieve against a tidal wave of Saracen knights who were all armoured with chain mail, round shields and wickedly curved scimitars?

Edward ordered me: 'Escort Lady Leonora back to the palace, Hamo, as swiftly as you can.' He looked out again at the advancing Mamluk army, one of the few times I ever saw him truly discomposed, and whispered to me so that Leonora could not hear: 'God preserve us, Hamo. I did not dream that armies such as this existed.' Then he remembered his regal duty to lead by example and resolved: 'God has sent me on this mission and, whatever He has in store for me, I must bear with Christian courage.'

I watched Edward stride back to rejoin his retinue and thought to myself that I did not have to bear anything with Christian courage. I would escort Leonora back to the palace, make an excuse to leave her, run down to the harbour and, whatever the cost, hire a vessel to carry me away from certain death at the hands of this terrifying infidel army. I had no doubt that in a matter of hours, despite the intervening walls of Acre, I would be feeling Saracen steel being drawn across my throat and dying in screaming agony.

I escorted Lady Leonora back to the royal apartments. News of Baibars arrival was already creating an atmosphere of panic within the palace. Servants and officials were darting to and fro, all with the same haunted expression on their faces.

As soon as I dare, I informed Leonora: 'Excuse me, my lady, but there are some urgent tasks I must attend to.'

Leonora stared at me, wild-eyed with terror. 'Don't leave me alone, Hamo. I don't want to be alone when I die.'

'I will send your ladies to comfort you,' I replied in desperation. 'What good am I as a comfort?'

'God sent you to me, Hamo. Have you forgotten? You are small but you are very strong. You may be able to defend me from the infidels.'

Lady Leonora, in her panic, had lost all sense of royal decorum. She even clung to my arm for a few moments. I cautiously made her release me and then poured her a goblet of wine. My hand was shaking when I handed her the goblet, and her hand shook as she took it.

The wine seemed to calm her nerves, or perhaps she was simply resigning herself to her fate. Neither of us had any doubt that nothing, not even the double wall defences of Acre, could possibly withstand the army of Baibars.

Leonora's ladies-in-waiting had heard the dreadful news of Baibar's arrival and had entered the royal apartments in search of their mistress. They were all sobbing as, I could well imagine, were the rest of the inhabitants of the city.

Lady Leonora noticed me edging towards the door of the apartments and cried out: 'Don't abandon me, Hamo. I need you, and so will Lord Edward.'

I considered that Lord Edward would not need my help but, as I looked at Leonora's pale, panicked and tear-stained face, I knew that I had to stay with her. I did not want to die but, in my way, I loved Leonora and I realised that if I ran away now I would forever be cursed as a coward and a nonentity.

'Madam!' I blustered, as if shocked by her suggestion, 'I have no intention of abandoning you.'

The royal ladies-in-waiting were not used to hearing me speak intelligently and I realised, in the tension of the situation, that I had slipped out of my assumed idiot character. The ladies seemed not to be surprised by my sudden coherence and even begged me to stay with them.

We men are but poor gullible fools when pleaded with to be manly by women, so I picked up my harp, gave them my most reassuring idiotic grin, and began to play. I expected, at any moment, to hear the cries of Saracen assassins bursting through the door.

We waited in those royal apartments for several long hours, strained almost beyond endurance, not knowing what was happening outside. We had been somewhat reassured by the arrival of a strong contingent of knights sent by Edward for our protection, and a message that the Mamluks were not yet investing the city as had been expected, but the unspoken fear that we were doomed remained with us.

After those long hours Lord Edward himself entered the apartments. He looked dishevelled and very tired but calm enough. He took in the sight of me entertaining the distraught and fearful women and said quietly: 'Thank you, my most faithful friend, for comforting my wife.'

Lady Leonora, overjoyed to see her beloved husband still alive, asked him: 'What is happening, my lord?'

Edward, fully comprehending his wife's intense fear, smiled reassuringly: 'Thank God, for the Mamluk army has departed. The danger has passed. Hamo, pour me some wine.' He sat down wearily in an armchair.

I did as Lord Edward commanded while he thanked the ladies-in-waiting but indicated they should leave. I handed the wine to Lord Edward and he ordered me to stay and play soothing airs while he talked to his wife.

Lady Leonora, now weeping with relief, said: 'Praise be to God that we are delivered from the infidel, but why did they not attack us?'

'Because they do not need to,' Edward sighed. 'This sultan, this man Baibars, is a shrewd commander. He knows that if he flung his army against the walls of this city then they would suffer catastrophic losses, even against such a small defending force as ours.'

'Then why did take the trouble to come here at all?' Leonora asked.

'This display of his might was to send me a message. He came here to display his strength but also his clemency. He has released all the prisoners taken from the siege of Montfort Castle. The citizens of Acre, who are not all Christians, have witnessed this strength and this clemency and will be thinking "why should we die defending this city when Baibars will spare our lives?". He has shown me his power, the size of his army, the number of his men. I have a few hundred knights and attendants. He is saying to me that I cannot possible defeat him in open battle and, God forgive me for agreeing with him, but he is right.' Edward, plainly shocked and dispirited by the events of the day, took a long gulp of wine.

'Then what is to be done, husband.'

Edward shrugged, trying to remain confident. 'We must do what we can to recover the Holy City, as God wills it. We are here and we must do our Christian duty, whatever the opposition and whatever the outcome.'

I thought of Dolores tucked up comfortably in our bed at Westminster while I was stuck here in this baking prison, serving a militarily impotent master, and still facing the prospect of an agonising death. I became almost overwhelmed with anguish.

Soon after the shocking and demoralising demonstration of how numerous and formidable was the Mamluk army ranged against him, Edward received a report that propelled him into a savage fury. It was a fury of an intensity I had never seen before, despite having witnessed many displays of his Angevin temper in the past; a fury that made me sorely fear for my friendship with him, and even fearful for my life.

A messenger despatched by Charles of Anjou brought the

devastating news that Henry of Almain was dead. He had been murdered, and when Edward was informed of the identity of the murderers, he was seized with an almost insane lust for revenge.

The murderers were none other that Guy and Simon de Montfort, the two sons of Edward's mortal enemy, Simon de Montfort. The two sons had fled England after the death of their father at the battle of Evesham.

Edward ordered a holy mass to be held for the soul of his cousin that, thankfully, I was not required to attend. I was left alone to reflect, poignantly, bitterly, on the fate of my secret half-brother.

Later on that same day, however, Edward summoned me to his chamber on the pretence of playing a game of chess. I say 'pretence' because he was drinking copiously, which was unusual for him, and quite unable to concentrate on a game of chess, even if he had been interested.

He was wearing the simplest and plainest woollen tunic, as if he were somehow punishing himself or paying a penance. Having not been apprised of the purpose of his summons I had to employ all my iron self-control to prevent myself quaking with fear because it had been me who had persuaded Edward of the need to send Henry of Almain on his fateful mission. I was in dread that the blame for Henry's death would somehow attach itself to me.

Edward made a show of actually playing a game but between every move he would stop and stare into the distance, sometimes for several long moments, and sometimes muttering curses and imprecations like a man demented.

Edward, all royal protocol forgotten, was pouring me goblet after goblet of wine, so that I was compelled to match him drink for drink. I managed to avoid drinking them all without Edward noticing by pouring them away when I staggered to the garderobe for a piss, but I could still feel myself becoming slurringly drunk.

With the courage borne of wine, and mourning for a lost half-brother, I eventually asked Edward to tell me exactly what fate had dealt to his cousin.

Edward said: 'Henry had reached Viterbo, which is just outside Rome. The two de Montfort brothers, by evil coincidence, had also arrived in Viterbo. They somehow heard that Henry was hearing mass in the church of Saint Silvester. They went to the church and stabbed him to death. In the church, Hamo! Not since the murder of Becket a hundred years ago has there been perpetrated such an infamous deed, to violate the sanctuary of a church in such a way. Then they dragged Henry's body outside and mutilated it some more, saying that it was in vengeance for what had been done to their father at the battle of Evesham. Poor Henry did not even fight in that battle! Their real intention was to take their revenge against me. I cannot get the thought of poor Henry's mutilated body out of my mind, that is why I drink. We were childhood friends. He was my most trusted adviser and companion.' [23]

Edward paused to take another long draught of wine. A cruel and sly expression suffused his face. His drooping eyelid twitched and the dangerous sibilant lisp became more pronounced. 'I will have my revenge on whoever did this, Hamo. If only I could take my army there and root out the perpetrators!'

Edward thumped the table so hard that goblets and chess pieces jumped up into the air.

The rest of that mournful evening is lost in a fog of wine and the intense feeling of relief when it became apparent that Edward did not hold me culpable for the fate of Henry of Almain.

JULY 1271

Another affliction was sent to test our mettle during the next month of July. The weather became unbearably hot. It was impossible to find relief despite an occasional moderate cooling breeze off the sea. All we could do was stay in the shade and pray for night to fall.

Lord Edward, however, had recovered his ebullient spirits and, always restless for action, conceived a plan for an attack on a castle named St. Georges Lebeyne, which was situated some twelve miles from Acre.

I sensed much apprehension among the knights and squires as they prepared for this mission. They were not afraid of Baibars but they were very afraid of the unaccustomed heat. They dare not, however, refuse Lord Edward's zealous commands.

The remnants of this disastrous enterprise came straggling home late at night. Leonora despatched me to the palace courtyard to aid the comfort of Lord Edward in any way I could.

The knights were being dismounted and stripped of their chain mail armour. The memory of the stench is something that turns my stomach to this day. The knights were not able to remove their armour during the day, which meant that, when need arose, they had to piss themselves, and this was mixed with the sweat from their bodies.

To add to the brew, most of them were suffering from diarrhoea or, even worse, dysentry, owing to the unfamiliar Eastern diet of fruit, raisins and honey, and such like. Most of them were also suffering piteously from heat stroke.

The squires and pages were unable to hide their disgust at

having to perform these gruesome tasks, and the knights were too debilitated to take umbrage at such disrespectful disgust.

I had never before seen Lord Edward looking so ill and distraught. Although the expedition had managed to seize some cattle and some crops, the attack on the castle itself had failed abjectly.

I had obtained a large flagon of cooled wine that Edward drank down in one gulp and then ordered me to fetch some more. Later, he slept for several hours but was still exhausted and much chastened when he awoke.

Once again, however, Edward's natural high spirits reasserted themselves and, a few weeks later, a lavish feast was held in the great hall of Acre Palace. All of Edward's senior commanders, those who had survived the disastrous raid on St. Georges Lebeyne, were present. I remember this feast very well because also present were three men who, to my intense chagrin, distracted attention away from my tumbling and fooling.

They were a Venetian merchant family named Niccolo, Maffeo and Marco Polo. These three men were clearly insane but highly amusing. They had travelled to Acre from Cyprus and were returning to the country called Cathay, which I had vaguely heard of, to resume trading with the inhabitants.

They related concocted stories about this country but, despite all our derisory and mocking laughter, we could not shift them from their delusions. They claimed that this Cathay was as big as all Europe combined, that there were many cities, each one containing many more thousands of people than cities such as London, Rome or Jerusalem.

They claimed that the inhabitants had never heard of God or Jesus Christ, and that their nobles lived in more opulent conditions than we could possibly conceive. They talked of man-made rivers hundreds of miles long, they talked of ships so large that even the royal cog would fit into them four times and, most laughable of all, the Polos claimed that these strange yellow people had spent centuries building a defensive wall that was many hundreds of miles long in order to keep out their enemies!

All these fantasies about Cathay were most amusing but Lord Edward, after the meal had been taken, brought the company back to the serious business of the evening. He stood up to his full impressive height and announced: 'Gentlemen, we have seen the strength of the infidel army. Let us be frank and admit that it is formidable, much more formidable than the combined forces of we, gathered here tonight, can consider challenging. There is, however, an army as large and as formidable to the north of here. If we are to defeat Baibars, we must seek an alliance with the Mongols. I have already sent emissaries north with messages of greeting and respect to Abagha, the il-Khan of Persia, proposing an alliance to our mutual advantage. Gentlemen, it is our only chance to rid the Holy Land of the infidel.'

Why do you shudder, boy? You cannot believe that the Christian Lord Edward would seek the help of the brutal barbarians who have laid waste to most of Asia and half of Europe? He was desperate, I can tell you, and he would have made a pact with the Devil himself in order to free Jerusalem. His strategy seemed to be succeeding because the Mongols drove the Mamluks out of Aleppo but then Baibars advanced to meet them and the Mongols withdrew. Even the mighty Mongols were afraid of Baibars. So, brother, this was God's judgement on Lord Edward's strategy, and my liege lord was contrite and desolate.

So, after months of effort, we had arrived at a situation where the Mongols had been frightened off, the Christian crusaders were bottled up, harmlessly impotent, within their own walls, and Sultan Baibars was in complete control of the Holy Land.

Lord Edward was outmanned and had been comprehensively outmanoeuvred and, was desolately aware of the inadequacy of his crusading forces. Being an energetic and proud prince, he felt the frustration and humiliation keenly.

So the entire Christian garrison of Acre drifted into months of impotent inactivity. I filled the long hours with various schemes to make myself richer but I longed to be back in England. I was also putting on weight, thanks to endless eating and drinking to relieve the boredom, and I was uncomfortably aware that my abilities as a tumbler and acrobat were waning. Fate was waiting to take a hand in that issue but, in the meantime, we received news that finally ended any hope of retaking the Holy City.

In April 1272, Baibars agreed a ten year truce with every other city, faction and army in the Holy Land. Every one, that is, except Acre under the command of Lord Edward.

Edward's strong Christian and moral convictions would not allow him to accept such a truce. As a result, the other cities and factions that had previously supported the crusade, now saw Edward as a threat to this new-found peace and stability in the region. But Edward refused to comply with what he regarded as a shameful capitulation to the infidel.

Thus we remained in a stalemate situation in which Edward could not venture out to attack Baibars but equally Baibars could not attack Edward by breaching the walls of Acre without losing many men.

However, Baibars did launch an attack on Edward, and it was in a way that changed my life forever.

JUNE 1272

The seventeenth day of June was Lord Edward's birthday. On that evening he and Leonora had enjoyed a private meal together in the royal apartments. It was a serenely mild and balmy night and, looking out of the narrow palace windows, the eastern sky was filled with glittering stars, and the hazy silver disc of the moon appeared larger than usual.

After they had partaken of their meal I was summoned to entertain the royal couple with gentle ballads and harp music. I found them blissfully happy in each other's company.

In honour of the occasion they were both dressed more grandly than normal when alone together in private, Edward in his surcoat embroidered with the royal arms and Lady Leonora radiantly beautiful in a light blue and silver gown that displayed her black hair and sparkling brown eyes in full loveliness.

Their daughter Joan, born only two months before, was gurgling happily in her crib. I sat cross-legged on the carpet beside Joan's crib and, as the evening progressed, I noticed that Edward was well in his cups. I was aware that he had been drinking more than was good for him, Lady Leonora had remarked upon it, but we both agreed that it was simply owing to the frustration of his present situation and that, once relieved of this impotent impasse, he would return to his normal abstemious habits.

The evening was drawing to a close when one of Edward's closest and most loyal friends, a Savoyard knight named Otto de Grandson, requested admittance. Edward consented and de Grandson was ushered into the royal presence. Edward greeted his friend cordially and beckoned him forward. 'Otto, my friend! Come in.'

De Grandson bowed low to Edward and then to Lady Leonora. 'A thousand apologies for interrupting your celebration, my lord. Masruq ibn Mansur requests a private audience with you as soon as possible.'

'Masruq ibn Mansur?' Edward repeated blearily. 'Who is he?'

'He is the leader of the group who have defected from the camp of the infidel Baibars.'

'Ah, yes, of course,' Edward nodded.

A group of seven deserters from Baibar's army had arrived at the gates of Acre seeking sanctuary a few days before. They claimed they had been senior officers but had been put under a death penalty for various offences, and that they were deeply opposed to Baibars's savage policies against certain enemies.

They had been admitted and had, indeed, furnished useful information about the movements and composition of the Mamluk armies, even if the English crusaders were unable to act upon such information.

In an irritated tone, Edward asked: 'Could this not wait until the morrow? Why does he wish to see me now?'

'He has brought you a birthday gift on behalf of the Mamluk deserters,' de Grandson answered. 'He desires to help you celebrate your birthday by presenting it to you tonight. It is a very handsome gift of a gold casket containing jewels.'

I noticed Lady Leonora's eyes widen greedily at that statement.

De Grandson continued: 'Masruq also insists that he has just learned some vital information that you should know about without delay.'

'Will he not tell you what this information is, Otto?'

'No, my lord. Despite all my threats and cajoling, he will not tell me. He insists this information is for your ears only. I warned him that you were enjoying your birthday privately with Lady Leonora but Masruq is most insistent.'

Edward thought for a moment and then looked at Lady Leonora. 'Would you mind, my dear, if I interrupt our evening to hear what this Persian gentleman has to tell me?'

Leonora, no doubt thinking of that casket of jewels, answered: 'Of course not, my lord. I well know that your duty must come first in all things.'

Nevertheless, Edward slammed down his goblet of wine with no little annoyance and began to rise from his chair. He was swaying slightly as he asked: 'Has this man been searched for weapons?'

'Yes, sire,' de Grandson answered. 'He is unarmed.'

'Searched thoroughly?'

'Yes, sire. I searched him myself, even in the depths of his nether regions. Forgive my crudeness, Lady Leonora.'

Lady Leonora inclined her head to reassure de Grandson that it was perfectly all right, and then Edward ordered: 'Very well. I will give him audience in the next room. Will we need the interpreter?'

'I think not. This man speaks passable Latin.'

I considered that there was something deeply suspicious about Masruq ibn Mansur's request. I was a master of the art of deception and I had learned much about the fanatical piety and subtle intelligence of the Saracens during my time in Acre. There was no earthly reason why this man Masruq should need to impart information to Lord Edward immediately, even if the army of Baibars was, at that moment, flinging themselves against the walls of Acre. The casket of jewels could easily have been presented to Edward much earlier in the day and was suspiciously like the bait in a trap.

I could see that Edward, despite his irritation, was desperate to glean any little success or advantage over Baibars and that he was, quite possibly, walking into that trap. Edward's recent vigorous drinking habits had become well-known and it would be reasonable for an enemy to assume that, late on the evening of his birthday, his judgement and reactions would be impaired by wine.

I sensed grave danger. I had to remain in character as the idiot jester so I began to rock backwards and forwards on my haunches and moan as if in pain.

Edward stopped and looked down at me. 'What ails you, fool?'

I looked at him, trying to stamp an expression of alarm on my face, and intoned, as if in a trance: 'The lamb presents itself to the lion, the sparrow flies towards the hawk, the leopard offers himself to the father of conquests.'

'Hush, stop your babbling, Hamo,' Lady Leonora said.

But Edward, despite being befuddled by drink, understood my warning. An epithet applied to him in his younger days had been 'the leopard' and an epithet applied to Baibars was 'father of conquests'. Quietly, he instructed me: 'Stand by the curtain, Hamo, and watch this man.'

There was an elaborately brocaded curtain separating the dining chamber with a larger chamber that Edward used to receive visitors. I could peep around the edge of this curtain and see the large wooden armchair, almost like a throne, which Edward would use when receiving those visitors who were paying homage. He settled himself into this chair and ordered de Grandson, waiting at the entrance to the apartments, to bring in Masruq ibn Mansur.

Masruq entered the apartment. He walked slowly in an almost regal manner. His long black hair and beard flowed down to a long robe of green silk embroidered with gold filigree work. His aquiline nose looked aristocratic and the expression on his face was serene and not at all tense or apprehensive.

For a moment I thought I had been mistaken in my suspicions but then I realised I had seen such a serene look on the faces of habitues of vice dens in Acre. It was caused by a drug named hashish.

Masruq held the jewel casket in his hands, with arms stretched forward, as he approached Lord Edward. Masruq bowed. Edward inclined his head in response and then the gold casket fell to the floor, scattering jewels all over the carpet.

Masruq, seemingly from out of nowhere, was brandishing a long thin dagger. Leaping towards Edward, Masruq brought down the dagger with bewildering speed. Edward just had time to raise his arm and the dagger ripped into the muscles of his upper left arm. Edward cried out in pain and then raised his long right leg and kicked out viciously at Masruq.

By this instant I had thrown back the curtain and was hurling myself at Masruq with all the force I could muster. Edward's kick had provided a split second reprieve by throwing Masruq slightly off balance as he was raising the dagger to strike again.

I crashed into Masruq and we both went toppling over to the floor. Masruq struck his head against the edge of a side table as we fell. Using all my strength I managed to seize the assassin in a headlock but his dagger arm was free and he plunged the knife into my leg time and time again before Lord Edward, blood streaming down his arm, came to my aid and kicked the knife out of Masruq's hand.

Masruq struggled to free himself from my grip but I grabbed his long hair, twined it around my hand and pulled his head back violently until his eyes were popping out of their sockets. I took his chin with my other hand and wrenched his head until I heard his neck snap. Masruq went limp in my arms and I angrily thrust his corpse away.

I could see my warm sticky blood spreading over the carpet as Edward, deeply shocked, stumbled backwards on to his throne. Lady Leonora was already at his side and was attempting to staunch the flow of blood from his arm. Otto de Grandson had burst into the apartment, quickly surveyed the scene with a horrified expression, and was calling frantically for help from the royal servants.

I could feel myself losing consciousness but a frightening thought occurred to me from stories I had heard in the drinking dens and markets of Acre: perhaps the dagger had been poisoned? Gathering the last of my failing wits I shouted to Lady Leonora: 'Poison! Suck out the poison!'

Although she was weeping and shaking and as pale as winter, Leonora understood my meaning and I saw her tear open the sleeve of Edward's surcoat and, without hesitation, put her mouth to his wound. Then I fell into a deep black void with the despairing certainty that this was the end of my miserable life.

I awoke with an almost unbearable throbbing pain in my leg. I found I was in bed within a very long and airy white-washed room with a vaulted ceiling. Golden light streamed through the high and narrow windows. I remember thinking that perhaps I was in heaven, although I doubted God would admit me after reviewing my lamentable catalogue of earthly sins.

I gingerly turned my head and saw other beds, at least thirty, arranged in a line down each side of this room, most occupied by fellow sufferers.

When my wits returned fully I noticed that my bed space was more comfortably appointed, in every respect, than all the others. I had been given a side table furnished with a decanter of wine and a bowl of oriental sweetmeats.

A monk in a grey habit was attending the sick further along the room. He noticed that I had become conscious and, ignoring other pleas for help, hurried to my bedside. He said anxiously: 'I will inform the doctor that you have awoken, sir. Is there anything I can do for you?'

'Drink,' I managed to croak, realising that my throat was chokingly dry. 'A drink, please.'

The monk poured wine, which was cool and well watered. As he was helping me to take a few sips, I asked: 'Where am I?'

'You are in the hospital of Saint Thomas of Canterbury.'

In my groggy confusion I asked: 'Canterbury? Am I back in England?'

'No, sir. You are still in Acre. I will fetch the doctor.'

'Wait,' I said, plucking at his sleeve. 'Lord Edward? Does he still live?'

The monk stared at me wildly and answered, almost in a panic: 'I will fetch the doctor.'

The monk scuttled off. I lifted the linen sheet covering my

naked body and looked down at my aching leg. It had been bandaged and smeared with some sort of substance that smelled quite sweet.

I began to doze off again, immensely relieved simply to be alive, but the monk returned and gently shook my shoulder to rouse me. 'The doctor is here to see you, sir.'

I looked beyond the monk but I could not see anyone else except a young woman who was dressed in a long grey habit with a hood concealing her hair. 'Where is the doctor?' I demanded.

'This is Doctor Trotta,' the monk replied, indicating the woman as she moved towards my bed.

'No, this is a woman. I want to see a doctor.'

'Signorina Trotta *is* the doctor,' the monk insisted. 'She is treating Lord Edward as well.'

The dark-skinned woman, more like a girl, aged no more than twenty, appraised me with her deep brown eyes. She laid the palm of her hand on my forehead and the coolness of her touch was heavenly. I asked: 'You are treating Lord Edward?'

Doctor Trotta nodded.

'Then he lives?'

'Yes, he lives, but his wound is infected. He is dangerously ill. Unlike you.'

Her voice was soft and soothing, but no-one likes to hear their malady belittled, so I challenged her: 'How do you know? You cannot be a doctor. You are a woman.'

Doctor Trotta did not appear to be offended by my statement and simply smiled, but the monk leapt to her defence by saying: 'Doctor Trotta is a most respected doctor. She studied at Salerno and is here in Acre studying the works of Arabic doctors.' [24]

'Arabic doctors?' I snorted. 'What can such infidel savages teach us?'

This time it was Doctor Trotta who answered. 'It is they who have saved your life and, much more importantly, the knowledge they have discovered is helping me to save the life of your master, Prince Edward.'

'In what way do you mean?'

'The salve I have applied to your leg is a mixture of herbs and honey that has been found, by those Arabic doctors you despise, to staunch the flow of blood and to prevent gangrene.'

'Why, then, is Lord Edward's wound infected and mine is not? Was the assassin's dagger poisoned?'

'No. I suspect it was infected when Lady Leonora attempted to suck out the poison that she imagined was on the assassin's dagger. Many infections are spread through the mouth. I have not told her that is so.'

'Nonsense,' I snorted. 'I am tired of your lies. What sort of quack mountebank are you?'

Ignoring my insult, Doctor Trotta asked: 'I understand that you are Lord Edward's fool, and that you are a tumbler and acrobat as well.'

As soon as she had asked the question, I realised that my self-imposed mask as an idiotic halfwit had slipped completely. In an instant, I became aware that I was desperately tired of that role and that I wanted to discard it. It was if I sensed what Doctor Trotta was going to say next.

She said gently: 'Your wound will heal but your leg will never again be strong enough to allow you to perform tumbling tricks. You will, most probably, be able to walk again, but it will always be with difficulty. I am very sorry.'

I looked into her eyes expecting to see glee but all I saw was genuine compassion. She said: 'I will return tonight to examine your wound. Call me if the pain increases or if you suffer any other reaction.'

Doctor Trotta turned and left the room. I watched her slim and elegant figure with a warm feeling of security and assurance. I said to the monk: 'I have never heard of a woman being a doctor.'

'She has been here only a few months,' the monk replied, 'but I have seen her perform such miraculous cures as our dear Lord would have been proud of. If anyone can save Lord Edward's life, it is she. Now, Lady Leonora has been informed that you have woken. She asked to be informed and she wishes to see you as soon as she can leave her husband. Do you wish for food?'

'No, I am not hungry, but pour me some more wine.'

The monk did as I asked and then left me in peace.

As I sunk back into a slumber, all I could see was the face of Doctor Trotta. Like all self-seeking rogues I feel humbled and ashamed when faced with genuine goodness and piety, even then as my mind lashed in protest at my painful and crippled fate.

Many hours later, it must have been late in the afternoon, I was awoken by the monk. As I was blearily gathering my wits, two young monks began erecting folding screens around my bed.

'What is happening?' I asked.

The elder monk answered, unable to conceal his excitement, that Lady Leonora had arrived to visit me and did I feel well enough to receive her? I replied that I did but I needed a drink and to use the chamber pot before she was admitted.

·   After these preparations had been completed, Lady Leonora entered the ward, fawningly accompanied by the monk. Leonora was dressed in the modest grey woollen habit of a nun, her head hidden from view by a hood, wanting to attract no attention and ensure that her visit was entirely informal.

A padded stool had been placed by my bed so that Leonora could sit down beside me. After the screens had been closed around us, Leonora smiled at me sweetly and took my hand. 'Bless you, Hamo,' she said softly. 'Thank you for the life of my husband.' She raised the back of my hand to her lips and kissed it.

Flustered by her plain sincerity and by this unaccustomed intimate honour, I replied: 'I only did my duty, my lady. I am distressed to hear that Lord Edward still suffers, even while I thank God for his survival.'

Leonora gave me back my hand and patted it reassuringly as she said: 'Good Doctor Trotta is confident of his eventual return to health. She says that Lord Edward is a strong and fit man and she is doing all within her power to return him to us.'

'She seems to be a remarkable woman.'

'They say she is one of the best doctors in Europe. It is fortunate that she happened to be here in Acre.'

'Something has been puzzling me, my lady. From where did the assassin Masruq produce the dagger to attack Lord Edward?'

Lady Leonora shuddered at the memory. 'Otto de Grandson inspected the casket of jewels that the infidel was carrying. The dagger had been artfully concealed within the lid of the casket to spring out when required. Masruq knew that he would be searched for weapons before ever being allowed into the presence of my husband, but no-one suspected that a weapon could be concealed in such a way. But you suspected it was a trap, didn't you, Hamo? You tried to warn Lord Edward, and thank God you did.'

'I think it must have been God who gave me such a warning,' I smiled.

Lady Leonora smiled back. 'Well, Hamo, you have given me many gifts in the past but none that can compare with saving the life of my dear husband. Is there anything I can give to you as a reward?'

'My only wish is to go on serving you and Lord Edward, but Doctor Trotta tells me that, thanks to the assassin's dagger, I will no longer be able to perform as a tumbler, or even a fool, with the skill worthy of your distinguished selves. I am afraid I will not be of much use to you ever after.'

Lady Leonora laughed in the most sweet and delightful manner. 'Such nonsense, Hamo! Do not concern yourself about your place in our affections. Such a faithful and trustworthy servant as yourself will always be in our service, whatever your capablities. And you can still sing and play for me, and tell those dreadful jokes of yours.'

'I'm afraid the biggest joke from now on will be me.'

'Is there nothing you wish to ask for, Hamo?'

I could have asked for a barony here, an estate there, or gold and jewels in abundance, but such things were rewards that royals prefer to bestow at the time appropriate for them rather than when requested by a lackey, even when he has been invited to claim his reward.

I replied: 'There is just one favour I wish to ask of you, my lady. You, and my dear wife Dolores, are the only ones to know that I am not the half-witted imbecile everyone else believes me to be. I find I am tired and increasingly strained by pretending to be so. You know that God performed a miracle to release me from the prison of my mind's imbecility. Could I now have your permission to let Lord Edward, and everyone else, know that I have been miraculously cured of my imbecility.'

Leonora frowned, so I quickly added: 'I do not mean admit that I was cured many years ago, but pretend that I was cured by God for saving Lord Edward's life.'

The frown cleared as Leonora considered my request. 'Very well, Hamo, but my husband must never know that you have been cured for many years.'

I would have to be very careful how I juggled both of my royal benefactors, but I really did feel tired of wearing my imbecile jester's mask. I could not enjoy my wealth, or my estates, or the company of intelligent men, or beautiful women, without them thinking me sadly retarded.

Saving Edward's life in such a dramatic fashion was the perfect opportunity for my 'miracle cure'. I was now in such good favour that no-one could possibly threaten my position in the royal affections.

I said: 'All I ask, my lady, is that I tell Lord Edward of this recovery myself, when Lord Edward himself has recovered from his wounds.'

'Very well,' Lady Leonora agreed.

We reminisced about this and that for a long time until candles began to be lit and dusk filtered into the ward. Leonora noticed that my eyelids were drooping and, indeed, a dreadful lassitude was overtaking me. Leonora bid me farewell and I drifted back to sleep, dreaming of Lady Leonora's sweet rose lips on my hand and of Doctor Trotta's cool palm on my forehead.

After a few more days I felt strong and well enough to leave the hospital. I was carried back to the palace on a litter and allocated a small private chamber one floor above Lord Edward's apartments. I was even allotted my own servants exclusively to cater to my every need. Being accorded such privileges confirmed how well I was in favour for having saved Lord Edward's life.

Lady Leonora visited me every day to report on how her husband was recovering, and recovering rapidly he was, thanks to the skill of a doctor who looked no older than a schoolgirl.

Doctor Trotta also came every day to inspect my wound and I was surprised to find that I looked forward to her brief visits above all else in my life. I could not understand why my heart raced with delightful abandon every time she entered my room. Dolores was the only person I had truly loved in my life. I dismissed my feelings for Doctor Trotta as simply the natural gratitude of a patient saved by the ministrations of a pretty girl.

As soon as I was able to walk unaided, save with the help of a crutch under my arm, Lord Edward summoned me to his bed chamber. I hobbled into his presence and was shocked by his appearance. I tried not to let my expression betray so. He was pale and haggard and had lost a lot of weight. His smile when he saw me enter was warm and sincere, and when he spoke he seemed to be in lively spirits despite his suffering.

I lowered myself, with difficulty, on to a chair that had been placed by his bed especially for my comfort. I kissed his hand in fealty.

'Hamo, my faithful friend. I give thanks to God for your recovery and for your courage in saving my life. Never was a prince better served by anyone.'

'And I likewise thank God for your recovery, my lord. The loss of my humble existence would affect nothing, but the loss of your life would have been an immeasurable catastrophe for England and the whole Christian world.'

Edward looked downcast and answered: 'I wish I could share your opinion of my usefulness, old friend. I have achieved nothing very much in God's service here.'

'My lord, you once gave me leave to speak to you honestly, without dissimulation, when the need arose. The illness caused by your wound has lowered your spirits, as it lowered mine, but allow me to reassure you that no prince could have achieved more to make this holy crusade a success than you have. The French contingent abandoned you because of their crass folly in attacking Tunis. Given the resources left at your disposal, no leader could have done more, not even King Richard the Lionhearted. Perhaps this is God's way of telling you that you are needed in England.'

Edward grunted. 'More like Baibars's way of telling me to go back to England.'

'Reverse the situation, my lord. You are confronting, with a handful of men, a seasoned warrior like Baibars, who has thousands at his command, in his own territory. If Baibars came to England on a mission for his God, with a handful of men, and faced you on the battlefield of England, with the same resources in your possession, what would the outcome be? You would triumph over him as you triumphed over de Montfort.'

'You are right, Hamo,' Edward said wearily. 'Do you think I should return to England?'

'Perhaps this is God's way of telling you so, my lord. I have seen the joy in Lady Leonora's face at your recovery. All England will rejoice likewise. You are well-loved, sire, not just by your family but by all the people of England. Perhaps your true destiny is to return to your realm and be a good son to our liege lord King Henry.'

I fervently hoped that my reasoning was persuasive enough for Edward to abandon this infernally frustrating and dangerous crusade.

Edward was deep in thought for a long moment, and then he said: 'I think your counsel is sound, Hamo, but I will think some more on this matter. But come, I am dwelling on my own misery at the expense of yours. Doctor Trotta tells me that your leg has healed well.'

'Indeed so, my lord, but I am afraid that the assassin Masruq's dagger has destroyed the usefulness of my leg. I will never be able to serve you as a tumbler, or even as a jester, in the way to which you are accustomed and entitled by your rank. I am sore afraid that I will not be allowed to serve you in any way.'

Lord Edward smiled broadly. 'Fear not, Hamo, for even if I wished to discard you, my dear wife would not let me. She adores your music and your singing and your jokes. You have been a comfort and consolation to her on many occasions.' Suddenly serious, he continued: 'What reward can I offer you for the services you have rendered to me for many years? You have given me my life. What can I give you in return?'

This was the ideal opportunity to free myself from the shackles of my self-imposed imbecility. I answered: 'I am overwhelmed by your generosity, sire, but the only reward I wish to ask of you can be granted simply by your blessing.'

'Speak then, Hamo.'

'Sire, you are the only person in the world who knows that I am not the dim-witted fool I pretend to be. It is an act that has, I believe, allowed me to serve you well on many occasions. Now that I can no longer serve you as a jester and tumbler, I do not think such a pretence will be of much use in the future. I am growing older, my lord, and my legs have been destroyed by assassin steel. My body tires and will not spring me around as once it did. I yearn to be able to enjoy the intercourse of other men and women without being thought of as a nincompoop. I yearn to serve you, openly, with all my wits, and I seek your permission to be myself, who I truly am, and that is all I ask of you.'

Edward nodded, clearly not comfortable with my proposal, as Lady Leonora had not been, but unwilling to appear an ungenerous prince to the man who had saved his life. Eventually he conceded: 'I would be happy to grant your request, Hamo, but what will you tell people to account for such a miraculous transformation.'

'Miraculous is the word, my lord. My reward from God for the saving of your life is the restoration of my wits. May I be so bold as to say that Lady Leonora has already remarked on the lucidity of my speech and has thanked God for it. I think that everyone will accept the mysterious workings of God's mind and accept that this is my reward for saving the life of England's future anointed sovereign. If you confirm that it is so, then it will be so.'

Edward, to my relief, accepted my argument. 'You have spoken well and wisely, Hamo. I will issue a proclamation to that effect. Also, I am releasing you from your duties as court jester.' He smiled at the expression of dismay on my face. 'Fear not, I am teasing you,' Edward continued. 'I hereby create a new post for you, Hamo. You are to be Marshal of the Revels. You will supervise all my other jesters and musicians and organise my entertainments. I command you to stay by our side and entertain us with your good humour and guide us with your wise counsel.'

'Thank you, my lord,' I said, kissing his hand again. I felt overjoyed and mightily relieved to be free of my lifelong performance as a moronic clown.

Edward called out to a servant to bring us wine and we talked and drank until we both felt the need for sleep.

I quit Lord Edward's apartments and saw Doctor Trotta walking towards me down the rush-strewn corridor. She was carrying the instruments of her trade, which were wrapped tightly in a white linen cloth.

I wished with all my heart that she could observe more than a short ill-favoured fool hobbling along on a crutch. She never seemed to smile and yet her face and her voice were always full of kindness and concern.

'Signor Pauncefoot, I am gratified to see you up and about. Does it pain you to walk with the crutch?'

'No. Thanks. My leg feels much better. Thank you. Thanks to you.' I cursed myself for being hesitant and tongue-tied, something I never was except in pretence. 'But what of Lord Edward? He still seems weak and poorly.'

'He is, and he will feel so for many days to come. The wound in his arm became badly infected. The only way to cure such a condition is to cut away the infected flesh and clean the wound until the body can fend for itself. Tell me, what is your opinion of this English prince?'

Doctor Trotta's question caught me off guard. I was wary about her reason for asking. I replied cautiously: 'He is a most courageous and generous man.'

Doctor Trotta considered my reply and then said: 'Never have I treated a man, let alone a prince, who bore with such fortitude and courage what I had to do to him. To have to cut away his flesh in such a manner, and he never once has complained or cried out, even when the sweat has been rolling down his face in his agony. I would be happy to serve such a prince. Your country is fortunate.'

SEPTEMBER 1272

In late September the Mediterranean winds turned favourable and, to my intense relief, Lord Edward announced the abandonment of the crusade. The English army embarked and set sail for Sicily.

The voyage to Sicily seemed interminable, even with the relief of a stop at Cyprus, and took more than a month to complete. Edward was still weak from his wound and found the sea voyage very arduous.

NOVEMBER 1272

We finally arrived at Palermo and Lord Edward was greeted at the dockside, with all due ceremony, by Charles of Anjou, the king of Sicily.

Edward was still seethingly resentful of the manner in which Charles had diverted the French crusading army to Tunis to serve his own ends, but Edward was compelled to be cordial to Charles because the English army had perforce to travel through Charles's lands in order to return to Gascony and then England.

Charles invited Edward and Leonora to spend Christmas at his palace in Trapani, on the west coast of Sicily. Edward was reluctant to spend so much time in the company of King Charles but he was weak and exhausted from the long voyage and his physicians insisted that a long rest would restore his vigour for the arduous land journey to come.

So we embarked again, this time for a thankfully short voyage along the coast to the cosmopolitan port of Trapani and its beautiful crescent shaped harbour.

A few days after we had settled into the lavishly appointed royal palace, Edward introduced me to King Charles as the court jester who had saved his life from the assassin Masruq. Charles looked at me with the arrogant disdain he reserved for the lower orders but, because I was so well in favour with Edward, he was obliged to treat me with a modicum of respect.

Christmas at Trapani was a pleasant experience, with ample food and wine and entertainment to relieve the tedium of endless church services, but we were still languishing there in the middle of January.

I was becoming very anxious to return to England and sometimes, in the darkest hours of a Mediterranean night, despairing of ever seeing home again. Then Edward received visitors who changed his life, and the life of England, forever.

JANUARY 1273

E dward and Leonora were spending an evening in the company of King Charles and his wife, Margaret of Burgundy. A formal evening feast, attended by various dignitaries and nobles from both the English and Sicilian camps, had been held in the great hall, and then the two royal couples had retired to Charles's private apartments to relax.

Relations between Edward and Charles had warmed considerably, thanks to Margaret of Burgundy, who was a charming and humane woman, and the convivial atmosphere was improving Edward's spirits and health, and he was no longer anxious to depart the island.

I had been summoned to entertain the royal spouses with songs and harp music. The royal apartments of Trapani Palace had been built with large windows, larger than any I had ever seen in England apart from in cathedrals, which afforded a spectacular view down to the harbour and the coast. It was a cloudless and moonlit evening and the ships in the harbour and the activity in the town were clearly visible.

King Charles's seneschal requested admittance to the royal presence, which was reluctantly granted, and announced that there were four emissaries who had just arrived from England and who begged an official audience with Lord Edward at once. Edward asked King Charles's permission to receive these emissaries, which Charles readily granted.

Looking back all these years later, I am sure that we all suspected the reason for the arrival of these distinguished visitors, but nothing was said. It was fortunate and appropriate that the royals were still attired in their grandest and most regal attire following that evening's feast.

Edward remained standing while Lady Leonora seated herself in an armchair next to him. King Charles and Queen Margaret retired to the far end of the apartment where they seated themselves so as to observe the meeting.

The four emissaries were ushered into the room and bowed to the assembled royals. I recognised all four of them. There were two earls, who were among Edward's most loyal friends and supporters; the bishop of a diocese, I cannot remember which one; and the archbishop of York, the most senior churchman in England after the archbishop of Canterbury himself.

Edward nodded to them in greeting but said nothing. Such a party of eminent men could mean only one thing and the air became almost unbearably tense with expectation.

Having been seated in a chair at the side of the room, unable because of my wound to sit cross-legged on the floor as I was used to, I had unobtrusively risen and silently moved into a shadowy corner of the candle-lit apartment. I did not want to be noticed and possibly ejected from this momentous encounter.

The archbishop of York moved towards Edward and bowed again. 'My lord, we thank God to have found you safe and well at last. It behoves me to be the bearer of news that is at once so sad and yet so joyous for the realm of England. Your father, our liege lord King Henry, is dead. You, Edward, are now King of England and Duke of Aquitaine.'

Edward took a deep breath and I could see that he was employing all his iron self-discipline to control his emotions. Despite their many differences and quarrels, he had loved his father deeply. He asked: 'When did my father die?'

'Last November, sire. He had been very ill for a fortnight and, despite the prayers of the entire realm, God saw fit to call him to Heaven. He did not suffer and Queen Eleanor was with him at the end. He was interred in Westminster Abbey a few days later. The ceremony was magnificent, sire, and all the magnates of the land attended.'

Edward was deeply affected by this news and clearly wanted to dismiss the emissaries before his emotions overcame him. 'Thank you, gentlemen,' he said quietly. 'I know you must have had a long and arduous journey to find me. I am sure that King Charles will be happy to provide you with comfortable accommodation and refreshment.'

Instead of moving to leave, the archbishop, uncomfortable in his responsibility, continued: 'Sire, it is my duty to report more sad news.' He looked uneasily at Lady Leonora. 'Your son, Prince John, has also passed away. He died last August. I'm afraid the doctors, despite their best efforts, could do nothing to save him.'

Lady Leonora was gripping the arms of her chair so tightly that her knuckles had whitened. Unaffected by the news of King Henry's death, the news of the death of yet another of her children had gripped her cruelly.

Edward looked down at her and saw her distress. He turned back to the emissaries and again hinted that they should leave now, but the archbishop was relentless in the quest to unburden himself. 'I have also been instructed by the royal council to inform you of the death of your uncle, Earl Richard of Cornwall. He was taken by an apoplexy in the spring of last year.'

I could not control a gasp of shock as I heard of the death of my father. Fortunately King Charles and Queen Margaret, who were within earshot, were intent and transfixed by the scene being enacted before them and did not notice my involuntary spasm of grief.

Edward looked down at the floor, breathing heavily to control his emotions, but then asked: 'Who is heading the royal council in my absence?'

'Sire, the task has fallen on Robert Burnell, with the approval of Queen Eleanor, who is giving him the benefit of her wise counsel.

I am instructed by the council to say that your presence in England, sire, is sorely required as soon as possible, and to give you this letter.' The archbishop handed Edward a parchment roll.

From my hiding place in the shadows I listened to this announcement with high vexation and, as Edward read the letter from the royal council, I felt like punching the wall in anger.

To hear that my father was dead, and then that Robert Burnell was ruling England and perhaps cuckolding me at the same time, was devastating news. I was mightily cheered, however, by the thought that this news meant we would have to return to England as soon as possible instead of lotus-eating in Sicily.

The English emissaries were at last finished with their onerous duty and were ushered out of the royal presence. As soon as they were gone, Lady Leonora – or Queen Leonora as she was now – began to weep piteously for the loss of her son.

Edward looked at her with anguish but before he could move to comfort her, King Charles and Queen Margaret came to Edward and kneeled before him to kiss his hand. Thus the change from prince to king. Charles was the king of a strong domain but Edward was now the king of a considerably stronger domain and Charles, no doubt thinking what an excellent ally he had made, was eager to show his respects.

He then rose and embraced his brother king with the words: 'Edward, I am truly sorry for the loss of your father and your son and uncle, but I rejoice that you have come into your inheritance and I pray that God will always temper your justice with courage, prudence and honour.'

'Thank you, Charles,' Edward replied softly.

Queen Margaret, a most kind and charitable woman who had also lost a child in infancy, had comforted Leonora and then hugged Edward and kissed him on the cheek.

Edward turned to his beloved wife and, as she rose from her armchair, he took her in his arms and they both broke down in piteous sobbing.

Charles and Margaret discreetly moved away to allow the couple their private grief.

I had witnessed Edward's tears after the battle of Evesham but that grief was not as deeply felt as this, and I was touched and transfixed by this display of genuine human emotion from such normally cool and lofty personages.

Prince or pauper, every human being has but one father and the death of a father, especially one as well loved by his son as King Henry had been, is a grievous blow. Henry had been on the English throne for more time than most folk could even remember, and it was a peculiar feeling to think that he was no longer there.

I had lost a father in Richard of Cornwall and, with Henry of Almain also gone, I had lost any possibility of ever proving my birthright and claiming my rightful inheritance.

Edward soon regained control of himself and summoned Leonora's ladies-in-waiting to escort her back to their bedchamber and attempt to alleviate her distress.

He then turned to Charles and Margaret and apologised by saying: 'I am so filled with conflicting emotions. I regret inflicting you with my weakness.'

Queen Margaret tried to offer consolation. 'To hear of the loss of your father and your son in one instant is too much for anyone to bear, sire. Your tears are worthy of you as a devoted son and father, a true king and a good Christian soul.'

Edward managed a wan smile. 'In truth, Margaret, I grieve not for a son, but I am devastated by the loss of my father.'

Charles looked at Edward almost critically and asked: 'You grieve for your father but not your son?'

'I am not callous, Charles, but my son John was a new-born infant when last I saw him. I did not know him. I can make more sons, but a father is irreplaceable. He was my father and my king and, despite his many faults and weaknesses, I loved him dearly. He ruled England for over fifty years. It does not seem possible that he has gone.' The three royals stood in respectful silence for a moment, then Edward said distractedly: 'Please excuse me. I must return to my wife.'

'Of course,' Charles said. 'You should rest. You will have much to do in the morning.'

Including, I fervently hoped, issuing orders that we would be returning to England immediately.

As Edward was leaving he caught sight of me lurking in the shadows. He stopped and said: 'You are still here, Hamo?'

'Please forgive me, sire. I did not know whether to leave and interrupt those fine gentlemen or to stay and risk your wrath at remaining.'

He beckoned me out of the shadows. 'Fear not, Hamo. If it were not for you I would now be a corpse in Acre instead of king of England. You have witnessed my tears before. I may now be a king but I am still a loving son and father. Come, walk with me, as best you can, back to my chamber.'

I picked up my harp and, hobbling along trying to keep up with Edward's long stride, I ventured: 'It will be good to see dear old England again soon, sire.'

'Indeed it will, Hamo, but it will not be soon.'

We had reached the door of Edward's chamber and I blurted out: 'But sire, you heard what the archbishop said. You are needed back in England. Robert Burnell may be a competent administrator but the country needs a ruler. And there is the coronation to consider. Until you are crowned and anointed, your power as the king is unconfirmed and limited.' I realised that I was stumbling into dangerous territory and quickly said: 'Forgive me, sire, I speak too freely.'

Edward smiled at me and replied: 'God bless you, Hamo. I know you speak out of love for me, and for England, but there is no need to worry. I knew, before I ever left England, that my father was ill, and so did he. Before my departure on crusade my father transferred all the royal castles and estates to me, and trusted lieutenants have been placed in charge of every one of them. That letter the emissaries delivered told me that the day after my father's death, my peace was proclaimed in Westminster Hall. After my father's funeral, all the magnates of the land swore allegiance to me. My authority and my kingship are unimpeachable. As you have said, Robert Burnell is a competent administrator, but that is all he is. There is no threat to my authority, Hamo, and no need to rush back to England. I will deal with matters in Gascony first. Now, good minstrel, perhaps you will allow the king of England to get to his bed.'

I bowed as Edward entered his apartment and closed the door behind him. I stood in the antechamber and cursed. It would still be weeks, perhaps months, before I could return to the comfort of my own land and my own home. Eventually I hobbled off in search of wine with every intention of getting myself very drunk.

1273

We began our journey north through the mainland of Italy as soon as the winter weather allowed. In the cities that we passed through, such as Bologna, Parma and Milan, it was apparent that King Edward of England had already become a legendary figure.

He was regarded as a true hero of Christendom for leading a crusade, albeit an unsuccessful one, and the story of how his wife, now Queen Leonora, had sucked the poison from his wound after the attack by the Saracen assassin, had been told and retold throughout Europe. The fact that there had been no poison in the wound was conveniently forgotten, as was my part in the whole affair.

When Edward became aware of this legend and how it was spreading, he remained silent about my role in saving his life and all the credit became attached to Leonora. There was nothing I could do to prevent such a false legend circulating so I had to accept the situation.

Early in June we crossed over the Alps. Waiting for Edward on the other side of these intimidating mountains was a delegation of bishops and nobles who had journeyed from England to greet their new king. They urged Edward to return to England without delay, but Edward would not hear of it. He was determined, now that his power as Duke of Aquitaine was untrammelled, to arrange his affairs and administration in Gascony to his own satisfaction.

Thus followed long tedious months stuck in Gascony. I became more and more frustrated and could think of nought but getting home to England and Dolores.

The only relief from the monotony was that Lady Leonora gave birth to another son. He was christened Alphonso after Leonora's half-brother, King Alphonso of Castile.

It was not until the end of July that, to my relief and jubilation, we arrived in northern France and boarded the royal cog to take us back home to England and the coronation.

AUGUST 1274

F ine weather and favourable winds ensured a smooth passage from France, for which we were all thankful, and we disembarked at Dover on the second day of August in the year 1274.

Gathered to greet the new king on his return home was a panoply of the highest nobles in the land, headed by Edward's mother, Eleanor of Provence, and his brother Edmund.

It was a gloriously warm summer day at Dover Castle. The ceremony of greeting and fealty took place on a lush meadow outside the walls of the castle. Several magnificent and gaily colourful tents and stalls had been erected around the ancient Roman pharos to shelter and refresh the nobles and the hundreds of retainers, officials and servants in attendance.

I stood in the background and watched Edward affectionately embrace his mother and brother and then, while seated on an elaborately carved and bejewelled throne made especially for this day, receive the homage of the host of magnates.

I took several long and deep breaths of the warm English air and felt a sense of contentment and satisfaction I had never experienced before.

After four years in exile I had returned to the security and promise of England. I was as well in favour with the most powerful man in the realm as it was possible to be. I had saved his life, and he called me friend. I was expecting some form of reward and the imminent coronation ceremony would be the appropriate time for King Edward to grant me that reward.

Dolores had not travelled to Dover to welcome me home but I accepted the excuse that she was needed at Windsor Castle to help care for the royal children.

I had hobbled away to the top of a grassy slope that afforded a better view of the ceremony and sat myself down on the warm grass to ease the strain on my wounded leg.

As the ceremony was drawing to a close I saw a man walking towards me up the gentle slope. I recognised him, with a tightening knot of anger in my gut, as Robert Burnell, the man who coveted my wife and the shrewd politician who had been governing England as head of the royal council. He had, according to official documents, with a phrase that twisted the knots of my jealousy and resentment even tighter, 'occupied the king's place in England' while we had been away on crusade.

Burnell was dressed more kingly than King Edward. He wore an elaborately embroidered blue and gold surcoat, short red cloak trimmed with white fur, and red leather boots. He smiled at me as he approached.

I did not smile in return, and I did not allow him the courtesy of immediately standing up. I continued to sit languidly in the grass.

Burnell appeared unconcerned by my disrespect and began: 'Welcome home, Pauncefoot. We were all overjoyed to hear of your courageous act in saving the king's life and we thank God for rewarding you by releasing your mind from the prison of imbecility.'

A smile played around Burnell's mouth. Was he mocking me? He was a consummate diplomat and I could not tell whether he was sincere or not, but I decided to act out the charade.

I rose to my feet, determinedly not showing the pain of such effort, and stood up straight to face him. 'Thank you, Master Burnell. It is good to be home and with my wits about me. I have no doubt that I shall need them all now that you have risen to such exalted heights.'

'Well, it seems we have both risen to exalted heights. We must both be careful not to fall down. Perhaps we can cling together for mutual support.'

'As no doubt my wife has clung to you in the years of my absence.'

Burnell shook his head as if hurt and disappointed by my attitude. 'You do your wife a grave injustice, Pauncefoot, not to mention myself. Your wife, as far as I know, has been chastely devoted to you while you were away on holy crusade and I, while acknowledging that she is a most comely woman, would not dream of offending the sanctity of your marriage by any improper behaviour.'

'Your reputation suggests otherwise, your Grace.'

Burnell, among his many other offices, was the Bishop of Bath and Wells, a clerical appointment that had not prevented him from indulging in many affairs and siring many bastard children. [25]

Burnell shrugged off my barb equably and pointed down to where Edward was receiving homage from a procession of local worthies. 'That man is not like his father. He is a strong man and nobody's fool. If we are to help him rule this country with justice and efficiency, it would not help his reign, not to mention our security, for you and I to be feuding. From what I have been told, Edward calls you friend and trusts you as much as any man in the world. You have played your hand brilliantly and I admire you for it. Will you accept my apology for any wrong I have done you, and accept this hand of friendship in the interests of the peace of the realm.'

Burnell held out his hand. I knew he detested me as much as I detested him. It was a shrewd move on his behalf to win me over to his side. If I now refused to take his hand then I would appear petty and small.

I decided to subtly play the awestruck neophyte at such tactics, disarm his suspicions, and give myself time to plan how to bring him down. I had little doubt that Burnell was thinking similar thoughts.

I took his hand and bowed, but not too low, and replied: 'You speak handsomely and generously. Let us then forget the past,

Robert, and look to the bright shining future that King Edward's reign will bring us.'

'Excellent,' Burnell beamed. 'I look forward to conversing some more at the banquet later tonight.' He turned and strolled back down the slope to lurk ingratiatingly near to his royal master.

The next morning the royal entourage set off on the journey to London and the coronation. We stopped overnight at castles in Tonbridge and then Reigate. In each castle the new king and queen were lavishly entertained by the resident earls, who spared no expense to curry favour with the new monarch.

All along the route we encountered cheering groups of peasants and citizens eager for a glimpse of their new king. The weather was perfect for them to view their new liege lord, being sunny and bright but not too hot.

As we trotted through the Kent countryside I was summoned forward to ride with Edward. He was in a charming and mellow mood and smiled at me warmly. 'Well, Hamo, it is good to be home.'

'I have to confess that it is, sire, and the people are according you a right royal welcome befitting such a great king.'

Edward waved regally as we rode past another knot of cheering farm workers. 'I have not yet proved that I am a great king, my friend. That remains to be seen and decided by the Almighty.'

'But, sire, if I may make so bold, I think the mantle of greatness already envelopes your shoulders. You have, for a long time, been acknowledged as the most courageous knight in Europe. You despatched the usurper de Montfort in open battle and restored your father to his throne. You have travelled to the Holy Land to do battle with the infidel on God's behalf. And the incident of despatching Sultan Baibar's assassin has become legendary throughout Europe. You have been cheered and feted all the way through Italy, France and now England. You are healthy, tall and well-favoured. If all such as this does not add up to greatness then my name is... Robert Burnell!'

I had taken a risk by using Burnell's name in jest but, fortunately, Edward laughed. 'All that you claim for me, Hamo, is a satisfactory start but does not yet add up to greatness such as enjoyed by a Caesar or an Alexander. I will need wise counsellors such as Burnell. I have decided to appoint him Chancellor of England after the coronation.'

That casual announcement was like a dagger through my heart, although I had fully expected Burnell to receive such an appointment.

Edward continued: 'Burnell is a capable administrator and did an excellent job in controlling the realm as head of the royal council after my uncle Richard died.'

'Burnell is a clever and ambitious man, my lord.'

Edward looked at me askance. 'I know what your words infer, Hamo, but I am not a man to be led by the nose like my father, God rest his soul. I can control Burnell. But what about you, Hamo? What are you ambitious for?'

'Me, my lord?' I protested disingenuously. 'My only ambition is to see my dear wife again and to sleep in my own bed.'

Edward actually clapped a hand on my shoulder. 'God bless you, Hamo. You have served me better than any man alive. I have kept you away from Dolores for many years and I thank you for your loyal service. You shall have your bed, and your wife, and I think we can find something else for you as well, my friend.'

That was it! The promise, or half-promise, I had been waiting for! How best to respond? Disarming modesty and flattery was always safe. I said: 'To hear a king such as yourself call me friend is the greatest reward I could dream of, sire.'

Edward smiled lightly, but then the smile faded as we rode past a black iron gibbet that was hanging from a tree. Inside the gibbet was encased a corpse that must have been several weeks old.

Edward said: 'There are many injustices that need remedying in my realm, Hamo. There has been an increase in lawlessness in my absence. There are many men in this kingdom who, unlike yourself, covet more substantial rewards than my friendship. They are ready to impinge on my rights as king as they once impinged on my father's rights. Many of those rights are still in their hands, or so they think. I had to serve a hard apprenticeship as a prince, Hamo. Perhaps harder than any prince has ever done. But now I am king I am determined to restore peace and justice to this land and to take back the rights and privileges that are mine, as the sovereign anointed by God, which have been traduced by these overmighty barons and earls and sheriffs and judges. I will be the arbiter of rights and justices in England, Hamo, and no-one else.'

Edward became aware that his speech was overheated but it was a true glimpse and summary of his inner feelings, as was to be proved in the future.

We entered a village named Crowhurst. The villagers lined the single street of modest huts to cheer and wave. Edward smiled at me and remarked: 'At least I seem to be beginning my reign with the love of the people.'

We rode into sight of Windsor Castle and found hundreds of people gathered outside the walls to welcome the new king. Edward, riding slowly but guarded by a watchful host of his knights, looked magnificent in an elaborately embroidered silk surcoat over ceremonial gold and silver chain mail, and returned the cheers with regal waves of his hand.

We rode into the castle and found another reception committee, this time merely dozens strong, waiting for Edward. Leonora, quite naturally, was anxious to embrace her children, who had been brought out to welcome their parents.

Dolores was carrying the baby Prince Alphonso. She caught sight of me and smiled hesitantly but cordially enough. Queen Leonora kissed her old friend, petted the baby, and after a brief ceremony of welcome and fealty, the royal family withdrew to their chambers for rest, refreshment and reunion.

Having been given no instructions as to what I should do, I ordered a servant to fetch me food and wine and bring it up to my private chamber. I found it little changed although Dolores had spruced it up with flowers and put up her embroideries as wall decorations. It felt strange to be back home and completely alone.

It was growing dusk and the servants had lit the candles before Dolores returned. I had laid down on the bed and fallen into a light sleep. I felt someone shake my shoulder and opened my eyes to find her looking down at me.

'Welcome home, husband,' she said pleasantly, and kissed me on the forehead. 'I see you have put on a little weight.'

'While you, my dear, are as lovely as ever. I hope my return gives you as much pleasure as it gives me.'

'My mistress wrote to me and explained how well you had behaved and how you saved Lord Edward's life from the assassin. I am proud of you, and proud to call you husband.'

Dolores kissed me again, this time upon the lips.

'Now that I am even more in favour with Edward than I was before, and him now being the king, not just a mere prince, I have no doubt you see riches and titles in the offing.'

'And what if I do? Do you not?'

I could not help smiling. 'I tease you, my dear. Of course I do, and my friend Edward has already promised me my reward after the coronation.'

'What is it to be?' Dolores asked eagerly.

'I don't know, he did not tell me. But I hope for high favour. Did Leonora tell you that my wound has finished me as a tumbler and acrobat?'

'Yes, but she said that you are still highly valued for your harp and your jokes.'

'Indeed, but for how long? The favour of princes can be fickle. I took the precaution of bringing back some of the riches of the East with me. Fetch me that box.' I pointed to a small iron-bound strongbox that I had placed on a sideboard.

Dolores did as bidden and returned to the bed with the heavy box. I opened the strongbox with a key that I kept on a silver chain around my neck. I lifted the lid. Dolores gasped when she saw the contents.

There were pearls, gold and precious jewels in abundance. Dolores lifted out one particularly fine ruby pendant, mounted in a gold frame, and gazed at its lustrous colour in the candle light. She put it back in the box and was pensive for a few moments. 'You know well that, back home in Castile, I was set to marry a rich old grandee. I did not love him. I was forced to marry you. I confess that I do not love you and I never will. But you have risen to heights of which I did not believe you were capable. I am Queen Leonora's best friend. You are one of King Edward's friends. I am secure and comfortable and I lead a more interesting life than I would have done stuck in a backwater in Castile. After the coronation perhaps we will be even more exalted, thanks to your efforts. I am satisfied with you as my husband.' She smiled down at me. 'Is there anything I can now do to satisfy you.'

After four years in the East exiled from carnal comfort I was well ready to accept Dolores's tempting offer, and for the next few days she was as attentive as a dutiful wife could be.

I well knew, as she had admitted herself, that she would never love me, but I was content with her declaration that I was an acceptable husband. We were both older, wiser and more mellow. I could look forward to the coronation in a few days time with fine hopes for the future.

Two days before the coronation I decided to make a visit to my house in London.

I had shown Dolores only a small portion of the riches I had garnered in the East. I was anxious to secrete the rest, together with some valuable documents, in a secure and hidden niche I had constructed with my own hands within the house.

I considered that it might be difficult to absent myself from Edward's service while immersed in the coronation ceremony and festivities. I asked permission from Edward to be released for a few hours and he readily granted permission but with a stern admonishment to ensure that I returned in good time to take part in preparations for his coronation.

Dolores had told me that the house was locked, with the windows shuttered and barred, and the servants granted leave of absence to celebrate the forthcoming coronation. It was an ideal opportunity to carry out my purpose. I did not tell Dolores where I was going.

The weather was fine and it had been dry for many days so the roads were in good condition and I could easily ride to Westminster and back within a day.

I arrived at the house in the late afternoon. Despite the warm weather I had donned a hooded cloak so that I would not be recognised. I tethered my horse at the back of the house and let myself into the grounds through a gate in a wall that gave access to the kitchen garden.

Being careful not to be observed, I carried my jute sack full of precious objects and rolls of documents to the back door, which led into the kitchen. I stood among the pots and pans and, just to make absolutely certain that the servants were not using the house for any unauthorised purpose, I listened for long moments to make sure it was unoccupied.

I carried my goods out of the kitchen and into the main room. With the windows shuttered it was very dark and I put down my sack in order to light a candle. As I did so, I heard voices from upstairs.

I drew my dagger and listened, considering whether I had been imagining things, but the voices, a man and a woman, carried on talking. I surmised that a pair of servants had decided to use my house for a secret tryst. The thought of mere servants rutting on my bed made me lividly angry.

Brandishing my dagger, I tiptoed up the stairs as quietly as I could. The voices were definitely emanating from the master bedroom. The door was ajar but not fastened. I could tell from the amount of light filtering through the door that the bedroom window shutters had been opened.

I was making ready to burst into the room but hesitated when I heard a child's voice, which was also emanating from the bedroom.

I kicked open the door. A man was cradling a toddler in his arms, watched by an older woman whom I recognised but whose name I could not place. The man I certainly recognised and the shock of seeing him standing in my own bedroom made me witless.

It was my hated rival, the man who was designated to be the next Chancellor of England, Robert Burnell.

For a moment he looked equally shocked to see me but he recovered his senses and his equilibrium faster than I did. 'Pauncefoot,' he said quietly, 'this is an unexpected pleasure.'

'What in God's name are you doing here?' I asked lamely, unable to comprehend what was happening. 'And what is this woman and this child doing here?'

Burnell answered coolly: 'This woman is Mary Stradden and she is about to take this boy back to my estate in Shropshire.'

I remembered that Mary Stradden was one of Dolores's maid servants, but I could not fathom what she was doing in my house with Robert Burnell.

Mary Stradden had been terrified by my sudden dagger-wielding appearance and the boychild, who was about three years old, looked equally frightened.

'Who is this boy?' I asked.

Burnell stroked the boy's dark hair and replied: 'This is my son.'

'And are you the mother?' I asked Mary Stradden, but knowing that she was probably well past the age for childbearing.

Mary Stradden was sore afraid to speak, and Burnell simply looked at me until, at last, the realisation dawned. 'Dolores,' I breathed.

Burnell placed the child in Mary Stradden's arms and said: 'Take him to where I instructed you. My men are waiting for you outside. Take good care of him and you will be well rewarded.'

Mary Stradden was only too relieved to quit the room and escape from whatever was going to happen.

I waited until Stradden was out of earshot and then challenged Burnell. 'So, as soon as I had left on crusade, you were cuckolding me?'

'Yes,' Burnell replied simply.

'Did you think I would not find out about this child?'

'If you had not returned at this instant, you never would have found out. Dolores knew that you would never accept another man's child and also that she would never be allowed to leave you, so the child will be brought up by me. Dolores was fervently hoping that you would not return from the East. I was heading the royal council here at Westminster while you and Lord Edward were abroad. I could visit the child as often as I liked. Dolores has been very happy. And so have I.'

Enraged by jealousy and humiliation I leapt at Burnell and grabbed him by the collar of his fancy linen shirt. 'Now I will kill you, Burnell. Let us see how happy that will make you and my dear wife.'

'You will do nothing of the kind,' Burnell choked back, trying to push me away, 'unless you wish to ruin yourself at the same time. Kill me if you must but how will you explain to King Edward that his valued chancellor was found murdered in your own house. Mary Stradden, and all my men, know that I am here. You could not get away with such an act of murder, as you did once before.'

That last statement sent shock waves of fear through my mind. 'What do you mean by that?' I demanded.

Despite the pain of my grip, there was a glint of triumph in Burnell's eyes. 'The body of Peter Pauncefoot, found in a barrel of brine in the cellar of his own inn on the night you disappeared from Portsmouth. Nobody knows of this except me. Let us talk sensibly about this situation, like men of the world. Edward is about to make me Chancellor of England and I know he plans a high reward for your services. Whatever our differences now, we can work together in the future, or we can destroy each other. I saw right through you from the start, Pauncefoot. The idiot jester act and now the miraculous recovery of your senses. I decided to find out who you really were and what you were up to. Come, release me, let us sort things out.'

Despite my almost insane rage I realised that Burnell was right. To kill him now would be to lose everything. I released my grip on his collar and he staggered back and sank down to rest on my bed. 'Good,' he breathed, rubbing his neck. 'Good.'

While recovering my wits I realised that Burnell had tricked me. He was correct that I could not kill him, here and now, but he could not possibly have any proof that I had murdered Peter Pauncefoot, even if the circumstantial evidence indicated so.

'I am letting you live, Burnell, but do not think you can frighten me with tales of Peter Pauncefoot. I know nothing of what happened to him after I ran away from the inn. How many people know about this child?'

'None, except Mary Stradden. Dolores came to live on my estate before she reached full term. Only Stradden knows about the birth, and she has agreed to look after the boy. No-one knows that you have been cuckolded. Your dignity is safe. I know you will always hate me for this. Now you have knowledge of me that could harm me, and I have knowledge of you that could harm you. As I have said, we could destroy each other or we could work together. I urge you to be sensible.'

We talked for a long time and reached agreement. We both knew that we would eventually try to bring each other down but, for the time being, it was for our mutual benefit to tolerate each other.

Burnell departed but I sat thinking for a long time on the bed, the bed that Dolores had shared with Burnell as well as me. I felt an almost unbearable aching emptiness.

Eventually I bestirred myself and went downstairs to conceal the treasures I had brought with me, and then rode back to Windsor Castle.

It was late in the evening when I arrived back in my chamber at

Windsor. Dolores was sitting in an armchair sewing an embroidery by candlelight. 'Husband!' she said, when she noticed me standing there. 'Where have you been? I have been looking for you all day!'

I poured myself wine from a flask on the sideboard and pulled up a chair to sit opposite her. She looked at me expectantly.

I said softly: 'I have been visiting our home in London, my dear. I have been entertaining some unexpected visitors.'

Dolores was suddenly tense with expectation. 'What do you mean? Who were they?' she asked tremulously.

Slowly, I answered: 'Mary Stradden... Robert Burnell... and your bastard child.'

Dolores put down her embroidery on her lap. 'I had hoped that you would never find out.'

'No?' I said, and took a long draught of wine. 'You also hoped that I would not return from crusade, didn't you?'

'You have not been able to give me a child. I love Robert Burnell. I wanted his child, not yours.'

'You mean you did not want to be the mother of some stunted fool, even as you are forced to be the husband of a stunted fool.'

'Yes,' Dolores replied simply and calmly.

'And all the assurances that you were satisfied with me as a husband have been lies?'

'Yes. I despise you. Your touch, your mere presence disgusts me. I have been forced to act the satisfied wife, simply to persuade myself to carry on living. Even so, I could not do so.'

'So, after all these years, I am still the duende, the hateful monster?'

'Yes.'

'Nevertheless I am your husband and, as your husband, you are my property and subject to my will. Robert Burnell and I have come to an arrangement. You will never have anything to do with him again. Do you understand that?'

'Did he agree to that?'

'Yes, my dear. I am not the first husband that Burnell has

cuckolded and your child is not the first bastard he has fathered. Robert Burnell is interested in one thing only, and that is his personal advancement. You have been a pleasant dalliance but now he is to be Chancellor of England, he cannot afford to consort with a married mistress such as you.'

Dolores nodded. 'What of me? Will you get rid of me?'

'By no means, my dear. How could I? You are the queen's best friend. You are untouchable. I fully expect that our dear King Edward is going to reward me handsomely after the coronation for my many services to him. I will not humiliate myself by putting aside an adulterous wife just at the hour when all my life's work is about to come to fruition. From now on you will be a dutiful wife in all respects.'

'And what if I refuse?'

'Then Queen Leonora will hear how you gave birth to a bastard son after cuckolding her beloved jester and Edward, who you know full well to be a pious man and devoted husband, will hear the same thing. He will not allow his wife to be served by a woman who abandoned the care of the royal children, while he was away serving God on crusade, in order to give birth to her own bastard child. You know that to be true, don't you my dear?'

'Yes. Will I be permitted to see my child again?'

'Perhaps. God did not allow me to know my mother so I know how painful it is to be deprived of maternal love. Despite what I think of you and Burnell, the infant is blameless and I would not wish to condemn him because of the sins of his mother. In the meantime we will have a child of our own.'

'That will not be possible,' Dolores replied, in a whisper so soft I could hardly comprehend.

'What do you mean?'

'I had difficulty while giving birth to... to my son, and it did something to me inside. The doctors tell me that I cannot have any more children.'

I hurled my wine goblet against the wall and watched the dregs run down. I said: 'Tomorrow we must ride into London with our royal master and mistress. Make sure you are prepared. Now get out of my sight.'

Dolores fled into our curtained off bedchamber. I listened to her while she cried herself to sleep. I drank until I was insensible, until her grief, and mine, was driven out of the dark evil caverns of my mind.

AUGUST 18TH, 1274

The next day was a Saturday. In the early afternoon Dolores and I took our place in the seemingly endless entourage that was to accompany Edward on his ceremonial ride into London.

My head was aching, eyes stung by the sunlight, and my throat was bone dry. I was dubious whether I could manage the ride without disgracing myself en route.

Dolores and I did not look at each other and we rode side by side in stony silence. When we entered London, however, our sorrows were put aside, overwhelmed by the magnificence of the welcome that had been prepared by the citizens for their new monarch.

Every street was lined with throngs of cheering people from all sections of society, from the highest to the lowest. Almost every house and shop was hung with silks or gold cloth, adornments that must have represented considerable expense for the loyal subjects who had bought them.

The people of London, knowing how Edward had detested them in the past, were seeking to make amends by a spectacular display of joy and fealty.

An immense amount of work had been accomplished at Westminster in preparation for the coronation and subsequent festivities. New stables, lodges and kitchens had been constructed and every piece of spare ground had been given over to temporary buildings to house and shelter the hundreds of guests. In case of rain, covered walkways had been set up between Westminster Palace and Westminster Abbey.

I did not see Edward for the rest of the day and, not being needed for any other preparations, I went to our private apartment in Westminster Palace while Dolores attended Leonora in her coronation preparations.

I spent the rest of the day brooding and agonising over the situation with Dolores. The happy life I had envisaged had been brutally shattered by her infidelity. I had been fooled by her protestations that she considered me an acceptable husband. Her true opinion of me had not changed since the first time she had set eyes on me in Burgos. Her bitter hatred had poisoned my life forever. And the most bitter poison was that I still loved her.

AUGUST 19TH, 1274

On the next day, Sunday, Dolores and I entered Westminster Abbey to take our place in the congregation to witness the coronation. Huge stepped wooden galleries had been built along the north and south transepts. The stage where Edward and Leonora were to be crowned had been built so high that mounted knights could actually ride underneath it. It had been planned so that every member of the congregation had a clear view of the coronation ceremony.

Hundreds of banners hung from the vaulted ceiling and the earls, barons and other senior knights were mounted on their best steeds and dressed in their most elaborate finery.

When the congregation had settled, a procession of bishops and archbishops, some carrying golden crosses, some swinging censers, preceded Edward and Leonora into the abbey, all accompanied by the massed abbey choirs singing liturgies from the balconies above us. This spectacle was lit by hundreds of candles and flaming torches.

After a round of solemn prayers, Edward made an offering at the altar to Edward the Confessor and St. John the Evangelist, asking for their guidance and wisdom. Then Edward and Leonora climbed up the steps on to the coronation platform, upon which two richly decorated thrones had been placed.

Edward, seated on his throne with Leonora beside him, took the coronation oath under which he swore to protect the Church, to administer fair justice, to suppress evil and lawlessness, and to protect the rights of the Crown.

Then Edward alone descended again to the altar where, standing on a marble mosaic adorned with religious symbols, he received unction from the Archbishop of Canterbury.

Edward disrobed down to his undershirt while the archbishop anointed various parts of his body with holy oil. Then a form of holy oil called chrism was poured over Edward's head. This was the moment that the new king's reign was blessed by God and the gifts of the Holy Spirit were bestowed upon him.

Edward again ascended the steps up to the coronation platform for the ceremonial re-dressing as king. He donned a golden tunic, was girded with the great sword Curtana, and a mantle woven with gold was placed over his shoulders. A gold ring was put on his finger and golden spurs attached to his heels. Then he sat down on his throne next to Leonora, donned the golden coronation gloves and then received the golden rod and golden sceptre.

Next came the crowning itself. A magnificent golden crown studded with rubies and emeralds was placed on Edward's head.

But then, in an astonishing deviation and to gasps of surprise from the assembled onlookers, Edward immediately removed his crown. In a ringing voice he declared: 'I swear by Almighty God that I will never take up this crown again until I have recovered the lands given away by my father to the earls, barons and knights of England, and to aliens.'

By this dramatic and unplanned departure from the ceremony, Edward stated, in terms that no-one could misunderstand, his determination to win back all the rights that had been taken from his father and his detestation for those who had stood against the anointed monarch in the recent civil wars.

Leonora was crowned in a much simpler ceremony and then the royal couple descended from the stage and, once again preceded by a throng of senior churchmen, left the abbey and walked to the great hall of Westminster Palace. Here, two new thrones had been erected for a ceremony of investiture.

As I was leaving the abbey, one of Edward's stewards approached me and told me that my presence was required at this ceremony. I was seized with excitement because this summons could mean only one thing. In Edward's first official ceremony as anointed king, he was, at last, to reward me for my many services.

I entered Westminster Hall to find that several dozen especially invited participants were already present. Edward and Leonora, still dressed in their coronation finery, were seated on their thrones.

Several young men, the favoured sons of some of the highest nobles in the land, approached King Edward in turn to be knighted with the great sword Curtana, a very high honour.

I was disgruntled, but not surprised, to see Robert Burnell in attendance. As one of the first to he honoured, he was proclaimed as the new Chancellor of England. I caught Dolores gazing at him with undisguised longing.

Many more distinguished men were summoned before the new king to be awarded titles or other official positions and appointments.

All this seemed to drag on interminably and Dolores and I were the only two left waiting when Edward's seneschal came forward and instructed us to approach the thrones.

Dolores was called forward by Queen Leonora and, with Edward watching with unfeigned pleasure, was created Lady of the Bedchamber, the most senior and intimate position in Leonora's entourage.

Then the seneschal called me forward. Leonora smiled at me graciously as I limped, with difficulty, up the stone steps and approached Edward's throne. I bowed, and as I did so my injured leg gave way and I fell to the floor in front of the king. To gasps of surprise from the other courtiers, Edward stood up and raised me to my feet.

'I'm so sorry, my lord,' I whispered.

'Fear not, old friend,' Edward whispered in reply.

Edward remained standing as the seneschal handed him a sword contained in a finely wrought leather scabbard and belt.

To further hushed expressions of surprise from all the other courtiers, Edward personally buckled the sword around my waist, a hitherto unprecedented honour. He kissed me on both cheeks and then proclaimed in a voice that rang around Westminster Hall: 'No man in the realm has served me more faithfully than Sir Hamo Pauncefoot, made here by my hand to be baron of the manor of Abinger, member of my royal council, and Marshal of the Revels for life.'

Edward smiled down at me as I kissed his hand and then stepped back. I hobbled backwards until protocol of distance allowed me to turn my back on the king and descend the steps.

He had made me a baron! It was more of an honour than I had ever hoped for or expected. The only higher rank, apart from royalty itself, was earl, but that rank could only be obtained by inheritance or marriage.

Edward had rewarded me with the highest rank available to someone born in my station. I did not know where this manor of Abinger was but, as baron, I would be entitled to all the revenues from the estate, which certainly would possess a fine manor house.

Everything I had worked for since that fateful day when the young Edward flung me into the sea had now been achieved. I was mercifully free of the need to act like an imbecile, and now I had the money and status to enjoy life to the full.

Dolores looked at me as I approached her, uncertain as to how to react. 'Congratulations, husband,' she finally said. 'It seems we are both well in favour.'

'Indeed,' I replied. 'If only I had a loyal and faithful wife to share my good fortune.'

Edward and Leonora had risen from their thrones and were now leaving to change their garments and to rest and refresh themselves while the great hall was prepared for a sumptuous feast.

Dolores excused herself from me, no doubt with relief, while the servants began bustling in carrying trestle tables covered in fine linen tableclothes.

I left the great hall to amuse myself and bask in the glow of my new status by touring the stalls, amusements and attractions that had been set up all around the palace. I remember that these attractions included a miraculous fountain of real wine that passers-by could sample in any quantity they desired.

Some time later the hunting horns of the heralds announced that Edward and Leonora were returning to begin the coronation feast.

I hurried back to the great hall to find the dozens of long trestle tables laden with food and drink. There were sides of bacon, pork, boar, beef and venison; capons, swans, cranes and peacocks; pike, eel, salmon and lamprey. I had never seen so much food in one place. To my immense satisfaction I was summoned to dine at the salt, on the dais above the common throng, at the long table where Edward was sitting.

I was with Edward's family, Eleanor the Queen Mother, his brother Edmund, his sister Queen Margaret of Scotland, her husband King Alexander of Scotland, and Edward's most trusted friends and supporters such as the Savoyard knight Otto de Grandson and several earls, including Roger Mortimer, the fearsome Marcher lord who had saved my life at the battle of Evesham.

An unwelcome sight, however, was Robert Burnell sitting with us among the favoured. Below us sat hundreds of other guests who were not so exalted by rank or favoured by the king's friendship.

I was already well in my cups but I was well practised in holding my drink. The exalted personages sitting at the salt were clearly not enamoured of being accompanied by an upstart neophyte like me but I did not care. As long as I enjoyed the king's favour, so publicly displayed in the same hall earlier, the rest of humanity was irrelevant. Dolores had not returned to join in the festivities but, for the time being, I did not care about that either.

The evening wore on and more candles and torches were lit until the great hall was ablaze with golden light.

Eventually Edward and Leonora, and the other members of the royal family, no doubt exhausted by the day's dramatic events, rose to leave. We at the salt made to struggle to our feet but Edward insisted that we remain seated and carry on enjoying ourselves. The other revellers in the hall, however, perforce rose to their feet to bow as the new king and his family departed to enjoy a personal and private celebration.

I was deep in conversation with Otto de Grandson, who had been with us on crusade and who had assisted Edward after the assassination attempt. He was one of the few military noblemen who deigned to talk to me. I had noticed Robert Burnell looking at me curiously and, in my drunken state, I inwardly renewed my determination to engineer the downfall of that clever gentleman as soon as possible, be he Chancellor of England or not.

The conversation at the salt, and at the tables below us, became more congenial and relaxed now that the royal family had departed. The assembled magnates sat back and loosened their elaborate ceremonial clothing to make room for yet more food and wine.

I looked around Westminster Hall with a warm glow of contentment at my good fortune. Up in the temporary galleries minstrels were playing soft airs; along the sides of the hall and in between the columns, tumblers and jugglers performed their skills; servants and retainers toiled up and down carrying platters of food and drink and carrying away empty vessels; hundreds of candles and torches in wall sconces cast flickering shadows on the walls and roof beams. Below us at the common tables the voices and laughter were increasing in volume as more and more wine, ale and mead was consumed.

As to be expected on such an auspicious occasion the general discussion at the salt turned to the turbulent events of Edward's life leading up to this coronation. The subject of the battle of Evesham was broached and I began to pay more attention to my noble peers. Most of the men at the table were aware that Edward felt remorse for the slaughter at Evesham and so refrained from discussing it in his presence, but now were free to do so and, as all the women had also departed, the conversation was becoming more and more bawdy.

I noticed Robert Burnell looking at me as if to ensure that I was paying attention. Then he cut across the conversation and called over the table to Roger Mortimer, the man who had slain Simon de Montfort, and in a voice much louder than necessary requested: 'Tell us about the gift that you despatched home to your wife after Evesham, my lord.'

Mortimer belched loudly and laughed, as did most of the other nobles, who plainly knew the story well. Mortimer sat back expansively, looking at the amused and expectant faces of his companions, and took a long swig of wine before replying. 'My wife said it was the finest gift I ever gave her. It was the head of Simon de Montfort.'

I was aware that de Montfort's body had been hacked to pieces during the battle, I had witnessed the atrocity myself, but I did not know that Mortimer had sent de Montfort's head to his wife as a token.

Burnell continued: 'I understand that you added a little extra gift in de Montfort's mouth, my lord?'

'Yes,' Mortimer guffawed. 'It was his cock. And he had a big one!' We all laughed heartily at the thought of Earl Simon's appendage. 'My wife asked me why mine wasn't as big!'

'And wasn't it strangely marked?' Burnell persisted.

'Yes!' Mortimer cried in delight. 'A big lozenge-shaped birthmark on that big cock of his.'

An almost uncontrollable wave of nausea flowed through me as the implication of what Mortimer had just said struck me with the force of a war hammer.

I pushed my chair back, stood up and mumbled an apology as I stumbled away from the table. The nobles gazed at me curiously as I stepped down from the salt and hobbled towards the doorway, pushing the tumblers and jugglers out of the way, until I plunged outside into the cool night air.

I found a shadowed place, leaned against the wall of Westminster

Hall and vomited on to the grass. I took deep breaths as I watched, uncomprehending, as the clouds scudded across the moon and the whirligig crowds of revellers, laughing and shouting in celebration, carried flaming torches to light their way through the maze of tents and kiosks spread out on Westminster Common. The River Thames seemed to be flowing like molten iron. The sound of revelry and mirth roared through my head, echoing off the stone walls, my senses overwhelmed with dizzying madness as my life turned over and over and over like a gigantic water wheel ploughing relentlessly through the wretched stream.

I stood breathing heavily and trying to recover my shocked senses when a hand grabbed my shoulder and pulled me around.

Robert Burnell looked at me with a wolfish grin of triumph, relishing my discomfiture. 'Well, well, well,' he whispered venomously, 'the newly created baron is the bastard son of Simon de Montfort.'

I pushed Burnell away and attempted to brazen it out. 'What nonsense are you babbling? I felt ill and came out here to clear my head. Leave me in peace, Burnell.'

Burnell put his hands on his hips and regarded me with an amused grin. 'You are the bastard son of de Montfort, and I have proof of it.'

'You have no such proof.'

'On the contrary,' Burnell replied, 'I have ample proof. I have proof that your so-called father, what was his name, Peter Pauncefoot, could not have fathered you because he had lost his manhood to a French sword. I have sworn testimony that you disappeared on the night your surrogate daddy's body was found in a barrel of brine. I know you hated him and that you probably murdered him. I have testimony from people whom you asked about that strange birthmark on your real daddy's cock. Oh, you hid your inquiries well behind that mask of idiocy that has served you so effectively but when I first heard Mortimer tell that grisly story of his, I realised what you were trying to find out.'

I became aware that I was swaying as my wine befuddled mind battled to refute Burnell's accusations. Then my natural instinct to survive reasserted itself and I realised, with thrilling clarity, that I had the perfect argument to refute Burnell's claims. 'I cannot be de Montfort's son. I am the son of another noble and the man who told me so is someone who you cannot interrogate with your sly methods.'

I saw the hesitation in Burnell's face.

'Who told you?' he asked.

'Our new king and liege lord Edward himself.'

'He knows of your real parentage?' Burnell was now thoroughly discomfited.

'No, he does not know, but he confirmed, with his own lips, who my real father must be. You see, the birthmark on his manhood was but one clue to my real father's identity. Another clue was that my real father was once married to a woman whose name was Marshal. I am the son of Earl Richard of Cornwall, who was once married to Isabel Marshal, the daughter of the Earl of Pembroke. This was told to me by Edward himself. I cannot be the son of de Montfort because he was not married to a woman named Marshal. So take your threats and shove them up your arse, Burnell.'

For a moment Burnell appeared confused and defeated by my riposte but then, to my confusion and consternation, he began to laugh, a gulping and cackling full-throated laugh of derision. 'Oh, Pauncefoot, you poor deluded creature! It was all so clear and certain in your mind, wasn't it. You think de Montfort was not married to a woman named Marshal, but you are wrong! He was once married to Eleanor Marshal, who was the daughter of John Lackland and who took the name Marshal when she married her first husband William Marshal, Earl of Pembroke! Oh, this is priceless. You poor deluded fool!'

Burnell had to wipe the tears of derision from his eyes with the sleeve of his surcoat.

In my befuddled drunken state I desperately considered the

THE CHRONICLES OF PAUNCEFOOT AND LONGSHANKS

other clue to my real father's identity. It was the rampant lion with pointed tail on his coat-of-arms. This lion featured on Earl Richard of Cornwall's coat-of-arms... but a rampant lion with pointed tail also featured on Simon de Montfort's coat-of-arms, and on his banner that I had carried during our advance at the battle of Evesham. I had unwittingly connived in my own true father's defeat and death.

Baffled and defeated by this stunning revelation, all I could think to do was fall back on a lame threat. 'I'll ruin you, Burnell, if you try to use this against me. I'm going to ruin you anyway, just for cuckolding me.'

Burnell actually leaned forward and patted me reassuringly on the shoulder. 'Hamo, I have no intention of using this against you but, just in case anything untoward should happen to me, I have left detailed documents about what I have found out with one of my trusted clerks. If I should die in suspicious circumstances they will be handed to King Edward. See how long your favour lasts with our new king when he discovers that you are the son of his hated enemy. And he might begin to wonder whether the de Montfort brothers were informed about the whereabouts of his beloved cousin Henry of Almain, information that led to his murder.'

'That's a lie! I did no such thing and you have no proof!'

'That, alas, is true, but now that I know you are de Montfort's son, I will create such proof.'

'You have not the stomach for such work.'

'You think not, master baron? Do you think that I rose to become Chancellor of England by picking flowers?'

A glimmer of hope pierced my drink sodden brain. 'My surrogate father was a notorious liar. He might have known about de Montfort's birthmark and made up that story about my being his father. It still does not prove that de Montfort fathered me. He probably was not even in England at the time. And why should he stay in a common inn if he was in England?'

Burnell put his hand on my shoulder again. 'Hamo, you really must stop underestimating me if we are to work together. Simon de Montfort came to England in secret in early January of 1238. He was to marry Eleanor of England, once Eleanor Marshal, the daughter of the late King John and sister to our late lamented liege lord Henry. Now Henry approved of this marriage but the earls and barons, not to mention the Church, did not approve and the marriage had to take place in secret. Earl Simon landed in Portsmouth incognito and, unable to stay with any of his noble friends and run the risk of being recognised, he stayed at the St. Nicholas Inn overnight. I have sworn statements from the retainers who were with him that night. No doubt he fancied one last fling before he married and your dear mother, impressed by de Montfort's wealth, stature and aristocratic status, and no doubt completely bored by a husband with no functioning cock, could not resist Simon's advances. Nine months later, in September, out pops Baron Hamo Pauncefoot of Abinger.'

I could no longer think of any argument to gainsay Burnell.

He grabbed me by the collar of my tunic and pulled me towards him. 'Listen, Hamo, I do not want to ruin you. I admire how cleverly you have raised yourself up by pretending to be a harmless idiot. You are a shrewd man, like me. I want you to work for me now, use your wiles in my service and that of our liege lord Edward.' I recoiled from Burnell's hot stinking breath in my face. 'You are my creature now, Hamo, and you know it. Serve me well and you retain your status. Serve me ill and you will be destroyed. Do you understand?'

I nodded. What else could I do? Burnell had won. He was right. He had proof that I was the son of Simon de Montfort. If King Edward was informed of that fact then my barony, hard won by years of struggle and danger and awarded only hours before, would be snatched away, together with my life in all probability.

I remembered how I had hidden in the pot cupboard to overhear de Montfort talking to Edward, how I had come to hate de Montfort's brutish square face, how he had humiliated me when in his captivity, and how I had watched his great sword sweeping down to kill me at Evesham before Mortimer impaled him with his lance.

All the years I had dreamed that I was the son of the noble and chivalrous Earl Richard of Cornwall I was, in fact, the son of the renegade traitor who had attempted to seize the realm.

I had no choice but to serve Burnell.

He put his arm around my shoulder. 'Come, my friend, you look as if you could do with another drink. Let us rejoin the festivities on this happy occasion.' He led me back towards the door of Westminster Hall but stopped outside. 'Oh, one more thing I want you to do for me, my friend. You can have Dolores back, I have no interest in her any longer, but I want her to raise our son. I want you to raise him as your own so that he will one day inherit your barony. That will give you some assurance of my good faith and save me the trouble and expense of taking care of another bastard. There is a pleasing symmetry to all this, don't you think, Hamo. You are the bastard son of a powerful man and was brought up by another, weaker, man. Now you, the weaker man, will bring up the bastard son of this powerful man. Do you agree to this?'

Once again, I meekly nodded my head. What else could I do but wait, and watch, and burrow for the weakness and sickness that lies at the heart of every man, even a man like Robert Burnell.

My faithful but admonitory amanuensis, Brother Godfrey, closes his eyes and desires to sleep. Yes, write that down, you dozing halfwit. What's that you ask? Is it true that Mortimer sent his wife the gift of de Montfort's head together with the extra 'gift' in his mouth? Yes, boy, it is entirely true. Your good Christian conscience does well to make you shudder in horror. Perhaps you now understand what manner of men, and women, I had to contend with.

But come, it is late and we have written enough for now. I will save the second part of my story for another day. Yes, I know you are curious but be patient.

You already know that I outlived them all… Burnell, Dolores, Leonora, King Edward, even Edward's son. In the next chronicle, I will relate how I struggled to escape the thrall of Robert Burnell, the fate of Leonora and Dolores, the fate of my 'son', and how I fashioned Edward of Caernarfon and watched his father grow to detest him.

I will relate how, standing side by side with my friend and liege lord King Edward, I aided the subjugation of Wales and, by conniving in the darkest and most Godless crime that I ever witnessed, almost brought about the subjugation of Scotland.

I will relate tales of plagues, sieges, plots, intrigues, executions, massacres, cruelties beyond imagining, and bloody battles that haunt me to this day.

But now you are nodding off, Brother Godfrey, and my eyes also grow heavy. Confession is good for the soul but my mind is weary and tormented with the burden of sins past. I pray that the balm of sleep brings consolation to my tortured soul and ease to my corrupting body.

NOTES

1. The cog was the predominate merchant and military ship of early medieval northern Europe. They were clinker built with rounded bow and stern, fore and after castles, and with a broad beam. The square sail was carried on a single main mast, thus they could not sail into the wind but could be operated with a small number of crewmen. Historical records confirm Pauncefoot's estimate of the size of this fleet as it required 300 vessels to transport King Henry's army.

2. Lord Edward was born in June 1239 at the royal palace in Westminster. He was the first born son of King Henry III and Queen Eleanor of Provence. Edward was named for Saint Edward the Confessor, an earlier Anglo-Saxon king of England with whom Henry III was obsessed. Henry was a peaceable and pious king who deeply admired the same qualities in his pre-Conquest predecessor.

Edward's birth was greeted with joy throughout the land. Hardly anything is known about Edward's childhood and education and it is a pity that Pauncefoot did not see fit to write anything about Edward's early life. The events related by Pauncefoot, when Lord Edward wept while waving goodbye to his father, are confirmed by the 13th century historian monk Matthew Paris. Paris writes: *'The boy stood crying and sobbing on the shore, and would not depart as long as he could see the swelling sails of the ships'*. Paris makes no mention of Pauncefoot's extraordinary intervention in this touching scene but any historian of the time would be careful not to offend the heir to the throne by making mention of it. Why was King Henry leaving for Gascony, and why was Lord Edward sobbing so piteously? Gascony had been granted to Edward in 1249 but that did not mean that Edward could rule Gascony himself. Gascony had been in a state of rebellion owing to the harsh regime of the royal lieutenant who had been ruling Gascony. That lieutenant was King Henry's brother-in-law. His name was Simon de Montfort. To the south of Gascony was Castile, the most powerful kingdom in medieval Spain, and the new king, Alphonso, was invited to intervene by the Gascon rebels. Alphonso saw the opportunity to add Gascony to his own empire and threatened to invade his neighbouring territory. King Henry of England was warned by the panicked citizens of Bordeaux that if he did not act swiftly then his lands in Gascony would be lost, hence his departure from Portsmouth with his army.

Edward, despite having been granted Gascony, was not allowed to accompany his father on this expedition and it is much more likely that Edward's bout of uncontrollable tears, the scene witnessed by Pauncefoot, was much more owing to Edward's frustration at not being allowed to play a manly part in protecting his own lands than it was to being deprived of his father's company for a few weeks. Henry's army had considerable success in quelling the rebellion in Gascony and the slippery King Alphonso of Castile, seeing his opportunity dwindling thanks to the presence of such a powerful English force, decided to negotiate. His negotiations hit the jackpot, and so did Lord Edward. It was agreed that Edward would marry King Alphonso's young half-sister but Alphonso wanted to be certain that his future brother-in-law would be a man of sufficient substance and wealth and insisted that Edward be endowed with lands worth £10,000 per year. Thus Edward became the richest landowner in the realm. King Alphonso wanted to meet his future brother-in-law and so, in May 1254, Edward was preparing to embark on his first-ever journey to foreign lands, to the exotic kingdom of Castile and, being a healthy and lusty young man, must have been excited and intrigued by the prospect of meeting his new bride, a woman who would one day inspire Edward to create one of the most romantic gestures of love in all history. She was the elegant, mysterious and beautiful Leonora of Castile. *(Leonora has now become known in Britain as Eleanor of Castile but, in order to avoid confusion with Edward's mother, Eleanor of Provence, we have retained throughout this narrative the Castilian form Leonora by which Pauncefoot, in his original manuscript, habitually refers to Edward's bride.)*

3. This extraordinary brawl between the seamen of Yarmouth and Winchelsea is confirmed by historical records. The men of Winchelsea were, indeed, jealous that the men of Yarmouth had provided Queen Eleanor with such a fine ship compared with their own. Several sailors were killed during this fight and it is fascinating, albeit appalling, to know that Pauncefoot incited and then manipulated this intense rivalry to his own advantage, albeit unintentionally.

4. As Pauncefoot was often travelling in, and making reference to, the royal wagon, it is necessary to explain what they were like. The roads and bridges in England and Gascony were in a shockingly bad condition and travelling was slow during the summer but well nigh impossible during winter weather. Most men, including the king, travelled on horseback, which was much more comfortable than a normal cart or wagon. Women also rode on horseback and, at this period, rode astride the horse. The more demur sidesaddle fashion did not appear until the later Middle Ages. Royal ladies such as Queen Eleanor of Provence and Princess Leonora of Castile could not be expected to travel in such an undignified manner and travelled in the luxury of the royal wagon. And luxury it was, the word 'wagon' now giving little indication of the nature of these glorious and immensely expensive machines. They were drawn by several horses, controlled by the postillion, and were built on a solid wooden chassis. The spokes of the wooden wheels were elaborately carved and expanded near the hoop of the wheel to form pointed arches. The upper compartment was formed like a long tunnel with the highly decorated but weather-proof outer covering fastened to rounded beams which, being visible inside the wagon, were also elaborately carved, painted and decorated. Imagine the shape of one of the prairie schooners of the Wild West but much longer and much more decorative. The sides were pierced with windows and hung with silk curtains so that the royal lady could look out at the countryside. The inside, equipped with all necessary 'conveniences' for my lady's comfort, was hung with tapestries, and the wooden bench seats were strewn with embroidered cushions and pillows so that the lady could recline or sleep or sit and talk with her attendants, or be entertained by Hamo Pauncefoot. Despite this appearance of luxury, however, the state of the roads made the journey noisy and jerky and, certainly compared to our modern modes of transport, would seem maddeningly slow and uncomfortable.

5. Bartholomew Pecche had been Edward's tutor since 1246 and had previously been responsible for the care of Edward's sister, Margaret. Such a man must have been trusted completely by the royal family and it is understandable that Edward was so upset at their perceived betrayal. The last thing that history tells us about Bartholomew Pecche and his two sons is that they did indeed sail to Gascony with the intention of attending Edward's marriage but, after arriving in Bordeaux, they are not mentioned again in any document. Pauncefoot's actions now explains their sudden absence from Edward's history.

6. A brief explanation of the titles Pauncefoot mentions here, as used during the late 13th century. The office of Chancellor had much less to do with finance than its modern connotations. The Chancellor was the Keeper of the Great Seal, and the monarch's closest spiritual and temporal adviser, more like a modern Prime Minister. The Great Seal was used to authenticate all letters, laws and documents that were issued by the king and thus the Chancellor, and the clerks working under him, was the direct conduit between the king and his officials in every shire and parish. The Wardrobe was the main spending department of the state and thus the Keeper of the Wardrobe, at this time, was the office more akin to the modern Chancellor of the Exchequer. The modern reader may also wonder why Pauncefoot almost invariably refers to Edward as Lord Edward or, occasionally, Prince Edward, instead of His Majesty. Early medieval monarchs were more down-to-earth than their later successors and the title 'His Majesty' was not used until some 100 years later as insisted upon by Richard II.

7. In this cynical, sceptical and increasingly irreligious modern age, Pauncefoot's pantomime in pretending to be given messages and the gift of tongues from God seems insanely risky and outlandish. Such a view, however, is to misunderstand the medieval mind. It was an age of deep religious faith in which God was seen to be working, quite literally, in everyday affairs, all the time. Signs and portents were seen in events which, to us, would seem of no consequence whatsoever: the appearance of a flock of birds, an oddly shaped cloud, unusual weather conditions, and so on. Many people from all strata of society were genuinely convinced they had seen angels, just as many modern people are convinced they have seen flying saucers or ghosts. People in medieval times slept upright in bed for fear that if they slept laying down and their mouths fell open then the Devil could enter them through their mouth.

In one well-known true incident, Edward was playing chess and moved from his seat just seconds before a huge lump of ceiling fell down exactly where he had been sitting. To the modern mind it would be attributed to luck. Edward, in all seriousness, attributed it to the direct intervention of the Virgin Mary because he had so often visited her shrine at Walsingham. To the medieval mind, Hamo Pauncefoot's conversion after being entered by the spirit of God would be completely feasible and acceptable.

8. Pauncefoot's account of why Leonora and her ladies, dressed in the latest Castilian fashions, were laughed at by the Londoners during their progress through the city is confirmed by Matthew Paris. Paris also notes how the installation of carpets in Leonora's chambers offended suspicious English notions of soft foreign luxury. It is interesting to speculate how such a derisive reception may have affected a young and impressionable girl such as Leonora of Castile, who was only too well aware of the English hostility to foreigners that was current at the time, and this reception may have contributed greatly to her later self-serving attitude and makes such an attitude more understandable and, perhaps, forgiveable.

9. The infamous sacking of the priory at Wallingford (now in Oxfordshire following the local government re-organisation of 1974, not Berkshire as it was in Pauncefoot's time) is mentioned, with shocked disgust, by Matthew Paris, and gave rise to severe doubts about Edward's fitness to be king and increased the hatred felt for King Henry's spoiled Lusignan gang. Pauncefoot's account, however, confirms that Edward was visiting his formidable uncle at the time and was not personally involved in the violence, although it certainly reflected badly on him to be on amiable terms with such Godless ruffians.

10. Pauncefoot's brief mention of the stone columns tends to confirm modern archaeological evidence that the roof of Westminster Hall was indeed, at that time, supported by two rows of stone columns. The spectacular and magnificent wooden hammerbeam roof which can still be seen today was not constructed until the next century by master carpenter Hugh Herland. It is also to be regretted that Pauncefoot did not give us more description about the general layout of parliamentary sessions at this time, and his equally regrettable vague descriptions of Westminster Palace as a whole, of which very little is now known. His account of this confrontation between the gang of earls and King Henry accords closely with historical records.

11. Ask English citizens about Magna Carta and all will have heard of it and most will have a fair idea of its implications. Ask about the Provisions of Oxford, however, and few will know anything about them, even though they are arguably as important in English legal and administrative history as was Magna Carta. For the first time in English history, the monarch was compelled to recognize and be controlled by the decisions of a parliament, and parliament was to sit three times a year at set times, not simply when the monarch decided to hold one. The Provisions of Oxford, although modified by the Provisions of Westminster and later annulled by the pope, are the true foundation of English parliamentary and constitutional authority.

This momentous change in governmental authority was communicated to the sheriffs of each English county in Latin, French *and* English, the first time since the Norman conquest of 1066 that an official government document had been issued in the English language. The Provisions of Oxford, therefore, instilled in England an enduring determination for not only freedom, the rule of law and constitutional government, but also a new sense of Englishness and English national pride, rather than the feeling of being a vassal state of French overlords.

12. Pauncefoot's account of this poisoning clears up some puzzling features of this fairly well-documented incident. Because of the reports about the earl's loss of hair and nails, some historians have attributed the cause to simple food poisoning, such as mercury in fish or lead poisoning that, in the fevered political atmosphere of the time, was hysterically transformed into a poisoning plot. The use of wolfsbane (also known as aconite or monkshood) explains the oral burning sensations experienced by the de Clare brothers, as well as the vomiting symptoms. It is possible that Richard de Clare's hair loss was caused by mercury or lead poisoning due to something he had eaten or drank the day before, and it is medically conceivable that this earlier poisoning actually helped to alleviate the effects of Pauncefoot's wolfsbane poison that so quickly carried off de Clare's brother William. What is certain is that Walter de Scoteny (or Scotney) was executed at Winchester Castle in May 1259 having been found guilty of this assassination attempt.

13. The nature of tournaments at this time differed greatly from the usual modern idea of two knights jousting in the lists, which became popular many years later, primarily during the reign of Edward's chivalrous grandson, Edward III. Tournaments in Pauncefoot's time were mainly conducted as a mêlée, or mock battle, in which two 'teams', sometimes consisting of hundreds of participants, would seek to outflank and capture each other on a playing area often miles in extent. A successful participant could win wealth and fame so competition was fierce, resulting in many severe injuries and frequent deaths. It was Edward I himself, many years later, who issued a statute ordering the use of blunted weapons during the mêlée to reduce the number of casualties. Edward considered that skilled English knights were much better employed in his real battles against the Welsh, Scots and French, rather than laying uselessly injured after a tournament.

14. The Treaty of Paris, agreed on December 4th, 1259, attempted to resolve the 55 year dispute between England and France over the French lands from which Philip II had ejected King John 'Lackland' in 1204. Louis IX agreed to stop aiding English and Gascon rebels, and Henry III agreed to renounce Anjou, Maine and Poitou but retained possession of Gascony as Duke of Aquitaine. Crucially, however, Henry's control of Gascony was subject to being a vassal of the French king to whom he had to pay homage. It is easy to see why Edward, as a hot-headed and ambitious heir to the throne, was appalled to find his future inheritance being signed away and decided to throw in his lot with Simon de Montfort. Such an alliance was fraught with danger for Edward. The fact of the English king having to be a vassal of the French king when ruling Gascony seriously undermined the English king's authority in that province and thus the Treaty of Paris proved unsatisfactory from the start and was one link in the long chain of events that eventually led to the outbreak of the Hundred Years War.

15. Strathbogie was the name of Edward's favourite hunting falcon.

16. According to the historical record, Edward arrived at the New Temple and announced that he had come to view his mother's jewels and was simply granted admission. Then, once inside, Edward showed his true colours and his men smashed open the treasure chests with iron hammers. Pauncefoot's account of the siege and consequent bloodshed tells a much more dramatic story and it is entirely possible that this unsavoury incident was subsequently covered up by the chroniclers on Edward's orders. Edward would not wish to incur the wrath of such a powerful body as the Knights Templar and may have sought to suppress all knowledge of his role in this break-in. The New Temple is now better known as the world famous Temple Church, made even more famous by the novel and cinema film *'The Da Vinci Code'*. In Edward's day the church was outside the city walls of London.

17. It is known that this incident deeply embittered Lord Edward against Londoners. Quite apart from the love that Edward felt for his mother, despite her many faults and failings, she was an anointed queen and, as a future anointed king, Edward regarded this insulting and dangerous attack on his mother as a scandalous lack of respect and breach of natural authority. His attempt to take revenge for this, and other examples of gross disrespect by Londoners, would result in disaster, as Pauncefoot later relates.

18. Historical accounts of Edward's courageous dash for freedom have varied considerably in detail but all roughly correspond with Pauncefoot's account. Edward's exultant cry as he made his escape in to the trees has been quoted for centuries but has always seemed improbable, but Pauncefoot has herewith confirmed the veracity of that quotation.

19. Pauncefoot's account of how Simon de Montfort junior escaped Edward by rowing across the moat of Kenilworth Castle clears up a mystery. Another contemporary account, more prosaically, states that Simon was never in danger because he was actually within the castle when the attack took place. A scurrilous rumour circulating many years later stated that, after the raiding party had arrived at Kenilworth, Edward was most reluctant to press on with the attack and had to be shamed into doing so by Roger Clifford, who advanced with his banner flying, thus giving Edward no alternative but to follow. Such a rumour seems to confirm Pauncefoot's account of Edward's reluctance to carry out the raid but it is unconfirmed by any other source and, given Edward's undoubted courage, is most likely a lie intended to discredit his reputation. Another interesting historical fact is that news of young Simon's vulnerability at Kenilworth was brought to Edward by a female transvestite spy named Margoth! Pauncefoot does not mention such a person and it may have been an alias or disguise used by Pauncefoot himself that he has forgotten or does not wish to admit to. Whatever the truth, Edward's attack at Kenilworth succeeded well with many of the enemy being killed and, as Pauncefoot confirms, many high-born hostages being taken.

20. This comment confirms the account given by other contemporary sources and is one of the very few actual quotations to have come down to us intact through the centuries from this time.

21. Contemporary accounts of the battle of Evesham differ but Pauncefoot's eye witness account corresponds closely with modern historical research. Edward did suspend the normal rules of chivalry and came up with the ruse of using de Montfort's captured banners to fool the enemy. Now we know who suggested such a devious ploy. Pauncefoot's account of the course of the battle again corresponds with what is already known. There was, indeed, a 'death squad' detailed for the sole purpose of killing de Montfort. It was Roger Mortimer who inflicted de Montfort's death blow with a lance, although through the neck rather than under the arm as Pauncefoot relates. It is entirely possible that Pauncefoot, in the heat and terror of battle, mistook what he saw. What is certain is that de Montfort's body was subjected to dismemberment in the savage manner that Pauncefoot describes. Accounts relate that it was actually Roger Leybourne who found King Henry wandering in confusion on the battlefield and conducted him to Lord Edward and safety. Given Pauncefoot's self-serving nature it is entirely possible that he took the credit for saving the king, or wishes posterity to think it was him. Evesham was a decisive battle, and the bloodiest battle that had been fought on English soil for literally centuries.

22. As Pauncefoot relates, King Henry III was now reinstalled as sole ruler of England. His son Edward, to a far greater degree than before, was now the second most powerful and influential figure in the land, and was able to influence his father in ways that he had not been capable of before the overwhelming victory at Evesham. De Montfort's son Simon had arrived at the battlefield too late to take part in the fighting but in time to witness his father's head being paraded around on a spike. The victory at Evesham had been so complete that the baronial cause, as led by de Montfort, collapsed. The garrisons at Windsor Castle and the Tower of London surrendered immediately. Edward made good on his oath given to God at St. Egwin's monastery, as witnessed and recorded by Pauncefoot and, thanks to Edward's promise of clemency, the garrisons at Wallingford and Berkhamsted surrendered without any punishment. The only significant garrison still offering resistance was at the mighty Kenilworth Castle, to where young Simon de

Montfort had retreated to carry on the struggle. The first thing that King Henry had ordered after the battle of Evesham, when he had recovered his wits, was the seizure of all lands held by de Montfort's supporters. The triumphant royalist magnates rode off in all directions to grab their share of the spoils.

After recovering from the trauma of battle, Edward's success and happiness must have been abundant. He was securely placed in the affections and the counsels of his beloved father and he had been reunited with his beloved wife. Edward travelled to Chester to oversee the retrieval and security of his estates in the north. He returned for a parliament ordained by King Henry to be held at Winchester in September but his happiness was tarnished by two events. Edward learned that his daughter Joan had died. She was only a few months old and Edward had seen very little of her before her demise. By far the more distressing event, for the realm as a whole, was King Henry's decision that under no circumstances would the estates owned by anyone who had supported de Montfort be returned to them. They were to be disinherited forever. This decision immediately created a resistance movement as disgruntled de Montfort supporters stood by helplessly as their lands and wealth were mercilessly ransacked by royalist magnates such as Gilbert de Clare and Roger Mortimer. With nothing to lose, these disinherited men began a troublesome campaign that would take many more months to suppress. Advisers wiser than the king, such as his brother Richard of Cornwall, quit the court in disgust at Henry's foolish vengeance, as did several other nobles. Edward also disagreed with this harsh decision but he could not abandon his father's side. King Henry's wrath directed at the rest of the country was bad enough, but his lust for revenge against London, shared by Edward, was merciless. The king threatened to besiege the city and when a party of some forty eminent Londoners threw themselves on Henry's mercy in order to prevent the siege they were promptly imprisoned. The city surrendered and the king and Prince Edward entered the city at the head of their army, held a grand ceremony to reinforce their new rule, and proceeded to ransack the city for spoils.

23. All Europe was shocked by the sacreligious manner in which Henry of Almain was murdered, and the great Italian poet Dante, in *'The Divine Comedy'*, written long after the murder, consigns Guy de Montfort to the seventh circle of Hell for his foul deed.

24. Pauncefoot's physician may possibly have been the most famous female physician of the early Middle Ages, who is variously known as Trota, Trotula or Trotta of Salerno. She wrote many treatises on medicine, mainly on female conditions, but many scholars question whether she actually existed, with these medical works being written by a man under a discreet pseudonym. It is not certain in which century she actually lived and the year in which she is treating Pauncefoot is later than the time she is thought to have lived. Despite doubts about her identity, what is certain is that the pioneering medical school at Salerno became famous for the education of 'wise female healers', who were known as the 'mulieres Salernitane'. Trotta's existence and reputation may have been denied and blotted out by men who, just like Pauncefoot, were unable to believe that a woman could not only become a doctor, but a doctor superior in skill and knowledge to any male doctor of the time, especially in the treatment of female maladies.

25. Here Pauncefoot's memory plays him false because Burnell was not appointed Bishop of Bath and Wells until long after this encounter. Pauncefoot's estimate of Burnell's sexual morality, however, is accurate.